Girls on the Home Front

Annie Clarke's roots are dug deep into the North East. She draws inspiration from her mother, who was born in a County Durham pit village during the First World War, and went on to became a military nurse during World War Two. Annie and her husband now live a stone's throw from the pit village where her mother was born. She has written frequently about the North East in novels which she hopes reflect her love and respect for the region's lost mining communities.

Annie has four adult children and four granddaughters, who fill her and her husband's days with laughter, endlessly leading these two elders astray.

Annie Clarke
Girls on the Home Front

arrow books

1 3 5 7 9 10 8 6 4 2

Arrow Books
20 Vauxhall Bridge Road
London SW1V 2SA

Arrow Books is part of the Penguin Random House group
of companies whose addresses can be found at
global.penguinrandomhouse.com

Penguin
Random House
UK

First published in Great Britain by Arrow Books in 2019

www.penguin.co.uk

A CIP catalogue record for this book is available
from the British Library

ISBN 9781787462571

Typeset in 10.75/13.5 pt Palatino by Jouve (UK), Milton Keynes
Printed and bound in Great Britain by Clays Ltd, Elcograf S.p.A.

MIX
Paper from
responsible sources
FSC® C018179

Penguin Random House is committed to a
sustainable future for our business, our readers
and our planet. This book is made from Forest
Stewardship Council® certified paper.

To Catherine in Thirsk
Sister Newsome – my mum
Betty, my pal, who worked at Bletchley Park

Acknowledgements

Of course there's a great deal of background reading when writing about the past. So huge thanks to Google and *Bomb Girls* by Jackie Hyams. Thanks also to a fellow bus passenger who was a bomb girl (filling factory) during the war – fascinating. And my mum's anecdotes from her time working at the Royal Victoria Infirmary in Newcastle, not just nursing miners, but those whom the nurses felt were munitions girls (this was never confirmed – secrecy was paramount). She also had a couple of pals who were indeed munitions girls, though it was only much later that they felt able to share their reminiscences with me. Thanks also to Michael Rowan for reminding me about papier-mâché footballs.

My fabulous pal Betty was at Bletchley Park during the war and aware of the need for secrecy when I was teaching her writing group way back when, but she finally loosened up and told me much. Oh, how I miss her. She was *so* clever, and so mischievous. Again, there are many books on the subject: *The Secret Life of Bletchley Park* by Sinclair McKay and *Station X* by Michael Smith are just two of them. Him Indoors, a computer buff, has also been really helpful. However for a few years we lived close to Bletchley Park and of course visited, and saw and learned much. Do go if you can. Talking of Him Indoors, he has, as an ex-submariner, been able to bring some sense to the munitions with which the girls worked, and the technology at Bletchley Park, so he may have one of my chocolates. As always, any errors are my own, and my eternal thanks to everyone who has shared their knowledge. I am in awe of their courage, endurance and humour.

Prologue

The bus rattled their bones and teeth, or so thought Fran, but her stomach was rattling enough with nerves anyway as they headed for the Ordnance Factory, which was so secret that it must have no name and never be talked about.

'Spark Lane sounds about right,' she murmured to her friend Sarah, sitting next to her.

Sarah muttered, 'Well, our Davey should be good with codes, thinking of his crossword solving and setting.'

The bus slewed right around a corner, throwing them to the left. Sitting in front of them, Maisie, who had worked at the Factory for a while, braced herself and yelled, 'Oy, oy, Bert, steady the buffs, lad.'

'Lad, eh?' he called back. 'Wish I were, pet.'

The seats were just wooden slats, and Fran felt the wheels hit every clod thrown from the tractor as the farmhands had roared from one field to another, ploughing while the weather lasted. In the distance she could just see the pit-heads of the mines.

'I'm right nervous,' Sarah muttered.

Across the aisle, Beth, their other old schoolfriend, gripped her hands together and said quietly, 'Me an' all, but we'll know all about it any minute now.'

Fran peered ahead and there, in the distance, were what looked liked huge air-raid shelters covered in grass, and what seemed like hundreds of one storey brick buildings

1

huddled beneath a lingering mist, the whole of it surrounded by a high wire fence where guards patrolled. Mrs Oborne, who sat next to Maisie, both of them from Massingham pit village too, snatched a look back at Fran and Sarah and whispered, 'It's best to have these factories where the bombers can't find 'em, eh, so most are in misty areas.'

Beth reached across the aisle and pulled at Fran's sleeve. 'What did she say?'

Fran repeated Mrs Oborne's words just as Maisie turned. 'Aye, same as me last one. Right glad about it we were an' all when we heard the beggars poking about the skies.'

Beth stared ahead, then at them. 'Bliddy hell.'

Quite, Fran thought, as all three girls sat back while Bert ground through the gears, almost seeming to feel his way in the deepening mist, until finally he drew into a siding. The bus jerked as he parked. 'Bliddy old cow,' he muttered. 'Needs a new engine.'

Ahead, Fran could see large double gates with security guards on duty and a high fence around the perimeter. She found herself fingering the crisp pass in her pocket, her mouth dry. Suddenly it was real. Now she knew where Mrs Oborne, Maisie and the others were actually going day after day, or night after night, when they just said, 'the Factory'. For a moment she wished she was still working in the safe but boring office in Gosforn as a shorthand typist.

But last year her mam had lost the baby. Betty was too early, too small, and had drawn breath for only a few minutes before slipping away with the dawn, her da had said when he came down into the kitchen. He had stared at nothing in particular, just stood with his back to the range, then whispered, 'Who can blame the poor wee lass. We're a world at war and I reckon she took one look and said what's the bliddy point?' He petered out, just went on standing there.

Fran had worked on in the office, but as her mam failed to thrive she'd gone to the Labour Exchange in Gosforn and asked for war work. One where she'd earn decent money, she'd added, having heard the rumours around Massingham about some of the women finding well-paid work in a new factory. Then she'd be able to pay someone to help with the washing and give her mam a break.

In the Labour Exchange they'd told her she had to be over eighteen. She was nineteen. She had to work shifts. She would. Sarah had come with her and as Fran agreed, so had she. The woman had hesitated. 'It's dangerous, but no war work is a walk in the park. The pay is good, and trust me, you will be helping.'

Bert cut the bus engine and called, 'Hoy yourselves ladies. Work awaits.'

The women groaned, rose and started to make their way along the aisle and down into the siding, which was clearly a turning point for all the workers' buses. Fran, Sarah and Beth followed, glad to be out into the cool, damp air. They walked in a convoy to the gates, showed their passes and were beckoned through. Beth whispered, 'Why the bliddy hell did I sign up for this?'

The other two sighed and exchanged looks. Fran knew it was what they were all feeling, but trust Beth to actually say it. They followed a guard along the wide roadway, seeing a stream of women wearing overalls entering the grass-covered mounds over to the left, so perhaps they were actually bunkers, where the more dangerous work was done?

There was no time to watch because the guard was setting a cracking pace, and Fran hurried along with the others, eventually turning left onto a path which led to a large, low brick building, but then they were all large. The guard left them, pointing at a double doorway. Mrs Oborne led the way, calling, 'Follow yer leader, pets.'

3

The women laughed as they passed into a corridor and then turned into a windowless room lit by a couple of bare light bulbs There were two women and a man standing at the far end, the women wearing black overalls, the man green, all of which contrasted with the whitewashed bricks. Fran's heart sank just as Sarah nudged her, for the man was Mr Swinton, a dour bullying crosspatch of a Geordie from Sledgeford, near Massingham. He wore a badge that said *Foreman*. The two women wore black caps and badges that said *Security* and their names.

One, a woman of about thirty, whose frown was deep, stepped forward. She smiled, and her face was transformed. 'Welcome, ladies,' she said. 'Mrs Raydon and I are security officers. Some of you are new, so will the others forgive me as I go through the usual pep talk, or perhaps that's too optimistic a description. You see, new girls, I have to tell you what it is you've signed up for.' She held up her hand, only it wasn't a hand, it was an arm that ended at the wrist. 'I made a mistake. I became careless and had a mishap with a detonator, and you may well find yourself working with these, so be careful.'

Fran gasped, along with several others. Miss Ellington continued to smile. 'This is a filling factory, and it is work which is simple, but needs total concentration and steady hands for you will be filling armament cases of varying descriptions with explosive powders. These cases include detonators, shells, bullets, rockets, bombs. You are not only handling these powders, you are breathing them in and they can cause rashes, changes in skin and hair colouring and so on. Not always, but they can. We do our best to transfer you to the sewing shop or somesuch if this becomes a problem to you. Sometimes you feel sick, sometimes you get a bit emotional, sometimes . . . Well, let's not dwell on it, but we do what we can to give your bodies a change of scene.'

4

She pointed to Mr Swinton's overall. 'Yes, made by a "resting team". Not Mr Swinton, just his overall. We had no pattern for Mr Swinton so he created himself, indeed he did.'

As the others laughed, Mrs Oborne whispered, 'Miss Ellington's a devil for riling the old bugger. Gets right up Swinton's nose.' Fran could see Swinton glowering beneath his bushy, grey-tinged eyebrows as he moved his weight from foot to foot, and then rose on his toes, before subsiding and repeating the pattern.

Mrs Raydon took over. 'Now, ladies, a few crucial rules. You must not – ever – say where you work, not to your mam or da, not to the lady in the corner shop. Do remember we have to assume that even walls have ears, or so the posters tell us. Also remember that if our troops have no weapons capable of firing, they are in mortal danger, and what's more, we will lose the war. If you do your work efficiently, diligently, you will be part of the process that allows them to survive and crush the enemy.

'You need to know very little except your own particular task. The less you know, the less you can inadvertently discuss. Here, in this sector, you are likely to be working with one of the following: a fuse pellet – which helps the detonator to spark the explosive in a shell, or the detonator itself, and not forgetting the explosive, which we call The Yellow. You will come to understand why. All of these are bad-tempered little beggars and need careful handling.'

Mr Swinton now stepped forward. 'Don't be fooled. There are those within our own population, our own community, who would do us harm, so if you are vulnerable to flattery, to blabbing, you might be drawn into certain actions, or into explaining how the site is protected. If you do reveal what you are not supposed to, if it is discovered that you have spoken of your work, or helped the enemy in any way at all, you *will* be arrested and imprisoned.'

5

Fran thought of how she'd told Davey she had signed up for war work in a factory, and swallowed. She had told him nothing about what it was, or where it was, because she didn't know. All she'd known was that it was secret and this is what she'd said. It was then that Davey, Sarah's brother, had come up with the idea of calling it Spark Lane between themselves because the canny lad had guessed. Now, listening to Swinton, she felt it better to just call it 'the Factory'.

Miss Ellington was speaking again. 'Of course, there are rumours of our existence as we have so many employees – we Geordies aren't daft – but no details have been leaked. So make up your own fibs if you have to say anything.'

Miss Ellington then explained that the Factory complex covered hundreds of acres, and that it was none of their business to know how many workers were required, or their tasks. 'When you arrive at the start of each shift you will come to this room, or one similar, for every section has its own facilities. Once here you will divest yourselves of anything metallic, including wedding rings, and put them in the envelopes provided, and these will be kept safe until you leave at the end of your shift.'

Mrs Raydon took up the thread. 'You will also leave matches in the envelope provided. You will wear only cotton for fear of static. If you wear even a hairgrip within the working area of your section and it drops, it can cause a spark. If you drop a detonator, if you, well, become in anyway careless . . .'

On cue, Miss Ellington waggled her arm in the air. Fran thought they had their routine down to a T.

Mrs Raydon nodded. 'Need I say more?'

Mr Swinton cut across Mrs Raydon. 'We need a perfect product so if you make a mistake, we must know immediately. We can't have flawed weapons going to the front.

We canna say any of this too often, and you will hear it often, believe me.'

Mrs Raydon explained that all the buildings were well spaced out so an explosion would cause minimum damage to any of the other sectors. Each wall had a strong skeleton structure, but with a centre constructed to give way easily in order to minimise the effect of an explosion. 'In order for work to continue, in other words.' There was a pause. Mrs Raydon finished, 'That's what's important, pets. The work must continue, whatever happens.'

Beth muttered, 'And bugger the workers.'

Fran sighed, but Miss Ellington had heard. 'Exactly, young lady. An explosion is usually your own mistake, but it might be something worse. If, for instance, you take a hairgrip into a work area, it will in all likelihood be considered sabotage. Therefore, if that grip is discovered upon your person once you are clear of the changing rooms, you will be removed from the premises and will, probably, face serious criminal charges. Throughout the shift, we, or others concerned with security, will float around keeping an eye out for lack of concentration or carelessness. That is our job. We do it well.'

Mr Swinton waved his hand around. 'While you're in this sector, this is where you'll change into the overalls provided, wearing them over your day clothes which should be cotton. Checks will be made. You will don turbans and felt boots, if required, since we can't have any sparks from shoes. Over there, along that bench against the wall, are the envelopes for your dangerous articles. Place your shoes beneath if you are required to change them. Mebbe in time we'll get a separate security room for your articles. Miracles happen.'

He coughed. 'Today the trainees will start in the sewing shop, the others will follow me. Trainees, there's no need for you to know any more than that they are following me.'

Miss Ellington took over. 'A hint. If anyone asks, you are working in a factory making thingummybobs, and then change the subject.' Miss Ellington waved her hand to Mr Swinton, Mrs Raydon and herself, and then encompassed the room – 'At the start of every week you will be reminded of all that's been said today. Remember, you know nowt. You say nowt about nowt. You work eight-hour shifts, or longer if needed. These shifts rotate weekly – mornings, afternoons or nights. You do not complain if we have to work a seven-day week. We have a war to win.'

Mrs Raydon stepped forward. 'Any questions?'

Valerie, from Sledgeford, where Beth now lived, put up her hand. 'We get fed, I 'ope, otherwise it's a bliddy long day. The bus takes near on two hours.'

Miss Ellington grinned. 'Don't you worry, you won't fade away. There's a canteen.'

Mr Swinton pointed to the clock. Miss Ellington nodded, serious now. 'Time to get on and take the place of the night shift. Remember: "Be like Dad, keep Mum", "Walls have ears" and ... Well, bear in mind every other poster you've seen. And end the war with two hands, I beg you.'

Chapter One

September 1941, Massingham Colliery Village

Fran Hall smiled at her mam, who had emerged from the scullery, wiping her hands.

'You tek care now, our Fran.'

Fran shrugged into her shabby mackintosh, wound her scarf around her neck, then hugged her mother. 'I love the way you always smell of soda suds, Mam, it's right cosy.'

Her mother laughed and patted Fran's back. 'Aye, well, that says more about you than it does about me, pet, for I'd like to smell of a bit more'n suds. A dab of French perfume might do it, eh? But maybe for you, pet, it's all about the washing soda you hope to use when you're wed to yer man, eh? There's a time when even ironing his drawers is romantic, but that doesn't last long, let me tell you.'

The two of them laughed. Fran squeezed her mam and her heart twisted at how thin she still was, but there was no time to dwell on that because the grandfather clock chimed three forty-five. It was the one thing of value that the Hall family had.

'Pass your plate from the table, Fran Hall, or are you thinking the butler'll do it? And be quick about it, mind, or you'll be late for the Factory bus. Then Sarah'll hang about for you and you'll both miss a day's pay. Which'll please both your das, but let's not get into that.'

Fran snatched up her side plate, on which lay the crusts of her bread and dripping. Her mam swore it kept the chills from their chests, even during the warmest of summers. Now her mam tutted. 'Crusts make your hair curl, bonny lass, and we're on to winter soon, so you need to keep the chill away. Besides, it's wartime, so don't waste good food. Mind you and Sarah have a good dinner in the canteen at the Factory, which I heard you girls call it as if we don't know what it really is. But aye, we know from the posters these walls might have ears . . . I can see their lugs growing every day, flappin' in the draughts—'

Fran grinned. 'Draw a breath, Mam, for the love of God, or you'll have a turn.' Her mam took the plate and Fran headed for the door saying, 'Just don't go on about it when you're out and about.'

Her mam sighed. 'Teaching a dog new tricks, eh . . . Lugs open for spies, lips tight shut till us find 'em. Go on with you, and don't forget your bag and your gas mask.'

Fran was laughing as she unhitched both from the back of the chair, slipping the bag over her shoulder and patting its patchwork. 'Oh Mam, it's a miracle you didn't sew me into existence too, but let's face it, it would have been a darned sight easier than all that heaving and push . . .' She faded away. How could she be so daft? She reached a hand out to her mam, who had stopped dead in the scullery doorway. 'Oh Mam, I didn't think.'

Her da's voice came from the hall doorway. 'Aye, ye do far too much "not thinking" by a long chalk, Fran Hall.'

Her mam stepped into the kitchen, the plate still in her hand. 'Oh hush, Joe, the bairn's got a bus to catch.'

'She's no bairn, which as I recall, she took pains to tell me not so long ago, eh?' Her da glared at Fran, but then dug in his trouser pocket for his handkerchief and held it to his mouth.

Fran looked at her da, who was coughing up muck now, black muck, but no blood. *Not yet, not yet.* It was a sort of mantra against black lung. He stomped past her to the back door, pulling aside the blackout curtain. He opened the door to the clatter of pitmen as they headed along the back lane to Auld Hilda, the pit, and reached out to grab his boots from under the old chair at the side of the step that he had set up as a footwear shelter. It was a shelter that doubled as the place where he'd plonk himself down at the end of a shift and survey the yard.

Her mam spoke firmly. 'Best be on your way, our Fran. Be safe, bonny lass.'

Fran passed her da, who was slumping onto the chair at the head of the kitchen table, ignoring her, and looking tired, unhappy and out of sorts. She wished he wasn't so cross with her, on top of everything. She walked across the yard, swinging her gas mask, slowing by the old pigeon loft where the hens now roosted. She lingered, waiting just as she had done for the last month for those words – 'Be safe' – from her da, but none came. Instead it was she who called out to him, as she had since she had been a child, 'Be safe, Da.'

She lifted the sneck and stepped into the back lane, keeping tightly to the side as the miners almost marched along for the early shift at the pit. As she was about to close the gate she heard her da call, 'Be safe, our Franny.'

She could hardly believe it, and thought for an awful moment that she'd burst into tears in front of all their neighbours and friends. She could hear the relief in her voice as she replied, 'I will, Da, and thank you.'

She walked on feeling as though a great weight had fallen from her shoulders. Be safe, she thought. Oh, be safe. She swung around, stared back at Auld Hilda's pithead standing a bit over half a mile out, with its winding gear stark against the moonlight, and said, 'You take care of my men, d'you hear, Auld Hilda.' It was what she'd done ever since she could talk and her da had gone on shift, and then her older brother, Stan. She'd once asked who Hilda had really been, but no one knew, or cared.

She repeated herself as she set off again, and the miners continued to pass her, 'You take care of them all.'

She wondered if Stan still missed the hewing, the heaving at the coalface with his pickaxe, his marrers – this world. She had asked him in one of her letters when he'd started his first year at Oxford University, and he'd replied, *How can you not miss something that's in your blood and bones, and aye, in your bliddy lungs too?* She'd imagined him laughing as he wrote it.

She'd asked Davey if he would miss it if he were Stan. Davey, her canny lad, the one she loved and had always loved, said he'd miss her more, then kissed her. She was seventeen, he eighteen, and that had been two years ago. It was the first time they had kissed, and it sealed what they had both known.

Mam had said that seventeen was too young to set your heart on someone, but there was nothing she or her mam could do about it. It had always been Davey for her and her for Davey, right back to when they were wee bairns. They just fitted together, two halves of a whole, and everyone nodded, smiled and accepted it. Just like they accepted the kingfisher that owned the beck, and the slag heaps that smouldered day and night.

She hurried on, turning right and staying to the side as the men coughed, gagged and stamped along, their gas masks slung over their shoulders such a part of them all now that no one noticed any more. Some slammed their yard gates behind them before slipping into the stream with their bait tins hanging from their belts or hands, their caps pulled down or over to one side. Their mufflers were pulled up against the pre-dawn dampness of this September morning. Some were talking to one another, some nodded to her, all said, "Ow do, pet?'

'Be safe,' she muttered each time, looking ahead to where Davey would come along with his marrers, Sid and Norm, and all the time her heart was singing because Da had said, 'Be safe.'

So, at last she was forgiven for not going into the armaments factory office, where it was clean, respectable and safe, and where she'd use the skills he had grafted to pay for, as he had yelled a month ago. 'Grafted – and what do you do? Go and bliddy work with ammunition so's I might as well've shoved you down the pit and set you to work on the fuses.'

She could hear him now, and her own voice as she'd shouted back: 'It's supposed to be a secret. You mustn't say those words about the Factory or you'll end up in prison, and me an' all.'

She slowed now, staying by the wall and looking up at the night sky and still the men passed and her da's voice roared in her head. 'I'll say what I bliddy like in my own house, and I say you won't do it.' He'd been standing by the range mantelpiece, which was what he always did when he was making a point about some fat-arsed politician, as he called them, or when his children's school reports had said could do better, if only he or she tried. This time, he'd rammed shreds of tobacco into his pipe, as though pulverising the Hun he'd fought in the First World War, and stormed out.

Fran set off again, nodding to the pitmen, knowing that the same thing was going on in the Bedley household too, but both Fran and Sarah had dug in their heels. Fran turned right out of the back lane which ran between her own terrace, Leadenhall Terrace, which fronted onto Leadenhall Street and Litton Cottages, and set off towards the bus shelter but the echo of her da's voice followed her, as loud as if he was here beside her.

'It's bliddy shift work, grubby and dangerous, like the bliddy mines. In t'office you'd've been fiddling with typing keys, wearing clean clothes, getting on, working your way up. And I don't give a rat's arse about what Sarah does. Thee and she'll always do what t'other does, yer always have and always will. Two bliddy peas in a pod, but that's nowt to write home about when you're daft as brushes.'

Her mam had called from the scullery, 'Language, Joe. You're not in Auld Hilda now.'

Fran had said, 'And it's more money than in the bliddy office—'

'Enough.' He'd flung his unlit pipe onto the mantelpiece and stared down at the range before turning to her and saying in a voice that was full of rage and pain, 'You're saying I can't look after your mam, and it's up to you to pay for the washing and ironing? You're saying I can't look after me own family? You, a bairn, saying that?'

He'd stepped towards her, drawing back his arm, and Mam had yelled, 'Joe Hall, don't even think of laying a finger on our Fran, d'you hear me? What in the name of goodness . . . ?'

At the memory, Fran slowed, and almost stopped, but then shook herself for she had a bus to catch. She crossed Dunbury Street onto which Sarah's terrace fronted, then their back lane. The pitmen were clattering through it, but it was the quiet in the Halls' kitchen she heard. A quiet broken only by the spluttering of the range, and it was this she had concentrated on as her da's arm fell to his side. It was spluttering because Mam had used slack gleaned from the slag heap. It was coal from Massingham Colliery that burned quietly, coal delivered weekly to every miner's house from the pit, as decreed by the fair and decent owner,

Mr Reginald Massingham. She remembered thinking this, and even as she did so she had wondered – why?

A couple of pitmen passed and called, "Ow do, pet?'

'Be safe,' she called back, but her mind was on the coal and thought perhaps her brain had been trying to find something normal to concentrate on as the shock reverberated, but then young Ben had come in from his friend's house, where they'd been trying to solve a crossword her Davey had set them. At his entrance, Da'd shaken his head, yelling that at least Stan had got out, and away, and he'd picked up his cap and stomped out. Perhaps he was heading to the canaries in the Canary Club shed on the allotment, where he'd find Sarah's da and talk about their daughters' behaviour.

Sarah, her best friend, who had worked in an office too. Sarah, whom she had started school with. Sarah, who was Davey's sister, and who now worked in the same section she and Beth had been directed to – detonators, not that Fran or Sarah had told their mams and das that.

Fran sighed. Poor Da, he had had such hopes for her, but the war would end, and then she could type until the world ended. Perhaps she should have said that as he left, but it was her Mam who had spoken on the heels of the slammed door. 'He fears for you, for me, and for Ben. He wants to be the one facing any sort of danger. He wants to be the one supporting us. You have to try and understand that to have a daughter bringing home more'n him and being in danger is more'n he can bear, because it makes him fear he is not the man of the family. 'Tis all right for me to make me proggy rugs and sell them, because it's safe and just pocket money, but— Oh, he'd never strike any of us, he just ran out of words. You need to know that, Fran.'

'Of course I know that,' Fran said as she hurried now, for the bus had pulled up at the bus shelter where the women were milling. Yes, she knew it, but nothing would stop her working, because her mam was still thin and weak from the septicaemia that had struck after Betty was born and died, all within the space of half an hour, and she needed help, and that was that.

What's more Madge had been pleased to take in the washing, and there was enough left to save for a doctor, and one day there'd be enough for a headstone for Betty.

Fran walked past a group of miners getting a move on towards the pit as the hooter sounded. One nodded at her and called, 'The old man up, is he, pet?'

'Oh aye, and raring to go, Mr Corbitt.'

'That'll be the day,' Eddie Corbitt laughed.

Fran smiled. They all loved her da because he was not only a hewer, but also on the rescue team and would put his life in danger to save the men. Well, they all would, of course.

She lifted her head and breathed in *her* world, the one she had always known: the sulphur carried on the breeze from the slag heaps, the noise of the boots as shifts began and ended, the clank of the pit gear, the train that steamed to the main line, just past the Long Pull, where you could buy sweets and beer before there had been such shortages. She loved the gleam of the train tracks that ran across the square and the sound of the coal as they shovelled it into the firebox. It was Massingham coal, built with their pit-men's blood and toil. *Theirs*, these men like Da, Tom Bedley, Eddie and Davey, and Stan before he left.

Ahead, the bus exhaust was huffing out into the fading night. The girls and women were in groups, some smoking, and she laughed aloud to think of her mam on her Thursday-night Air Raid Precaution duties having to call, 'Put that light out.' Her mam said she felt a right fool because smouldering behind the smokers were the slag heaps, which could be beacons for any bombers, though none had ever come this way.

They hadn't even found the Factory, but if they did, wouldn't that be an explosion big enough to end the bloody world, or theirs at least? There were air-raid shelters on the site, but they weren't the huge bunkers she had seen; those were, it was whispered, where shell and bomb filling was carried out and were designed like that to contain any accidental explosions.

She saw Davey then, marching along with his marrers, though that was an overstatement – slouching, coughing and talking was more like it. She knew exactly when he saw her, because he hurried ahead, his boots slamming on the cobbles. They stood close. He smiled, reaching out his hand for hers. 'Well, bonny lass, another day, eh?'

'Da said it as I left, Davey.'

'Be safe?'

'That's the one.'

He leaned close and kissed her forehead. Sid groaned as he approached. 'Just put her down, Davey, for pity's sake. You've had your breakfast, no need to eat another.'

Norm dragged Sid on as Davey lifted her hand, kissing it. 'I'm right glad, my sweet bonny lass.'

She heard the bus driver hoot. She had to go. 'Be safe, lovely lad. Can you still come with me after shift to sort out the buyer of Mam's proggy rugs?'

His grip tightened. 'Oh Franny, I do wish just for once in your life you'd done as your da wanted and stayed beatin' hell out of a typewriter, not doing whatever you Factory girls do. But all I'll say for now is be safe yourself. Course I'll come to give him hell. I pumped me tyres up ready and'll make sure yours are all reet. You've the address? Does—'

He stopped. His marrers were calling out that he'd be

17

late for shift else he got a wriggle on. He dragged himself away and Fran hurried towards Sarah, who was waving to her from the queue, calling, 'Howay, pet, get some steam behind you or Bert says he'll leave love's young dream, and see how she bliddy likes that. Was that reet, Bert?'

The other women were piling on to the bus and laughing, and one called, 'Same every morning, afternoon or evening with you two, Fran Hall. Time you wed the lad and were done with it.'

Another, Maisie this time, called out, 'Their mams say they're too young. But right canny they are, and even manage to match their shifts. I don't know how, do you, Sylv?'

Her friend shook her head, her faded headscarf keeping her hair in order as she clambered on board.

Fran heard Davey calling then, but she was already on the step and had to strain to hear. 'Sarah has something for you. I'll be waiting with both bikes, if you still want to go after . . . Oh never mind. I love you, bonny lass. Don't be too hard on—'

She couldn't hear any more as he was fast disappearing down the alley, so she moved up into the bus and along the aisle, Sylv walking ahead of Sarah and calling, 'Full speed ahead then, Bert. Divint be lazing about. Get your foot down, for the love of God.'

'Bliddy hell, the cheek of it,' Bert huffed, putting the bus into gear while the women laughed and the bus lurched off. Fran steadied herself as she made her way along behind the others as they peeled off into seats, until finally she bumped into Sarah, who had stopped at a couple that had an empty aisle seat opposite, next to Mary. Sarah threw her muffler onto the single seat to bagsy it for Beth, whom they'd pick up at the Sledgeford stop, then slid along the double to the window. Fran joined her. They were over a wheel arch so would be shaken up good and proper. The slatted wooden seat was as hard as it always was, and cold. Bert swung the bus round the corner and headed down the winding lane towards Sledgeford.

'What did Davey mean? I couldn't hear him. What've you got for me?' Fran asked.

Sarah snatched off her hat and began tucking up into hair slides the escaped strands of her long, flyaway blonde hair. She had put it up in a French pleat that was even now disintegrating and was ramming the hairpins back in as she muttered, her blue eyes dark with anger, 'Didn't he tell you? He is a toerag. A bliddy toerag. I'll have his guts for garters, copping out like that.'

Maisie called from the seat behind them, her Woodbine bobbing up and down on her lower lip as she spoke, her eyes squinting against the smoke, 'That's men for you, in't it, Sylv?'

Sylv laughed. 'Reckon you've a point, Maisie.'

Chapter Two

The bus jolted as it swung round the ancient Hanging Tree on the corner and set out for the next village. It was said that highwaymen had been hung from the oak tree, and on a stormy night you could still see one dancing a jig on the end of a rope. Fran had believed it when she was young and couldn't pass beneath the branches, but such stories reverted to the fiction they were when one had to grapple with real life. She had told Mam so a couple of years ago, and Mam had hidden a laugh, though not in time.

'Mam . . .' Fran had wailed.

Her mam had merely kissed her and said, 'You enjoy sorting out your grappling while you're young, bonny lass.'

Stan had been there, giving his boots a spit and polish to keep out the wet before he headed over to see Beth, who lived two streets down and whom he had courted before she broke his heart. He had added, 'Aye, do that, pet. The grappling doesn't get sorted, it only gets worse.'

He and Mam had laughed quietly together, both dark-haired, dark-eyed – well, all the Halls were. The slack had spluttered, the oil lamp flickered, and the smoke from Stan's roll-up drifted towards the ceiling.

Fran smiled at the memory. Did Stan think of their kitchen while he scratched his head over his books amongst the dreaming spires of Oxford, as the vicar had begun calling them?

'Given to fancies, the new young vicar be,' her mam had said as they'd left the Reverend Walters looking at himself in the haberdasher's window, or was it young Molly Higgins he was pursuing?

Fran started laughing at the thought, but as she did so, Bert dodged a rabbit that tore out of the hedge at the same time as an owl burst from the tree and swooped over the bus. Sarah and Fran ducked, as did Maisie and Sylv behind them, then they all burst out laughing, though it was strained. An owl could be a harbinger of bad news.

'I'm crossing my fingers,' said Sarah.

'Don't be daft, pet. It's a load of rubbish and I for one'd like to see a million of 'em rather than them bombers that's just hit Newcastle, the buggers,' Maisie said, coughing and then drawing on her Woodbine again. 'Can't be doing with superstitious nonsense when bombs is the real-life buggers.'

Fran thought of that evening and Mam and Stan talking about grappling with life. It made her sit up straight. What was it Davey had said? 'Don't be too . . .'?

Just as she started to ask Sarah again, Sylv muttered, "Ope me uncle Sidney's not one of them that's copped it. Mam's setting off to check tomorrow, cos the phone lines're down. Fifty dead, thousands injured . . . Well, maybe hundreds, but that's bad enough. Don't know what me bairn'd think? Right fond of his great-uncle he is.'

Sarah looked at Fran and whispered, 'Aye, it could be us one day an' all, if someone does something bliddy silly in our sector, or the bombers find us.'

Fran shook her head, half singing, 'Don't be daft, we're invincible, we're the Factory girls.'

Bert called out as he changed down through the gears and splashed across the ford, 'We'll be pulling up at the Sledgeford Club any minute for the next load, so anyone who forgot to "go", you'd best get to the netty in the club yard and be sharp about it, for I'm not stopping until Minton.'

Several rose, leaving the cushions they had brought with them to make the seats more bearable. Once they'd squeezed their way down the aisle, others came on, with Fran and Sarah's friend Beth third in the line. Fran waved, then pointed to the seat across the aisle.

'She's got her face on her, so she's in a bad mood, again. But it must be awful to not know if someone's all right,' Sarah whispered.

Fran smiled as Beth sank onto the seat next to Mary and in front of Edith Wilson who lived near the corner shop in Massingham. Beth just snapped, 'Must be nice to be a pair, just as it were at school – you two leaving me on the outside.'

Fran ignored Sarah's nudge and tried to make her smile gentle. 'So, still no word from Bob?'

Beth pressed her lips together and stared ahead, then shook her head. 'Bliddy seats get no better, nothing does.'

Sarah leaned past Fran. 'I just know he's all right, Beth. His letters have got caught up or his minesweeper's busy, or whatever they've put him in now. If it were worse, you'd feel it in your gut, or have been told.'

Although one of them said the same thing almost every day, Beth looked at her, relief lighting up her face as she grabbed at Sarah's words. 'Maybe you're right. I haven't seen an owl fly over the house, so that's something.'

Maisie was clambering back on the bus, shrieking as she missed the top step and fell forward.

'Tek more water with it, our Maisie,' Mrs Oborne called from the front seat.

'Come on, come on, if you're five minutes late they'll dock you fifteen minutes and so far we're just that – five minutes late,' Bert yelled, starting up the bus again.

As the women hurried, Mrs Oborne called, 'Less of the bossing and more getting your foot down, Bert Evans.'

But Bert, not wanting his pay docked either, was already

storming along, swerving round panicked cock pheasants, or if not, clipping them. They were considered fair game, so someone could fetch them home for tea without expecting the Massingham gamekeeper's knock on the door.

As they rushed along the lanes, they seemed to be driving through a forest of slag heaps that glinted like ashes in a grate, brightening as the wind swirled and seeming to fade when it died. In the light from the moon Fran checked her watch. Dawn wouldn't truly come until after they'd started their shift at six, by which time Da and Davey would have reached the pit, waited for the cage to take them down the pit, and then traipsed along the seam, all half mile or more of it, bending and crawling, to the coalface where work would begin. 'Be safe,' she urged again, not realising she'd spoken aloud until Beth said, 'I'm a cow. I forget that we've all men we want to keep safe. Right sorry, both of you.'

Fran felt the pressure of Sarah's arm and said, 'We don't need to say sorry to one another, and anyway, it's not as though we girls are sitting about all day sunning ourselves in the lap of luxury and drinking cocktails. Who the hell knows what accident is going to come and bite us on the bum, or snatch off a hand like Miss Ellington, and if we think about it more'n we do, we'll like as not end up in the nuthouse, along with the whole of this bus.'

Sylv tapped her on the shoulder. 'You speak for yersel', lass, though when I think of it, it might be a nice rest in one of them padded cells.'

They all grinned as Fran reached for Beth's outstretched hand and squeezed it. 'You're worried about your man, and there's Sarah a poor old spinster, with not a lad in view to mither about.' She ignored Sarah's pretend punches, and all three collapsed into laughter.

'Aye . . .' Sarah said, trying to speak and breaking down

again, until finally she spluttered, 'They keep running off soon as I show interest, canny blighters.'

All three of them were laughing again, and everything was all right, for now. Beth let go of Fran's hand and took her knitting from her bag to continue with the sweater she was making her Bob for when he finally came home. As Fran's mam said, you did what made things better, and there was sense in that and it was no one's business. But Fran and Sarah still wondered if Bob would appreciate bright yellow.

Maisie leaned through the gap between the seats, trying to whisper over the roaring of the engine. 'Her Bob'll look like a ruddy canary, but I daresay he'll treasure it so much he'll keep it locked away safely in a drawer for evermore – what do you say, hinnies?' She winked at the two girls, leaned back and lit another Woodbine.

Fran supposed a husband would do exactly that, possibly out of love for his wife, but more likely because he didn't care to be the butt of tweet-tweet whistles wherever he went. It was then that she saw the envelope Sarah had dragged from her mac pocket and was holding out to her.

'This is what our Davey were talking about, bonny lass.' She only called Fran bonny lass when there was something wrong.

Fran looked from her friend to the letter, her mouth dry. Was Davey chucking her? But he'd sit her down and tell her if that were it, surely? Besides, he'd said he'd see her later. Her heart was beating so hard she could hardly breathe. Or had he signed up? But he couldn't; he and Stan had been hurt in the same fall and with their wonky legs had both been turned down.

'Why's Davey writing to me? I don't want it, Sarah, and besides, the sun's not up yet, it's still too gloomy.'

'You have to have it. It's from your Stan, you daft thing,

24

not our Davey.' Sarah was whispering because she didn't want Beth to hear any mention of Stan's name. It would be embarrassing for them all, yet again.

Fran said, in a whisper that matched Sarah's, 'What on earth? He can't have signed up? And why write to me? He should tell Da and Mam.'

Sarah put the letter in Fran's lap. 'The lad sent it to Davey because he didn't want your da peering over your shoulder while you read it and having a right palaver. Or that's what Stan put in the note that came with it. Stan wants you to break whatever it is to your folks, to sort of soften the blow.'

Bert had drawn to a halt at a T-junction. He turned left, heading east where the sky was lightening. Sarah picked up the letter and flapped it in front of Fran's face. 'Read the damned thing and then we'll know what you have to soften. You know what, I'm right fed up with these lads.'

Fran continued to stare at the letter, but Sarah just carried on flapping it. Fran ignored her, turned away and looked down the aisle, muttering, 'He's just a bliddy snot, and I won't do his dirty work for him, whatever it is.'

Beth looked across at them. 'Why are you fanning her? Come over all hot and bothered, has she?'

'Got a letter from her Stanhope,' Maisie called over, 'and doesn't want to open it.'

'For heaven's sake, Maisie, have another ciggy and mind your own bliddy business,' Fran snapped.

'Then open the damned thing, and put us all out of our misery. It's cool enough without yon lass fanning us all.' Maisie lit another Woodbine.

Fran snatched up the letter and drew it out of the envelope, conscious of Beth staring. What on earth have you done, our Stan? she thought. Failed your exams? But it's the vacation and you'd have heard before this. Or lost your holiday job with your professor? But no to both – you're Mr

Massingham's scholarship boy, so you couldn't, not with your brainy bonce. Debts? Well, pay them off yourself. I'm not forking out, nor is Da, and I won't soften the news if it's that. But no, Stan wouldn't; he was a good boy, always had been. She unfolded the letter and Sarah clicked on her small torch, holding it over the writing, and Fran read as the bus jerked and swung.

Dearest bonny lass
   I know you've had your troubles with our da over the work you're doing now and I've tried to write a letter to him and Mam about a decision I have made, but I just can't get going, so I'll tell them more about it when I come up, but I'm as yellow as that jumper you say Beth is knitting. (Yellow? So perhaps it were better she broke me heart when she did and chose Bob Jones, eh, otherwise I'd be tucked up by mistake in me da and Tom's cages along with their canaries.) Anyways, I want you to tell Mam and Da gently. Will you do that for me?

Sarah was reading it with her, and now they looked at one another. 'Tell them what, for pity's sake?' Fran snapped. 'He always was a one for mithering until he got things sorted in his head, but he should have done that before he wrote the thing.'

Sarah focused the torch again, muttering, 'He really seems over her, d'you think?'

Fran felt too angry to even care whether he was over Beth or not, for he wanted something from her that was going to upset her parents, just when . . . She read on:

I'm coming home, lass. I start in the pit on Monday.

Fran dropped the letter onto her lap. Coming home to the pit? He was mad. Their da . . . her mam . . . All their striving to pay for extra lessons. First it had been her, and now he was throwing it up too?

Sarah had dropped the torch onto her own lap, its slit beam playing on the back of the seat in front. 'He can't?' she whispered. 'Oh, he can't. What a kettle of fish, what a ... What about Beth? Will he mither over her all over again? Will she now Bob's away? Or ... howay, he's not coming back because Bob's out in the war and he sees his chance again? No, that can't be right. He wouldn't be such a cheat, and oh – imagine – we'd all have to lie to Bob's family and everyone. It'd be dreadful, so dreadful ... ' Sarah's voice began to shake before she fell silent for a moment. Then she whispered, 'Not Stan. He couldn't do that, could he?'

Fran only half listened, dreading the scene her da would make when she told him Stan was returning. How was she to break it? How could the lad do this? How damn well could he? Finally, as she folded the letter, and leaned back in her seat, Sarah's words penetrated and Fran closed her eyes. First he was coming home, which was almost the worst news her parents could hear, but if it was because of Beth ... No, that would break her da even further, not to mention her mam. She snatched a look at Beth, and away again. No, Beth was a married woman. No, it mustn't happen, and that was that.

Sarah lifted the envelope lying on Franny's lap and slipped it into her pocket, still shocked and confused, picturing the handwriting on the envelope sitting on the mantelpiece, which was where her mam usually propped Stan's letters to Davey. As always, she'd gazed at that royal blue scrawl and for a moment it was as though he hadn't really gone. As though their gang hadn't broken up.

She looked out of the window as they whipped past the fields. But the gang had broken up, and that was the sadness. Mark you, Stan and Davey were still as close as thieves, and Fran and she were too. When they were bairns, though, they'd been a gang as tight as a fist, but they had opened up to let Beth in when she had arrived in the village, because . . . Well, why had they? Ah yes, she and Fran, both seven years old, had taken Beth under their wings when she'd arrived in their class after her da changed pits from Darlington to Massingham. Stan had protected Beth too, as he had all of them, because he was the leader. But he had become more than a leader to Beth as they grew older, for he had loved the ground she walked on, until Bob came back to Massingham in his uniform, all signed up and different, and what happened, happened.

Would Stan reach out to them all again, if he came home? All, which would include Beth? Would Stan resist – would Beth? Sarah felt sick, but it was because Bert was taking them over an old bridge now, swooping over it, leaving their stomachs in the air. Yes, that was it, that's what it was.

She stared over the parapet beneath which ran Cold Beck, where bairns from Minton must have swum and played, and probably still did. They'd be bound to catch minnows in jam jars on strings, and race sticks beneath the bridge, and maybe watch a kingfisher as it darted from its perch in a willow. It's what all gangs did, and always had done, just as they had at Massingham Beck, just outside the village. She could taste the jam sandwiches they ate on the bank, hear the laughter as they swam, dived and raced across the deep water by the bridge. When she thought of it, the sun always played on the ripples, and the fire they built dried them.

Bert was driving beneath overhanging oak trees, their leaves still clinging, the green of them turning. Sarah again felt the breeze as Stan tied a rope to the old horse chestnut tree on the bank when she, Fran and Beth were ten, taking his time to pick the best and strongest branch for them all to swing on. In her memory Stan always seemed to be joshing them, picking them up when they fell or taking the blame if they were caught scrumping Farmer Brown's apples.

She still heard Stan's news when a letter from Oxford arrived for Davey, which was often. Her brother would tell her, though he wouldn't read the letter aloud, which was what she actually longed for him to do. She wanted to hear it in Stan's words – all about the town and the river, and the punts, which had taken time to become used to. Who had he taken punting? she wondered, but never asked. Somehow she didn't want to know too much.

He'd looked after them even after Beth had chosen Bob Jones instead of him and left the gang. Yes, he'd still looked after them, but it wasn't the same because Stan wasn't the same. His pain was the gang's pain. They'd wanted to help him, but how could they? Stan was the leader, and it had made her feel off-kilter not having that one person who stood so strong, and who somehow made her days softer, and safe.

Sarah leaned back, like Fran, and shut her eyes. Stan had soon left, Bob had gone to war, and Beth had bumped into them at the Labour Exchange and decided to join the Factory. It was almost the same, the three of them together again, but not quite. Beth had hurt their Stan, and she was prickly about being an outsider. Was that really because she had arrived at the school later, or because she felt embarrassed about cheating on Stan? Suddenly, savagely, Sarah wished Mr Smith had never left his Darlington pit. Shocked at herself, she opened her eyes and stared around her.

'Hey, Sarah Bedley, what's going on in that head of yours? You look as though you're about to bash someone.' It was Fran raising her eyebrows at her.

Sarah nodded. 'Course not. It's these seats, they're too hard. I were just thinking back to how it was when we had the gang, and life was so – oh, I don't know. Normal, I suppose.'

Fran squeezed her hand, 'I know what you mean.' Sarah gripped the envelope in her pocket as Fran picked up the letter from her lap, then peered at the bottom corner. 'Hang on, it says PTO.' She read on, in a low murmur.

Elliott the manager is making me stop on the surface at the sorting screens for a bit before I get back to hewing at the coalface. He says it's only right to think on me as a new pit-man. And Franny, don't let Da go mithering on about the Massingham scholarship. I wrote to Mr Massingham, and he says I can take it up again when the war is finished because he'll hold it over. He said it was good to be wanting to help the war effort. So, be sure to tell our da that too, and Mam, and that I'll be back Saturday evening, if the trains behave and the bombers stay off the line. Do this for your big brother, and I'll buy you a bag of chips. I'll bunk in with Ben in the attic room.

Bonny lass, don't show Da this letter. Just say I think if I can't go to the war, I'll bloody well hew for it. Just tell him that, bonny lass.

Stan.

Fran whispered, 'Turn off the torch, Sarah.' They both sat back in the lightening gloom, neither saying anything.

Maisie tapped Fran's shoulder. 'Your lad all right, is he?'

'Oh yes, Maisie. He's all right, except that he's a bugger.'

Maisie and Sylv cackled. 'Well, he's a man, isn't he?' Sylv said.

Beth was looking at the two of them. 'What's going on?'

'Nothing,' Fran and Sarah said together.

'Be like that then,' Beth sniffed.

'So, that's why the owl flew over the bus,' Maisie whispered, leaning forward and ramming her head between theirs.

'I could strangle him,' Fran hissed, wanting to cry.

'You couldn't catch him,' she heard Sarah whisper.

'Stan, not the owl.'

'I know, you daft beggar.' They laughed together, but there was only a strained humour in it.

'We both know this'll wreck Da's dream completely. First our Betty, then Mam not thriving, me in the Factory amongst explosives, and now Stan returning to the pit when he were set for a different world. And it's me that's to break it to him.' Fran snatched a look across the aisle at Beth, who was knitting furiously, and whispered, 'How's it . . . I mean, is he—'

'Don't. We just have to wait and see,' Sarah interrupted.

Fran stared out of the window, the fading moonlight glinting through the changing leaves, and hints of autumn already in the air.

Damn Stan, she thought, because he was right; it had to be her, a letter or a phone call would be too cruel, and an appearance out of the blue the bitter end. She tried to think of how she could set it all out for her da and mam before Stan came through the door. For if she didn't, words would be thrown that could never be taken back.

Sarah silently packed away her torch, then held out her hand, which Fran gripped. 'Aye, we have to wait and see,' Sarah repeated.

Fran sighed. 'I know, and just when I've had me da deciding to be kind and calling out to me to be safe . . .'

'You've work to do, so don't mither it, or you'll end all your problems, and the rest of ours,' Sarah said.

Bert went into a pothole and out again, the wooden seats spared no one, and Maisie groaned behind them. Sarah asked, 'So, will you still go with Davey when you get back today to sort out that man who's buying your mam's rugs too cheap? The one you reckon is selling them on to someone else? Or are you going home to talk to yer da?'

'He'll be pulling the cabbage at the allotment, or with your da at the canaries, so I'll go. Can't put off sorting out that idiot just to make things easier for another idiot called Stanhope.'

Beth listened to them laughing, but sat still, letting her knitting rest on her lap because she had heard what Fran said just now to Sarah about Stan coming back. After the war started in 1939, she'd been walking out with Stan when Bob had come home in his uniform to Massingham after his training. Right grand he'd looked too in his sailor's uniform, and it was as though Beth hadn't seen the lad before, though he'd been in the class above Stan and Davey. He'd gone back to serve on minesweepers out of Grimsby, but caught pneumonia, and been sent home for a few weeks' sick leave. She should have told Stan before he'd caught her with Bob in one of Mr Massingham's cornfields, but she hadn't, and that had been that.

She shut her mind against the look on Stan's face, and the burning shame she'd felt. He had begged her just once, the following day, to come back to him, but by the end of the week he had walked as tall as he always had, and within weeks he was as pleasant as he'd always been, though his eyes showed how he was suffering. She and Bob had brought the wedding forward so they could rent a house in Sledgeford and have a fresh start. It meant she didn't have to see Stan and the girls every day.

But Sledgeford wasn't really her home, it was just a

house, and she was lonely even though Fran and Sarah were friends again. Aye, achingly lonely she was. She'd taken to wondering, as she lay in bed, if she had made the wrong choice for if she'd stayed with Stan, he'd likely not have gone to Oxford, or if he had, she could have gone too.

Beth sighed, for she couldn't rightly remember Bob any more, but she could still see and hear Stan as though he were right in front of her. She continued to twist her ring, trying to get her head straight before she came anywhere near the detonators.

Chapter Three

They eventually neared the Factory as dawn was threatening to break over the mist-covered acres of buildings that housed the different sectors. Fran checked her watch. It was five forty . 'Well done, Bert,' she called. 'You've picked up that five minutes. No money lost today, lad, so I've decided it will be a good day.'

'You and whose army, our Fran?' he replied, parking the bus.

The girls on the bus called, 'She doesn't need an army, she's a Hall.'

They filed off, grumbling about their numb or sore backsides, sure they had the slatted seats imprinted on their flesh. They walked in a crocodile to the gates, and as always it reminded Fran and Sarah of class trips to find fallen leaves they'd take back to draw round and colour in. They showed their passes at the gate, and still in a crocodile walked along the wide roadway with their guard, turning off to their section's changing rooms, where they would put on their blue overalls, turbans and felted shoes, unless it were messy work, in which case it would be spark safe Wellington boots. They would also divest themselves of any dangerous articles.

There were already some women changing, having arrived from other towns and villages. There was one newcomer, though, standing to one side of the white tiled room and already tying up her blue apron-type overall, then smoothing it over her smart black skirt, and pulling out the collar of her pink blouse so it lay along the collar of the overalls. Her bare legs looked cold, as she pulled on the Wellington boots over her bare feet. Oh, so she had worn nylons?

Fran snatched a look at the coats hanging on hooks. Yes, sure enough there were a pair of stockings hanging from a smart coat pocket. The girl was now wringing the turban she had been designated, and looking wildly about her.

'Nerves,' whispered Beth to Fran.

Mr Swinton was standing by the far door, as was usual at the start of a shift, as if he was guarding the way to their various workshops, his hands balled up in his pockets. The girls thought he did that to remind them he had fists. He hadn't used them as such, to anyone's knowledge, but he wasn't above pushing and shoving as he passed by in the corridor. Fran was waiting for it to be her turn, which it would be, she was sure, for she was a Hall and the sister of the scholarship boy – a scholarship his own son, Tim, had sat, and failed.

The bus 'team' slipped off their rings, or wrapped a plaster around, and checked for hairgrips and hairpins. Fran removed her belt, which had a metal buckle. How stupid. She'd meant to leave it on the chest of drawers in her box room. She stuffed everything into the envelope on which she'd written her name a month ago; it was growing increasingly tatty.

The new girl continued to stand there, but was now leaning back against the wall, still mashing her turban. Her mid-brown hair hung loose; her hazel eyes still darted about.

Once everyone had divested themselves of their contraband, as it was called, Mr Swinton snapped, 'Jewellery, matches, cigarettes, hairgrips, and anything else metallic removed? Then . . .'

He rose on his toes, and Franny's heart sank. He was going to go through his safety-and-security rigmarole. It wasn't even the start of a new week and therefore not obligatory safety procedure, but he was staring at the new girl. Ah, Fran thought, it's for her sake and it's going to raise the level of her nerves something chronic, poor thing, for she still looks like a rabbit caught in the gamekeeper's shotgun. A white rabbit, because she was so pale she almost matched the wall tiles.

Mr Swinton withdrew one hand from his pocket and jabbed his forefinger at the girl, directing her into the group, then returned the hand to its lair. She obeyed and stood next to Fran, who smiled. The girl's shoulders dropped in relief as she tried to smile back. Rising on his toes again, Mr Swinton spelled out the need for secrecy and shut mouths, for some lugs were always open and sabotage always a fear in a workplace such as this. It wasn't just explosions, but machinery that could be destroyed and therefore armaments stalled. He stared around at them all as though they were saboteurs in disguise, but they knew it by heart and no one took any notice except for the new girl.

Swinton drew breath and then launched into the remaining rhetoric, dragging his hands from his pockets and almost conducting as he extolled the need for care as they filled the bombs, bullets, shells and detonators, emphasising the burden of guilt should they become careless and kill not just themselves, but others.

It was the relish with which he said this each time that was unnerving, and summed up the strange darkness in the man, or that's how Mrs Oborne had put it in the canteen a couple of days ago.

'Strange darkness?' Maisie had reared up. 'He's a bliddy bully, that's what he is. Shoved past me on our way to the section last week. Whack went his elbow and straight into the wall went I, and he meant to an' all.'

Valerie had said, 'He don't like women, he really don't, and he's even worse since his wife walked out. Aye, she took a taxi from Sledgeford to Lord knows where a year or so back. Told the cabby to get the fee from the "auld bugger" an' all.'

Maisie had shot back, 'Good bliddy luck to her, and I bet the "auld bugger" didn't tip him.' The whole table had burst out laughing.

Mr Swinton was now running through the shift system: one week on the fore shift, 6 a.m. to 2 p.m., then the aft shift, 2 p.m. to 10 p.m., and after that the night shift, 10 p.m. to 6 a.m., though these were open to change, depending on circumstances, and what's more, change without warning. If more hours were needed, then they were needed. He ended on the declaration about mistakes, as per usual. 'Even a seemingly small mistake could mek you the murderers of your friends and colleagues, splattering 'em about the walls, legs and arms all over the bliddy place, but more'n that, you could also be responsible for our defeat. Errors must not be hidden, they must be declared, or worse damage could ensue.'

With that, Fran presumed he had finished, but he started again from the beginning as though they were deaf, or stupid, or was he just trying to make them late on shift and therefore lose money? She wouldn't put it past him. She looked at the floor and tuned him out, but that was just as bad because all she could think about was Stan returning to the pit, to danger, to a bad bliddy chest, to Da's cruel disappointment. She hated the damned war, hated it more than she had hated anything in her life.

'I don't see your hand being raised, Miss Frances Hall.

Too clever by half, are you? Or too lazy?' Mr Swinton was staring at her, his hands back in his pockets, writhing.

Sarah nudged her, raising her eyebrows to warn her not to inflame the man who had already shown many times since they'd begun here that he harboured a grudge against the sister of Stanhope Hall. But Fran couldn't stop herself and waved her hand in a deliberately languid way, answering, 'So sorry, Mr Swinton. I was just mulling your words of wisdom, so compelling were they.'

There, she thought, stuff that in your pocket and pound it to death. Sarah rolled her eyes, and smothered a grin.

Swinton bawled, 'Compelling, eh? Showing off, eh, and reminding us that your white-collared personage should really be in the office. Or maybe university, like that brother of yours.'

Sarah and Beth, who stood behind Franny, hissed, 'No, don't rise to him, Fran.'

Fran shook her head, as though she was shaking off their warning, because today she'd had more than enough of men being idiots. 'Not at all, Mr Swinton. I think safety is a very serious business. I am not desirous of causing an accident, of that let me emphatically assure you.'

Now Sarah dug her elbow into Fran's ribs while Fran watched Swinton's complexion reach an alarming red. She couldn't give a monkey's, quite frankly. His digs about Stan had been going on for too long. Everything was just going on too ruddy long, and how dare Stan dump the breaking of his news onto her? How dare her da be so cross with her – as he would be – when she told him? How dare the buyer of her mam's proggy rugs short-change Mam and her friends? And how bliddy dare this wretched bully go on day after day making all their lives a misery?

Swinton looked at the new girl now, who still stood next to Fran. 'You and Miss Cartwright should get on right well.

Both know long words, so you can teach us, can't you? Bring us up to scratch . . . Do you desirous – I mean, are you desirous of keeping your fellows safe, Miss Cartwright? Is that included in your plans at all?'

The girl standing next to Fran said quietly, in a posh southern voice, 'I just want to help the war effort, Mr Swinton, that's all, and this is where I was sent. Though I confess I hoped I was destined for the office, for I'm not used to . . . well, *this*.'

Fran winced. The girl had opened the door to a Swinton put-down, never mind ruffled a few feathers amongst the Factory girls, including her.

Swinton stood on his toes again. 'So, you're saying it's not where you want to be?'

The girl kept calm, though Fran could see her hands making fists in her pockets now – was it catching?

'If it's where I can help the war effort, then this is where I want to be.'

All the other women were torn between the worry that as the clock ticked towards five fifty-five they would be late to their workshop and lose fifteen minutes' worth of wages, and the rat-a-tat of the row brewing between the hated Swinton, Fran, who was one of their own, and Miss Cartwright, who was not, and who had seemed to look down on them. Though perhaps not, for with her final riposte she had recovered what had probably just been a slip of the tongue.

Fran was looking from Swinton to the phalanx of women, and suddenly Swinton looked tired and old and Fran felt mean and spiteful. What she'd done to Swinton was bullying too, mocking someone's limitations. Her mam would be angry and tell her it wasn't funny or nice. What's more, she'd be right.

'I'm sorry, Mr Swinton. You're reet, I was showing off, being silly,' Fran said.

At that moment Miss Ellington and Mrs Raydon, the security officers, entered. 'Sorry to interrupt, Mr Swinton, but we were waiting for your knock to let us know we could begin our spot check. It would appear that the timetable has slipped and the girls are about to be late for their shift?'

Miss Ellington, the senior of the two women, turned to the girls. 'But don't fret, we'll hurry, and besides, your pay won't be docked. We saw you arrive at the correct time.'

A wave of relief ran through the room and then someone said, 'Thank heavens for that. I felt my life draining out of t'bottom of me feet these last ten minutes. Would've been worse to pay for the bleedin' privilege.'

Mr Swinton's colour rose further. Perhaps he'll explode, thought Fran, almost regretting her apology since he was looking at her with such venom. So, would his explosion go down as an accident or self-induced? At least it would only hurt him, though there'd be a ton of bile to mop up. Davey, though, would say that it wouldn't matter if he did explode, because it would only be hot air that swept the room.

'Let it go now, Fran,' Sarah whispered, 'or he'll be even worse to you, especially when he hears Stan's coming back.'

The smaller of the women, Mrs Raydon, asked the girls if anyone was still wearing nylon or silk. Fat chance in this neck of the woods, thought Fran. Miss Ellington added, 'We have to ask as it was reported by the gate that one of you was, and might not know to remove them. We don't want any static to set off the explosives, do we, girls?'

Someone now said, as they usually did, 'No, Miss Ellington, too right we don't, but we'd like some nylons for afterwards.' It was a sort of good-luck charm, and made everyone but Mr Swinton smile. Miss Cartright put up her hand. 'I was wearing them, but they're in my coat pocket now.'

The women looked at one another. Sarah whispered, 'Stockings?'

Fran shrugged, after all they might be the girl's only pair and as it was her first day she thought she should be smart.

Mrs Raydon and Miss Ellington began checking each girl for metal, and asking if they were wearing cotton underclothes before passing them through the doors into the corridor and their 'work stations'. As the security officers drew nearer, Fran smiled at Miss Cartwright, who smiled back.

'My name's Amelia Cartwright.'

As Amelia turned around, Fran saw a glint in her hair. 'Duck down,' she whispered. 'Pretend to scratch your foot.'

Puzzled, Amelia did just that and Fran snatched the hairpin out. It could have killed her, as well as her fellow workers, if it had fallen and created a spark around the explosives, if that's where she was working, though as a new girl she'd probably only be in sewing. Fran palmed it. 'Get up,' she hissed as the women came nearer. 'Don't give Swinton an excuse to make a do of anything.'

Fran stepped back, seeing Swinton watching, and scratched her upper arm, tossing the grip towards one of the individual envelopes on the bench and praying it landed near one. It did. Swinton was approaching, pushing through the women. He reached her. Fran stared ahead and shoved her hands in her pockets.

'You need to check Frances Hall's overall pockets. She's just taken something from Miss Cartwright's hair,' Swinton shouted to one of the women.

Fran stared from him to Miss Ellington. 'It was fluff. Harmless but unattractive.'

Miss Ellington came across to Fran, and stood in front of her, her pale blue eyes expressionless. 'May I see?'

Fran had already run her fingernail along the pocket's

seam and now drew out the fluff that seemed to breed overnight.

'Harmless,' Miss Ellington snapped, and turned away. But then, holding her notepad beneath her handless left arm, she spun round to address Amelia. 'There is no quarter given for a mistake such as the one Mr Swinton thought you had made *if* you had left this room and reached any active area. If that had happened, *you* could have been responsible for death and disaster. So remember, had that been the case you would have been escorted off the premises and never allowed near an armaments factory again, or face an even worse penalty. And the same goes for you, Miss Hall.'

She addressed everyone now. 'However, I will remind you that it is not just up to the security officers or the foremen, it is up to you to check, check and check again whilst in the changing rooms, not just yourselves but your fellow workers. Is that not so, Mr Swinton? So anyone finding and removing such an article would be doing us all a favour – correct, Mr Swinton? What's more, that "someone" should be confident enough to do it without fear, don't you agree, and not receive a warning? After all, the thrust of your lecture is that mistakes must not be hidden.'

Mr Swinton looked as though murder was the only thing that he'd agree with at that moment, and Fran wondered how long the Factory would keep this man, who was a looming presence, a . . . But for once, Fran said nothing. What was the point? He wasn't on every day, and it wasn't Stan's fault that Tim Swinton had tried the scholarship exam and fallen short. But she didn't want to think of Stan, or anything to do with his idiocy while she had work to do.

Fran, Sarah, Beth and Mrs Oborne headed for the detonator section workbench, arriving a few seconds before six o'clock and took the place of the night shift workers, while Amelia, as a new worker, did indeed head for the sewing shop to find her feet. Maisie, Sylv, Valerie and the rest were elsewhere today, but from the yellowing of their skin they were either filling shells with TNT again or stemming – filling rubber 'somethings', or 'thingummybobs', as they called them, with chemicals from a large container – both of which could tinge the skin.

Maisie had experienced 'the yellow' in her first factory down South, when she was pregnant, and although she had been moved to the sewing sector in the later stages to allow her body to free itself of the chemicals, her baby had still been born yellow. Mother and baby had gradually returned to normal under the care of her mam in Massingham, and a transfer had been arranged to the Factory. Against Miss Ellington's advice, she had started in the shell-filling section rather than work in the safety of the sewing shop. When asked why, or even when not asked, Maisie would proclaim that she needed the danger money now she had a bairn, thank you very much.

As Fran thought about it, she nodded to herself. You would, if your husband had died at Dunkirk. She took a deep breath, taking a face mask filled with cotton wool from on top of the steel shield which made a barrier between the women and the detonators on the workbench. She tied the mask on and peered through the shield's Perspex window, seeing the trays of empty detonators waiting to be filled. She was as glad as everyone else was for the shield, since Miss Ellington's absent hand loomed large.

The detonator bench was at the top end of the sector and the tannoy played the same tinny music it played all over the Factory, so she barely noticed it as she collected a small container of fulminate of mercury from the hatch. She carried it back to the workbench as though it was her mam's

43

one and only bone-china cup and saucer, the one that came out at Christmas. Mark you, if she dropped Mam's cup all she'd get would be a clip round the ear, whereas if she dropped this mucky brown powder it was so sensitive it would blow her to kingdom come.

At the thought she smiled grimly beneath her face mask, for after all, that's what was needed in a detonator, so the least said about it the better. She pulled forward the first tray of detonators, and trickled the fulminate of mercury into each one, gripping the container in case it slipped and fell, taking care always to keep her hand steady and wary of getting any of the powder on her skin. Even more so after Miss Ellingham had said it could seep into the body through the skin and lungs, and could perhaps cause 'the rash'. Well it certainly did that to Fran, and several of the Massingham women.

Miss Ellingham had also told them of the olden day hatters who had gone mad after breathing in the mercury vapour given off in the curing of the hat felt and scared the women half to death, making them extra careful, which was clearly just what she had intended. Fran continued filling the detonators hour after hour, tray after tray, collecting more powder from the hatch, and filling more detonators which were brought along by Mr Swinton, or one of his supervisors. She filled, filled, filled, and then again. All along the bench the girls sat on stools, working, not allowed to speak in case it disturbed their concentration.

The itching increased around her mouth, but why think of that, because she itched all over her hands and arms too, and she just had to get on with it. Dermatitis, they called it at the Factory. Only some of them suffered, others had tougher skins – Maisie said that therefore those who were affected were special and must be princesses who would feel a pea under a dozen mattresses. She had preened as she said it. Fran smiled as she filled the next, and the next. She was still trying to breathe lightly, but then smiled again, for if she did go bonkers or got blown up, at least she wouldn't have to worry about Stan any more. She'd be sitting on a cloud instead.

She had a rhythm now, and was only aware of the music on the tannoy from time to time. Sometimes a message from the office disturbed the music. She wished it wouldn't for none of them wanted to be distracted. She longed to scratch her face, but didn't. For a moment she wished she was back in the bazooka section where she'd been sent for a few days. All she had to do there was push a cartridge into each of the beggars rather than muck about with powder which helped her rash. The trouble was, the pay wasn't as good because there was little risk. Fran blinked, forcing her mind back to the detonators.

On and on they worked until midday, when they broke for chips and egg in the canteen. Over Woodbines and the bread they used to scrape up the remains of the egg yolk, Amelia told them she came from Guildford and wanted to do her bit. She'd hoped for the WAAF but her parents thought armaments work would be less dangerous because she would be an office worker, so here she was. Her laugh was high-pitched with hysteria. 'I had no idea,' she said. Then repeated it. 'I had no idea what it's like to be a factory girl.'

The others looked at one another, half offended, half wanting to comfort her, but how? 'There's a war on,' Beth muttered. 'You'll get used to it. We all have to.' Beth's blue eyes were almost as pale as Miss Ellington's. She had said before how she wished for green eyes to go with her red hair.

Fran tried to soften the sentiment. 'Just think how someone out there will be so grateful that you've saved his life, just make sure the powers that be know you are capable of office work and they might transfer you when there's an opening.'

Sarah, ever practical, asked, 'What about your digs?'

'Mrs Miles is a horrid woman, and her cooking is so bad everything ends up like shoe leather, even a fried egg. How can that be?'

The others laughed and those that hadn't finished passed over some of their chips. 'Eat up, pet,' Valerie from Sledgeford urged, 'and I'll see if me mam can take you in. We have our own hens.'

With half an hour of the lunch break to go, someone started the sing-song, this time with 'Stormy Weather', which they always chose when there'd been a two and eight with Mr Swinton. It was Beth's voice that soared on the words 'Since my man and I ain't together . . .'

Then Sarah, Fran and Sylv took them all straight into 'A-Tisket, A-Tasket', with the women getting to their feet and dancing off their chips. Maisie even grabbed Mr Swinton and twirled him around until he remembered himself and shrugged her off.

Miss Ellington, who was on the next table, dived into the sing-song with 'Over the Rainbow', and as usual some of the girls failed to reach the top notes but Fran's voice soared true and bold, supported by Beth and Sarah, all of whom adored singing, and even as bairns had pretended they were wireless stars, swirling and twirling as they sang on the bank of the beck until Stan and Davey threw acorns at them.

While the rest of the canteen joined in the singing, table nine, two along from them, played dominoes and Fran guessed they had money on the winner, the prize being a cigarette. As the clock ticked away the minutes, the catering staff sang their own version of 'I'm in the Mood for

Love', which was vulgar and funny, and involved cooking implements. Finally, they ended on 'All or Nothing at All', with Amelia surprising them as she harmonised with Fran's powerful rendition as they all belted out the second line, 'Half a love, never appealed to me', and for Fran it was true: there were no halves in her feelings for Davey.

On they sang until Maisie, up on her chair, conducted a final refrain, 'No, no, all or nothing at all.' By this time everyone in the canteen was on their feet, including the domino players, and the song was repeated twice, ending in laughter, which continued as they all made their way back to their workplaces. There was no overtime today, but they would be in on Saturday all day, as the management had ordered, though not Sunday, or not that they knew yet.

Fran murmured, 'As Stan's coming back in the evening on Saturday, I'll be there to hear all the shouting, worst luck.'

They took their places and worked on, and as the clock moved to one fifteen, Fran eased her shoulders, but not for a moment did her concentration waver as she returned to filling yet another tray, even though her eyes ached, and her mask seemed to grow hotter and hotter. Beside her, Beth coughed, and then again. 'Leave your container and step away,' Fran ordered sharply. 'No jogging, jostling or coughing with that beggar in your hand.'

Her words were muffled behind her mask, but understandable. Beth nodded and moved away, continuing to cough, and Mr Swinton interrupted his stroll round the huge area and headed for the girl.

'You were quite right to step away. Remember the rules. No jogging or jostling, and this includes coughing.'

'Yes, Mr Swinton, Fran's just told me,' Beth said.

Fran didn't stop work, her eyes always on the fulminate

47

of mercury as she trickled it into each detonator, and she wondered what Mr Swinton would say.

'Well, on this occasion Miss Hall is right. Just you remember that rules are set up for a reason,' he muttered. He thrust his chin towards the posters that lined the whitewashed walls with their warnings and continued his rounds.

Again, Fran felt badly about being so patronising earlier since Swinton carried a huge responsibility. On the other hand, that didn't alter the fact that he was a bugger. Beth returned to the bench, swallowed, stepped back, coughed again, returned, swallowed, waited a moment and then resumed her work, while Fran eased her shoulders again and as she did so she spared a thought for Davey and meeting him off the bus, thankful she'd be back by four if they left the Factory on time.

She finished another tray, paused and allowed herself a moment to think of him waiting for her, and while he did so he would be working out something he was setting for the crossword magazine based in London, and perhaps writing some articles on crosswords. Clever he was, her Davey. He had taken the Massingham scholarship, as all the evening-class boys had, ending up in a draw with Stan. There'd been no exam to decide, for Davey had given way to his marrer.

As Fran started to fill another tray of detonators a tickle started in her throat. Trying not to rush, she placed the container on the work bench, and stepped away clearing her throat, to find Beth doing the same. They both coughed, then Beth said to Fran, 'Thanks for reminding me before. I was mithering over Bob and didn't even notice I was coughing. I won't do it again.'

The girls stayed back, both coughing now, with Fran hoping it wasn't the powder in their throats and thinking how Davey had insisted to her, Sarah and Stan as they ate sandwiches and downed beers at the beck when the scholarship results had been announced, that he'd really rather Stan took the university place they'd tied for. He explained that he'd become more and more interested in crossword setting and wanted to get expert enough to run his own magazine, and he could do this while staying in the pit, near Fran. He'd also insisted that Stan needed to get away from the Beth 'thing'. Suddenly Fran was very conscious of Beth standing next to her. Mithering over Bob? More than usual? If so, why? Was it because Stan was coming back?

She remembered how, at the beck, Stan had wiped his hand across his mouth and tried to tell Davey they should retake the exam. "Tisn't a fair win, lad.'

Davey had stood firm, staring first into his beer, then at Fran, then at the beck just as the kingfisher had flashed out of the willow. 'Away from my Fran I'd not thrive,' he'd said. So what did Davey think about Stan turning his back on Oxford, having been given such a chance?

She smiled beneath her mask, knowing he'd say, 'There's nowt to mither over. He can go back when this lot is over, bonny lass.'

The two girls returned to the workbench. Fran reached forward to pick up another detonator just as the ground shuddered and somewhere there was a crashing explosion. Without a word, all the women put down their containers . . . carefully, carefully . . . stepped back and froze, as they had done before and would no doubt do again. No one asked what had happened for they knew - it was an explosion. They'd probably never know where, how, or who.

Fran's mind was racing as the noise reverberated, but there was just the one explosion so far, no others had been set off. They stood, waiting. It had sounded like an artillery shell exploding, or even one of the bombs – but no, that would be in the bunkers unless one was being moved to the testing site. Nearby there was a crashing and rumbling, like walls falling. Sarah gripped her hand.

After a moment Miss Ellington arrived and had a word with Mr Swinton before they both started to walk the 'roadways' between the tables, which were well spaced to restrict damage in case of an accident. 'Carry on, nothing to do with us. Fifteen minutes to go, targets still to reach, ladies.'

The clock ticked on as they began filling again, but they worked even more carefully, carefully. It wasn't the first time this had happened, and it wouldn't be the last. But it wasn't them – this time. Though it was someone.

'Yes, yes, all of me to go home, not nothing at all,' Sarah whispered softly behind her mask, her eyes full of unshed tears. Fran and Beth smiled sadly. All three whispered that refrain, their eyes meeting, wondering – who? All the while the clock ticked.

They laid down their tools at the precise moment the clock reached two, seeing the next shift approaching their workbench. They washed and changed, recovered their possessions, showed their passes again at the gate, and streamed to the bus.

'Had a good sleep, Bert?' Fran murmured as she hurried on board.

'Less of your cheek, young Fran, or I'll tell your da to tan your hide.'

Their laughter was forced, but they must laugh, they must smile, it was all part of carrying on. They forged down the aisle and this time Fran sat with Beth while Sarah sat across the aisle. There were two free seats behind them, for Maisie and Sylv. Bert started the engine just as Maisie panted up and scrambled on, having a quick word with Bert, who paused, then nodded. He started to pull away as

Mrs Oborne in one of the front seasts called, 'Hang on, Bert, Sylv's still to come.'

Bert took no notice and drove on. The women on the bus immediately fell silent and there was no singing as Maisie, quiet for once, made her way up the aisle, ignoring everyone until she took her seat behind Fran, who turned once Bert was half an hour from the Factory.

'Sylv?'

Maisie's hand shook as she took a puff from her Woodbine. She leaned forward and spoke. 'Keep bliddy mum, but a lad were taking a shell for testing on a trolley down the main roadway, a bloke bliddy millions of yards ahead with a red flag, and another behind with another bliddy flag, and the shell just rolled off, hit the wall and exploded. The walls're built to implode, as yer know, and the lass was passing on the other side. She's all reet, or will be, or maybe will be, and she's got all her hands and fingers and even her thumbs.'

Fran murmured, 'Hospital?'

'Oh aye. I'll nip round to her mam, who'll keep the bairn, but there'll be no trip to see Sylv's uncle Sidney for a while.'

Fran turned to the front when she saw Maisie's swollen eyes welling again. Maisie had mentioned nothing about the lad who'd been shoving the trolley, which said it all.

Next to her, Beth closed her eyes. 'Bloody Hitler.'

Sarah leaned across the aisle and whispered, 'That's why the owl flew over us.'

Fran didn't know if it was or not, but none of the women had died today, only a wee lad. She sat back, closed her eyes and wouldn't cry. Damn it, she wouldn't. Instead, she dragged her sleeve across her face and whispered, 'Damned mucky powder gets everywhere.'

It was only as Bert drove the bus round the tight bend,

which signalled they had another hour and a quarter to go, that she led the bus in singing 'Abide with me; fast falls the eventide.' They sang for the lad who'd been shoving the trolley, whoever he might be. But if he was from around here, they'd learn soon enough,

Chapter Four

At Massingham, Sarah saw her brother Davey waiting for them, safe, bathed and bushy-tailed, and felt better. She followed Fran off the bus and watched as they stood together, her brother and Fran. They were strong, loving people she could lean on. Davey waved and she returned it. 'All right, lad?'

'Aye, you too?'

Sarah smiled as the wind rustled her hair, which had fallen free of its pleat, yet again. Perhaps it was time she had it cut. If she was ever transferred to a section working with moving parts of a machine, she didn't want it getting caught, and scalping her. Perhaps Madge could cut it, because whether there was machinery or not, it would be easier with the turban. Well, she'd ask, but not today. She was too tired. She hurried home, wishing she had her own man, someone to hold her as Davey must hold Fran, as Stan had held Beth . . . No, she didn't want to think of that, or what might be about to happen.

Davey slipped his arm round Fran, who leaned into him for a moment, smelling her man's scent, a residue of coal and sweat. She felt his lips on her forehead and just wanted to rest in his arms for ever. Davey shook her slightly. 'Come on, pet. Let's get going, eh?'

The pair of them cycled towards Denton and Davey talked into the silence, telling her that his mam had been pulling up the last of the lettuce from the allotment, though they were all seeded and floppy and not worth the hassle, and that he'd had time to wash in the tin bath in front of the range after his da had had first dibs. They were riding single file now, in case of tractors. 'It's the sluicing that's important,' he called over his shoulder. 'What's the matter, hinny?'

Fran shook her head as she dug down with the pedals as they crossed the rising bridge over the beck, then soared down the other side. 'It's just one of those days. I can't tell you why, you know I canna, but what with Stan and his news, and knowing I have to face Da, Davey, I'm wondering how you feel? Do you really not mind passing on the scholarship and staying here, only for him to chuck it up?'

At that Davey braked and threw his bike on the verge. As the wheels spun, Fran braked too, and Davey turned and caught her handlebars. 'Off the bike, now,' he ordered. The wind was snatching at his cap and muffler, bringing the scent of sulphur from the slag heap on one side and of freshly turned earth, where Farmer Murphy had ploughed the harvested cornfield, on the other.

She dismounted and he lowered her bike to the verge, then pulled her to him, kissing her mouth, her eyes and then her mouth again and again, until she kissed him back and she in turn pulled him tight against her. They stood together as a tractor roared round them, pulling a load of baled straw from the second of Murphy's fields. Davey coughed as the straw dust tumbled in the air and fell around them.

He dragged his arm across his mouth, then held her again, and his voice was fierce as he said, 'Listen, lass. When I do or say something, it's because I mean it. I do what's best for me, and you, and me family. Me, do you hear – and you are best for me. Where you are, I am. I divint like the thought of dreaming spires or whatever Vicar Walters calls them. I want me magazine. I want our house, our

54

bairns, you. You, do you hear?' He lifted his head and shouted at the rooks pecking at the furrows behind the drystone wall. 'It's this canny woman I want, need, love, so what's she got to say, eh?'

He pretended to listen to the birds as a few lifted into the wind. 'Ah, even the birds say you've to listen, pet. Listen hard and you'll hear the truth. Remember that. I say as I feel, no games, no lies, no code. What I say is what I mean, and I mean I love you, and always have, always will, just as I tell you every day, daft lass.'

She leaned back in his arms, knowing he wouldn't let her fall, and then she held his face and kissed him, saying against his mouth, 'You canna know how much I love you because it's too damned big and it drives me daft because I can't show it.'

He grew serious. 'You can, but we won't till we're married, and as to that – your mam said not yet, so not yet it is. But what we have to do is get on to this Bill whatshisname today, to get him to offer your mam, and mine, more for the rugs. You're right when you say he's knocked 'em down once too often. It isn't right, when they thread them strips through backing to make what look like bliddy works of art and are then diddled. But I'll leave you to do the haggling, cos I'm no match.'

She kissed him once more and then hauled her bike up again and they cycled along together while she filled him in on Swinton and how badly she'd behaved by using words as weapons.

He listened, but simply said, 'He needs diminishing sometimes. He's a bully, but you don't want him to target you more than he does, so keep your tongue still. I'm always surprised he's employed there when you think that boy of his, Tim, went to the Blackshirt meetings. Little Fascist, he were. Mebbe still is.'

She panted as the road ran out of tarmac and they struggled along a rutted lane. 'The lad didn't go for long, though, did he, and if he were a threat he'd be in prison, I reckon, and he isn't. Bit like Mr Massingham's whelp, Ralph, though I reckon that was because his da sat on him pretty damn quickly. Good man, old Massingham. We're right lucky.'

'Aye, he is that, but the lad is a jumped-up brat, all trousers and no—' He stopped. They laughed and turned back to the subject of Bill Norton, who last Christmas had bought her mam's proggy rugs at the Miners' Club local sale, saying they were presents for his relatives. He'd been back to Leadenhall Terrace many times since then, not just knocking on the front door, but knocking her mam and Mrs Bedley down in price if he bought two or more. 'So, he has a bliddy big family or he's selling them on, or that's what you reckon?' Davey asked.

'Aye, I reckon he's marking them up somewhere along the line and selling them on. Me mam nor yours doesn't know how to ask the question or say no, but I'm not having it. She doesn't know we're doing this, nor does your mam, so keep your trap shut, lovely Davey.'

They reached the better road and turned right, heading for Denton pit village, pedalling slowly over the cobbles, looking for Norton's house on Brownley Terrace, while the slag heaps loomed and the pithead winding gear rattled above them. They finally found number 12, but it wasn't a house, it was a shop selling household goods and bric-a-brac. 'A shop, eh, bonny lass? Well, what d'you know,' murmured Davey. They leaned their bikes against the window, peering in, but saw none of Fran's mam's rugs, his own mam's, or any others come to that. Just a load of buckets, mops and so on. 'Are you going in?' Davey asked.

Fran stared at him. 'Howay, lad, we've come all this

way just for the sake of our health, so we'll just potter back, shall we?'

It was such a close mimicry of her da that they both laughed. Davey kissed her and said, 'If you still had your pigtails, I'd pull them, then knot them.'

She nodded. 'I reckon you would an' all.' She took a deep breath and entered. A bell jangled above the door and Bill Norton appeared from the back room. He raised his eyebrows when he saw Fran. Davey followed her in, taking off his cap and standing close beside her. Bill raised his eyebrows even further. 'A shop, Mr Norton?' queried Fran.

'Well, I never said I hadn't.'

'So, you've been buying my mam's rugs at cut-down prices for your shop?'

He shook his head, looking from Fran to Davey, who still stood by her side, motionless but with his blue-scarred hewer's hands visible, balled into handy fists. 'No, for relatives, as I said, pet.'

Fran moved closer to the counter, her bad day brewing up into a storm. 'I'm not your pet, and no, that's not true. You've been selling them on, but not here, that's clear, and why would you? Because here the wives make their own. So where? But that doesn't matter, does it? All that matters is that me mam gets a fair price for them, cos she works by the light of the oil lamp till her eyes ache.'

He shook his head. 'That's nowt to do with me. I'm not forcing her to sell them, she wants to, and what's more, I like to buy 'em. I've a living to make, and a middleman can't offer top price—' He stopped abruptly.

Fran shook her head. She had thought it would be harder than this. 'So, you're a middleman, and now you must listen to me, Mr Norton, because I have the rest of the evening to stay here, in your shop. You see, I don't need me tea, I had dinner at the work's canteen and what's more, I've had a

57

hard day, a really hard day, and I'm right angry because I have things to do when me da's had his tea that I'd rather not do. So, if you don't want me here, stopping you from shutting up shop, tell me who buys me mam's rugs.'

Mr Norton shook his head, placing his hands on his counter. 'You've no right. Your mam was happy with the price or she'd not have sold 'em.'

Fran nodded. 'Yes, I expect that's right enough, but the thing is, I'm not happy, so you'd best offer a better price or you'll get no more.'

He shook his head. 'Then I'll have no more.'

Fran nodded, turned and left. Davey closed the door behind them, hearing the bell jangle. 'Now what, lass? Yer mam won't be laughing if'n she's no buyer any more.'

'We talk to the missus.'

He rammed his cap back on and grinned at her. 'Be kind, because I think that's steam coming out of your lugs.'

She led the way round to the side of the house, intent on finding a way into the Nortons' yard via the back lane, but there was a side door to the house itself, and she knocked. It finally opened, and a woman in a stained overall with a roll-up in the corner of her mouth stood there, her arms crossed. The cigarette wobbled as she said, 'Aye?'

Fran smiled. 'Your man wanted to give me the name of the people he sells the proggy rugs on to as I know someone who can collect 'em cheaper, but it's gone right out of his head. I reckoned you'd know, cos you mebbe do the accounts. Somewhere in Newcastle, isn't it?'

The woman sighed. 'Aye, forget his bliddy head if it weren't sewn on, daft wallop that he is. Briddlestone's Unique Crafts.'

Fran smiled. 'Right you are, and ta for telling us.'

The door was already closing. Mrs Norton said, 'He should get himself a brain,' and banged it shut.

Davey shook his head. 'Will he give her hell for telling us?'

Fran just grinned. 'Think of the pair of them and work out who gives who hell.'

She returned to the shop. Jangle went the bell. Mr Norton looked up. 'One last chance, Mr Norton. A fair price would be another five bob each, eh?' she said.

'They're not worth it,' he said. 'Just a bit of tat, and you can tell your mam I said that, cos I will when I see her next.'

Franny's qualms about her next move disappeared out of the window. She turned on her heel, with Davey following her out yet again.

'Toerag,' she said. 'Now I'm going telephone Briddlestone's. I'm not having me mam's work being spoken of like that.'

Davey dug in his pocket and drew out some coppers. 'There's a phone box over there, bonny lass, and remind me never, ever to cross you, or I reckon you'll have my guts for garters, and stuff a few of them in me mouth while you're at it. By, lass, you've not changed a bit since you gave your Stan a belt round the ears when he called our Sarah a – what were it? – a dozy dumpling after she'd swung across the beck and fallen in the water.'

'Well, that's only because you were going to punch out his lights, so I thought it were best it were me. I don't hit so hard.'

They had to wait as there was a queue of women at the telephone box, but what did that matter, Fran thought, for she had Davey's arm around her shoulder. They spoke of nothing much except love, which was everything. After twenty minutes the phone was free, but there were others behind. An elderly woman in a headscarf said, 'You going to be long, bairns? I've got me tea on the stove.'

They sent her into the box first, while they talked to the

59

rest of the queue. At last it was Fran's turn. As she waited to be connected, she watched the old lady limping to her back alley, with Davey helping her. It calmed her anger as she finally spoke to Briddlestone's, explaining that she had taken over the buying and selling of the proggy rugs from Bill Norton, who no longer wanted to be involved, and that she would lower his price by four shillings a rug if delivery by rail would be acceptable, rather than their Briddlestone's van picking up from Denton. She actually had no idea if that's what they did, and waited, barely breathing.

The voice at the end of the telephone told her to hold on and she would be transferred. Fran repeated her offer to the man who came on the line. He conferred with someone else, and came back. 'Aye, that'll do nicely.' A price was agreed that gave her mam and Davey's an extra ten shillings a rug, which went to show how high Norton's markup had been. Briddlestone's explained that even though there was a war on, there was a steady market because each one was well made, with a unique pattern. In fact, they sold them on to stores in London, where there was still money and a nostalgic hankering for the traditional crafts. 'Something to do with the war, maybe,' the bloke said.

He continued that the war had come too close a few days ago, with Hitler's bombs dropping on Newcastle but missing Briddlestone's, this time. He agreed to write to her home: 14 Leadenhall Terrace, Massingham to confirm the new arrangements. He also wanted Mr Norton to understand that they were still interested in receiving other products to supplement their range. They returned to Bill Norton's shop and reported Briddlestone's request for other products, but, Fran insisted, banging the counter, he must agree not to return to Massingham, ever, or Fran would report his unprofessional behaviour to Briddlestone's. Shaken, Norton agreed.

The cycle ride back always seemed quicker, she and Davey agreed as they pedalled into the wind. Once in Massingham, Davey turned off into the Bedleys' back lane rather than going with Fran to her house because his mam would have tea on the table and her clipped ear was much worse than anything Fran could deliver. Fran was laughing as she opened the gate into their own yard, relaxing a bit as she saw that her da's boots were not under his chair, so she could put off the conversation she had to have, for a little at least. She put her bike away behind the old pigeon loft as the hens clucked, amazed that she had forgotten the message she had to deliver for even a minute. Worse, she had forgotten about the lad who had been killed by the shell, and Sylv lying in hospital.

Her mam opened the door, and stood on the step wiping her hands on her tea towel. 'Howay, lass, Davey picked up your bike and said you were off on a ride to blow the cobwebs off but you must be fair weary. We heard about young Jimmy from his mam's neighbour. Eighteen and no life lived—' She stopped, then continued quietly, 'Sledgeford is sorrowful today. But Sylv should be all right, so that's right good.'

'Aye, a bit of a day, one way and another, Mam, but some good news. I bumped into Norton, and you and Mrs Bedley're to get another ten bob for each rug if we package them up and send them by rail to Newcastle, where they'll be picked up by Briddlestone's.'

'My,' her mam said. 'Well, that's right grand, really it is, oh my word.' As the two women entered her mam flapped her tea towel to cool herself, excitement in her voice. Fran grinned to herself as she hung up her shabby mackintosh on the peg on the back door just as Ben tore into the yard, his boots flapping because his laces were half undone, as usual. He was shouting, 'I done it, quicker than ever. I'll drop in on Davey later. Stevie did it too.'

Mrs Hall laughed as he yanked off his boots on the outside step and rammed them under his da's chair, pushing them to the back and storming into the house in his socks. 'What's that you said, lad? What've you done, as if your sister and I don't know.'

Ben flung himself onto his chair at the table, laughing too, his dark hair in his eyes. He swept it back. 'The crossword Davey's just set, Mam. You see, he wanted to mek sure a bairn could crack it, cos the magazine has said he can set some crosswords for a column for under-thirteens. He said he'd give us each a bob when he gets his fee if'n we could brek it in an hour.'

Fran crept up to him and grabbed his hair. 'I reckon this mop needs a cut, don't you, Mam?'

Ben shrugged her away. 'Keep your mitts off, Fran.'

But his mam was bearing down on him with scissors. 'Happen you're right, Fran. Have a go, would you? Madge is busy with a couple of young 'uns already today. And you sit still, lad, or you'll lose your lugs.'

Ben crossed his arms and sank back into his chair, sulking. Fran caught the towel her mam threw from the ceiling airer and wrapped it around his shoulders. 'How would sir like it?'

Ben shrugged. 'You'll do it how *you* like, our Fran, like you always do, but since you came back today, not like Sylv, I'll let yer. But not too short.'

Mam and Fran looked at one another and Fran recognised the shadow of fear in her mam's eyes. She concentrated on cutting his hair, which matched hers exactly in its colour and was her mam's colour before she'd lost the babe and been so ill. Since then, grey had come into the rich darkness. While she worked, Fran said, 'I'm sorry to vex you with the Factory work, Mam, but there's a war on, and I'm very very careful.'

'Aye, pet, I know. It is what it is, eh?'

Her da's voice broke in then from the doorway. 'At least Stan has the sense he were born with.'

Fran closed her eyes, and stilled her hands. Ben said, 'Come on then, our Fran, brush off the bitty hairs round me collar – they itch. I've to get to our Davey with me crossword.'

Fran finished while Ben told his da what he meant and Fran had to listen to Da, walking to the scullery in his stockinged feet, telling Ben that if he kept on like this, he'd be one for the university too. Da always wore socks because unlike some of his marrers, he didn't mind the bits of coal that fell into his boots and caught on them, saying they'd catch on his bliddy skin otherwise. Not that he usually swore in front of his womenfolk, but she'd grown up hearing her da and Stan talking as they walked through the yard while she was up in the box room, doing her homework.

Mam called through to the scullery. 'Did you finish taking the sickness dividends at the Miners' Club today, our Joe?'

'Oh, aye. The early shift came in to pay up. I'll put it in t'bank on Monday.' He returned to the kitchen and patted his torn jacket pocket, then drew out a stout brown paper bag and hid it behind the cushion of his armchair, which bulged stuffing through the splits. He laid the accounts book up on the mantelpiece, and while he was at it, grabbed his pipe and baccy. He stood there for a moment, letting the heat from the range soak into his aching limbs.

Fran wondered if Stan remembered the ache, the cough, the scrambling along roadways bent double, and sometimes lower than that. Did he remember lying on his side while he hewed at the coal face when the roof was too low to stand, or sitting on a tiny stool winkling out the layers?

Silly stupid bugger, she thought, and him with the same broken bones as Davey, so he could easily have stayed amongst Vicar Walters' dreaming spires. Was it really because of the war he was doing it? If so, why not before? Or was it Beth, alone now Bob was at sea? But what did it matter? Fran still had to tell her parents.

Ben was tugging at her arm. 'Wake up, our Fran. Am I done?'

Fran tweaked his ear and came to stand in front of him, pulling up strands of hair either side of his head. They seemed the same. 'What d'you say, Da, is our bairn tickety-boo?'

Her da laughed. 'Aye, I reckon so.' He raised his voice. 'When's tea, Mam?'

'Now.'

Her mam came out and while Fran carried the towel into the yard and shook it free of hair, her mam laid the table.

The meal seemed to go quickly, and as always Fran only had half the amount the others had as she'd already eaten at dinner time.

The two women washed the pots while Ben rushed off to see Davey. Then her mam made a cup of tea and while it mashed Fran wiped down the table and her da resumed his place at the mantelpiece, pressing down the baccy into the bowl of his pipe. He lit it with a taper from the grate, sucking to draw the flame in the bowl while keeping his finger over the top. Without turning he said, 'I hear from our Tom that his Davey had a letter from Stan, with one for you along wi' it.'

Fran stood quite still. Why hadn't she realised Tom, Davey's da, would have seen the letter? For heaven's sake, they'd have been nattering together in the Miners' Club as they took the contributions for the sickness insurance, which Mr Massingham matched. So it was bound to come up.

Again, she felt pure rage, hurt and worry, for her mam had come to the doorway of the scullery, the teacups on the tray, curiosity vying with anxiety on her high-cheekboned face. Fran moved to take the tray from her and placed it on the table, just as her da turned from the mantelpiece to face the room. 'Well?' he said.

Fran was standing by the table, still covered with its threadbare spotless tablecloth, forcing herself to stay still and not fiddle with her hands or tear at her hair, or run from the room. 'Aye, he wrote because—' She stopped when her da spoke, pointing the stem of his pipe at her.

'I also heard that there's a sorrow in Sledgeford this day as a lad is lost, and there's a grandmother caring for a bairn in Massingham until his mam is out of hospital. But if that mam had worked in the office, she would have been safe.'

'Oh Da, don't. Just don't,' Fran pleaded.

'At least our Stan—'

Fran held up her hand. Her da coughed, dragged out his handkerchief, and held it to his mouth. The mucous was black. The grandfather clock ticked. It had been her grandda's. He had died of black lung, his wife of grief, so they said. For a moment Fran looked from one to another full of fear for them. She swallowed, trying to find some courage. It was she who balled her hands now, as Swinton and Amelia had. Her nails dug into her palms as she turned full square to her da.

'Stan is coming home. That's what was in the letter. He wanted me to tell you, to prepare you, Da, and you, Mam. He's going back into the pit because he—'

Her da didn't shout, he just seemed to groan, then fold up achingly slowly, finally slumping into his armchair. He dropped his pipe onto the proggy, spilling ash. Fran ran to pick it up, rubbing the burn with her fingers, blackening and burning them. She held it out to him, but he looked at her as though he didn't understand anything.

Her mam came and touched Fran on the shoulder. 'On your feet, Franny. I'll tek the pipe.' Fran moved away, and her mam stood in front of her husband. 'Here's your pipe, bonny lad. Tek it, and put more baccy in it, there's a canny one.' She kept on, almost crooning the words until at last they reached her husband.

Da looked up and did as she said, then rose to his feet. Only then did Fran notice that he had a hole in the heel of his sock, and somehow it made her da even more vulnerable. Her mam moved to the table and sat. She poured tea while her husband filled the bowl of his pipe with trembling hands. Fran watched as he breathed heavily, in and out, in and out. It's what he had always told his bairns they should do to gather their wits. Her mam topped up each cup with milk, her hands quite steady, but the beads of sweat on her forehead showed the effort required.

As though exhausted, her mam nodded to Joe's cup. Fran took it to the mantelpiece. Her da ignored her as he drew on his freshly lit pipe. Only when it was glowing red did he say, not looking at either of them. 'Well, our Frances, perhaps you'd tell me why our Stan has done this?'

Fran stayed by the mantelpiece, one hand gripping it. She copied her da's breathing, in and out, in and out. 'What he said, Da, was to break it to you, because it wasn't the news he wanted to burst on you in a letter, or news simply to arrive with him, through the door.'

Her da continued puffing on his pipe. Her mam said nothing, just sat with her hands in her lap, her cup of tea steaming.

'He said he couldn't go to war, but he could hew for the war effort. He said he'd written to Mr Massingham, who has offered to hold his scholarship over until war's end. He means to do his bit, Da, like you did in the First War. He said he has to hold his head up, for he is a Hall.' Stan hadn't said that, but he should have done, to try and make Da understand.

At those last words, her da looked at her. Their eyes met and there was a glimmer of the old Da there, amused, understanding, and dear. The old Da, before she'd defied him and gone to war herself. He said, 'He shouldn't have got a lass to break the news, our Franny. He's got soft, has our Stan, and he didn't say he wanted to hold his head up, for that's what you think about yerself. He's a pitman. He'd just say there was nowt else he could do.'

He looked past Fran to her mam. ''Tis all been for nowt, our Annie. All of it.'

Annie Hall shook her head. 'They're your bairns, Joe Hall. You told yer da just the same when t'last war started. What you needs now is to get off out and get yourself sorted. Shout at Stan if you must when he comes, then accept it, but no shouting at our Franny. I'll not have it. What if Sylv's da had railed at her last night, or Jimmy's da? No, I'll not have it. Pit families stick together. Now go and see Tom Bedley and Simon Parrot and them canaries of yours, lad. This minute.'

Fran and her mam watched him to the door, which he closed behind him, but didn't slam. Her mam looked at her. 'I'll darn that sock when it comes out of t'wash.' That was all. Pit wives were all the same, stoic, daily expecting the accident hooter, and blessing the end of the shift if they hadn't heard it and they had their man for one day more.

Joe Hall clattered in his boots along the Bedleys' back lane. He lifted the sneck on their back gate, and strode across the yard. Sarah heard him and met him on the back step. 'Me da's howay to the shed, Mr Hall.'

Joe tipped his cap. 'Reet.' He turned on his heel, and felt the hole in his sock that had been growing all shift. He'd put on another pair tomorrow and Annie'd darn it after washday. He clattered along the back lane, thinking that for a few weeks she'd darned nothing, done nothing after he'd had to carry the bairn to the funeral parlour. All white and cold the bairn, Betty, had been, and somehow something had broken in his mind. A fear had grown, because now he knew that the worst could actually happen to his bairns.

He stopped a minute as the Bedleys' back lane gave way to Main Street, feeling the breath leave his body and his head swirl, his throat thicken and his eyes fill, but he made himself breathe slowly, and all he could think of was that his remaining precious bairns were so full of life and promise, and so wonderful, that he blessed the ground they walked on. Though he could still have whacked them two older ones good and proper, that he could.

He reached the shed that the Canary Club had set up at Simon Parrot's allotment. Strange that, a parrot who liked canaries, folks said, and how can it be a club with three members? Well, it can, they'd said, and shut your noise. Joe tapped on the door in case any birds were flying free, but no shout reached him. He entered. Simon and Tom were sitting on the bench, facing the cages.

'How do,' he said, at the same time as they. He sat alongside the two of them and looked at the neat rows of cages they'd built, stretching from floor to ceiling and then the full-size flight cage along the length and breadth of the adjacent wall, where the canaries were flying and singing, white ones and all. He liked the white ones and had bred a few, and even had a few bairns in the top cages.

There were seed husks on the floor of the shed, and the clean smell of sawdust, even though it was full of the cage droppings, but after the pit every smell was clean. Had Stan remembered the stink? The rats, the mice and the blacklocks like giant cockroaches. The squeezing of the coal as the weight above strained the pit props and ceiling planks. Had he remembered the jagged rock as you lay full length to hack at the face? Had he? Daft bugger.

'Run yer fingers through this lot, Joe, and stop looking as though your Fran were hurt today at that damn place. 'Tweren't our lasses and that's what you have to remember, or so our Simon said when I mithered in 'ere a moment ago,' Tom said.

Tom was pointing at the sack of seed standing on the ground in front of Simon, who sat in the middle of the bench. 'We reckon there's not enough hemp, eh, Simon, and too much red rape. Have a gander and a fiddle, Joe.'

Joe sank his hand into the seed. This part of his world was calm, here, with his marrers, and birds. Aye, no matter what other muddle the rest of his life brought, here was calm. 'It'll do, lads, an' sort out the mites for the little fellas all reet.'

Tom rose and tied chickweed to the bars of each cage. 'Give us an 'and, Joe.'

Joe did, and slowly, slowly he felt as though his feet were beginning to rest on solid ground. As he found that balance, he felt growing anger for his son, who had thrown his scholarship to the wind. After the war it'd be given again, so he said, but who knew when the war would be over and who would win? Or even if Massingham would be around then. If not, and that sly young whelp Ralph with his fancy talk and schooling took over all that his father had built, what price would a scholarship be then?

He helped tie the chickweed while Simon strolled along the flight path and the cages' nest pans, which had birds sitting on eggs. Silly bugger, silly, daft bugger, his son was, but the battle wasn't over. He could always face him, and bring his own words to bear and send him back. Yes, that's what he could do. He joined Simon, and pointed to one of the birds. 'Best little sitter, she is. Nowt to look at but knows what she's about, and she can't half turn out a few show birds.'

'Aye, that she can, our Joe, that she can.'

At home, as the clock ticked and bedtime loomed, Fran sat at the table, relaxing as her mam wrapped her inflamed hands in the sphagnum-moss poultice that her own mam had used, and her grandma before her; it was not just absorbent, but antiseptic.

'There you go, pet,' Ma murmured as she always did when tucking in the torn strips of sheeting that passed for bandages. 'That'll keep the itch at bay, so we'll keep at it, eh. What about your trunk?'

'No, Mam, that isn't bad. It's me hands that are worst.'

Sarah's mam would be treating her daughter's hands in the same way. It not only seemed to keep the rash there under control, but also helped the severity and spread around her trunk.

'I don't think it'll work on the yellow stuff you had to work with a week or so ago, but at least that were only for a couple of days till the worker came back off sick, or so I reckon, though you won't say owt about owt so I'm talking to meself. I reckon there's some fumes where you are now that makes the rash grow—' She suddenly stopped and Fran smiled as her mam looked around the room before finally whispering, 'Enough said, eh?'

She touched Fran's cheek as Fran said, 'Aye, Mam, best we don't.'

Her mam carried the hessian bag of fine dried moss back to the mantelpiece, and the jam jar of her mixture of goose grease and moss back into the scullery. She returned, smiling slightly. 'We must do as we're told, our lass. Can't have one of Hitler's men earwigging, then sabotaging all the work and hurting you into the bargain. I'm not having it.'

Fran roared with laughter. 'Then that's decided. No sabotage at the Factory, or the wrath of Annie Hall will descend on the Nazis.'

Her mam laughed too, and it was a real one, which was getting to be a habit, unlike the pale imitation that had existed for months after the babe, and Mam's sickness. Fran hugged her mam gently, feeling as she had since that day that this woman must be treated like one of her da's canary eggs, or a detonator shell. At that thought, she shook her head because using that image summed up how the world had changed.

Her mam seemed to read her mind, and said, 'Don't fret, our Fran. I'm much more meself these days, and there's no way I'm going to break into bits. That's past. Away to bed, as you'll be up before the sparrows again tomorrow. Take no notice if there's a dark cloud over your da in the morning, for I believe our Stan was wrong to lay it on your shoulders, and your da will feel that too. And it's for your da and me to remember that it's not our lives you're all living. Not ours at all . . .'

Her mam returned to her armchair where she'd work on her rugs until Joe came in from the canaries or the Miners' Club, which is where the men would probably drift to.

Fran climbed the stairs and walked into the box room. She stared out of the window, across the village. The slag heap was doing what it did, the winding gear was standing sentinel as the night shift set things up for the fore shift or did maintenance beneath the ground. Nothing changed, but then you found everything had changed. War and pestilence . . . She laughed. Well, war at least. Pestilence was another matter and so was the plague, and as for locusts, none of these had arrived. Ben might feel it had when Stan arrived home, if his mutterings as he had headed for bed earlier this evening were anything to go by, the loudest being, 'It's a bugger cos I'll have to share me bed with the big lug again. He's a bliddy pest.'

'Language, lad,' their mam had snapped.

Ben, standing in the doorway, had shrugged. 'Well, his feet're cold and he divint cut his toenails short enough.'

Fran laughed again, her breath misting the window, because her mam had replied, 'Just like your da's, but not the toenails. I daresay yours are cold an' all, lad, and you know you're hankering to see him again, as he hasn't come back for the vacation, or whatever he calls it.'

And that's the trouble, she thought. I could strangle the tyke, but I want him back. It's not right without him.

Chapter Five

In the Hall kitchen just before four in the morning on Saturday, Fran's da shouldered his way past her, heading for the back door. He hauled his boots out from beneath the old chair by the back step, and put them on. He was wearing a different pair of socks.

'Be safe, Da,' Fran said.

He didn't reply as he tugged his cap down and stamped across the yard, jerking up the sneck and disappearing into the back lane. She shrugged into her mackintosh and followed him outside, knotting her scarf, easing her bag and gas mask, listening to him clattering along the alley with all the other pitmen, and sighed. She was about to call goodbye to her mam when she heard the hinges of the gate creak as Da peered back into the yard. He stood there, defiance in every fibre, as he muttered, 'Waste of bliddy money getting you trained to type, but if yer have to be the bliddy fool yer are, and yer brother too, be safe.' He slammed the gate and stamped off, joining the endless stream of men flowing through the darkness towards the pit.

Her mam was behind her on the top step, the wind snatching at her flowered overall, her arms crossed in the moonlight.

'He swore,' Fran said.

'Aye, well, he loves yer, and it's all moving a mite fast for him. Just like you should be, if you're to catch your bus. Just think, our Stan'll be home later today. Oh, just think—' It was as though her mam was excited, but at the same time, subdued. The colliery hooter sounded, and her mam's hand went to her mouth. Now Fran saw the fear in her eyes, for da, and Stan.

Fran nodded, reached out and gripped her hand, then ran on to Main Street, seeing Davey and his marrers in the flow. He stepped out and caught her. 'Hey, spare me a second.'

He swung her round and kissed her. She laughed against his mouth. 'I love you, Davey Bedley. Right up to the sky and back again, but I'm late for the bus, or the bliddy bus, as me da would say this mornin'.'

Davey was grinning, his cap at its usual angle off to the left. Sarah was at the bus stop but had obviously heard because she called out, 'You best get into this queue, or we'll all be swearing at you. And you, David Bedley, get on to your work, for pity's sake.'

Fran snatched another kiss and he gripped her hand. 'One day,' he muttered. 'One day . . .' She backed away, as he did too, and she longed for the time they'd share a colliery house of their own, with bairns. She'd type his articles and then he'd start up his magazine . . . She paused, wondering how you would put in the crossword's straight lines for the printing firm? He was still watching her, and she him, and he called, 'Be safe, bonny lass. And don't yer fret, I'll tek care of our Stan.'

Then he was off and running as Sid shouted, 'For the love of God, man, shift yer arse.'

'You be safe too, you daft galumphs,' Fran called after them all.

She turned and ran as Sarah laughed, standing back and watching as Maisie waltzed Fran to the steps of the bus, saying, 'Don't think of Stan, just tek it day by day, eh?'

The driver was Bert again, but on Monday it would be Cecil driving them in for the 2 p.m. start when their shifts changed. Maisie shoved Fran ahead of her down the aisle. Sarah brought up the rear, singing, 'Put your left foot in, and your left foot out . . .' and the women all shouted, 'Then shake it all about.'

Fran, Sarah and Maisie did just that as Mrs Oborne called, 'Decorum, please, lasses.'

Patsy from Lindon Lane called, 'Who's he when he's at home, Mrs Oborne?'

The women fell about laughing as Bert hooted his horn and yelled, 'All aboard for the crazy farm.'

Sarah shoved Maisie down next to Patsy, who'd been beckoning to her. Would she be taking over Sylv's shift as well? Sarah sat down on the spare seat next to Mrs Wilks, then Fran took the double behind so that Beth could be one of a pair today. Mrs Wilks continued her knitting. She was in the sewing department at the Factory – the clean room, as they called it, meaning it was chemical-free. She'd be training all the new girls in cutting out and running up their blue overalls until they had come to grips with the Factory, and she herself was less yellow and itchy when she'd return to 'active duty'. Sitting back, Fran wondered if one's innards went yellow as well? She wanted to think of this, for Stan was coming back today, well, it would be in the evening by the time the train arrived, if there was no bombing . . .

'Got an eyeful, have yer, Franny?' Mrs Wilks said.

Fran came back to the present. 'Sorry, I was just thinking . . .'

'Aye, we heard your Stanhope were on his way back. Bit of a facer for yer da, I 'spect.'

'Oh aye, more than a bit. I could strangle the beggar, Stan, not me da.'

Bert was driving down Main Street and then out into the countryside, leaving Massingham behind. They winced as he bumped in and out of the potholes. Everything was as usual, but then again it wasn't. What was Sylv doing, and her bairn not yet two? And what about Stan? Had he left Oxford and its spires yet?

Fran sighed and stared ahead, thinking again of Mrs Wilks's innards, then the canaries in the shed, and remembered the day her da had sold his pigeons and gone over to canaries, as Tom had done. He and Tom Bedley were like twins, so if one did something, the other followed. It was Tom who'd sold up his pigeon loft first, saying it was too much of a do to take them out in their baskets to the start of the race, and then wait for them to return and clock them in.

As Sarah said, it wouldn't have bothered him if he'd got a good racer, but he hadn't, and the pair of them had laughed because neither had Franny's da. The two marrers had then joined forces with Simon Parrot. They made a bit of money, breeding and selling them on.

Would that happen to the pit ponies, too, one day, when they weren't used any more? Would the pitmen who ran them, and who looked after them on their summer holidays, buy them up and keep them bankside to gallop, toss their heads and generally live in clover?

At Sledgeford, Beth clambered on with a wide smile. Sarah turned and smiled at Fran, but it didn't reach her eyes. Fran sighed, and watched as Beth headed for her, knowing Sarah was worried that Beth and Stan might spark up again. Where would that get anyone? Nowhere, except pain and chaos all round, and it seemed to be niggling at Sarah like an open wound.

Amelia followed, and then Valerie with her thumbs up for all to see. For a moment Sarah and Fran were puzzled and then Valerie shouted, 'Me mam's taking in Amelia.'

Mrs Oborne shouted, 'No more shoe-leather suppers for

her, then. But maybe she should have stuck it out and started a cobblers?'

They set off again and the sing-song began – of course it did. In spite of Jimmy dying and Sylv being hurt, the world had to go on, and the work too. Fran sang to stop the thought of Stan in the pit, as though it wasn't bad enough with her da and the lad she loved being down there already. And what about Sarah, Beth and all the other friends who handled explosives? Whichever way any of them turned, there was—

Beth nudged her. 'Sing up, pet. We need your voice today of all days.'

Fran sang and soon she thought of Stan back in the gang, and the beck that they must go to tomorrow, as they were all off work. Should she ask Beth to cycle over from Sledge-ford? But that decision had to wait.

She began to hum and, tucking her arm in Beth's, the two of them stood and swayed to the rhythm of 'Smoke Gets in Your Eyes'. Maisie and Sarah rose as well, and soon all of them were singing, with Bert hooting from time to time to keep them company.

In Oxford the same day, Stanhope Hall slung his carpet bag over his shoulder, feeling it thud across his back. He loped down the last flight of the stairs leading to the Porters' Lodge. The door into the quadrangle was open and the early-morning light flooded in. The air in Oxford was clean and clear; standing in the doorway, he drew in a great lungful, enough to last for as long as the war. He then smacked on the porters' bell. Mr Carter came from the back, where he had been sorting the letters that had arrived. He took Stan's keys and said, 'Good luck to you, Mr Hall. You take care now.'

Stan smiled. 'Thanks for all you've done, Mr Carter. I

hope your son makes it through – keeps his head down, in other words.' He left some pound notes on the counter.

'That's uncommonly civil of you, sir, but I think you might be needing these yourself.' Mr Carter pushed them back. 'And may I say that in that colliery of yours, I hope you keep *your* head down, and don't knock it against anything sharp. I have to say I admire you, and it's Oxford's loss.'

Stan tipped his cap, picked up two pounds and left two. 'Let's divvy it up, eh. Your words are kind, but I'll see you again when this lot is over.'

Mr Carter smiled. 'I'll be here, sir, never fear. Perhaps you'll have the same room.'

Stan grinned. 'You never know. Must go, I have a train to catch and then a sister to beard. Right angry she is an' all. Thinks I should have told Mam and Da meself, or so Davey, her lad, warned when he rang me last night to confirm I was coming, and hadn't changed my mind.'

Mr Carter laughed. 'The female of the species tend to take their pound of flesh, Mr Hall, then forgive you.'

Stan nodded. 'This one will certainly take a great mouthful, but as for forgiving . . . The jury's out on that.'

He waved, turned and headed out without a backward look, mostly because he felt sick every time he moved his head. This morning the green of the lawn seemed brighter than ever, the lavender in the corner beds still buzzed with bees and the central fountain trickled. It reminded him of the beer he had sunk with Professor Smythe, but he needed to get back in training if he was to go not only to the club after his shift but down Auld Hilda too and not make a fool of himself before his marrers, Sid, Norm and Davey. Something struck him then. That's if they still were his marrers? He'd walked away . . . The thought bothered him far more than leaving this place.

Last evening, Professor Smythe had insisted on pint

after watery pint to thank Stan for being his wingman, as he was wont to put things now his son was in the RAF. Stan strode through the arch to his left and along the gravel drive, forcing himself to appear fine while it felt like a sledgehammer was destroying his skull from inside. The Oxford wind was battering his sinuses into the bargain too. It was a hangover the likes of which he hadn't had since he'd staggered home from the Miners' Club every Friday night, only to wake in the morning wishing he were dead.

He reached the road, grateful that the prof had not only paid him for his vacation work, but had rammed £10 into his hand as they separated outside the pub, saying, 'You'd better return to us, Stanhope Hall. You're bound for a first if I know anything about anything. Shame to let it slip away, eh? Think of me when everyone's back for the Michaelmas term including the freshers, expecting praise just for breathing.'

Stan was about to cross the road and head for the bus stop when a red roadster swept towards the kerb and screeched to a halt in front of him. The wheel arches gleamed, and Ralph Massingham's white teeth weren't far behind. Stan sighed. They'd managed to avoid one another since they'd started at Oxford in the same year, as they were at different colleges, so what did the jumped-up bugger want?

Stan checked his watch, then half saluted Ralph, who had a case strapped to the rack on the sloping rear of the two-seater, open-topped monster, whose engine he hadn't yet cut.

"Ow do?' Stan said.

There was something about the son of the mine owner that still, after all the years he'd had the misfortune to know him, set Stan's teeth on edge and made him more of a Geordie pitman than ever.

Ralph drawled, in a way that made Stan want to punch out his perfect teeth, 'Good morning to you, Stanhope. I heard you were heading off about now so I parked further along and waited out of the way of a delivery van for some considerable time, I might add. You see, I have a better idea for you than the train. It'll save you a fare, which no doubt will be a source of relief to you.'

Stan shook his head. 'I've booked.'

Ralph's flashing smile faltered.

Just then, from further up the road, they heard, 'Hello . . . I say, hang on.' Both turned as Professor Smythe waved frantically from about thirty yards up the slope. 'Still here, Stan, no chocks away as yet? Good. Good. You see, I meant to say last night . . .' Professor Smythe broke into a trot, but pedalled back to a walk almost immediately, which was a relief because the old boy's stomach was stressing his waist-coat buttons.

Stan smiled, pleased to see this man again, a man who had nurtured him since his arrival. It was part of Smythe's duties as Mr Massingham's scholarship liaison officer, but he'd gone above and beyond. Apparently, he'd been given that duty because he and Massingham were members of the same club in London and, like Reginald Massingham, Smythe was passionate about the fulfilment of potential, no matter what the background. Somehow, the professor had the ability to make his scholarship boys feel like they were on a par with any one of the privileged students, and in a very short time they all came to love and respect his incisive mind, foibles and all.

'Oh God, not Father's bumbling chum,' Ralph muttered. His remark incensed Stan and he hurried to meet Smythe, his carpet bag banging as he ran; eager as much as anything to get some distance between him and Ralph.

Professor Smythe stopped, pressing his hands on his

knees and panting. When Stan arrived, he straightened. 'Splendid, my boy, saves me toiling all the way down and spending more time than I need to with that totally irritating whelp of dear Reginald's. His mere presence on this earth is a great waste of oxygen and one wonders how he can be so unlike his father. The apple has undoubtedly fallen far, far from the tree on this occasion. It's the car I recognised – can't see the visage under that tweed cap. Such a large peak, don't you think? Indicative of rather a small . . . Well, let's leave it there.'

'What can I do for you, sir?' Stan murmured, trying not to smile and mindful that time was passing and he needed to catch the train.

Professor Smythe held up a finger. 'I just remembered I should have said that your crossword friend, David Bedley, must contact me if he feels he would like to reconsider the opportunity of a scholarship after this wretched Hitler business is sorted. You see, I had to discuss one or two things with dear old Massingham in the club last week and he reminded me that there was a draw in the exam, with you two lads coming up equal trumps, which, sad to say, had slipped my mind.'

Stan nodded. 'I did tell you, Professor. I still feel bad about it.'

Professor Smythe looked amazed. 'No, don't. It was his decision and it seems to me he is making good use of his brains, no doubt while he's hacking away at the coal. Oh my word, what ideas must be churning in his head with each bash of the pick, for he sets such intriguing crosswords. Dear boy, I do thank you for showing me the magazine to which he contributes. I of course mentioned it to Reggie Massingham, who even took the magazine away . . .' He drifted off, then muttered, 'I say, I really must get it back.'

Stan prompted. 'So, what was it you forgot, sir?'

Professor Smythe turned back to him, as though not quite sure who he was, but then gathered himself. 'Ah yes, Reggie made it clear that he would be more than happy to provide a subsequent scholarship for your marrer – that is what you pitmen call your friends, isn't it? Oh, but I've already touched on that. What was it I wanted . . . ?'

Stan forced himself not to look at his watch because he owed a lot to this man who had encouraged him to push himself further than he thought he could go. But Professor Smythe's eyes had yet again taken on the distracted gaze that meant his mind was toying with some irrelevance, as though the world did not exist. But exist it did, as pedestrians wove round them, their gas masks over their shoulders and sometimes nudging the two men. The bus to the station passed by, but there was another due in ten minutes, and if he caught that he could still get his train.

The professor tapped Stan's arm. 'Yes, that's it – marrer. Named thus, I seem to remember, because the roots of the marrow grow underground.' He frowned and stared earnestly at Stan. 'But surely don't the roots of all plants? However, let me not travel along unnecessary trails of thought.'

Oh, please not, thought Stan. The professor suddenly focused, his finger in the air, ignoring a drayman carrying a barrel on his back from the brewers' lorry parked alongside, who bellowed, 'Mind yer back, matey.'

'I know what it was, Stan. I'd so like you to give this little missive to your marrer David. It is a page or two of jottings on what I think could be an effective improvement on the setting of his recent fascinating and original form of crossword that's to be placed in the column for advanced aficionados. You know, the one in which the clues are virtually a code one has to break? I have suggested moving said clues up a level, using a key. There are several that contain such a wonderful use of anagrams, but Bedley's are more than that – they are more demanding. Yes, indeed. I've provided just the merest of nudges, for I am no expert. Indeed, I bow to his expertise and should he wish to correspond . . .'

The professor paused, this time dodging out of the way of the returning drayman, presumably carrying an empty barrel this time. 'It does make one think . . .' He stopped again, with a look on his face that indicated he was indeed about to plough along yet another furrow.

Stan took the notebook from the professor's hand and stuffed it in his jacket pocket. The professor came back to earth and they shook hands.

'I must go, sir. Many thanks for all your help – I mean it.'

Professor Smythe held on to his hand for a moment, looking at the blue pitman scars, and a sadness seemed to sweep over him. 'Such is the badge of a miner – trapped coal in your wounds. May you return, dear boy. You must all return to us, you simply must. But I do believe that young David Bedley would be most useful to the war doing . . . Ah well, I will be discussing this more with Massingham. Senior, of course.'

He looked beyond Stan to the car and tutted, then turned on his heels and wafted back towards the centre of town, his scarf somehow billowing, though the wind had died. Stan stared after him. He loved the fellow, but he simply couldn't stay in Oxford. How could he, and call himself a man, when there was work to be done at the pit now so many young pitmen had left to join the war? Besides, he was trained to lie on his side or his back, or to kneel, as he forced his pick into the living, breathing coal. For that's what he felt it was: a real and worthy opponent that he could face up to, even with his damaged leg – an appendage that was no use on the front line, apparently.

Stan checked his watch again and decided to walk to the station. He turned just as the blast of a car horn alerted him to the fact that Ralph Massingham was still parked at the side of the road. He was beckoning to Stan, waving the peaked Harris tweed cap and revealing goggles hitched up onto his forehead. Stan sighed, but the boss's son was still that, and it was the boss who controlled whether Stan's family had work and a house, or not.

He still had time to catch the bus, so he sauntered back towards Ralph. The cap had now been replaced, but the goggles remained on the lad's forehead and his scarf was still wound several layers deep round his neck. The fact that he looked like an idiot was neither here nor there, though the fact that he had suspect political affiliations wasn't. Or was Stan being unfair? He drew near enough to hear the engine as it ticked over. After all, Stan had been to a Communist meeting. But that didn't make him a leftie; in fact, he'd thought the speaker a thug and a dreamer, if you could be both ... He stopped himself from playing with the notion, or else he'd become like Professor Smythe – unfit to survive anywhere but in a seminar at precious Oxford University.

He came to a halt by the side of the roadster.

'What was it you were saying, Mr Massingham? I've not seen hide nor hair of you since we both arrived, and now I'm off home and you are not, so whatever you need I doubt I can help. Or was it something you'd like me to take to your family? I'm sorry to be rude, but could you make it snappy, because I must get my train.'

Ralph patted the passenger seat beside him. '*Au contraire, mon brave.* It is I who can do something for you. I heard on the grapevine that a Massingham scholar, a known clever clogs, was tossing up these esoteric dreaming spires in favour of returning to the murky depths of my father's pit.

84

I knew it could only be you, as Pater has held over the Massingham scholarship examination for the duration of the war. Your pure and patriotic gesture made me feel it was incumbent on the son of said Massingham Colliery owner to relinquish his place here for the interim and do the same – do my bit, as it were. You shamed me, my hewer friend. So, although you said you had booked your ticket, do just strap your little bag and gas mask on top of my case and we'll set off.' Ralph revved the car and dropped his goggles over his eyes.

Stan stared at the pit owner's son and was careful in his reply. If it had been the senior Mr Massingham he would have leapt into the car, for the man was a decent and good bloke. 'Kind of you, Mr Massingham, but I repeat that I have a ticket, so won't trouble you with my little bag and my hewer's arse on your fine leather.'

He stopped. Good Lord, he was getting as bad as Fran. The thought conjured up an image of him arriving at the door of number 14 Leadenhall Terrace in the owner's son's car. It would make the row that was to come a million times worse.

To his surprise, Ralph laughed, and again patted the seat. 'There's room for your hewer's arse, lad. Besides, Father said to pick you up and we don't ignore his wishes, do we, and frankly it's a good idea to have company on a long drive, don't you think? If you're worried about a chill, we can draw the hood up and protect your chestnut locks.' Ralph's eyes had become like cold grey stones. It was his familiar look when issuing instructions to 'commoners'.

Ah, if Mr Massingham had suggested it, well and good, he could accept that, and what's more so could his da, Stan thought. Besides, it would help no one to set himself against the whelp, as Ralph was commonly known – without affection. He nodded. 'All reet, Mr Massingham. Thank you kindly.' In spite of intending to assert his roots, he thought he still sounded like Uriah Heep. Any minute now he'd wring his hands.

He sorted out his carpet bag, rescued his gas mask from it, and settled himself in the passenger seat, tightening his scarf and tugging down his cap as Ralph pulled into the traffic.

Chapter Six

Ralph drove like a blithering maniac, just like he always had around Massingham, roaring round bends, screeching to a halt at junctions and scaring the horses of the milk vans they sped past. Stan made himself stare ahead impassively, refusing to be scared or embarrassed as they were cursed. On and on they motored, heading across country and then setting course for the north.

Ralph talked for the first hour about Classics, about which it became evident he knew bugger all, so Stan merely nodded and said every so often, 'Oh really.' By the time they were beyond Birmingham, Ralph had quietened down, and once past Leicester he was ready to find some lunch. 'What about you, old boy? Fancy a bit of tucker at some roadside hostelry?'

Stan had his sandwiches in his carpet bag but could hardly sit in the car stuffing his face while the master took luncheon, so he agreed and did the polite thing by offering to pay, hoping that Ralph would find some sort of a café. Not a bit of it. He swept through the arch of a coaching inn and skidded to a halt in front of a glass-walled restaurant, showering gravel everywhere. Ralph didn't bother to open the door, but vaulted out of the car and strode towards the double doors without a backward glance.

Stan's vaulting days had ended with the roof fall in Sour Seam a couple of years ago, so he opened the door and eased himself out, trying to straighten up without appearing to wince. He shook his leg, then headed into the restaurant, checking his watch. Davey had said Stan's da was on the fore-shift when he'd telephoned the Porters' Lodge yesterday evening, so at least they could have the face-to-face row over and done with before bedtime.

Ralph was sitting in an alcove, his cap and jacket being borne away by the waiter. He beckoned to Stan, who joined him. A large a la carte menu was placed before each of them. A multitude of knives and forks glinted either side of the place settings. Stan sighed, and hoped the menu wasn't too extensive, which usually meant expensive. Though how could it be, with rationing beginning to bite? But he was wrong. Three courses later, with Ralph having chosen the most expensive dishes from each, as well as a beer, though no wine, thank heavens, they left, Stan's wallet some pounds lighter.

But Stan had also had a beer and it loosened his tongue as they continued to fly along, his fury at the price of lunch adding a touch of venom. 'So, Ralph,' he shouted above the throaty roar of the roadster, 'you were in Germany for the Olympics with Swinton's boy, Tim, weren't you?'

Ralph stared ahead, but Stan caught the momentary tightening of his grip on the steering wheel. There, you bugger, he thought, that'll teach you to cost me an arm and a leg. Unwilling to let the venom seep away just yet, Stan added, 'With some group or other, wasn't it?'

Stan knew perfectly well there were suspicions the group had been allied to the Blackshirts, or, in other words, the British Union of Fascists. Why on earth had Massingham senior allowed that? The talk was that he hadn't realised the connection and once he'd cottoned on, it had been the end of all such nonsense.

Ralph drew his silver cigarette case from the breast pocket of his tweed jacket. 'Take one out for me, would you, Stan? And have one yourself.' He tossed it onto Stan's lap.

Stan eased one out part way and waved the case in front of Ralph, who placed the cigarette in his mouth before dragging out his lighter and flicking it alight. Stan closed the case with a click and returned it, taking out his own Woodbines and lighting one with a match as Ralph said, 'Yes, a few chums and I got together and off we went. Seemed a shame to miss all that sport. Tim Swinton came along to make up the numbers. He's a handy boxer, don't you know, so a good man to have around if things get out of hand. Not that they should – can't think why I said that.'

Oh, good catch, Stan thought. Smoothly done. A few chums indeed, what utter tripe, and you can't think why things should 'get out of hand' ... ? But he moved on. 'So, what did you feel about the Jewish situation, and Freemasons? What about—'

Ralph was laughing. 'Oh, for goodness' sake, young Stanhope. The publicity about the situation bore no resemblance to what it was actually like. We were there for the Olympics, and the beauty of Berlin. I remember a bit about youths in uniform, but they were merely Scouts. The press made their usual fuss about things – it's naive to believe all their rubbish. Besides, I was a mere lad. It *was* a few years ago, laddie. Good God, thousands were there. The British participated, that shows it was all right.'

'What was Berlin like then?' Stan asked.

'Like any city. I particularly liked the wide streets and, quite frankly, the sense of order. But let's talk about you for a moment. Never been to Russia? I heard you were at some Communist rallies – or do we call them "anti-Fascist"?'

'One. I was curious. But there's little to choose between the Fascists and the anti-Fascists, quite frankly. Load of buffoons, the lot of them, throwing their weight around, saying they know best, but each meaning they would stuff in a dictator and get rid of those they don't like.'

'So speaks the great scholarship boy, eh? A statement, not a discussion.'

Stan looked sideways at Ralph. 'You're right, it was a statement, but look at what's happened: Stalin and Hitler, two dictators up to no good, just showing they're greedy bastards intent on ruling the bliddy world, no matter the cost.'

Ralph flicked his cigarette stub into the road. Stan's Woodbine had burned down long ago. 'Stan, war is such a bore, don't you think? Much better to make some sort of compromise peace and all just get on in one Western big empire, with some sensible people with proper ideas at the top. Then at least the trains would run on time and the West could stand against the East. Or that's some of the thinking a while ago, so I gather.' He flashed a look at Stan, who was shaking his head in disbelief. Ralph laughed. 'Don't worry, old boy, only jesting.'

Stan said nothing. What on earth was the point? And perhaps the idiot *was* only jesting. On and on they travelled. After they had tucked Ripon, with its tiny cathedral, behind them, Ralph said quietly, 'I met a nice girl – Dagmar was her name. I was sixteen, as was she. I thought I loved her, but of course I couldn't have. Far too young, and best not pursued under the circumstances. Lord knows what she's doing now, probably wedded to some burly officer.'

Stan said, 'In Ripon?'

Ralph shook his head. 'Berlin, idiot.'

'Ah.'

The wind was bitter now, the sky clouding over, and as he thought of Ralph missing Dagmar, Stan faced what – or who – he had been pushing away since he'd decided to return: Beth. He swallowed. It was her existence that had almost changed his decision to return because he didn't know how he'd feel to be near her, and he couldn't bear the pain to start all over again. He stared at the countryside, anything, to steady himself. 'I heard they tidied up the place, pulled down the Nazi posters for the visitors,' he said.

Ralph's laugh was hearty. 'In Ripon?'

I'll give you that one, Stan thought, happy to fence with him if it pushed away Beth, which it did.

'Berlin during the Olympics.'

'Lord, how should I know? They certainly weren't in evidence when I was there, but we had a trip out to see the autobahn. We could do with a few straight roads like that, let me tell you.'

'You're tired? Shall I take over?'

Ralph snatched a look at Stan through his goggles. 'Can you drive, old boy?'

'Of course. It's not just philosophy, politics and economics I've picked up from the Prof, you know.'

Ralph seemed to be considering, but finally shook his head. 'I'll give it a bit longer.'

The light was fading as they approached Durham, and Ralph said, 'It's all right, I'll drive on. I prefer to be in control. But perhaps if we do it again?'

'Aye, but we won't, not until the war is over, and Lord knows when that will be. But thanks for the ride, and to your da for suggesting it.'

They drove on, past fields with stone walls, and then headed through pit villages, skirting the slag heaps, and Ralph said suddenly, 'It's such a bloody mess, isn't it? And it stinks.'

'Aye, but it's what keeps the country going.' Stan had been going to say that it kept Ralph in nice cars and all, but it sounded petty.

At last, as the evening fell, they approached Massingham, with its smouldering slag heaps and the pithead with its winding gear against the skyline. Stan said just as they reached the outskirts, 'Drop me here, if you would, Ralph. I'll head down the lane and can cut across to the village.' In the distance he heard the whistle of the train taking coal to the main line and realised just how much he'd missed it, and the smell – all the things that bothered Ralph so much.

'Lord, no. I'll take you to your door, old boy. Leadenhall Street, isn't it? But perhaps no one will be at home. Your sister works at the Ordnance Factory now, and the lad is still at school?'

Stan swung round to stare at Ralph. 'Fran? How did you—' He stopped. No one should know. How the hell had Ralph heard? If he blabbed, Fran could get the sack.

Ralph shook his head, as though irritated, and muttered, 'Sorry about that. Er, I shouldn't say who . . .'

'Oh, your da? Yes, I see,' Stan said.

Ralph smiled, then, his voice eager, said, 'Yes, that's right. But . . . don't say I said anything. I'm a bloody fool. I usually know when to keep my mouth shut. Bit weary is all, old boy.'

Ralph turned left off Main Street into Leadenhall Street, cruising slowly along the row of terraced houses, pulling up at number 14. Stan hardly ever used their front door and it felt odd, as though he was a visitor. Well, he wasn't. He was home where he should be. He dragged money out of his wallet for the petrol, and said, 'He told you where we lived an' all, did he?'

Ralph had vaulted over the door again. 'What is this, an interrogation? Where you live is hardly new to me; after all, we own the house.' This was said quietly, coldly.

Stan said, 'Aye, and we work for it an' all, so it's you scratch our back, we'll scratch yours, I reckon.'

The two stared at one another and Stan realised that Ralph hadn't changed one whit from the jumped-up little snot he'd been as a boy, the one who'd waltz through the village bragging about whatever his new toy was that week. Well, Davey'd shown him back then what was what good and proper when the whelp had deliberately destroyed their papier-mâché footie, the twerp.

Stan opened the door and stepped from the car, praying his leg would take his weight after being cramped for so long. It did, just as Ralph laughed, 'I owe you a lunch. A good one.'

Stan unstrapped his carpet bag and gas mask. 'Nay, lad, no need. And I need to give you money for petrol.' He came around to the whelp and handed him a few notes. Ralph hesitated, then took them.

Behind Ralph, the front door opened. Stan saw Fran standing there and his heart lifted. Ralph turned and snatched off his cap. 'Ah, Fran Hall. Delighted to renew our acquaintance. I was just telling your brother that I owe him lunch, so do come too.'

Fran looked from one to the other, taking in the notes in Ralph's hand, and the car, and raised her eyebrows. 'I don't have time to eat dinner in a restaurant, thank you, Mr Massingham. Hello, Stan, brought door to door, eh? Getting ideas above yer station, lad? Though I see you're paying for the pleasure.'

At that, Ralph looked down at the money in his hand and passed it back. 'Certainly not, old boy. You had already bought your train ticket.'

Stan shook Ralph's hand. 'Don't fret about a meal in return. Good luck, and see you in the pit sometime.'

Ralph smiled. 'Oh, you will, you will. Elliott has agreed that you'll be my marrer, Stan. I asked; he obeyed like the good manager he is. Seems like a good idea, don't you think, as we have a bit of a bond already? Oxford, you know.'

Ralph walked with Stan to the front door and held out his hand to Fran. 'And I hope that we'll meet again soon, Fran Hall.'

Fran shook his hand. 'The name's Frances, Mr Massingham.'

Stan moved to kiss her, and as he did he whispered, 'Remember, he's the boss's son, and owns our house.'

She merely looked at Ralph. 'Nice of you to bring our lad back, Mr Massingham, but I expect you're tired and your da will have a nice glass of wine picked out for you and will be wondering where you've got to. Best not to come in and keep him waiting. You and Stan can catch up at t'pit Monday morning – fore shift, or so Davey's heard. You remember Davey? He took your football after you, the boss's son, busted ours up good and proper down the back alley. Best you get some rest tomorrow. You'll need to be bright-eyed and bushy-tailed.'

Stan recognised the suppressed fury in her voice and suspected some of it was really directed at him; the football incident had been years ago. He did wish she hadn't said it, though, for Ralph was—But Fran was grabbing Stan by his sleeve and hauling him in through the door, calling over her shoulder, 'You take care now, Mr Massingham.'

Stan's thanks joined his sister's as she slammed the door.

As Ralph climbed back into his roadster he smiled, but there was no humour in it. That was one lass he needed to get to know again, indeed he did. Not only was there a lingering sore of a score to be settled with Davey, but Fran Almighty Hall's bloody rudeness back then, and now, had just been added to the bill. By God, it had.

Fran shook her head at Stan as they stood in the passage at the foot of the stairs. 'Well, our lad, not quite the way to come home, is it? Tucked up in a roadster in the company of the boss's son. Not exactly set to please our da, but then you've not pleased him, nor me.'

Stan dropped his carpet bag and held out his arms. 'Don't give me a hard time, for the love of God, our Franny. I've been all day in that damned car when I could have been reading on the train an' all because Mr Massingham senior thought it a good idea. Give us a hug. Your big brother is home, pet.'

She shook her head. 'You're a great dolt, you know that? So I've to worry about you an' all now.'

He pulled her close and hugged her so tight she could hardly breathe. Finally she hugged him back and laid her head on his strong, familiar shoulder, but there was no pit smell, just a clean college smell. She said into his jacket, 'So, it's because of the war that you're back, nowt else?'

Stan eased her away. 'What else could there be, except I want to see you all, especially our mam. How's she looking, Fran?'

The door to the kitchen opened and their mam stood there, saying, 'Ask her yourself, bonny lad.'

He stepped into the warmth and light of the kitchen and held her in his arms before swinging her around. 'By, you're looking grand, Mam. Better'n I hoped.'

A voice came from Joe's armchair. 'So, you've given it all up, eh, to grub in the coal when you could have got away?'

As Stan turned to face him, his da rose and stood by the fireplace. Stan recognised the action and braced himself for the row, recognising the pain in his da's face. It was the same pain he'd felt when he caught Beth lying in the corn with Bob Jones, knowing he'd lost her and his future.

'I'm going back, Da, when the war's done. Mr Massingham is holding the scholarship over, so I still have my future.'

His da kept his back to him and Stan waited as he packed his pipe with baccy, lit it and drew on it until it glowed red. Only then did he turn. 'So, yer think you'll survive, do yer, to have a bliddy future? Down there, with the coal squeezing, and the tubs roaring along the rails. What makes yer so different from the rest of us, Stanhope Hall? What makes yer such a damned fool as to give up that world and come back here?'

Stan knew that Fran had followed him in and was waiting near the kitchen table, but his mam had retreated to the scullery, which was wise. 'I have to do my bit, Da. Even the Prof's lad is. How can I not, when I'm yer son?'

His father jabbed his pipe at him. 'So, yer'll go on shifts, yer'll forget the look o' the sun. Yer'll start to cough. Yer'll forget yer book learnin' cos you'll be too damned tired, and are yer forgetting the blacklocks? Them damned beetles that march on yer bait, yer drinks . . . What about the stink of pee cos yer divint have a netty down there? And the dust which'll blind yer, fill yer hair, the coal that'll cut yer and most likely muck up yer other leg?'

Stan wanted to go to him, hold him close, because the pain was still there in this man whose chest he could hear rattling from where he stood. 'Da, I—'

'Da nothing,' roared his father. 'Don't come here with your posh ways, driven to the door by the boss's boy, that namby-pamby, bloody Fascist. What t'hell be he doing back?'

'Da, he went to a couple of Fascist meetings and the Olympics, that's all, like lots of us did. Remember, I went to a Commie one to see what was what, and stuck me head into a Fascist one. Load of buggers, the lot o' them. Ralph's come back to the pit cos he wants to do his bit. His da seems to think it fine, anyway, and what can we say or do about it when they own the house? Think on it, Da. Perhaps he's

96

changed from the spoilt brat he was?' Though even as he said it, Stan didn't believe it.

His da was shaking his head. 'I divint heard such bollocks in the whole of me life. Changed? Do his bit? What does he know about doing his bit, wi' his soft hands on the pick. But I divint care about the lad, it's you, yer damned great fool, I'm shoutin' at because it's not too late.'

'Da—' Stan tried again.

'I'm not telling yer this for the sake of me health. I have yon sister o' yours doing a damned fool job, I have you back here, and I look at ye and wonder what it was all about, that's what I ask meself. What were all the strivings for, when you throw it back in me face?' He was still jabbing the pipe stem at him, his hands gnarled and scarred, his nails torn and thick with coal. Stan expected Fran to leap in at the mention of her name, and was glad when she didn't. Why draw the flak when she didn't have to? This was his fight.

'It's not about you, Da. It's what I want – need – to do. Look at Davey, look at me marrers, hewing away, keeping the engines of the country running. I can't hold me head up, Da, not if I don't do this.'

'What if yer bliddy 'ead gets knocked off while yer holding it up? That's what I want to know. But that be it, what do I know? I divint got learning, so what does I know? Thick as two bloody planks I be, but don't yer think I won't be bloody awkward an' all, every time I see yer daft face, and yon sister of yorn too.'

Fran stepped forward now, as Stan thought she might. 'Da, that's not fair, you've had yer go at me. Stick with Stan.'

Her da just stuck his pipe in his mouth, sidestepped her, strode to the back door, picked up his cap and muffler from the hook, grabbed his boots from under his chair, and slammed the door behind him.

Stan stared at the range, which was burning good coal, quiet coal which Mr Massingham Senior insisted the pitmen were still to be allotted every week, even now when the pits were under the management of the war cabinet, or whoever the hell it was. It was coal he'd be hewing again on Monday.

The door slammed open again and his da yelled from the step, 'And I'll not have that Massingham whelp here again, d'yer hear? And to think he'll be in t'pit buggering about and being a bliddy danger. Knows about the blacklocks, do 'e? Rats running up inside his trouser leg, do 'e? The world's gone bliddy mad. First 'Itler, now you bliddy bairns. Bliddy mad. And you can still change yer mind, so tell me tomorrow and I'll stick yer on a train back t'south, that I will.'

The door slammed shut, again. Well, thought Stan, I hate the blacklocks and all, but so does every pitman. He waited, and it was as though the whole house did too. Then he heard Ben's feet on the stairs and his younger brother rushed past Fran and Mam, who had appeared from the scullery, and hurled himself at Stan, holding him tightly.

'Da's gone down the back lane – I watched from Fran's box-room window. And Mam and Fran have sorted two mattresses in the attic room so I don't have to have yer bliddy cold feet on me. And da's really angry. He only uses 'divint' when his rage's boiling fit to spill over the whole of County Durham and it's all yer bliddy fault, our Stan.'

'Language,' Fran and Stan shouted together.

Mam disappeared to the scullery again, shouting in her turn, 'If you've had yer dinner with his lordship, our Stan, you won't want the tiny bit of lamb we got special, though it'll be lost amongst the carrots and potatoes.'

'And dumplings,' Ben shouted.

Stan laughed. 'Try and keep me from it, Mam. Da's vegetables, is it?'

Fran set the table while Mam dished up a plate for Da for later. The two of them brought in the food, setting it on the table. As her mam sat, and both boys picked up their knives and forks and dug in, Fran saw the contentment on her face because her family were back. It would help the healing of her even more, she knew, but only if the menfolk stayed safe, and united.

She watched Stan gobble up his food as he always used to, and though she could still wallop him, she felt . . . She couldn't quite find the words. Then it came to her. They were a family again, which was something that had been taken from them when wee Betty was buried, for then a cold wind had blown through their lives. Their world had been rocked, and how could they recover? Well, here they all were, just as they'd always been after her da had been in a rage, and her da would come round and be, as he'd always been, if not pleased, then accepting.

'Eat up, bonny lad,' Mam said. 'Your da will be back later. He'll be in the club or with the canaries. He knows you won't go back. War is war and he went into the last one, so he'll blow himself out, you'll see. But to get your feet back on the ground, you two boys can do the pots, as we women brought it to you, eh?'

The groan from Ben made Fran laugh. It was all going to be all right, just so long as Stan didn't find he still cared for Beth, or she for him.

Chapter Seven

The next morning, Sunday, Fran was at the box-room window as the miners on the extra shift clattered towards the pit. Da should be one of them, Tom Bedley too, but Da and Stan had been bellowing at one another for the last hour. Suddenly there was silence and Fran held her breath, waiting.

She heard Stan shout, 'I'm staying, Da, and that's that. Besides, Mr Massingham wants me to partner the whelp until he gets the hang of things, and I owe the man, but not the son. And you remember that difference, Da.'

Her da's reply was so loud the whole of those along the back lane must have heard. 'The whelp will only cause bliddy havoc wherever he bliddy well puts his bliddy great feet, and that's a good reason, if you won't listen to owt else, for going back to bliddy Oxford, and taking him with you.'

Stan bellowed back, 'Oh, for pity's sake, Da.'

Silence again. The pitmen were still passing and she heard one of them shout, 'Howay, Joe Hall, Tom's on his way. Save your breath for Auld Hilda.'

Fran agreed with her da. No one in their right mind would want that nincompoop anywhere near where real pitmen worked because he couldn't have changed that much from childhood. What a pillock he'd been, lording it over them on his school holidays. But the owner was the owner, and the order had come down, so that was that.

She heard the back door slam and peered through the window. Her da was crossing the yard, stopping by the hen-feed barrel and throwing grain through the chicken wire.

For a moment he watched the hens come from the old pigeon loft with a fluffing of feathers, then he threw the scoop back into the barrel and slammed the lid down. He clumped to the gate and opened it. She pressed her nose against the glass, seeing him meet Tom Bedley, who looked so like Davey and Sarah, and the two of them set off towards the mine, heads down, talking, her da gesticulating.

She waited a minute, opening the window and leaning out to make sure that her da wasn't going to spring back in like some jack-in-a-box and start another round of bellowing, then headed downstairs for her own bread and dripping. She met Ben on the landing. 'By, Franny, they were loud enough to wake the whole bliddy village, that they were.'

'Don't swear,' she muttered, pulling him back by the collar. 'Ladies first.'

He came down behind her, muttering, 'There's no lady anywhere near me, that there isn't.'

She said nothing until they reached the passage, then she whipped round, grabbed his ear and laughed. 'Take that back or I'll skelp you, you little toerag.'

Ben squirmed. 'Pax, pax, you're the best lady there's ever been, and I want me bread and dripping, so get off.'

'Don't you two ever grow up?' Stan called from the kitchen.

Ben tore ahead of Fran, who yelled, 'What happened to ladies first?'

'That was then,' Ben yelled, bursting into the kitchen and hiding behind their mam.

Fran followed. 'I'll swing for you one day.'

Stan was sitting on his chair at the table and slurping his tea. 'Swing? Aye, that's an idea. Let's get on to the beck, and see if the rope's still there. Maybe the kingfisher, or his bairn at least, will be there too. Mam, are you coming? We'll take a bit of bait and spend the day out. What d'you reckon?'

Fran, who was chewing her bread and dripping, thanked her mam for the mug of tea she set before her and added, 'Oh, we'll get Davey and Sarah too – it'll be the gang, plus Ben. Ben, d'you feel like scooting round and getting them sorted? Tell Davey to make his own bait; he's got a pair of hands, same as Sarah.'

Ben was off and out of the house, wiping his mouth on the back of his hand.

Fran looked at her mam. 'Come too, Mam. The sun's out and it's right nice.'

'Nay, lass, Mrs Bedley's on her way and we'll work on sorting our proggies. If we're selling to the big stores direct, we reckon on starting a cooperative of workers to produce the goods, but their work 'as to be good enough. We've drawn up a list of the lasses we think will be happy to do it.'

Her mam was pulling out her proggy frame and putting it on the end of the table. Stan leapt to his feet and helped, while both Fran and he grinned at one another.

Stan said, 'Aye, we've bred our own boss, an' all. What d'you think you've been and gone and done, our Fran? There'll be no peace now. She'll have us cutting up the blankets once she's dyed them, see if she doesn't. It'll be like we're bairns again.'

'Aye,' said their mam, 'and any nonsense from the pair of you, and it'll be a clip behind the ear, let me tell you.'

At the Bedley house, Sarah was helping her mam lay out a finished proggy rug on the existing kitchen rug to see how it looked when it was down. 'It's grand, Mam, just right, but listen, are you and Mrs Hall sure you want to do this, get a group together, have Briddlestone's expecting delivery, that sort of thing? You work hard enough as it is.'

'Oh, stop your mithering, pet. I make them anyway, so why not get paid proper for doing it? And it'll be reet good because while we're all working together we can have a bit of a natter. It's what we need, you know – something to think about other than the war, and the pit, and yon Factory place. It'll be canny, you mark my words.'

'Are you putting all the money into a pot and divvying it up? Or is everyone getting paid for what they produce?' Sarah asked, sitting back on her heels as Mrs Bedley eased herself to her feet.

'Mrs Hall and me'll have to sort that out in some way that's fair, then put it to the others and see what's what.'

Sarah, still hunkered down, traced the pattern, smoothing the strips of rag she and her mam had cut from old blankets and felted jumpers. She realised the blue sweater of hers that had felted in the wash had been incorporated into the centre of the design.

Mrs Bedley went on, 'Mrs Hall telephoned the man at Briddlestone's about their needs and he said they're thinking of using them for wall hangings in London and want the shaggy *and* the smooth, so they've asked us to make some samples of both. We've got Mrs Smith – Beth's mam – from Langton Terrace, too, and a few more, including Mrs Oborne when she's off shift. Some of them have young bairns an' all, and as they need the money most, we reckon to take 'em on. Their men can help to make the frames, if the lasses can't do it.'

There was a knock at the back door and Sarah sprang to her feet, finding Ben stotting and jiggling on the back step. The lad always made her smile because he was so like Fran, with the same grin and enough energy to turn the world around.

'Sarah, our Fran said we were all to go to the beck for t'day. So, put yourself some bait together, and Davey must too. She says you're not to do his, cos he has mitts too. Where's he, anyways?'

103

Davey had crept up behind the lad and now yelled, 'Right behind yer, Ben.'

Ben jumped sky-high, then turned. 'That's bliddy dangerous. I could have fell and broke me legs, Davey.'

'Language, young Ben,' Mrs Bedley called.

'But Mrs Bedley—'

Davey lifted up the lad and whirled him around, Ben shouting, 'Let me go, I'm not a bairn.'

Davey put him down, ruffling the lad's hair. Ben shrugged himself out of Davey's reach, sticking his hands in his pockets. 'Don't know why I came to ask you, because you don't deserve to come to the beck, so you don't, Davey Bedley.'

'Howay with you, our Ben,' Davey laughed. 'If your sister's going, d'you think wild horses'd keep me away?'

Ben grimaced. 'I don't want any kissing and hugging. It's daft, and right soppy.'

Sarah stood watching these two, loving every second. It was as it always was, and now Stan was back it would be even better. In fact, it would be perfect, especially if . . .

'Stan's coming too?' she asked.

Ben was backing towards the gate, smoothing his hair, which would not lie flat, just like Fran's. 'Oh aye, we're all going.'

'All?' Sarah asked.

Davey pulled a face. 'What, you don't want our Ben? But he's part of the gang.'

Sarah grinned. 'Aye, wouldn't go without the lad. Just checking.'

For a moment she'd thought Ben had meant Beth too and something had twisted inside her.

Chapter Eight

Fran and Stan cycled round to the Bedleys', Ben sitting on Stan's crossbar, his cap pulled down hard, while Stan pedalled with his knees stuck out. As they reached the back gate and Stan dismounted, Ben muttered, 'Yer look like a bliddy stork, so yer do, our Stan. I should have a bike of me own, now you've taken yours back.'

Fran raised her eyebrows. 'Tip his cap over his eyes if he swears again, Stan.'

Slouching over to the gate, Ben lifted the sneck and yelled, 'We're ready and off, so if you're not, then bliddy catch up.' He sauntered into the Bedleys' yard, hands in his pockets.

'What on earth's the matter with the lad?' Fran whispered to Stan.

Stan draped an arm around Fran's shoulders. 'I reckon big brother is back, and little brother isn't about to take it lying down. He'll settle.'

'He'd better or he'll get the feel of my hand across his backside.'

Stan, who was peering into the yard, turned around, laughing. 'No need to do a thing. Move up a bit and have a look.'

Fran did, and there was Mrs Bedley whipping her tea towel across Ben's legs as he stood on the step. 'I've told you before – language, young man, language. Once more and I'll skelp your lugs an' all.'

Ben backed away. 'Aye, Mrs Bedley. Just let 'em know we're ready, if yer please.'

He sloped past Stan and Fran, while Mrs Bedley winked, then said, 'Nice to see yer back, young Stan, even if yer Da don't agree. Yer keep that little tyke on the straight and narrow, eh? Too smart by half, that's his trouble. He'll be following yer to Oxford, you mark my words – that's if I don't get me mitts on him beforehand.'

Ben came to stand beside Fran, muttering, 'That bliddy hurt, that did. Like a whip, it were. By, she's got a good throwing arm.'

Snatching off his cap, Fran smoothed his hair, replaced the cap and said, 'She's right. You've a future, lad. Just learn who to show off in front of, and who not, and for the last time, stop swearing.'

Stan was leaning forward on his handlebars. 'Listen to the women, our Ben. You'll go far, but only if you remember there are some rules that shouldn't be broken, and swearing in front of ladies is one of them.'

Ben's frustration got the better of him. 'Fran swears and she's a lady.'

Davey came limping across the yard. 'Fran's no lady,' he yelled.

Fran just watched him – that golden hair, which after a day in the pit was thick with black dust, those blue eyes that were so alive – and waited for Sarah who was running across the yard to the shed, to take him on. Sarah grabbed her bike and barged into her brother so he had to hop out of her way. 'You don't deserve our Franny, loopy lugs.'

Mrs Bedley was flapping her tea towel. 'Away with you. I've work to do at your ma's.'

Finally, they were heading along the back lane, Ben sitting on Davey's crossbar now because his was the bigger bike. Stan tipped his cap at him as he overtook, telling Ben he was a little snot, while Sarah, following Stan, called, 'Take no notice, Ben, you're too big to be a little snot. You're a big one.'

Even Ben had to laugh, and he called after them, 'So what rules can be broken?'

Stan's reply was thrown over his shoulder. 'Ah, that's for you to find out, but not yet. It'll be when you're of an age.'

Fran grinned as she rode alongside Davey, but heard Ben, who was holding on tight to Davey's handlebars, mutter, 'What the bli—' then stopped. 'What does that mean, when it's at home?'

Fran and Davey just laughed, and soon they reached the tarmac of Main Street. From here, they followed one another like ducklings, then Sarah quickly overtook Stan, calling out as she did, 'You've been away so long, bonny lad, you've probably forgotten the way, so best follow the leader, eh? If you can catch me, that is.'

'Leader, eh? Fighting talk, our Sarah. Get yer best foot down, pet, for you're going to eat me dust.' With that he put his head down and overtook.

'Come on, Davey, get yer head down, man, and yer legs working on the pedals as though they mean it,' Ben shouted, ringing Davey's bell. 'We're after yer, Stan.'

Soon they were all racing, scorching past hedgerows and drystone walls while the slag heap smouldered and pigeons fluffed, then settled in the furrows of the newly ploughed fields shooing off the seagulls that had flocked onto them in search of grain. Fran listened to the laughter and added to it. She shouted along with everyone else as the lead changed with each spurt, the bait tins clattering and the bells ringing. Finally, they were off the road and jerking and winding along Cod Lane – which meant Cold Lane – avoiding the potholes and tractor ruts, puffed out and full of laughter and relief.

Stan was back, and was the same lad he'd always been. Da would forgive him, Fran knew, because his anger was born out of love and fear. All three of his bairns understood that, more so since Betty. She looked up as brakes squealed ahead of them, seeing Sarah gaining on Stan as he turned off down a single lane path. Ben groaned as he bumped on Davey's crossbar and hung on for dear life until they all arrived at the beck, almost but not quite together. Sarah, who had taken the lead by overtaking on the grass verge, threw her arms up in the air and danced about, singing, 'Who's the winner, who's the best?'

Davey and Fran braked to a stop and Ben leapt down grumbling, and rubbing his bum. 'Well, Davey cycles like an old woman, so he does, which means, Sarah Bedley, it's not much to say you're the winner, so bliddy there.'

Sarah and Fran looked at one another. 'Language,' they both yelled, as Ben took off over the beck bridge, with them tearing after him while Davey and Stan shouted, 'Get the tyke and throw him in, cos we haven't a tea towel to whack him with.' The lad's laughter drifted on the breeze as the men clattered across the bridge to join them.

Ben stormed along the the bank and on to the lane that ran on between the fields where the Massingham sheep grazed. The girls slowed, still laughing, but panting too. 'That'll wear the little devil out,' Sarah coughed.

They walked back to where the boys were sizing up the swing rope which still hung from the branch where Stan had tied it years ago. 'D'you reckon it will still take us?' Davey was muttering.

Stan hauled on it, lifting his feet off the ground, swinging slightly. The branch creaked, or was it the rope? Fran wasn't sure. Whichever it was, nothing gave. Stan pulled again. 'Davey, come and let's try it with the two of us, just to be sure, eh?'

Together the boys dangled, letting the rope take their weight while the girls watched, then eyed the beck. It was running sluggishly, but then it always seemed to because it was so deep here, having been dammed by generations of the village bairns who had left just a narrow overflow. Further on, in the shallows, it seemed to rush along.

Davey punched Stan lightly on the shoulder. 'Well, lad, if you've done nothing else of any great importance except swan about in Oxford, yer have at least strung up a rope which has lasted the test of time. As good a memorial as any, I reckon.'

Fran and Sarah laughed, then Sarah blurted out, 'It'd read, "Here swung Stan Hall, and here dropped Stan Hall, with the biggest splash known to man, but then he floated because of all his hot air."'

Fran grinned as Stan approached Sarah and chased her round and round till she begged for mercy. Davey slipped his arm round Fran's shoulders while Ben slouched back along the lane, arriving at the beck, his boots still half laced. It was getting to be a habit and he'd trip and break his neck. But Ben was looking at Sarah, who had called 'Pax' and was bent over, trying to get her breath. 'You're right about Stan,' he said. 'But Davey'd be as bad or worse and float clear to the moon, no need for a balloon.'

They were all laughing when a voice called from the bridge, 'Your mam said you'd be here, so I thought I'd come to join the gang again?'

It was Beth, and it was a question. Fran froze, Sarah too. They looked at one another, and then at Stan, who had stood stock still but just for a few seconds, and now he took hold of the rope and swung it out across the beck. He caught it on its return, watching it, not Beth. No one spoke, not even Ben, who was peering from one to the other, puzzled, but Davey's arm had tightened around Fran.

Finally Stan looked up at the bridge. 'Well, Beth, bonny lass. Here you are right enough.' He didn't sound quite right, and it was Davey, letting go of Fran, who beckoned Beth over. 'Get on down. We were just testing the rope. Did you ride from Sledgeford? By, a bit of a way when the wind's against you.'

Fran and Sarah walked towards Beth as she came off the bridge. Fran was struggling to feel the friendship that had been rebuilt at the Factory, while Sarah muttered, 'She shouldn't have come. It should have just been us, until we'd settled. It's not her place to be here, it's bliddy not.'

Linking arms with her friend, Fran whispered, 'Aye, it's too soon, and not fair on Stan. She should have waited to be asked, so she should.'

They stopped, feeling angry and upset but all they could do was to wait for Beth to prop her bike against the hedge this side of the beck, however as she was about to do so she called, 'It looks a bit lonely propped here, when the rest are across the other side.'

Sarah said, 'Aye,' but Fran said nothing because now she saw that Beth was wearing lippy and she wanted to wipe it off the girl. They only wore lippy at village dances these days, and only a little at that. She swallowed. Sarah said, 'By, look at her lips. How bliddy could she?'

Beth came along the path, waving to the lads, and linked arms with Sarah who felt the girl trembling. They turned to walk back to the oak, and Sarah could find no words, and wanted to pull away, because Stan's face had that empty look, when a few minutes ago he had been happy. Fran said, 'How long did it take you in this headwind?'

There was no reply and Sarah saw that Beth only had eyes for Stan, while he now stared down at the water and Davey kicked at tufts of grass. Sarah looked up at the sky expecting clouds, for the day seemed to have darkened, but there were none. Then Ben joined Stan at the rope. 'Don't just mither about then, our Stan, are we going across on it, d'you think? I've not done it yet – you said I were too young.'

It seemed to break whatever spell was being woven and Sarah felt Beth's trembling cease as Stan and Davey spun into action, lifting the lad while shouting at the girls to get to the other bank and catch the hooligan, or he'd swing back across the beck and dangle over the water like a lost mayfly. Fran ran, and Sarah too, but Beth stopped by her bike, hauled it free of the hedge, and only then followed.

Fran and Sarah spurted ahead, and over the bridge, Fran yelling, 'Not yet, not yet, Ben.'

At last they were in place, Fran and Sarah either side of the flight path, ready, because it didn't matter whether or not Beth arrived in time, for they could manage just the two of them. Sarah snatched a look, but disappointment gripped her, because here the girl was, throwing her bike down on top of theirs and taking up position as the back-stop. Fran and Sarah exchanged a look, but what could they say? Davey and Stan were running Ben back, having hitched his foot in the loop they'd knotted years ago. They let him go, and Ben whooped as he swung over the beck into the hands of the girls, who dug their heels in. Fran and Sarah hung on to the lad, and then changed their grip to the rope as he was dragged back and back towards the edge of the bank, but Beth let go and the other two girls were dragged out, over the water, with Ben calling, 'I can't get me foot out of the loop.' Fran yelled, 'It'll take us to the other side, all three of us.'

But it was no good, and Sarah felt her hands slipping on the rope, and Fran was going too, and they plunged into the deep beck while Ben finally loosened his foot and plunged in too.

The cold of the water took Sarah's breath away. Down

she went, mouth shut, her mind frozen, then her hands started working and her legs were kicking until she rose to the surface, her boots heavy with water, her clothes dragging at her. She coughed and spluttered as she watched Ben emerge, followed by Fran and finally Beth, who must have jumped in. Why? She had let go. Sarah caught Ben's collar, but he shouted, 'I can swim by meself, Sarah. Stan taught me, didn't he?'

Sarah shook him, laughing into his face. 'Make sure your boots don't come off, you dafty. This'll teach you to do 'em up proper.'

She released him, treading water, laughing at Fran, who flicked her hair from her eyes and nodded towards Beth, grimacing. The girl was holding her head high above the water, her lippy in place, splashing and watching only Stan. The sight chilled Sarah. She watched Stan and Davey look at one another, nod, run back, then forward, towards the beck, jumping high off the bank and bombing into the water. They surfaced, Stan in front of Sarah, and Davey near Fran. The boys, including Ben, beat at the water, splashing until the girls couldn't see. 'Don't you dare pull us under like you used to,' shouted Davey.

Sarah could recognise an invitation when she heard it, and saw him winking at Fran. The two girls ducked and dived, each pulling one of the lads way under, as they had always done.

Beneath the water, now that Sarah was used to it, it was clear and quiet and she opened her eyes. She saw she had grabbed Stan. Suddenly awkward, she let go of him and rose until she was level with his face. He reached out, gripping her arms and holding her still. Bubbles escaped his mouth as he looked at her, as if confused, and she knew then he had thought she was Beth and felt a tearing sadness. But still the leader of the gang held her steady, as he had always done, and at last she relaxed. He was back, they were all together, and whatever happened, they *were* still that gang.

She smiled, holding her breath, though bubbles escaped to join his, rising, rising. He smiled back and it seemed an endless moment, here, suspended, hearing nothing, just seeing him, only him. But then there was a flurry and Ben started dragging Sarah away, while Beth pulled at Stan. They all kicked to the surface and broke into the fresh air.

The four of them shook their heads and the splashing water caught the sunlight. Davey and Fran were turning their fire from one another onto the other four. Sarah looked for Stan, but he was diving for Ben's legs now, and the lad was beating the water to scare him off. She knew, though, that something had happened to her in that long moment alone with Stan, but she wasn't sure what. As the water drenched her, and Ben drew back his arm to send another surge against her, she swam as the others did, and laughed too, her skirt floating up as she slipped down, down, before surfacing and lolling about in the water, looking up at the sky.

It was then that she understood *what* had happened to her, it was the realisation that the gang had its leader back, and there was a safety in that, a safety that was almost the same as it had once been. Almost, because Beth was surging towards her now, her pale blue eyes alight and her smile wide. Her auburn hair streamed behind her like a mermaid's, though her lippy had been washed away. Sarah felt chilled again and looked back at the sky, which was now darkening into bleakness, as the clouds gathered.

Sarah swam for the bank and began to scramble out, feeling strong hands at her waist, Stan's hands that had gripped her and held her steady beneath the water. He pushed her up, helping her, calling to Ben, helping him towards the bank, helping them as he had always done. But why did that have to include Beth, who had hurt him? Why?

She shivered on the bank as Stan hauled himself out. She reached down to Ben and after a split second hesitation, Beth. By the time they were all out, Davey and Stan were gathering wood for a fire, and soon it was ablaze, with Beth handing out Woodbines as they hunkered down. 'To warm us,' she said. It was Stan who lit them, cupping his match with his steady hands, hands that were scarred blue, and which Sarah wanted to touch. For goodness' sake, she told herself, as Beth did just that, running her fingers along the blue lines.

'Still got your scars then, Stan,' Beth said.

'Some scars never fade,' he responded.

For a moment no one said anything, but Sarah felt such a shaft of pain that she almost gasped. And at that moment, as she looked at Stan, at his hands being cradled in Beth's, she finally understood that what had happened to her in the water was more than just feeling safe, it was the birth of love, one so intense that she could scarcely breathe. Still Beth held his hands, and Sarah looked away, wanting to drag the girl from Stan, wanting to take her place, wanting to heal his scars, all of them, but especially his damaged heart so he could love again.

She drew on her cigarette, but then stubbed it out on the grass, savagely. She wished now they'd never decided to come to the beck. And that they'd never become friends again with Beth, and that her bliddy husband, Bob Jones, had never gone away.

'Stoke up the fire, bonny lad,' Fran said to Davey, who did so, squinting against the smoke of the cigarette lodged in the corner of his mouth.

'Come on,' he said, as he put the last piece on, 'I need a wood-gathering party, and be quick about it. We've got to dry off – can't have you lot shivering or sneezing at the Factory, and heaven forbid you should cough.'

Fran nodded at Sarah and Ben and they all set off to look in the hedgerows, though the two girls dawdled behind the boys. As she stooped to gather some dry wood, Fran whispered, 'I can't stand it if they start up again. He was hurt enough last time.'

Sarah looked over her shoulder to the fire, where Beth and Stan were in deep conversation. 'She's married, Franny, so I don't see how she can forget all about that.' But she was only trying to convince herself, which was daft, because in war, things happened.

The two girls found more wood, as they explored the verges. Their hair was blowing in the breeze, which was on its way to being a wind. Fran added some pine cones to the top of the pile Sarah was clutching in both arms. They had fallen from Murphy's pine tree, or so they had called it when they were bairns. Fran echoed Sarah's thoughts. 'It's war. Things happen. Even Davey noticed the lippy. But Beth mustn't – Stan mustn't. Can you imagine the bus journey? The tuts, the gossip, and Beth's ups and downs and then Bob'll come home . . .' She stopped.

Davey came out of one of the gateways leading into empty grazing pasture. He had a load, and Ben was laden too, but they'd also picked bits of lanolin rich sheep fleece from the hedgerows, which should burn a treat.

'Come on, you two girls,' he called. 'Let's have some lunch.'

Stan had moved to the edge of the bank and was staring down into the water, strangely calm, for when he'd recaptured his hands he felt there was nothing more to say to this girl he had loved once. Nothing, and the relief was almost a physical thing and why the hell had he said that about some scars not fading? Well, perhaps he hadn't known that the one Beth had created had indeed gone, and now he was glad she had come today, otherwise how would he have ever known he was free of her.

Beth came to stand beside him, her arm touching his. 'Oh, wasn't that the kingfisher, there in the willow?' She peered along the beck. 'I'm sure it was. Howay, Stan,' she leaned against him. 'It's just the same here as it always was. Everything's just the same – you can see that, can't you, Stan? I were a fool. Bob were a mistake, we can go back to how it was, be together again.'

Stan murmured, 'Aye, in a way you're right, lass. So much is still the same – all of this, who we all are . . .'

She swung round, gripping his arm, her face alight, but he put up his hand to continue. 'You're right, pet, we're the same, in a way – the gang – but we've grown, and aye, I like you still, course I do, but you and me? No, there's nowt there, for you, as well as for me. It's gone, but we're friends. You have Bob who weren't a mistake, lass, and I'm back into Auld Hilda with me marrers on the Monday, but with Oxford under me belt. Life's changed us.'

She took hold of his hand. 'But you said not all scars fade?'

He shrugged. 'I know, but it were daft, cos I didn't know mine had, yer see. Well, p'raps it were that I didn't recognise it had until I were deep beneath the water just now, and it were quiet and calm, and I watched our Sarah's breath rising in bubbles up to the surface, and they were small, beautiful, and since you left me I haven't noticed the beauty of life. It was then I knew that even the memory of the pain had left, and it were the habit of it I've been living with. Suddenly the beck made everything that happened between us all right and now I just want Bob home, and for you to be happy.'

'And if he doesn't come back?' she asked, panic in her voice.

'He will, I know it.'

'You can't know,' Beth snapped, turning away as the clouds darkened. No, he couldn't know it, so of course he couldn't *know* it was over, by watching a few bubbles. Bob wasn't here, but Stan was, so . . .

She looked for the kingfisher again as Stan stood strong and silent. No bird flew from the willow and no word came from Stan, but it would. She'd make sure it did, she thought, as she saw the others returning, and building up the fire again; Davey and Fran together, Ben and Sarah like brother and sister. Sarah whose escaping breath had caused Stan to realise he was free of Beth. Sarah's breath? It should have been her he saw, Beth Jones, and then he'd have realised something quite different.

She felt his hand grip hers, felt his strength, heard the kindness in his voice. Oh God, what a fool she'd been. He said gently, 'We're all still here, the *gang* is still here and that includes you, and we're all part of this grand community.' He let go of her hand and waved at the slag heaps, distant pitheads, the fields, the beck and lastly the fire builders. Beth looked around too, but saw only smouldering slack, drifting smoke and emptiness.

As though he realised, Stan said, 'Bob's probably on a mission, that's what happens in war and people can't write or phone, but once he's back this'll be home again too. Until then, I say again, we're here, all of us, getting through the war together as best we can, like grown-ups.'

Beth snatched a look at him, wanting to slap him. Was he saying she wasn't an adult? She turned and watched the other four deep in conversation. This was where they had played as bairns before she came, but was also where she had been absorbed by them once she arrived. The heaps might be smouldering, Bob might be missing, but Stan was right, the gang was still here and though it wasn't enough, she'd have to pretend it was for now.

She smiled at Stan. 'Look at those two, they are just "together", aren't they?' She was nodding towards Davey and Fran, who were laughing at one another.

Stan grinned and took her hand again. 'Oh aye, they'll be together, no matter what. They always have been really, two parts of a whole.'

She looked at his hand holding hers, feeling his power. She knew him better than she knew Bob. After all, Bob hadn't taught her to swim, it was Stan who had. She squeezed his hand. 'Aye, we're friends then, back to friends, and I was a right little baggage and I'm sorry for the pain.'

He kissed her hand. 'Don't be. We'd have drifted on, I might not have gone to Oxford, and maybe we wouldn't have worked after all.' Stan grinned and dug his hands into his pockets, then grimaced, then called across to the others. 'Nothing's as bliddy awful as wet pockets.'

'Language. Yer said never in front of a lady,' Ben yelled.

The others shouted, 'Where's the lady?' and they all laughed.

Over by the fire Sarah watched Stan and Beth, and Fran sighed, adding more wood to the fire, muttering, 'They were holding hands. He kissed hers. It's all going to start again.'

'It wasn't that kind of kiss. I reckon he were saying good-bye,' Davey said.

Sarah hung on his words, but she didn't really believe her brother, and in that moment she hated Beth with such a passion that she shocked herself.

As Stan and Beth joined them, Davey drew out one of

the sticks he was turning to charcoal. He examined it, and shoved it back into the ash while Beth collected the bait tins from the pile by the bikes and distributed them.

'Well, so where does today leave you two?' Fran asked, her voice almost rough.

Stan laughed. 'You're so tactful, Franny, so delicate, so—'

'Shut up and tell us,' Davey said. 'Am I right and you've got yourselves sorted, and we're back to the gang? Or are we all going to have to tiptoe about being embarrassed and—'

'The village women gossiping, and the girls on the bus, and Beth being smug . . .' interrupted Sarah.

They all stared at her, as startled by Sarah's sharpness as she was herself.

Stan laughed. 'Shut up, all of you. We're friends, just like we used to be, so that's that. Eat your hard-boiled eggs and whatever else you've got.'

Ben was already sitting down, opening his tin and scoffing his bread and dripping. 'I don't know what the hell you're all talking about.'

'Language,' they shouted in unison.

Beth was still looking at Sarah, and then she saw it, the love in Sarah's eyes as she looked at Stan, and Beth clenched her fists against the jealousy that overtook her. It was this girl's breath that had taken him away from her, but what if it was the girl herself? Her heart seemed to shrink inside her chest, her eyes filled. She looked away, at the bridge, the beck, the willow, swallowing, seeing the tremble in her hands. She clenched them and lifted her chin, for what did Sarah know of Stan? It was she, Beth Smith who had felt his hands on her body, his mouth on hers . . .

The afternoon wore on, the sun finally came out again and, in spite of it being late summer, it still helped dry them.

They scoured the beck from the bridge, looking for minnows. As Fran leaned on the parapet, the lichen rubbed off on her arms. She brushed it away just as the kingfisher swooped from the willow where the beck started its long bend, soaring almost to the bridge. They fell silent as it dived, found the minnow they hadn't, and flew off.

'It's still here, just like us,' breathed Fran as they all stared, first at the water and then along the bank, towards the willow.

'Aye, you're right, isn't she, Stan? It is still here, just like it's always been, so everything *is* still the same,' Beth said in an urgent whisper, but Stan, looking along the beck, didn't answer.

Davey slipped his arm around Fran and leaned in to kiss her neck, but before he could there was a hail from the lane where it met the beck path.

'I say, your mother told me you'd be here, Fran. Thought you might like a ride home as the day is cooling.'

They all turned at the sound of Ralph's voice. 'Why would she want a lift when she's got her bike?' Ben called.

Ralph sauntered towards the bridge as they all straightened, looking up, and Stan muttered, 'Remember his da owns our house and gives us our jobs, young Ben. You too, Fran, hard though it is to tolerate.'

Ralph kept walking and came to stand with them. 'Six people and five bikes. Who's had a free ride then?'

'I have, Mr Ralph. On the crossbar,' Ben muttered.

'Uncomfortable, I bet.'

'Not so bad, Mr Ralph, but since you're offering, a ride back would suit me right proper.'

Ralph looked taken aback, but no one laughed or smiled, just nodded. Fran thought she'd have to slip Ben a bob for that was a right canny move.

'That'd be kind of you, Mr Ralph,' Fran said and thought

she might just tug her forelock, but a look from Stan put a stop to such doings.

Ralph stared at them all, one by one, then smiled. 'Even better would be to let the little lad ride your bike back, Fran. Better for him to get the hang of it, and you can come with me. As you know, your Stanhope is to be my marrer, so it's as well I learn all about him, and you can fill me in.'

Fran shook her head. 'I couldn't possibly put my damp arse on your passenger seat, Mr Ralph, I just couldn't. So if it would be better for little Ben to cycle, please take Beth.'

Sarah joined in. 'She has to get back to Sledgeford and it's no time in the car, but a bit of a slog after a full day. What do you say, Beth?'

Beth nodded, but glared at Sarah, because this would leave the field clear for her and Stan, who also nodded, then smiled. 'Good idea. It's a hell of a ride back, Beth, and you've work tomorrow.'

So he did care. She said, 'I'd be right grateful. Ben can ride me bike back to Fran's and I'll pick it up another day, or shall we put it on the back of the car? You've a luggage rack, I think? We could tie it on. Or hang on, Stan could cycle it across sometime. Aye, that might be better.'

Sarah nodded at Ralph. 'Beth can fill you in about Stan – she *used* to know him quite well. And if you take the bus to us tomorrow after work, Beth, then Stan doesn't have to bike it across after his first day back in the pit. In fact, it needn't be tomorrow. You can pick it up any time.'

Fran agreed. 'Good idea. That solves it then.'

Ralph looked at Fran, his smile strained. 'Very well, this time.' He nodded to them all, his gaze lingering on Davey. He followed Beth, who was striding towards his car.

The others watched, and Sarah said, 'Sorry if I butted in, Stan, but cycling two bikes across is a lot after a day at work.'

Stan looked at Sarah and nodded. 'I'm glad, lass. Butt in all you like. Besides, best she has a lift back, it's been a bit of a day.'

As they cycled home, Davey thought of that long look from Ralph, so cold, so dark, knowing he'd seen it before. They cycled on, alongside the drystone walls, the shadows of the trees long in the waning sun, and he remembered now. It was when the whelp had kicked his footie at their goal, chalked on the Halls' back lane wall, and missed. The bet he and Ralph had made was that if Ralph missed, he forfeited his ball. Of course they'd have given it back, especially as it was his ma's present the year she died.

He remembered dashing off to collect the ball after the show-off had missed. It was right grand, leather and like gold dust in a colliery village, for who could afford such a thing? He was just about to hand the ball back when the whelp picked up their papier-mâché ball, made by Grandpa Percy, when he was dying from the black lung. Davey had yelled, 'Here's yer ball. It weren't a real bet. We was always going to give it yer back. That's the ball me Granpa made when he were dying, so tek this one, eh?'

But the whelp had looked at him like he'd just done now and kicked Grandpa Percy's ball as hard as he could at the wall, again and again, then stamped on it until it was in shreds. The gang, and the marrers, had been stunned into immobility, but then Davey had run at him. Ralph held him off; then Sarah, Fran, Stan and the marrers had started to run at the whelp too, but he had held up his hand and shouted, 'One step more and I'll get me da to take your houses.'

It had stopped them, and he'd gone on kicking and digging his studs into Grandpa Percy's ball until the scraps of papier mâché were scattered across the cobbles of the back

122

lane. 'There,' he'd said. 'Dead like yer grandpa. That'll teach you to cheek your betters. I'll have my ball back now.'

Davey had fought back his tears while Sarah cried. He'd picked up the ball, taken a step towards the whelp, and then the lad had laughed. So Davey had hunkered down, dragged his penknife from his pocket and stabbed the leather ball, wishing it was the whelp himself. As the air hissed, he threw it. 'Catch then, Master bliddy Massingham. I wouldn't have kept it, never would I do that, but . . .' He'd run out of words.

The whelp had just looked at it, then at Davey. 'You'll regret this,' he'd said. 'You better look after your things, cos I'll take them from you, every last ruddy one, you mark my words.'

'Penny for them,' Fran said, ringing her bell as she cycled beside him.

'When I saw his look it reminded me of when we were bairns and he brought his bliddy ball to show off. I had forgotten. But you know, the thought of it makes me ashamed. I stabbed a leather football his mam gave him, so I were no better'n him.'

Sarah drew alongside Ben and muttered, 'He started it.'

They were entering the outskirts of Massingham as Davey replied, 'Well, I made the bet.'

Stan drew alongside now there was room, so that they were cycling five abreast. 'He didn't have to take it. I just wish I'd got meself into gear, but I were so stunned. He were a weasel then, and probably still is. But we were bairns. He won't remember, surely. He's just kept the look, daft beggar and dusts it off whenever he can. Think of me at the pit with him. It won't be easy, cos the men aren't happy he's coming.'

Chapter Nine

The next morning, before dawn broke, Fran slipped up the attic ladder and poked her head through the hatchway into the darkness. 'Are you awake, bonny lad? No sleeping, it's heading for four in the morning and this isn't a place for dreaming about spires, or whatever it is you do.'

She heard Ben's grunt. 'Aw, shut up, Fran. He's downstairs and he trod on me on the way, so he did. I might not have his cold feet, I just have him steppin' on me, daft beggar.'

'Go back to sleep, lad.' Fran edged back down the ladder and then the stairs in her threadbare dressing gown, her bare feet making no noise. Her da would be asleep as he was on the afternoon shift, and hopefully her mam was still dead to the world too. Fran tiptoed along the passage, avoiding the holes worn in the linoleum. She thought they should take it up and just leave the wooden floor, but her mam said the dirt got in between the boards and wasn't hygienic. She neared the kitchen door, wondering why on earth she was doing this when she could be sleeping too, since she was on the aft shift, but it was two years since Stan had been in the pit, and the thought of the dangers for him had kept her awake. The least she could do was brew him some tea and make bread and dripping.

As she reached the kitchen she heard a murmur of voices, and eased open the door to see her da standing at the range with a frying pan full of bread and dripping and a piece or two of black pudding. He wore his old mackintosh and had bare feet. 'Da? I thought you were on late, like me?' Fran whispered.

Stan sat at the table looking embarrassed. 'He is, and he should be asleep.'

Her da didn't turn but just poked at the fried bread. 'Your brother's old enough and stupid enough to make up his own mind, I daresay, and if he wants to gan into the pit, then the least he needs is food in his belly.' He shrugged with embarrassment. 'And before yer start, our Franny, sit yerself down and yer can have a piece an' all, but put a lock on yer mouth and let your mam sleep. This isn't a party.'

Her da stood looking at her for a moment. Fran obeyed, winking at Stan, who said, 'Well, just hurry yer bliddy self then, Da. Else I'll be late.'

It broke the strangeness, and all three laughed. Fran watched as Da put a couple of slices on a plate and placed it in front of her, and then another plate of the same in front of Stan. He then pointed to Stan's old bait tin. 'Just for today, lad, I've put yer bait up. Two jam sandwiches and cold tea. Tomorrow yer can get theesel' out of the house, and be quiet about it.'

He disappeared into the scullery and washed up the frying pan. It was the first time she'd seen in him there since he'd done this for her on her first day at the Factory, though that time he hadn't spoken a word to her, not even to wish her safe. But they were weeks further on, and something in her da had softened into an acceptance of his bairns. She now realised that the words hadn't been important – it was the doing that had wished her safe. She shook her head. What a child she had been; it was as though the Factory was dragging her into adulthood.

As he came out of the scullery, wiping his hands on the old towel before draping it on the airer above the range, he passed her and she leapt to her feet and hugged him. 'I love you, Da, with all me heart. I'm careful, and Stan will be too.'

After a moment her da's arms came around her and he rested his head on hers. 'Yer my bairns, see. Yer my reason . . .' He trailed off, patted her, then let her go and walked to the door. As he opened it he called to Stan, his voice back to normal. 'Yer go to the pit clean if yer go from this house, and when you come back yer wash yerself clean of Auld Hilda's muck afore yer go into the rest of yer mam's house.'

Stan was standing, watching him. 'I remember, Da. You taught me well when I started in the pit after me schooling.'

'Well, Stanhope Hall, let me remind yer, you belong to our name, and will all yer life, and yer past will travel with you. As for you, our Franny, you will change yours, likely to Bedley. So behave yerself and bring no dishonour to the name yer brothers'll have to carry.'

He stuck his chin in the air and left, closing the door quietly. Fran looked at Stan, startled. 'What was all that about?'

Stan was wrapping the muffler round his neck that his mam had knitted and which he had worn for the two years he had worked in the pit, then slipped into his jacket. He opened the back door and took his boots from beneath the old vegetable box Da had found for his son's footwear. Standing on the step, he rammed in his feet. 'He'd just told us he loved us, and that we three bairns are his world. So, he had to break hard on us to pull himself together.'

Fran could hear the beat of boots along the back lane. 'Best get going, lad. Be safe.'

He set off across the yard, then turned, but Fran already had his bait tin and was waving it about. 'I don't know, you men. You'd forget your heads if they weren't stuck on.'

His laugh followed her as she made her way upstairs,

hoping for a bit more sleep, but doubting she'd get it. Stan was facing the pit, and at last she understood her da's fury at his bairns putting themselves in danger. But in war, what else could you do?

Stan caught up with Davey, Sid and Norman, who'd said they'd wait on the corner. Together they strode to Auld Hilda, which took longer than usual as he was hailed by what seemed like the whole of the shift weaving in and out around them, and then by the night workers who were streaming back. "ow do?' they called.

'Champion,' he replied as the wind snatched at his cap and he burned through his Dunhill, a packet of which his da had given him.

'Not for long, our Stan.'

'Any minute now you'll be like the rest of us.'

'Old afore our time.'

Laughter filled the early hours. His boots rubbed – he was used to wearing shoes with socks, but couldn't bear the trapped coal and preferred bare feet with his boots – yet he realised with a start that he really was happy to be back here with Davey and his marrers. He'd known he would be, but not quite so much.

As though he could read Stan's mind, Davey said as they walked, 'By, man, we've missed you, haven't we, lads?'

Sid shook his head, giving him a sideways look. 'Howay, not a bit, why would we?'

Norm muttered, 'It's them long words from yer our Davey's missed, used 'em for his crosswords, so he did, Stan, lad. It were like working with a bliddy dictionary so it were back then, so we'll be back to not making head nor tail o' a word yer say, man.'

They all laughed and within twenty minutes were entering the pit yard, and it was like it always was. He was home.

Then he heard his name being called by the bank overman, Tom Higgins.

'Hoy, Stan Hall, come back here, lad. No going down the pit yet awhile. Got to break yer in, so Elliot says it's the screens for yer.'

Davey spun round, walking backwards to keep up with the marrers as Stan headed towards the office near the gates. 'What? He's one of our best bliddy hewers, man.'

All around, the men were coming or going and the winding gear was busy – the wind, too, as it whistled through its struts – while up above it all was the waning moon.

'Not today, nor this week, then we'll see. Procedure, and he's to babysit you-know-who. Them's God's orders which were passed down to Elliot.'

'Reet, I'd forgotten. Short straw, I reckon, but catch yer later,' Davey called. 'Enjoy the screens, our Stan.' The men grumbled as Stan threaded his way through them towards Tom, and some whacked him on the shoulder.

'Bloody waste, we need you on the face.'

'Bliddy ridiculous, and who needs the whelp anywhere near here? It'll be bad bliddy luck.'

'Like a woman in the mine, him be. Aye, bad bliddy luck.'

Someone else spat then muttered, 'Him and his Black-shirt ideas shouldn't be here.'

'Aye, bring even more bad luck, it will.'

'Hush your rubbish. His da owns our houses.'

'Aye, well, his da's welcome here any day, yer know that.'

Tom the overman raised his eyebrows as Stan finally reached him. 'Sorry, lad, orders is orders. It needs someone he knows to keep an eye, and one trusted enough not to throw the little bollock under a pile of coal.'

Tom laughed and Stan grinned, though it was hard, for

he had hoped the pairing had been forgotten about. 'Where is he?'

'Over at the screens already.' Tom jerked his head to the right. 'Remember?'

'Oh aye, I remember, just didn't think I'd have to fiddle about on 'em ever again. I'm a big boy, our Tom.'

Tom shoved back his cap and smiled, his eyes tired. 'Ah, but the whelp divint be, our Stan. And maybe won't never be. You're with him on number-three screen, lad, and good to have yer back, even if it near bust yer da's gut when he heard. Steam there was, out of every orifice.'

Stan cut through the passing miners and headed up the slope to the massive open-sided shed where the sorting was carried out. There, waiting, was Ralph Massingham, wearing a Harris tweed jacket, clean trousers, polished brogues, a tweed cap and, to top it all, a yellow cravat. Well bugger me, where does he keep his brains? Stan thought, knowing the cravat wouldn't be yellow for long, and that what's more it made the idiot even more of a laughing stock.

Ralph was shouting something at Barry Woods, who was in charge. Stan was glad he couldn't hear over the clatter of the coal on the screens, and the noise of the winding gear as it brought miners up from the depths and took others down.

There were teams of men on the three screen belts, hard at work sorting the coal between gash and good as it rumbled along the belt, and he waved to Frank Tumbler, who'd lost half a hand and half a leg when a firing went wrong. There was also Sammy Street, too old for the face now. Learning the game were a couple of youngsters amongst the rest of the old or damaged. The lads would do as they were told and learn quickly, if he knew anything about Barry, who taught well.

Stan sighed and tapped Barry on the shoulder. 'I've to report to you, Barry,' he yelled.

Barry turned, cupping an ear, then saw it was Stan. 'About bliddy time,' he shouted into Stan's ear. 'And the best of bliddy luck with this fecking idiot wearing a fecking canary round his fecking neck.'

He stormed away as Ralph walked towards him, waving a languid hand and drawing out his silver cigarette case. Stan stared, just as much as the other men who were already hard at work sorting. Ralph placed a cigarette in his mouth. It was this that triggered Stan, who snatched it and flung it on the ground, grinding it into powder. 'You're here to bliddy work, not ponce about,' he yelled.

Stan pointed to the chute where coal was pouring down to the screens and from which dust billowed, gritty and strong. He showed Ralph what needed to be done, and together they watched the men for a minute, separating the stone and slate from the coal as it moved along the metal belts.

'Your da's modernising was halted by the war, so no shaking belts and it's up to us. Make the best of it,' Stan shouted. 'Chuck the gash onto one of the other belts; shove the good stuff through the holes.'

Ralph brought out a pair of black leather gloves. Stan sighed and the men grinned, their teeth white against the black of their faces. As they worked, Stan remembered it all: the splint screen or belt on one side for throwing splintered coal, a stone screen on the other, and the main screen, where the men sorted the wheat from the chaff. Stan nudged Ralph and pointed to the machine at the top end that tipped out the tubs, then the jigging machines that did the first sort, shaking out a fair bit of dust, and then the tumbling of the coal and crud from the chute onto the screens. 'There's a sort of symmetry to it all, but tomorrow you won't have any gloves left – they'll be shredded by the end of the day.'

Suddenly, Stan pictured Davey's Grandpa Percy's shredded football. Did Ralph? Clearly not, for he was bawling, 'Better them than my hands, old boy.' Ralph's voice broke, and for a dreadful moment Stan thought the lad was going to cry, but then he saw it was rage. Ah well, better that than tears, because the men would never let up if they saw even a hint of that sort of rubbish.

Stan started and was slower than the rest, but he soon remembered, speeding up, grabbing at the stone and slate, the splintered coal, and chucking them into their new homes, shoving the good through. Much slower was Ralph, who, after an hour, nudged him, shouting above the noise, 'When do we get a break?'

'What's the time?' Stan yelled, leaning close enough to shout into his ear. He was sure he smelled cologne.

'Seven o'clock.'

'Another four hours'll bring us to eleven – fag time.'

Ralph's expression was one to remember and those men who had learned to lip-read after months on the clanging, crashing screens roared with laughter. Ralph saw, and his face set. 'Get on with it,' Barry called from his platform above them, stabbing towards Stan and Ralph.

They worked for another four hours at the rattling metal screens. Ralph was struggling and Barry or Stan had to yell at him as he kept making mistakes. Ralph's lips almost disappeared as his anger grew.

Finally, Barry came down from his platform and tapped two men at a time to take a break. The screen kept moving and the remaining men kept working, the dust billowing and the grit crunching between their teeth. At last it was Stan and Ralph's turn and they walked away, heading towards the same supply shed the others had lolled against. Stan sat on the ground and unscrewed his flask of cold tea, while Ralph stood over him. Finally the owner's son nudged him with his no longer polished and shiny shoe. Stan looked up and Ralph shouted, 'Where's the canteen?'

Stan shook his head and pointed to the flask. ''Tis it. Share mine, lad. Cold tea or nothing. Jam sandwich? You should have asked your da, he'd have told you what was what.'

'He thinks I know all about the mine, just like he knows about it, and his factories, and . . .'

Ralph sank to the ground and leaned back against the shed, tearing off his shredded gloves and tossing them aside, picking at his coal-filled cuts. Stan drank half, then handed over the enamel mug his father had fashioned to fit the top of the flask. They each ate a sandwich from Stan's bait tin, leaving traces of blood and black grit on the bread. 'By,' Stan yelled, 'me hands have got soft, and me feet. The buggers ache.'

Ralph said nothing until Barry semaphored them to return to the screens and then the boss's son looked up as Stan stood over him. 'I've had enough. I'm going home.'

Stan nodded, hoping he would but knowing the lad would have to face his father and could never show his face at the village again. He said just this and Ralph's face set, then he took Stan's hand. Stan hauled him to his feet and led the way back.

Ralph walked as though his joints had stiffened and once on the screens he worked even more slowly, his hands too stiff to grasp the stones, slates and coal. Barry let fly at Ralph's head with one of the smaller stones, knocking his cap to one side. Ralph bellowed and swung round. Stan grabbed his arm. 'He does it to us all, it's how we learn.'

'It bloody well hurts,' Ralph shouted.

Stan grinned. 'Aye, that's why we learn.'

They worked on, and when Barry scurried down from his platform, he slipped on the last rung of the ladder, whacking his shin. He leaned down and touched the rung. Grease had been applied. Of course it had, Stan thought. Oldest trick in the book when there were new workers, as well Barry knew. Nonetheless, the foreman played the game and stormed along the screen. 'Who did that? Come on, you buggers, who be it?'

One by one the men pointed to Ralph. Barry squared up to the lad, knowing full well it wasn't him. 'I suppose you think that's funny?' It was also part of the game to test a new one.

Ralph drew himself up and shouted, 'I'll have your jobs for this, and your houses—'

Stan shoved him over, anything to stop him going on. Barry stared down at the lad lying at his feet; the men glanced at one another, disgust and fear on their faces as they returned to the screens. One said, 'By, puts me in mind of Grandpa Percy's footie smashed to shreds down the back lane, it do . . .'

'Aye, only big strong boys do that, eh?'

'Some never change, do they?'

There was a low laugh, which grew until it could be heard over the rattle of the screens and the rumble of the coal.

Ralph lay there as Stan hunkered down by his head. 'You get up, lad. You get up and yer laugh, and you nod, and you say, "Yes, it seems like it were me," as it weren't anyone else, and you take it like a man and pretend you like the trick. You do that and yer might rescue the mess you just shoved your nose into, because these men remember your Blackshirt meetings and your German trip, and lots else, like smashing up footballs belonging to one of their own, and if you're ever to be accepted, that's what you do. Now get up or get out – your choice.'

Stan stood and there was no helping hand this time for Ralph, who had to struggle to his feet, brushing himself off as there was a good half-inch or more of coal dust on the ground. He paused, and finally, as the muscles worked in his jaw, he nodded to Stan. He waved to Barry, who was back on the platform. 'Yes, sir. It was me, and I'm ready for my punishment. Shall I bend over?'

Stan sighed as Barry cupped his ear and leaned forward, bellowing, 'Come again, divint hear thee.'

Barry was making Ralph work for forgiveness. He'd threatened him and his men, and in spite of any apology he made, it would be tucked away in all their memories. What's more, the word would travel like wildfire around Auld Hilda that the boss's son had failed the test, so the lad would have to be whiter than white from now on.

Ralph repeated himself through gritted teeth, and this time Barry called, 'Nay punishment, lad. Back to work with you.'

Ralph said nothing more, just tucked in his chin and worked, though if his hands were as sore as Stan's, he'd not have a good night. At two o'clock the hooter went at last and, without a backward glance, Ralph left the pit, hurrying away stiff-legged. Stan caught up with him in the yard. 'Long way from Oxford, eh?' he said, walking along beside him. It was then he realised that Ralph had come by car. They stopped beside it. Stan saw the folded towel on the driver's seat. 'Good idea. Saves the leather.'

There was no vaulting over the door this time, but just an easing of sore limbs into the driving seat. Ralph looked up at Stan. 'Can't offer you a lift, old boy. The car doesn't need your hewer's arse on its fine leather.' Ralph's laugh contained all the fury of the morning, and the humiliation.

Stan merely shrugged. 'If you want to be part of the pit, and the war effort, this is the world you'll be working in, lad. If you make it more than it is, it'll be the harder for you, and you'll muck about with the good and true Massingham name. Just you think on.'

'I won't forget a thing, bonny lad. Not a thing about today, or anything at all, and I thank you for your part in it all,' Ralph said. The words were sort of right, but it was his eyes that disturbed Stan, for they were cold enough to freeze the beck.

Ralph roared away and Stan loitered, knowing that soon Davey would come up from the face wanting to know more about what had happened, for gossip travelled like wildfire in the pit. But while he waited, Stan's unease deepened as he remembered the threat Ralph had made to Davey as he left that day, clutching his stabbed football, along the lines that he'd take anything Davey valued from him.

That evening, Fran waited with the others outside the Factory for Cecil, who drove the afternoon shift and was often late. Mrs Oborne sighed, tightening her scarf and pulling down her hat against the wind. 'By, he's a devil. What does he do – doze in at the depot, or what?'

'Probably, lazy beggar,' Maisie joined in.

Sarah and Beth were stamping their feet against the cold, and Fran was thinking how full of stars the sky seemed on this cloudless night. Sarah muttered, 'Look at that, a bombers' moon, if there ever was one. Its size and brightness makes me shudder now, when before the war I thought it were a right good sight.'

'Aye,' Beth agreed. 'Not sure how it affects the navy. Does it make it easier to navigate? Do they still do it by the stars?'

Fran opened her mouth to reply, but Sarah muttered

quietly, as though to herself, ' 'Bob's the one to ask, after all, he'd know, and he's your husband, or have—'

Fran gripped Sarah's arm. 'Sarah, lass, steady on.' She turned to Beth. 'He's not been heard from yet, has he?'

Beth shook her head, her lips thinning. 'Or have—? What? What are you trying to say, Sarah? And no, Fran, he hasn't been heard from, and if you hadn't heard from your man for weeks, you'd wonder, you'd worry— And it's all very well for people to say he's out of contact, like many of the men are, but that doesn't bliddy well help me, does it?'

Beth had moved to stand in front of Sarah, who had somehow made Stan see the world was beautiful again, just with a few bubbles. Beth felt exhausted suddenly. Yes, it was just the bubbles, not Sarah. She pulled off her head-scarf, wanting to feel the cool wind in her hair, and turned away, but not before she'd heard Sarah say, 'Not many of us would make sure we were at Stan's side all the time at the beck if we were married, though, would we?'

Fran pulled Sarah away now, dragging her through the bus queue as Cecil drove around the corner with his slit headlights and drew into the siding. 'What on earth are you doing?' she hissed.

Sarah dragged her hands down her face, as though she was wiping her mind free of thoughts. 'Oh I'm sorry, I'm just tired, and she's just talked of Stan this and Stan that all day . . . and I've got a headache, and I bliddy itch, and I'm sick to death of mercury powder. It makes me edgy I reckon, but what if Stan goes—'

Mrs Oborne was looking towards them. 'Come on, you two. You're the last to get on.'

Fran pulled Sarah with her back to the bus, whispering, 'Stan's not going to let himself be hurt again. He's different now he's back, sort of free of worry and he's got more bliddy sense than to go there again, and anyway, he's not your responsibility, and ... well, you don't really think ...? Surely not?' They headed down the aisle while Fran ran over Sarah's words again.

Beth was sitting in one double seat, opposite another where Mary from Massingham sat. Before they reached Beth, Sarah leaned forward and whispered to Fran, 'I've made a daft fool of myself?'

'Aye, mebbe, or I hope it's daft. At least she's saved a place for us.'

Fran slipped into the seat next to Mary so that Sarah had to join Beth, who sat with her stoney face on. Maisie was behind Fran and boomed, 'I knew better than to sit there, after your fisticuffs.' Then she yelled down the bus, 'Come on, Cecil, get your bliddy foot down. It's gone ten and I want to see me bairn, and then get to me own bed.'

Sarah turned to Beth. 'Sorry, Beth. I was rude. I know you miss your husband and are worried. You're married, after all, we all know that, and it must be hard for you after you've taken your vows. I was stupid – tired, I reckon. I feel odd after a shift with the mercury.'

Fran thought that if Sarah had said married, or vows, once more she'd have had to slam a hand over her mouth. As the bus moved off, Maisie yelled, 'We met our targets, we're all whacked, so let's have a song, eh? Give us all some energy and mebbe make our Cecil be a bit careful, cos we all know he's an idiot behind the wheel.'

The laughter drove out all other thoughts and Mrs Oborne yelled, 'Come on, you three girls, lead us into "All or Nothing at All".'

Fran poked Sarah, and called to Beth, 'Got your voices ready?'

Sarah and Beth looked at one another, Beth said, 'Pax?' Sarah agreed, and they both laughed suddenly, then belted out the first line so that Fran had to catch up. On and on they sang, and it was almost as though Sarah and Beth were putting more and more into it, trying to be the loudest. 'No, no, all or nothing at all . . .' Cecil joined in, his baritone like a double bass, which, coincidentally, he played. He flung the bus round a bend, beside the memorial to a coach and horses that had gone out of control in 1859, killing the vicar. He dropped passengers at several villages this side of Minton Ford, then screeched on to Minton, dropping three there.

Having offloaded some passengers in Minton, he tore on and shuddered to a halt outside the Sledgeford Club, and Valerie, Amelia and Beth were amongst those getting off. Beth had admitted during lunch that her mam wanted her to give up the rented house and move back to Massingham as her da's chest was getting worse, and Amelia had raised her cup of tea to Valerie. 'Well, why not? It's nice to be living with a family. Better than chewing shoe leather, at any rate.'

Valerie had looked up. 'Is that all? Nothing to do with us being a lovely family?' She was laughing, but there'd been an edge.

Amelia had drawled, 'It's everything to do with being a lovely family, Valerie. Never doubt it. I expect your mother wants you back to mother you, Beth. She must worry about you.'

'It's really because me da's so ill and he misses me, and she needs someone else there.' Beth almost shook herself. 'Plus, I reckon she wants me to beaver away cutting up the old blankets for the proggy rug she's making in your mam's co-op, Fran. So it's all your fault, for it wouldn't have happened unless you'd gone to see the bloke and set it up with Briddlestone's.' She had been laughing, at last.

Fran shook her head. 'No, it's not me, it's Mam. She's like a ruddy dog with a bone now, and I reckon she'd snap and bite if anyone tried to stop their co-op. They are women possessed. But, lass, I'm sorry about your da.'

Now she waved through the window to Beth as Cecil roared off.

'I hope me da never gets black lung. It's a pig and a half,' Sarah whispered, wishing she hadn't be so tetchy, so mean because she was feeling like it again, at the thought of Beth in Massingham, near Stan and it was only because her da was ill.

Cecil swung the bus around another bend and Mrs Oborne shouted, 'By, Cecil, it's not a bliddy racetrack.' It's what she always said and it made no difference. By the end of the journey most of them felt sick.

Sarah clung to the seat in front and said, almost as though she was thinking aloud, 'Her da's ill, her bloke's not been heard from and I've been a right cow.'

Fran smiled and found herself saying, out of the blue, 'Ah well, maybe it's because you want her to leave the field clear for you, pet.' The moment she said it, she realised she meant it.

'What on earth do you mean?' Sarah snapped. 'He's our leader and we're all together, that's the main thing. And he's had enough heartbreak from that lass to fill a lifetime, and we don't need any more . . . Well, any more trouble, and I've the devil of a headache, so I have and if Cecil doesn't slow down I'll be sick.'

Fran yelled, 'For the love of God, slow down Cecil, or you'll have to clean the bus when we all get off.'

He took no notice, just rushed on beneath the overhanging branches of the oaks which lined the road. Fran looked at Sarah, her pale face, her obsession with Stan's heartache and she felt scared suddenly because life was getting far too complicated. Fran leaned her head against the window, suddenly desperately tired of the dark, the war, of black lung and the swirls of temper, of the doubt and uncertainty all around, and the mercury, the itching. And besides, her da's chest was getting worse.

She concentrated on the familiar slag heaps, on Davey, on light, warmth and life. Yes, she told herself, it's dark, but then the day comes, or the slag heap flares, and there's Davey, always there's Davey.

Davey was waiting for Fran at the bus shelter. He liked to see the bus coming: first its slit headlights, then the bus, and at last the girls toiling off and seeing Fran's face light up as she saw him.

He looked to the left, which was the way the bus would come, but then he heard a throaty revving and a backfire and saw the slit lights of a car shutting off. There was the slam of the driver's door. He knew before he saw the roadster that it was Ralph. What the hell was he doing here? He'd been on shift today, so should have scrambled home to get over being the buffoon they had all heard he had been.

Ralph came to stand in front of him, jangling his car keys. 'No bike today then, Davey?'

Davey shifted his weight from his bad leg to his good one. 'Unless it's invisible, no. I'm here to meet Fran.'

Ralph continued to play with his keys, eyeing the road to Sledgeford. 'It's a long way to— Where is it the bus is returning from?'

Davey shrugged. 'Who knows. Some things are best not talked about in wartime, as you should know.'

'Should I, more than you? You, the man who was too scared to take up a scholarship, or take another stab at it and let another set of exam results decide? It would, after all, have given your girl a better life. "Is Davey Bedley the best Fran Hall can do?" I ask myself. Then I answer, "Do you know, old boy, I don't think he is."'

Davey felt the air leave his lungs and he did what he had done under the rockfall. He breathed in and out slowly, counting to four each time, because it stopped him from punching the bugger's lights out, which he couldn't afford to do or his da would lose everything. But would Mr Massingham really chuck them out of the pit, and the house? He didn't know, that was the trouble.

'All I know is she loves me, and I love her,' Davey said calmly.

'Ah, love's young dream, but dreams fade when one of you is in the pit hacking up his lungs and, ah yes, the other is whacking, or is it dadding you pit folk call it, the filthy clothes against the outside wall, whack, whack, until your coal dust is filling *her* lungs, then she'll be in the scullery scrubbing them till her hands are raw. Such a lovely thing to wish on someone you love. I thought that today when I was working on the screens with imbeciles, rude ones at that.'

Davey turned his back on him, hunching his shoulders, hands deep in his pockets and the doubt born of Ralph's words niggling at his soul. As he stood there, others came to wait for their women, only to fall silent when they saw Ralph. Vicar Walters passed and doffed his cap. No one would ever doff a cap at Davey, or his wife.

He longed for the bus to come. As Ralph drew closer to him, Davey could smell his cologne. For heaven's sake, a man with cologne? Davey was conscious then that in spite of his bath in front of the range he smelled of the residue of coal and sweat. And there'd be no blue scars on Ralph's body, though they'd always stain Davey's. But now he thought about it, if the whelp kept on at the mine, he *would* have blue miners' scars. Had Ralph thought of that – for ever scarred and identified as a pitman?

He smiled grimly as he watched pinpricks of light emerge through the evening darkness and the bus appeared, taking the corner too fast. Of course, it was Cecil on the aft shift, the bloody fool. It was his Fran on the bus – precious goods. It grew closer, the brakes screeching as the bus slowed, then jerked to a stop. He turned and Ralph was just behind him, smiling and nodding.

'She could be taking a ride in a car if she was lucky enough to have someone like me, not rattling along in that boneshaker. Indeed, if she chose someone like me, she could instead be mistress of her own rather splendid home, wearing frocks and discussing menus.'

Davey couldn't believe the bastard's words. The bliddy cheek. Had he lost his mind, or was he just a bliddy fool? And why say this to him, why bother Fran? He stopped for a moment. Was he getting back at Stan for something? Was he less able than Stan at Oxford? Howay, he couldn't be doing with it. He pushed past the beggar and stood where he always stood, so that she'd see him when she started to alight. And here she came, and yes, her face lit up and she ran down the last few steps and flew into his arms, with Sarah not far behind, grinning.

But as he held Fran, Sarah's smile faded and Davey caught the whiff of cologne. And there was Ralph, standing close beside him.

'Ah, Fran. I have my car, so in the absence of your bike, ride with me. Sadly, only room for one.' He nodded to Sarah and Davey.

Fran stepped back and held out her hand. 'Evening, Mr Massingham. That's right kind, but I'm walking with Davey. I always walk with him for we're to be married. Not yet, but one day.'

Ralph shook her hand and as she squeezed, he winced.

'Mr Massingham has been on the screens,' Davey said. 'He's some way to go before he's safe for the pit or his hands harden.' He watched the muscles of Ralph's face working

142

and knew he'd made a mistake. He added, 'No one goes down until they've hardened up, Mr Ralph. Don't take it personal. It's good that you want to do yer bit.'

Ralph merely jangled his keys and said, 'Well, I'll let you all get home on Shanks's pony, by which I mean walking.'

Maisie was getting off the bus and cackled at Ralph's words. She didn't give a damn what anyone thought now her Derek was dead. Besides, she lived above the local shop her mam owned and wasn't beholden to anyone. 'By, you'd think we'd all been born yesterday, the way you talk, Mr Ralph, or were feeble-minded. My old bugger saw you in your Mosley uniform. Just the once, in Newcastle it were. Right smart. He liked the boots. Black, weren't they?'

Davey intervened, hoping to calm things for too many were at the mercy of this man's family and the air was fairly crackling with anger. 'Ah, that was a time when we were all trying out this, that and t'other.'

Maisie tossed her head and click-clacked along the road, arm in arm with Mrs Oborne, their heads close together. More laughter rang down the street.

Ralph said, 'She is mistaken. Whoever she saw, it wasn't me.' While he watched Maisie go, Sarah, Fran and Davey slipped away, with Fran holding Davey's hand tight and whispering, 'What's all this about? Does he think giving me a lift's doing Stan a favour, or just the opposite?'

'He was always a difficult lad, and real nasty with it, not like Mr Massingham at all,' Sarah said, walking the other side of Davey.

'Perhaps he doesn't like people bringing up his past. After all, lots went to meetings, then never again,' Davey said.

Fran muttered, 'But if he had a uniform, it wasn't just now and then, was it?'

Davey shrugged. 'He could afford one. Probably liked the look of it, that's all. Anyway, it was years ago.'

They walked on. Sarah, slipping her arm through Fran's, said, 'That still doesn't explain why he was here and came to the beck an' all.'

Davey wasn't really listening; he was wondering if Ralph was right, and he should have fought more for the scholarship if he wanted the best for Fran. But he'd really thought hard about it and couldn't leave her. Anyway, one day he'd have his magazine and then she could have help to dadd the clothes if she wanted it, just like she paid Madge to do it for Mrs Hall. He smiled suddenly, because if he said that to her, she'd dadd him instead. She might want to help with the magazine because she had such good ideas and that would be fine, but his Fran could do whatever she wanted when they were married. Aye, that she could, for he intended to be earning good money by then, so stuff that in your pipe and smoke it, Mr Ralph Massingham.

He looked down at Fran as she leaned against him while they walked, struck by the thought that she might not love him as much as he loved her. After all, Stan had said it were over with Beth, as though it had never been. People changed.

But would he and Fran? He couldn't begin to believe such a thing was possible.

Chapter Ten

Three weeks later

Fran and Sarah sat on the bus as they travelled to the Factory for the afternoon shift, feeling sick and their heads aching. Fran looked at her hands and compared them to Sarah's. 'Yours are worse, they're a real yellow now. You'd better watch it or your da will put you in one of their canary cages.'

Sarah pulled down Fran's headscarf. 'That's enough from you, our Fran.'

'Aye, well, we'll be in there together, Sarah, and your hair's blonde already so the green's fetching, and it at least tells us the powder has got past your tiny brain to your skull in order to tint your golden locks. Mark you, it's such a small brain it's no wonder it has.'

The two of them laughed, and it made Fran cough. 'By, me chest's one thing I can't blame on the chemicals, it's just this damned cold.'

'Aye, well, don't give yer cough to me. Mark you, Cecil's driving's a right pain and that doesn't help the sickness, but coughing isn't a good idea – something might slop out. And shut up about me brain, because yours isn't that grand. Your hair's got red strands to match Beth's, though hers has gone a bit sort of greenish an' all.' Sarah removed her scarf and pulled a long green strand of hair from her French pleat. 'Would you look at that. If it's not getting more green, I'm a Dutchman.'

Cecil screeched round the corner and onto the straight road leading to the junction with the Hanging Tree. Fran felt even worse as Sarah waved the strand in front of her face and flicked it away. 'Aye, it's green all right, but what can we do?'

There was nothing, just as all the complaints about Cecil's driving made no difference. Just like Fran's attempts not to be rude to Ralph when he turned up at the bus shelter day after day were doing nothing to stop her dislike turning to hate and fury—No, no, she mustn't even think about it, her mam was right to say ignore it . . .

She felt the rage tearing at her, though, and breathed slowly, looking out of the window at the countryside – her countryside, her slag heaps, the place she loved. She calmed down and instead watched as Sarah pulled out a hairpin and captured the strand, shoving the hairpin back in before pulling her faded old headscarf over it. This was stained yellow too, just like their sheets. Fran watched as Sarah knotted it under her chin with her yellow fingers.

Fran looked at her own hands. They weren't just *stained*, they were more like a couple of strange things that had attached themselves to her and needed shaking off.

She breathed in for the count of four, and out for four, making herself remember that once they spent time away from the stemming shop they'd recover. Her body would be the 'right' one again, though that wouldn't be any time soon. She started to breathe too quickly again, but it wasn't the stemming, it was Ralph, who kept turning up, wanting to walk her home. Why, when she looked as she did? Why? She shook her head. No, don't shake it, daft lass.

Instead, she pictured herself pouring powder into the drum in the shop, pulling the handle so that the powder came whooshing through a funnel into a rubber thingummybob, as they called the container. This powder was used

146

to fill shells in one or all of the other sectors, so it must be TNT, or something like that, but no one said. It was just 'the yellow'. All day they pulled the lever and the powder whooshed and filled the air, then settled on, and in, them – just ten of them from their bus – because this is where they'd been transferred. Nothing would explode, they'd been told, because the yellow needed a detonator and, she thought, a fused pellet, but it was all a guess, like everything at the Factory.

And who cared anyway, for they'd been moved from detonators to somewhere horrid but safe after someone had become careless and dropped half a tray. It had taken off the girl's foot. They didn't know her, but they'd seen her lying there, footless, and the blood, and heard the screams. They were now just along from the booster, or fuse pellet, shop, where millions of pellets were being wrapped to make them ready for use.

Would she and her marrers wrap the pellets, or go back on detonators? Who knew? Well, it might be bliddy safe in stemming, but the yellow settled on any hair that stuck out from under their turbans, clinging to their hands and floating onto their blue overalls, where it sank in until it reached their skin. Would it go deeper than that? she wondered. Would they breathe it in? Well, of course, but she mustn't think of it.

She tried to push away the nausea and dizziness, telling herself not to ask why. It was Cecil's driving, of course. She mustn't think of Ralph. Looking out of the window again, she saw that they were flashing past the trees lining the road, and that made her feel even worse. At least she wasn't having to worry about Stan and who he loved, or didn't, because all the girls felt so unwell no one was thinking of their love lives. She allowed herself to think instead of Madge, whom Fran paid to do Mam's dadding, washing

147

and ironing, because she was the one who had to do her best with Fran's sheets. The yellow never faded.

'I wonder what the powder is?' Fran muttered, for something to say.

'It's the yellow, daft lass,' replied Sarah. 'And that's all we'll ever know.'

Anyway, Fran thought, they'd feel better on the bus next week, with Bert driving the transport for the night shift. Fran hated the night shift – she found it difficult to sleep in the day, and she hated missing her Sunday with Davey even more, because her mam made her stay in, resting. If she wasn't working, that was. She stared down at her hands, then closed her eyes against the glare of the low early autumnal sun on changing leaves, and muttered, 'Yellow, yellow, everywhere. There might be no bananas, but I certainly feel like one.'

'Or a canary, more like,' Sarah muttered back.

They laughed together quietly as Cecil careered round another bend, whistling. Yes, Fran thought, Ralph might shove his way into her life for a few moments each day, but it was no more than that. It's what she and her mam, too, had decided. No more than that, and it was up to her to make sure it wasn't more.

Fran heard Mrs Oborne, who sat nearer the back because she didn't want to be at the front if Cecil crashed, shout loud enough to carry over Cecil's whistling: 'Night shift can't come soon enough. Just think, lasses, we'll get shot of this racing driver. I reckon I'll give Bert a right kissing on our first bus ride into work.'

They all laughed. Cecil broke off his whistling. 'If you lot got yourselves on the bus a sight quicker, I wouldn't have to rush.'

Mrs Oborne led the catcalls, while Cecil hooted his horn. As the noise died, Fran yelled, 'Wouldn't matter how quick we were, you'd still get your foot down. You're a menace, Cecil Woodward, that you are.'

As the others clapped, Sarah laughed fit to burst, then said quietly to Fran as the noise died, 'But nowt like the menace that damned Ralph's become. Three weeks now he's been turning up to meet you off the bus, almost shoving our Davey out the way. Not that he dares to touch our lad, but you can see he wants to, and I don't know what we can do to stop him?'

Fran didn't want to be dragged back to Ralph, but she had to say something. 'He and Stan are to go down the pit any day now, and the daft beggar won't have the energy to do anything other than crawl home.' Yes, she thought, that sounds tough enough. Yes.

Sarah agreed. 'Aye, wonder how he'll take to being tucked away in the muck? I bet he turns tail and buggers off back to Oxford. Sick of the sight of him, I am, lolling at the shelter. It's a bloody cheek. Anyone would think he was king of the walk.'

Maisie, who was sitting in front of them, turned round. 'Well, he is just that for the pitmen, in't he? He's the boss's son, and our Fran'll be getting ideas above her station if this goes on.'

Sylv, who had recovered sufficiently to be back at work, but only in the clean and safe sewing room, whispered to Maisie, loud enough for Fran to hear, 'She must be givin' him the come-on, else he wouldn't do it.'

Fran opened her mouth, but it was Sarah who poked at Sylv's shoulder. 'You wash your mouth out, you stupid moo.'

Sylv swung round, Maisie too, as Fran pushed Sarah back into her seat, hushing her. Sarah shook her head. 'I'm not having it. Sick I am of the looks, cos you haven't done anything. Let me tell you, Sylv Plater, and you, Maisie, while I'm about it: our Fran doesn't want him near her and neither does our Davey, and you'd damn well know that if you weren't so daft. It's just one of the whelp's games. You know what he's always been like – just causing a nuisance makes him happy.'

Fran felt a wave of sickness as Cecil roared on towards Sledgeford, its slag heap brewing up in the rising wind. She muttered, 'Oh Sarah, don't. He's not worth it. Ignore him, ignore it. Ignore the lot of them.'

But Sarah was leaning forward again. 'It makes me sick, do yer hear me, Sylv Slater, cos it's making me brother mad and miserable. Not to mention our Fran, and it don't help to hear you shouting your mouth off. Yes, it makes me sick.' Sarah suddenly sat back, her hand over her mouth. 'I feel really sick – not just that sort of sick.'

Behind them, Mrs Oborne muttered, 'It's the powder. It's not just the skin and hair that it gets into. I reckon our innards are bright yellow – stands to reason. Think on about Maisie's babe, like a bleedin' daffodil, it were.'

'What was the powder that time?'

'It were trinitro-something,' Maisie butted in, smiling at Sarah, wanting to be friends again. Sarah sniffed and turned away.

Mrs Oborne called, 'Trinitrotoluene, or summat like that. But that's too bliddy long to say, so call it TNT.'

Maisie continued, 'Well, that's what I were packing shells with at me first factory, and I reckon the yellow could be the same, but who knows, we're not told, and it won't stop at the skin neither until you lot leave the stemming shop. Why would it? You're breathing it in, after all. But anyway, the management'll move you if you get the rashes bad enough. Mark you, some other poor beggar will have to have a go, probably me, while you come into the sewing room.'

Sylv said, 'I reckon with all the chemicals in the air we're a right mess inside, as well as outside. Gives me the willies it does.'

Cecil slowed for a tractor that was coming the other way, both vehicles easing onto the verges, the two drivers stopping to shout at one another. It wasn't a row; it was just a talk. If Cecil had time for that, why was he always rushing? Fran wanted to run down the aisle and shake him, but it was only the powder making her edgy – well, making them all edgy. She looked out of the window at the drystone wall that was crumbling along this stretch. The drivers were waving to one another now and the bus jolted off the verge as Cecil headed onwards at the gallop, flying past some farm cottages.

Mrs Oborne said then, as though she'd arrived at a decision, 'Howay, I've got to say this, our Sylv, you need to stop being such a ruddy ray of sunshine, and yes, I'm being bliddy funny. Just put a cork in it for Pete's sake. The accident's made you a mithering Minnie, but you weren't the one who were killed, and what's more, you're in a clean area so not feeling out of sorts like the rest of us. So get some ruddy gumption or you'll be walking alone with only your mithering for company. And you can stop smirking, our Maisie. You could do with some gumption too. You just remember how your mam brought you up: if you haven't anything nice to say, say nowt at all.'

Sarah and Fran glanced at one another. Mrs Oborne usually kept out of things, but now she was part of the co-op she seemed to have changed into a mother hen. Gumption, eh? Fran thought. Aye, not a bad idea for you and all, Frances Hall.

For a while no one at their end of the bus said a word, just sat alone with their thoughts, which were only interrupted when they entered Sledgeford and the bus screamed to a stop, jolting them all forwards and then back again.

Beth came down the aisle, leading the charge because she hated the cold east wind. She was just as yellow as Fran and Sarah, and so too was Amelia, who followed her. Fran shook her head. It was ridiculous to think they were supposed to pretend they were working on something like sewing overalls or parachutes when they met friends on the street, for when did sewing anything have this effect?

Cecil drove on, screeching and swaying along the roads for what seemed like hours. Fran led the singing for some time, then Mrs Oborne took over with Beth's help when Fran's coughing became a nuisance. Finally, as they rounded the bend just east of the Factory, Cecil seemed to rush towards the gate, swinging into the parking area and braking so hard that everyone jerked forwards and back yet again. 'I truly will swing for him, so help me,' Mrs Oborne muttered.

Beth and Fran smiled at one another, for things were almost back to normal between the three of them but still not quite. But they were just too itchy, sickly and yellow to quarrel. And besides, Stan was on different shifts to them, so the gang hadn't met.

Stepping onto the firm ground, Fran wrapped her scarf tightly around her neck against the cold. At last she felt like smiling, thinking of her mam knitting it, or sitting round the table with the co-op, making not just rugs but plans for 'expansion' too.

Fran's da had muttered, as he stuffed the last of his baccy ration in his pipe, 'Better watch it, Ben. They'll be making you a new pair of proggy trousers any minute now, so they will.' Ben had grimaced while the co-op laughed, drowning Da's coughing.

Fran, Sarah and Beth linked arms as they walked to the Factory security gates.

'Honestly,' Beth said, 'the thought of our mams huddling

around the table, hatching plans and deciding whether to make the wall hangings with a Christmas theme reminds me of witches around a cauldron. I reckon they'll be making spells – ones that will shove the Germans back from the Russian towns.'

Fran squeezed Beth's arm. 'You're brave, or daft, because I might tell 'em you said that, and then you'll be whacked by one of their rugs, pet.' And what's more, she thought, I'll be the one doing the whacking if you start anything up with our Stan once we're feeling more the thing.

They showed their passes at the gate and moved on into the changing rooms. They hated the stemming-shop area in a way they hated no other. 'I hate feeling so sick,' Beth moaned.

Sarah muttered, 'Tell the foreman and he'll mebbe move you, if you wear your lippy, that is.'

Beth raised her eyes. They changed and checked one another for metallic objects and silk underwear, which always made them giggle. Then they gave Valerie and Amelia a quick once-over, before picking up their masks, which became just as yellow inside as they did on the outside by the end of the shift. Amelia whispered that she had an interview for a clerk's job that could be coming up in the office. 'It doesn't matter if I drop my pay. Daddy will make up any difference.'

Fran thought she hadn't heard right. 'Sorry, what did you say?'

Sarah answered, her voice loud enough to drown the chatter, 'She said it doesn't matter if she drops her pay, because her daddy will make up any difference.'

Beth, who was tucking up her hair in her turban, stopped. 'What? Howay, lucky for some, eh?'

Into the quiet, Amelia shrugged, the colour rising in her cheeks. 'It's not my fault if I'm used to better than . . .' She faded, looking around.

Beth stepped forward. 'Than? Than?'

The door opened and Miss Ellington appeared. 'Time we got you to your work stations, ladies, then the fore shift can go.'

Amelia rushed through the door, brushing against Miss Ellington, who called, 'My, someone's eager. Come back – I need to check you.' She waited in the doorway. 'Come on, ladies, check one another, then file past. Ah, there you are, Amelia.'

Amelia had re-entered and now stood in front of Miss Ellington, not looking at anyone else. Finally they all filed past the security officer and out of the door into the corridor.

All Fran could think of as she walked alongside Beth and Sarah towards the stemming shop, passing safety posters, war posters, secrecy posters, was how could anyone not have to worry about money?

Maisie caught them up in the passageway, whispering, 'That could be you, Fran, with no need to watch the pennies if you swap your pitman for the whelp, who anyone can see is licking his chops for you.'

Fran slowed, turning to look at Maisie to see if she was joking, mad or brave. Finally, she said, 'Well, there's no way I'm swapping Davey. Not now, not ever for anyone, and I don't give a damn about Ralph's chops, and that's the most revolting picture anyone could have painted. And I never thought to hear such stupid words from you, Maisie. Take a good look at yourself when you next pass a mirror, and any more of that and I'll punch your nose.'

Sarah moved between Fran and Maisie. 'Now I feel sick, really sick, again and I think this time it will be on your shoes, Maisie.'

She bent over and Maisie looked shocked and scooted around her, but Beth was in her way, her arms crossed, and wouldn't move until Fran said, 'Let her through, Beth. She understands, I reckon.'

Fran was shaking with misery, and ... well, she didn't know. Sarah resumed her place next to her and slipped her arm through hers, while Beth did the same on her other side. 'That'll learn her, silly fool,' Beth muttered.

Maisie called back, 'Can't you three take a joke?'

At that very moment, Fran hated the war. Well, she always hated it, but now more than ever. She wanted it to be over, for Maisie would never have said anything like that if her Derek wasn't dead. As they walked on, Sarah said quietly, 'I wonder if you and Davey should get wed now, to stop the gossip because I don't know how else we can stop Ralph. Marriage puts up a barrier, or should.' Silence fell between the three girls.

Beth muttered, 'If that's aimed at me, I'm not listening.'

Fran almost shouted, 'Oh, enough. Let's deal with Ralph, can't we?'

Sarah said, 'But what would your mam do without you and your money, Fran? And where would you live? You'd have to change villages and pits to get away from the whelp because he'd kick up. And then me mam needs Davey's money too, cos there's nowt for a rainy day yet, which is what he and I said we'd sort. But don't tell me da I said that.'

Fran noted that Sarah hadn't denied the previous remark was meant for Beth, but she couldn't deal with any more, so said nothing.

They passed a torn poster of a ship being torpedoed and the tannoy, which had been silent, burst into music. Fran and Davey had spoken of Ralph just last Sunday, and Davey had shrugged and said that Ralph was just a nuisance and to ignore him because he'd run out of steam. 'Remember what your mam said, Franny Hall,' he insisted. 'Which was we're not to be wed yet. War is war and you never know what's to happen. And she meant it.'

They walked on down the corridor, passed an emergency exit and suddenly Fran realised she'd slipped back into mulling over the whelp – again. 'That beggar's taking up too much of me brain, and I'm right sick of him,' she said. 'He's just a bliddy nuisance. Besides, we're the Factory Girls, we three. We have gumption, all of us have – everyone working here, everyone beavering away everywhere. Just remember what Mrs Oborne said: "Get some ruddy gumption". So I'm damn well getting some.'

Beth muttered as they walked down the corridor behind Maisie, 'I reckon threatening to punch our Maisie's nose meant you'd already got it.' The three of them laughed and it looked like the spat between the other two, which was never far from the surface, was over for now, before it had begun, and Fran started to relax. Beth continued, 'The whelp's messing about because of Stan, I reckon.'

Fran felt Sarah stiffen at Stan's name, and her heart sank, but it was all right because Beth went on, 'When they were both at Oxford I bet Ralph felt superior to Stan the pitman. Now Stan's the one who knows more, so Ralph's kicking out. Do you remember how he used to plague us, sniffing around the village? And there was that damned ball. Kicking out, yer see, just like back then. He's cruel, he has a nasty side.'

Fran murmured, 'But it can't be something so daft.' She stopped and grinned. The word gumption was running through her head loud and clear. 'No, it's not the footie, not Oxford, it's clearly because I'm as pretty as Marlene Dietrich and he can't resist me.'

The other two looked at her. 'Now that really is daft, our Franny Hall, unless he likes the colour yellow, like me Bob,' Beth said.

Sarah and Fran burst out laughing and, feeling more powerful than she had for the last three weeks, Fran said, 'You're the one that likes the colour yellow, not Bob, and where's the knitting? You don't do it any more.'

Beth flushed a little under her yellow skin, which created an interesting colour. 'Ah, well, you see I don't feel so lonely, because . . . well, because we're all together, feeling sick, looking a mess, so for once I feel we're all the same, and besides, when you feel like we do, anything else fades away to nothing. We're too busy trying to get through the day, and up out of the bed for the next one. Besides, you're right, all of you. What man wears yellow?'

Miss Ellington overtook them. 'Hurry along, girls, the stemming shop awaits your tender touch. And actually, no man in his right mind wears yellow, Beth, so good choice to ditch it. You don't want him to do the ditching.'

The three of them watched her rush ahead. Beth looked stunned. Finally she said, 'Oh, she meant ditch the sweater.' But it was as though, for a moment, she'd thought the security officer had meant *he* would ditch *her*.

They walked on and Fran hoped that Beth *had* felt threatened, because it seemed never to have occurred to her that there were two in the marriage, and if she was being silly, perhaps Bob could be too. Fran nodded to herself. It might be the shock that Beth needed, if she did still hanker after Stan, and that would be one less problem.

At 14 Leadenhall Terrace the women of the Proggy Co-op sat around Mrs Hall's table, their frames resting at a slant on their knees or on the table itself for those who could manage it.

In the centre of the table an old jam jar held the coppers the women had donated for the weekly tea and broken biscuits from Maisie's mum's corner shop. There was a hum of conversation as they all wondered how long the lasses would be able to cope with the chemicals, though they dropped their voices as they discussed this, glancing around to make sure the back door was shut.

Then they looked at one another, raised their eyebrows and burst out laughing. 'There's nowt like a co-op meeting to get the spies to rest their lugs against the door, is there?' Maisie's mam said. 'At Maisie's first factory, before she got herself transferred back here when her Derek got himself killed, she were right poorly, but she should have come back sooner with the babe comin' an' all. I reckon she were working on shell filling with TNT.'

Annie Hall shook her head slightly. 'Hush, Mrs Adams, we must say nowt – our girls could be sacked if it's known. Either way, whatever it is, it's made Fran right prickly – not just her skin, but her mood. Sort of snappy.'

'Aye, but is that because of the whelp hanging about?' Maud Bedley muttered, continuing to hook the navy-blue blanket strips through the hessian sugar sack. 'Canna work out why he's getting between our Davey and your Fran like that . . .'

Madge Field stopped for a moment. 'Me da says at least he's getting his hands dirty, which shows he's grown up a bit, and left his politics behind, but no one cares for the whelp. They think him a nasty piece of work.' She resumed work, forcing a short strip of red blanket through the hessian.

Audrey Smith, Beth's mam, said, 'I reckon with Stan coming back it could be that he thought it would look good if he came and did something as well. The boss's son an' all, pitching in. He'll have an eye on taking over some of his da's works and pits when he's finished at Oxford, I 'spect. He'll be showing off to his da. Cunning he always was and still is, and a right little snot. I remember him scrumping with some Sledgeford boys after his mam died, and they were caught. He told Farmer Stanton he were upset cos his mam had died and the boys had led him on. So they got the belting. What else could the farmer do when he was a tenant of Mr Massingham's? Aye, I reckon he expects his da to think highly of him for pitchin' in. Maybe he thinks them at the pit will an' all.'

The other women all laughed. 'Well, he divint know pitmen,' crowed Maisie's mam. 'You know, thinking about it, I reckon he's after Fran because she's Stan's sister, or could it be because he wants back at Davey for besting him in that football bet? The village hasn't forgotten, yer know, so p'raps he hasn't.'

The women all stopped working, their faces serious. At last Annie said, 'Nay, it's too long since, surely?' But no one seemed sure. Again there was silence, apart from the range spluttering from the slack.

Beth's mam nodded towards the firebox. 'Might be a might chilly working at the pit, when he's the boss's son, so if he started walking out with a hewer's sister, he might think it'd warm things up?'

Madge shrugged, adjusting her blue eyepatch. 'Be a damn sight chillier if he shouldered our Davey out of the picture. What's more, Annie, I can't see your Fran putting up with it. Her and Davey have been like twins since . . . Well, since I don't remember.'

Annie looked from one to the other, trying to get all her thoughts and memories straight in her head, then shook herself. The lads and lasses were all grown now, and not daft. She said, finally, 'I suppose we should think well of him, because he *is* mucking in. He'll get the message as regards Fran before long.'

Mrs Slater, Sylv's mum, rubbed her finger where it had slipped on her hook. 'She's told him enough, hasn't she, Mrs Hall?'

There was real doubt in Mrs Slater's voice and Annie snapped, 'You shouldn't have to ask. Whatever are you thinking, Jane?'

There was an embarrassed silence, broken only by the range and the clatter of hooks. Annie rose to make the tea, smiling as she did so, but inside she was furious. Not with Franny, but with Ralph and his mischief-making, and with the gossips. Even Joe was getting right annoyed with the whole business. Annie sighed. She'd said to Joe, 'What do you expect our Fran to do, slap him with a wet fish? He's the boss's boy and she knows that he owns us, so don't be so bliddy daft. And that's why Stan's biding his time too. More'n that, he knows our Fran can cope with the wee bliddy squirt.' She seldom swore and Joe had coughed and buried his head in his newspaper.

Annie poured in the boiling water and waited for the tea leaves to mash, feeling tired. She steadied herself on the bar of the range, wondering if she should have let Fran and Davey marry already? Yes, maybe that would be best. She would talk to Joe tonight. But where would they live? There were no spare pit houses and fat chance they'd get their own in the village if the Massingham whelp had any say in it. And good though Mr Massingham was, he'd choose his boy over a pitman, so they'd have to move and Fran would have to have her own house, and with that came bills, and housework, and cooking.

Annie Hall sighed, feeling the pain in her baby-bearing innards, aching at the very thought of the dadding, washing and ironing she'd have to do again. But not enough to stand in the way of Fran's happiness. And they could wait longer for a headstone for Betty. Who knew, she might sell enough rugs to pay for one.

But did Mr Massingham even know his son was trying to spark a pitman's daughter? Her thoughts drifted to the

Factory and a different anxiety took hold now. Maisie's babe had been born yellow, and Maisie had been right sickly before she was taken out of that section down south. Look at Franny – every day she seemed yellower, itchier and giddier. She had turned too quickly as she left the house for the bus and had almost fallen. By, she would have done if she hadn't caught the table and righted herself. But it wasn't just that. What else was it doing to her insides, especially if it was that blooming TNT? And this coming on top of that other stuff which gave them a really bad rash.

Annie poured cups of tea, setting them in the centre of the table. She took up her own rug. She preferred to make a proggy, but some liked to make a hooky, though they were both rag rugs, and Briddlestone's liked either. For a proggy she used short lengths of material of about five inches in length, and, working from the wrong side she progged or poked one end of a single short strip through the hessian with an adapted dolly peg, and then progged the other end of the clipped material through the hessian a tiny bit further along, and so it went on. In the end she produced a fairly ragged pile. Some though liked working with a hook. This involved working with a long strip of material, hooking it in and out of the hessian, creating a rug with a looped pile.

She found that using single short strips gave her a more flexible colour scheme, and allowed her to merge the colours, and tilted the frame to check the right side and smiled. Yes, grand it was and would look fine hanging on a wall. She'd need to bind the edges good and neat. By, fancy having the money to hang a rug on the wall, not walk on it.

She said as much now, and they all laughed. It was grand to have company like this. Madge cocked her head to one side. 'They can sling them on the ceiling for all I care, just as long as we get paid.'

Again there was laughter, and now Mrs Slater lifted her shoulders and said, 'They could swing 'em from the lights an' all, if they're not at it already themselves, as some says the naughty ones do in London. Right racy the goings-on, so they say.' By now they were helpless with laughter, and had to lay down their tools at the very thought.

Mrs Bedley leaned her frame against her chair leg and sipped her tea before wiping her eyes behind her spectacles with her handkerchief. 'By, you're a card, Mrs Slater, right enough, just like your Sylv.' She patted her mouth, looking around at them all over the cup. 'Let's forget the whelp. He'll move on to something, or someone, else. Let's think about the schedule instead, because Briddlestone's want to be able to distribute ready in time for Christmas. It seems that though the war is getting worse, there's still Christmas, isn't that right Mrs Hall?'

Annie smiled at her friend, the laughter wiping the worry from her. 'Right enough.'

So that's what they did, and it was Madge Field who said, 'Aye, it would be a grand thing if we could find another buyer too. There're others in the village that have war work in the fields, or ARP or WVS like us, who'd like to join us after their shifts. They're happy to be paid according to what they make as well, so that's not a problem.'

As one, they all looked at Annie, who nodded. 'I'll talk to Fran. She usually has good ideas.'

At the Factory, Miss Ellington called, 'Two minutes to eleven, girls. Thanks to those of you who joined us on the pellets and gave us an extra hour of your time. I know it's a pest when we have to switch some of you round to help out, but that's the nature of the beast. Don't hurry, finish what you are doing and then step back. Whilst I have you listening to my every word, I would just like to plead with you all to have your hair cut, or get your mothers to do it. It's so much safer when you come near any machinery. We don't want it getting caught up.'

No one took any notice, just worked on, including Fran, whose whole body itched, though her fingers were still nimble as she pasted and wrapped the fluted paper around what felt like the millionth fuse pellet and placed it in its stand, carefully, carefully, for she couldn't quite believe it exploded only if it met the right 'other'. After all, if it could boost the ignition of weapons, it could easily blow off her hands.

There was a certain symmetry to her life, she mused, as she wrapped another. If it wasn't the yellow, it was detonators, and if not that, it was fuse pellets, otherwise known as detonator boosters. And each and every one of these would contribute to the war. So, detonator, booster, the yellow. The words kept resonating in her head and she pasted and wrapped a pellet along with each one, creating something of a rhythm until there were no more.

She stood back, feeling her head whirl. She breathed in for four, then out for the same count, and it steadied her. She wondered if there were women in Germany as yellow as canaries too? And in Russia? What did Amelia say canary was in German? She stared at the bench, trying to think as the sector's foreman, Mr Hopkins, said, 'The target for today has been reached. Excellent effort, ladies.'

Those words always gave Fran a real sense of achievement and it was such a relief to work with the nice, sensible Mr Hopkins. Beth and Sarah on either side of her were smiling too, along with Amelia, Maisie and Valerie, who had all been seconded as well. They filed out of the section, past those heading in for the night shift. In the changing rooms they were joined by others from the stemming shop who had been asked to do overtime too. They washed, dragged on their clothes and finally Fran wound the scarf around her neck. A lovely red, white and blue scarf, because her mam felt it was her duty to be patriotic whenever and however she could.

The girls collected the belongings they had left for safety reasons and walked to the gate. Behind them, Mr Swinton hurried to catch up because he was cadging a lift to Minton with Cecil, who would be in a foul mood because he'd had to wait for them.

They showed their passes at the gate, then Fran walked along the tatty piece of tarmac ground with the others, aching with tiredness like everyone else. It was dark and they were guided by the slit headlights of the bus, but nonetheless they heard Cecil hooting, and everyone sighed together. 'Cecil must have a date with a beer.'

Sarah slowed down, gripping Fran's arm. 'Oh no,' she hissed. 'Look, Fran, it's him.'

By the light of the bus's headlights, Fran watched Ralph climb out of his roadster and stroll towards them. 'I was passing, Fran,' he called. 'Thought you could do with a lift. Stan mentioned you weren't so well.'

She shook her head as the women filed onto the bus, saying nothing, though several tutted. Cecil had left the engine running and Fran wanted to be on the bus too. She almost wept as she shouted, 'How did you know where this is? How? No one should.'

Ralph froze for just a moment and then Swinton paused beside them calling, 'I'm right glad to see yer, Mr Massingham.' He had shoved ahead of the girls, his hand out. Ralph stared as Mr Swinton reached him. They shook hands and Swinton said, 'Perhaps you can help, Mr Massingham? I want to know where me boy is. He wrote to say you'd been right kind and got him war work, but I'm wondering when he gets leave? We just got a postcard and—'

Fran grabbed the moment. 'Take Mr Swinton in your great big car, Mr Massingham. Then you can have a chat, eh?'

The bus was rolling forwards and Mrs Oborne was on the step, calling them. Fran, Sarah and Beth ran and leapt on, not looking back, and for once Fran was grateful to Mr Swinton. The three girls hurried along the aisle, holding on to the backs of the seats as Cecil roared up through the gears, taking no prisoners as the wheels spun and he scorched onto the road. They found seats together and fell into them, with Beth sounding surprised as she said, 'Well, I suppose we have to admit Ralphy boy has a few good points, if he took the Swinton boy under his wing.'

Sarah settled back in her seat. 'Just as long as he keeps his wings well away from us, eh.'

The girls grinned at one another. 'We've got one another, we three girls, and we've got gumption too, so what else do we need?' Beth said.

'A bit of shut-eye would do nicely, thank you,' called Amelia, sounding angry. 'Right now, if you don't mind.'

Sarah muttered, 'Well, forgive me for breathing.'

They all smiled, and shook their heads.

Chapter Eleven

October 1941

Fran, Sarah and Beth led the sing-song as they all half danced from the bus to the Factory an hour early for their afternoon shift, as instructed when they'd left the previous evening. It was a fine Tuesday afternoon, with even the birds hiding amongst the red and yellow leaves joining in, or so it seemed. Maisie turned and bowed to the trees; the others raised their voices. Even the men on the gate hummed along with them as they checked their passes. 'You must have been a beautiful baby . . .'

Once through, they headed for the changing room, where they would be directed to detonators, pellets, stemming or anywhere else they were needed. It had become the norm these days for Fran, Beth, Amelia and Sarah, and perhaps Maisie and Mrs Oborne, to be taken out of the stemming shop for the odd day or two to fill in for missing personnel.

Fran's mam still wrapped her daughter's hands in the sphagnum-moss mixture every evening, as Mrs Bedley did for Sarah. Annie had given some to Beth to apply herself and even Sarah had felt sorry for her, because how could Beth reach her own back? At least, she had muttered, she hadn't moved back to Massingham yet, so hadn't struck up with Stan. But was she going to? Neither she nor Fran knew.

They entered the changing room, pleased that for some reason they'd all begun to feel a bit more themselves. Was it the moss most of them were using, or were they just hardening themselves to the shifts, the work, the chemicals and the stress? Then Fran put two big bottles of water on the bench and Maisie said, 'What on earth?'

Fran told them that her mam had decided she should try to flush the irritants out of her system, so she had to drink all this each shift, and then more at home.

'Will you be allowed to take the bottles into the workshop?' Mrs Oborne asked, impressed, saying that she would do it too. It made sense.

They had let Fran through the gate, but had they been too busy humming to really check? She wasn't sure, but she wasn't going to go back and ask. They were all taking off their 'contraband' when the draught from the opening door made the bare light bulb swing, throwing up dancing shadows.

'Eh up,' Mrs Oborne called. 'The light likes a tune an' all.'

Miss Ellington, Mrs Raydon and several other women they hadn't seen before entered, all wearing black overalls. So, they were all security officers? The women were lining up, as though they were blocking the way to the works corridor. Fran clutched her bag. Had the guard said something? Were they going to take the water? Had she broken a rule? Would she be in trouble?

Miss Ellington stepped forward. 'A few changes, ladies. It has been decided by those who make decisions that from now on—But no, first let me tell you the history. On yesterday's fore shift, an unused match was found in someone's liberty bodice pocket. I cannot reveal why it came to be found, but she is even now being interrogated, and no matter if she is exonerated of the crime of sabotage, she will be dismissed, because who really knows if it was to be thrown into a machine to create havoc? The answer from the young woman in question was, "I forgot." I sincerely believe she did, but as I say, questions, questions.'

Now it was Mrs Raydon's turn to step forward. 'So, today everyone is to be stripped to their undergarments and searched—'

'Well, I'm not having Mr Swinton anywhere near me, I'm telling you now,' said Fran.

Miss Ellington hid a smile. 'No need for you to tell us anything, thank you, Fran. He will not be in this room for the search. Let us begin. Time is a-wasting.'

Amelia spoke now. 'I'm not used to communal undressing, Miss Ellington. Perhaps I could have a little cubbyhole, or something similar.'

'Or perhaps you could not, Amelia.' Miss Ellington shook her head. 'This isn't a polite tea party, it's a factory, and for the moment you are a factory worker.'

Amelia looked shocked, then furious.

The girls put their valuables in the envelopes as usual, feeling awkward and embarrassed. For as Fran said to Amelia, 'We aren't used to it either, Amelia. Whatever made you think we would be?'

Amelia was dragging her clothes over her head. Her underwear was rather splendid, but the same couldn't be said for the rest of them, so really they were the ones who should want cubbyholes, Fran thought. They were all avoiding each other's eyes.

They and their pile of clothes were properly searched. Then Mrs Oborne's bloomers and vest were patted down, then Valerie's, and Fran found herself watching the bare light bulb, for this was worse than feeling sick. Each member of the security team apologised, but continued and Miss Ellington told them all that they would be querying the necessity for this later on today. As the woman whose tight curls smelled of perm lotion finished patting Fran down, she whispered, 'Don't worry, for us it's like patting down a slab of meat.'

'Well, I might be a slab of meat to you,' Fran muttered, 'but I'll have you know I'm a Merle Oberon in me heart.'

The woman laughed and her face lit up. Others heard and they all vied with one another to be the most popular film star there in that room, in their shabby, well-worn underclothes. Suddenly the Factory women had taken back control and even Amelia said that she'd fight Fran for Merle Oberon, while Maisie sang, 'You must have been a beautiful baby . . .' At this point the security team joined in as they finished their task, finally stepping back, having found nothing. It was only then that the singing stopped.

'You can now dress, and pop on the overalls as usual,' Mrs Raydon announced. The girls and women looked at one another, and then smiled,

Once they were dressed, Miss Ellington held up one of Fran's two bottles, after tucking the other under her handless arm. 'Whoever these belong to, tell me you weren't thinking of taking them in with you?'

Beth said, 'Fran's mam was told by an old Great War armaments worker she met at t'market that she'd seen Fran, knew what she was was doing from her colour, and that she should drink water to flush the chemicals through. I think it's a bliddy good idea and I'm going to bring water tomorrow, so there.'

Amelia spoke over all the chatting and said, 'I also think that's a good idea. It makes sense, doesn't it? You flush a drain.' She paused. 'Well, I don't mean you're a drain, Fran.'

'I'd stop right there, lass,' said Mrs Oborne.

Amelia nodded. 'Perhaps I'd better.' She pulled a face, and there was embarrassed laughter from the women.

Miss Ellington and the other security women huddled together, talking, until finally Miss Ellington addressed them all. 'As long as your mother didn't say more about your work, so be it. And yes, it seems a sensible idea, but the bottles can't be taken into the workshops. They should be drunk here, and why not in the canteen on your break? In fact, I think the canteen should provide water for every shift.'

There was a loud rat-a-tat at the door. Mr Swinton called, 'All clear?'

'All clear,' called Miss Ellington.

Mr Swinton entered and saw Miss Ellington still holding up a bottle while Mrs Raydon now held the other. He reddened. 'Whose are those, may I ask? How did they get through the gates?'

'They're mine, Mr Swinton,' Fran sighed, knowing the fuss there was going to be.

Mr Swinton thrust his fists into his pockets. 'These were going into the pellet shop, which is where you will be working today? Glass, when broken, is a weapon. And anyway, what do these bottles really contain?'

Miss Ellington raised her eyebrows and Mrs Raydon said, 'Water, to flush the system before, during and after the shift, as an antidote to the chemicals flying about the place. Or in other words, nasty things.' Her tone seemed to indicate that she was looking at one of those this very minute.

Mr Swinton spun round, thrusting his chin out towards Miss Ellington. 'You have, I presume, tested said water, since you are head of this security team?'

It was Miss Ellington's turn to redden. Fran spoke up before the security officer could open her mouth. 'She was about to, because no one can be trusted – we know that. That's why she's holding one.'

Sarah folded her arms. 'Aye, that's right, Mr Swinton. Security is security, you've gone on about it enough.'

Beth nodded. 'But she gave us a talking-to first, to save you the bother.'

Mrs Oborne nodded too. 'Fair stung the air, she did. Made the light bulb flicker, she did.'

Everyone was grinning, including Amelia, as Miss Ellington removed the stopper. 'I'll try it now.' She did so, and Miss Raydon sipped the other. 'Water,' they both agreed.

Fran hoped against hope that Mr Swinton wouldn't put his thin, dry lips round the top of the bottles and test them too. But he did. She thought that beneath the yellow, she must be blanching.

'Had this gone into any of the workshops, it would have been a case for dismissal.' Mr Swinton spun on his heel and left, slamming the door behind him. The other security officers left on his heels, all except for Mrs Raydon and Miss Ellington.

Miss Ellington poured a little of the water onto a clean cloth she drew from her pocket. She wiped the tops, handing one of the bottles to Fran. 'Don't picture what's just happened; drink up and "think of England".'

The women laughed, while Sylv called, 'If she drinks the whole lot, she'll need to wee all shift.'

Miss Ellington nodded. 'Half the bottle only, then, Fran. I'll take the other to the canteen for your break, and see if we can't lay on water for everyone. Then you can finish this on the bus home. File out now, and Mrs Raydon will let you know where you're to go.'

Fran gulped it down as Mrs Raydon checked them off on her list. Finally, with half the bottle left, Miss Ellington took it from her and repeated, 'Such a sensible idea from your mam. You're on stemming again. If you need to wee, tell Mr Swinton and he'll send someone with you because, as you know, you're not allowed to wander about on your own. And do think of getting your hair cut.'

Fran thought of the Sledgeford dance on Saturday and

had no intention of doing any such thing, so said nothing, just as they all said nothing. Like the others, Amelia patted her hair before ramming on her turban, and watching her, Fran thought how strange it must be for her, the only southerner, the only posh girl. No wonder she got it wrong sometimes, and she made herself a promise that she would try to be kinder to the girl.

Stan clumped along the back alleys towards the pithead with Sid and Norm and the rest of the pitmen bound for the shift. He could hear Davey crooning above the sound of the hooter as the lad slung his arm over Stan's shoulders.

'Ah well, our bonny Stan, got sick of sorting someone else's coal hoyed up from the murky depths, did yer? Going to hew yer own, eh? We'll be keeping you out of mischief, never fear.'

Sid and Norm jostled them, shaking their heads. 'Nay, we'll not be doing that – he's a clever beggar, he can look after himself.' The four of them laughed as Davey tightened his arm around Stan's neck until he gagged, then released him.

'You're a bugger, our Davey,' coughed Stan, trying not to laugh.

'Aye, and yer love me for it,' Davey grinned. All four walked abreast, their bait tins hanging from their belts. Ahead of them their fathers walked together, ignoring their respective offspring. The winding gear was singing in the breeze, the slag heap smouldered brightly in the wind and Stan felt his heart lift. No more screens, just the job he knew like the back of his hand, working alongside his marrers, even if his muscles would have to relearn it all.

Davey muttered as they drew nearer the pithead yard. 'I doubt the whelp'll be arriving in his roadster today. He must know the pit'll be a sight more mucky than the screens, and that bloody silly towel all over the seat won't be worth a damn.'

Norm, looking behind, then in front, muttered, 'Can't see his da letting him have the Rolls.'

Sid held up his hand as though listening to someone. 'A little bird says it's the gardener's bike he has a loan of.'

They were still laughing and chatting when they reached the yard, passing the gate man, and there was Ralph, with a bike, a red face and a big frown.

'Howay, should have had a bet on it,' Sid said. 'How do we know if it's the gardener's? Still time though – a bob on it, someone?'

Stan kept his face rigid. A bike? He must not laugh. He waved. 'Ready for the fray, Ralph?'

'Pedalled all the way, lad?' asked Davey. 'By, and into the wind an' all.'

Ralph merely looked at him through hooded eyes.

'Bet your arse knows all about it?' said Norm.

Stan pointed to an open-sided shed where there were already a load of bikes propped against each other. 'They go there.'

Ralph stared at the ragtag and bobtail of bikes, even one without a saddle. 'I'll prop mine against the manager's office wall.'

After looking at Stan, who shrugged, then nodded, Davey walked over to Ralph and and stood in front gripping his handlebars, saying quietly, 'You won't. You'll put it with the others because you're trying to be one of the lads. If you want their help, you have to make a bliddy effort.'

Sid arrived beside Davey and said, 'And trust us, lad, you'll not half need their help, and ours.'

Stan watched the struggle on Ralph's face and for a moment he thought the lad would throw his bike on the ground in a paddy and stalk off and away home. The thing was, half of him wanted him to do it, but the other half wanted Ralph to succeed. Volunteering for the mine was crazy, but brave, and the lad'd soon stop this Fran nonsense. He must, or Stan would take Fran aside and insist that she let him interfere. Up to now, she'd been too bliddy stubborn, saying it would cause more trouble in the long run.

He heard Davey say, as the miners clumped past, caps pulled down and sideways, glances thrown, 'You're doing a good thing here, lad. Carry it through, proper like, eh, and it'll serve your name well.'

'Get your mucky hands off my bike, Davey ruddy Bedley, and don't lecture me. You've no right, and don't forget that, ever.'

Ralph shoved his bike straight at Davey and Sid, both of whom leapt aside, cursing. Stan moved to block Ralph's way, standing with his legs either side of the front wheel, thrusting his face just a couple of inches from Ralph's, smelling his cologne. Dear God, did the whelp never learn?

'Look, lad, we've tried this nicely, and now we'll try it t'other way. That's of course if you want any respect from the men, and if you don't want your da hearing what you just said, you jumped-up little arse. Now get that bliddy bike into the shed, shut your gob and follow us quick sharp. And for God's sake, don't wear cologne into a bleedin' pit.'

Stan brushed past Davey, Norm and Sid, who followed silently, heading towards the cages which were droning up and down taking clean men into the pit, and bringing out others who were weary, and black with coal dust. Stan checked for Ralph, but he was just standing by his bike, looking lost. Stan swung around and roared back, standing nose to nose with Ralph again. 'Your bliddy bad manners won't get you anywhere down there, yer stupid beggar. The blacklocks don't have ears, and the rats don't listen. They'll be up yer leg, quick as a wink after yer willy when yer doing a Jimmy Riddle, less'n we guide yer. Follow us now, this minute. This is your last chance, for I'm past putting up with your nonsense.'

Davey and the others had kept on walking, and still the fore shift pitmen clomped past, giving sideways glances, knowing something was afoot with the whelp. Stan stepped back, then, as the hooter sounded a warning for the start of the shift, Tom the overman called, 'Hall, get over here.'

Stan hurried over to the office, and Tom reminded him it was his job to keep the whelp out of mischief, above and below ground, so what was the beggar doing fannying about with his bike?

'What do you think I'm trying to do, Tom?' Stan shouted. 'Though I'd rather let him make a bloody fool of himself, because that's all he deserves. I'm heading for the cage, it might give him a scare and he just might get a bliddy move on.'

He stormed on, catching up with Davey. 'If we leave him, it might make him follow. I'm just fed—I mean, he's getting away with bliddy murder whichever way you look.'

Davey murmured, 'Well, if you include your sister and me in that, Fran thinks it's all summat to do with that bloody football, so if it is, it's partly my fault. I shouldn't have stabbed the bliddy thing. His mam gave it to him.'

They slowed as they approached the cages, and looked at the marrers and realised they'd heard and were shaking their heads, because they'd all been there. Stan thought of the silence as the shredded paper had fluttered down the back lane and the triumph on the whelp's face, even though he knew it was Davey's Granpa Percy's gift, made while he was coughing up his lungs, and dying.

He remembered how they had all stood alongside Davey, their arms crossed, feeling justice had been done with the piercing of Ralph's ball. As they waited for him to sling his hook, Fran had yelled at the whelp that he was a feeble minded spiteful boy who needed his arse whacked. Only then had he run off.

In a way though, Davey was right, stabbing Ralph's mam's ball was bad, but Mr Massingham had had it repaired, while all the Massingham bairns could do with theirs was to sweep it up, and burn it. Stan sighed, and said, 'I'll have to go and sort him out if he doesn't come.' The pit was the lad's chance for them all to build bridges, they were adults after all.

Ralph pushed the bike to the shed and shoved it hard against the others. What did it matter if it got scratched, it was only the chauffeur's. What's more, it'd teach the cocky young beggar to laugh as his master had wobbled off. What was the matter with these people, didn't they know which side their bread was buttered? He walked along with the other men to the lamp shed, where he knew Stan would have waited, as instructed by the overman, because the Massinghams owned all of them, every damned one.

Stan loitered while his marrers collected their lamps and two tokens each from the cabin. Davey joined him, muttering 'I'll wait with yer, lad.'

Stan nodded. 'No, Davey, you get on. He'll be along because imagine him telling his da he's walked off. Besides, he'll know he couldn't come into the villages anymore.'

Davey whooped with laughter. 'Well, that'd mean he couldn't wait at the bus shelter. Besides, even as a bairn he only ever visited to throw his weight around, and – wait one . . . Maybe that's why he's pestering the life out of Fran and me, just throwing his weight around in a different way?'

Both stood quietly, thinking, until Norm and Sid looked

around, raising their eyebrows. 'He's still not here then? D'you reckon we should go and find him?'

Stan shrugged, and they waited as other pitmen passed them. 'Nice to 'ave yer back in t'pit, lad,' one said, jerking his head. They realised why when they heard Ralph say from behind them, 'So, everyone collects a lamp, do they, and tokens? I can't remember what the trainer said. And sorry, chaps. Bad manners do not maketh the man.'

Stan exchanged a glance with Davey, who gave the slightest of shrugs. Norm said, 'Aye, man, that's reet. Two tokens it is, same as the other hewers, and them fillers who put our coal into the tubs, and the putters who shove 'em to the roadway for the ponies to take on to the cage.'

As the others went on, Stan and Ralph took a lamp, hung one of their tokens on a hook, and kept one for themselves, to hand in at the end of their shift. If they didn't they'd have the whole bloody shift looking for them, and as they waited for the cage, Stan explained how the system had saved him and Davey when the roof came down on them when they were working on a stubborn part of the face.

As the men moved forward to get in the cage he saw Sid, Davey and Norm had waited to one side for them. The banksman called out, 'Get a bliddy wriggle on, Stanhope Hall, anyone'd think yer don't want to get to work.'

All five of them squashed in with the others and Stan gripped Ralph's arm. 'Yer'll feel as if yer bread and dripping's in yer throat. Don't let it out.'

Around them men laughed, and Davey muttered, 'If yer do, spout it over our Stan, eh?'

The banksman hooked the chain over and said to Ralph, 'Yer listen to yer marrers today, sir. Can't have yer taken back to yer da with a broken fingernail, can we?'

Ralph's smile was weak, but his shoulders straightened. So, 'sir' was what they should call him? Stan thought, but that wasn't going to happen. Ralph was to be a hewer, it's what he said he wanted, and hewers weren't 'sir', not ever.

'Off yer go then, ta ta, lads.' The gate man pulled the chain across and they all fell silent. No one spoke, though the clamour of those waiting for the next cage continued, and then whoosh, down they went, taking the air out of Stan's lungs. Ralph leaned against him. Stan gripped his arm, hoping he wasn't going to faint.

'It's ruddy broken,' Ralph panted. 'We're falling.'

'Nay, lad, it'll slow soon enough.' Stan stayed still. He was home. He could smell the coal, the muck, he could hear the whispers around him, see Davey and Sid hard at it, quarrelling about who owed who a pint, and Norm counting in his head because he hated the bliddy cage, he said, whenever he got the opportunity.

The cage slowed, then slammed to a stop. Stan had bent his knees, but had forgotten to tell Ralph, who almost fell. 'Sorry, lad,' Stan muttered. 'Should have said. Had forgotten meself but me legs did it on their own.'

Edgar said from the back, 'Comes of swanning off to t'south. Makes yer soft, lad.'

Stan gestured.

'I'll tell yer da what yer just did with your finger, so I will,' said Edgar. 'And he'll skelp yer backside.'

'I'll hold our Stan while he does it, an' all,' Norm called.

'I used to stick newspaper in my pants when my teacher whacked me,' Ralph called.

As they left the cage and set off down the roadway which was lit by lamps screwed into the walls, someone called back, 'Bet it were *The Times* an' all. Thick as a plank, they say.' Stan and Davey winced. Would Ralph see the insult for what it was?

Ralph called back, 'Probably. Such good quality paper, don't you know.'

The men laughed and Ralph looked confused. They walked on, the wall lamps flickering along the wide roadway. Ralph walked alongside Stan with the marrers behind, though the other pitmen spread out, unwilling to be with the boss's son. They passed an overman working in his office.

'I thought you said we'd have to crouch?' Ralph said.

'Just wait, and save your energy, this is the best bit.' Stan coughed. 'And don't scuff the dust, for pity's sake. Lift your feet, and tread careful, man, or we'll all be eating coal dust, and don't trip on the rails, eh.'

On and on they walked, the ceiling lowering, the half mile of roadway lights long gone, relying on their own lamps now. Stan could hear the creaking in between the coughing, hawking and chatting of the men. Yes, he could hear it, and imagined the great weight of coal across the roof planks and behind the pit props, squeezing and squeezing, desperate to fill up this empty seam. He looked ahead to Davey, limping just as he himself was. Almost twins they were, marrers to the core, and howay, they'd even been hurt together. Always together. Stan bent lower, pushing Ralph down, calling, 'Ye'll have to bend yer knees, man. If yer too hot, take off yer jacket, but if yer do and yer leave it here by the side, the blacklocks'll take it over, or the rats, or maybe Mr Mouse and his tribe, so give it a reet good shake when yer pick it up.'

'Dear God,' Ralph panted.

On they went, Davey beckoning to Ralph to follow as he turned left down Menin Seam, which was even tighter. Norm and Sid followed, while Stan brought up the rear. They trod between rails along which the putter who shoved the tubs would come. That would be Ralph today. To give him his due, Ralph made no sound, just hunched down, plodding along, barely lifting his feet, but he'd learn,

179

because it might not be Stan behind him another time and he'd get a roasting.

They finally arrived at the face and Davey, who was already streaming with sweat, tore off his clothes, throwing them in a bundle to the ground, leaving him wearing just his drawers and boots. Ralph hesitated, then did as they were all doing. Work started immediately, the marrers heaving and thrusting picks into the cracks the blasters had loosened overnight.

Ralph said, 'Rather than push the tub, I'd prefer to work on the face.' Stan sighed but handed the lad his pick, showing him the ropes. Ralph stabbed at the coal, his gleaming white underwear already blackening from the dust. After about twenty minutes, he threw the pick down, gasping, 'I reckon you need someone to fill the tub, eh?'

Stan nodded gravely. 'We do indeed.' Ralph handed him back the pick, and started shovelling the coal into the tub, then shoving it back along the rails to the main seam where it would be hitched to the pony's 'train', as Stan had explained it.

Hour after hour they worked, and Stan remembered how they didn't even need a Jimmy Riddle because they were so dehydrated. At about eleven, the four hewers took a break, leaning back against the pit props. Stan faced Sid and Norm as he and Davey ate a jam and coal dust sandwich. Ralph arrived back with an empty tub brought by another pony 'train'. He joined them, carefully unwrapping his pâté sandwiches. 'God, I'm hungry,' he almost moaned, looking for somewhere to wipe his hands.

'Wipe 'em down yer legs, lad, or on yer trousers yer left in the heap ower yonder,' Sid said, nodding towards the small pile of clothes. Ralph stared at the clothes, then at his black-dusted legs, and just stuffed the sandwiches in his mouth, barely chewing before he swallowed.

'Make 'em last, bonny lad. One's enough. You'll get a bellyache because you'll be straight back to work,' Davey warned.

Stan saw the look on Ralph's face and cut across anything he might say to Davey. 'Bet yer right glad you were on the screens and toughened your hands.'

Ralph just looked at his sandwiches, and seemed to reach a decision. He folded half the second sandwich in the greaseproof paper, and replaced it in the tin. He slurped his cold tea and said, 'Quite frankly, I'd prefer to face a ruddy Nazi charge than sit my arse on jagged coal, trying not to hear the ruddy rats, mice and those infernal monstrous black cockroaches or whatever the hell they are.' He shuddered.

The other four laughed. 'Aye, that's just about a pitman's prayer, I reckon, but back to work,' said Stan.

They stood and Stan felt the waft of air from a ventilator door. He could hear the scrabbling of the mice, and somewhere the squealing of fighting rats. He collected his pick, then held it out to Ralph. 'Want an hour?'

Ralph shook his head. 'Let me get the hang of the tubs, eh? Tomorrow's time enough for the pick.'

Bringing down a wedge of coal, Davey muttered, 'Aye, lad, in your own time. You've done well today.'

When the bus arrived back at the shelter that evening, it was only Davey waiting for Fran. He watched his sister and the woman he loved step down from the bus, relief in their every movement.

'He's not here?' Fran almost whispered, leaning into him.

'I fancy he reckons he's paid me back over the bloody footie, if that's what it's all been about. That's what he said, weren't it, all them years ago? That he'd take everything from me, or somesuch. Well, mebbe the pit's making him grow up,' Davey said as he held her close, worried more by her thinness than by the whelp. She seemed better in herself, though, didn't she?

'Well, I damned well hope so,' Fran said. 'It's a long time to hold a grudge, and a long time to behave like a spoilt brat.'

'He's an idiot,' Sarah muttered. 'I'm off. I want to get to me bed. Davey, don't delay our Fran, she's fair done in. We all are.'

As Sarah walked off, Fran heard Stan's voice calling from the direction of the club, 'Hang on, Sarah. I'll walk you back. I've been helping me da with the sickness divvy.'

Fran smiled. For ages Stan had been too busy to spend time with any of them, but here he was. Would Sarah realise how much she liked Stan, not just as a friend but something more, or was Fran quite wrong? It would be so much better if Beth had heard from Bob, then everyone would settle down, so where the hell was he? She shook her head free of questions because there were no answers and it only made her more tired. Davey walked her back and left her in the yard.

'Go to bed, pet. You and Sarah look real tired.'

The back door opened, and Fran saw her mam framed by the doorway. 'Hey, Mam, you'll have Mrs Clarke calling you out for showing a light, and you an ARP warden an' all.'

'Hush your noise, Fran Hall. I'll do your itch and then you get to bed. How did you get on with the bottle of water? Away in, and let's hear all about it. And the whelp? Any sign? You've done as you was told, Davey, and given her a word about not being out late after the Saturday dance coming up, have yer?'

Fran kissed Davey, staying against his mouth so he didn't have to confess that he hadn't.

He kissed her hard, then held her close. 'You mean the world to me, bonny lass, and I should have said more about the dance. Now in you get.'

As Davey left, Stan came in the back gate, but instead of coming into the house, they stood out in the lane, smoking and talking, and Fran heard Davey say, 'I reckon that the pit's done the trick and Ralph's got over whatever it was.'

Chapter Twelve

Sledgeford Village Hall showed no lights the following Saturday evening as Fran and Sarah pedalled towards it. Even with the wind behind them, they were grateful to finally dismount and lean their bikes against the wooden building. No lights perhaps, but there were the sounds of a piano and a saxophone warming up. Fran grinned across at Sarah by the light of the half-moon. 'Got your dancing shoes, lass?'

Sarah laughed. 'Chance would be a fine thing. Bare legs, gravy browning, a pencil line down the back, and me old court shoes. What's more, I bet I can outdance you, bonny lass.'

Fran held out her hand. Sarah slapped it, asking, 'How much?'

'Tuppence.'

'Howay with you. Threepence at least.'

Fran spat on her hand, and held it out again.

Sarah shook her head. 'Urgh, tuppence it is, then, skinflint.'

Laughing, they entered, dodging through the dark lobby into the muted light of the hall. Beth called them over, her green-tinged auburn hair glinting and falling in large curls, her pale blue eyes almost dancing. She wore a red and green pleated skirt. Fran pointed from her hair to her skirt. 'By, a right good match, pet.'

Beth grinned. 'Aye, maybe, but it's our Bob's favourite for the dancing and it swings just right, and makes me almost remember his—' She stopped. 'Come on, we need to set out the tables.'

The small round tables were stacked in a room to the right of the stage and Valerie's mother, Mrs Hatfield, wanted one put out under the hatch into the kitchen, which was where the Women's Institute made jam for the war effort, using the extra rations of sugar they were awarded by the government.

'Right, lasses,' Mrs Hatfield ordered, signalling to them as though they were cars at a crossroads. 'Now you've set that one up, tek them other tables over yonder, quick as you can. See the time? It waits for no man.' She jerked her head towards the clock on the wall, which was showing six thirty. 'And a word of warning. You girls have to do a Sunday morning shift at the Factory tomorrow, so don't get yourselves too tired, eh?'

The girls lugged the tables out and placed them where she directed, and then sufficient chairs for those who wanted to rest their corns. Valerie and Amelia arrived with stacked cardboard boxes, each containing sandwiches on plates covered in greaseproof paper.

'A smearing of pickle and a sliver of cheese on slices of bread which were showed the butter,' Amelia muttered, 'but sad to say the pickle looked rather dry and old. Mrs Hatfield had a taste last night and it hasn't come back to greet her, so it must be all right. The Sledgeford corner shop donated it from some they made a couple of years ago. I have to say it's not the sort of "do" I'm used to, but it might be fun.' She walked off.

The musicians were resting on the stage on straight-backed chairs, surreptitiously sipping from flasks. Valerie winked at Sarah, Beth and Fran. 'I think we could do with some of that after our Amelia's comments. Tea doesn't touch the spot, does it?'

Fran grinned. 'What is it the men are drinking and where did they get it?'

Beth shrugged. 'Oh, don't ask, but if you go down into the Sledgeford pub cellar you'll remember there were a grand harvest of elderberries in '39. And back then there were still plenty of sugar which leads me da to say whenever anyone mentions Sledgeford: "That wine fair teks the top o' yer 'ead off, lass."'

'How is he?' Sarah and Fran asked together.

Beth just shrugged again. What could you say about black lung when it had got you good and proper? Fran thought of her own da and his black phlegm and knew it was what he and Tom Bedley dreaded above all else. 'A clean death is what I want,' her da had said more than once, adding with a cackle, 'Well, it'd probably be bloody dirty, but quick, eh. And not yet, if yer listening yer lordship.' He'd always look up at the sky then.

By eight the room was ready, the band, fully lubricated and red cheeked, were having a last-minute warm-up, and people had started arriving, including some from the after shift at the Factory, for they had started the shift early, as required, and finished early, as had been arranged. Fran was on the door with the draught whipping at her legs while Sarah and Beth helped Mrs Hatfield in the kitchen before bringing out the cups of tea on trays.

Fran took the money, and even made the vicar pay. He grinned as Fran said, 'Fair's fair, Vicar Walters: half for your plate, half for the war. And who knows, you might win the quickstep competition and get a sixpence back. Then you can let go a few hallelujahs in St Oswald's, or maybe a peal of bells.'

He smiled. 'Ah, Fran, you're forgetting the bells have to wait for victory, but I'll take the hallelujahs.'

Miss Walters, his sister, arrived in a flurry, pushing past

the queue, snatching up the vicar and dragging him onwards. 'He will chat so, Fran. Thinks he's giving a sermon, but he's nifty with his footwork, so I keep him on at the vicarage, so I do. I've joined your mam's rug-making co-op when teaching allows . . .' But then she was gone.

The queue continued, the sixpences kept coming, and when someone couldn't afford it, what did it matter, they were waved in anyway. Fran handed out a ticket to Mrs Oborne and her husband, a blue-scarred miner who could dance a nifty samba and then always grumbled about his back, loudly, which always made them laugh. If he did it tonight, she wondered if Mrs Oborne would tell him to show some gumption?

She was about to call after them when she heard Davey out in the lobby, berating Stan. 'You didna beat me, we got here even-stevens, and so, no, I won't pay yer entry, yer daft skinflint.'

They entered, all the marrers together, jostling their way through the door. Sid and Norm were in the rear, stuffing beer bottles in their pockets. Davey smiled. 'Ah, a pretty wench on the door, eh?'

Stan elbowed him. 'Nay, there are prettier ones on the floor, just waiting for us, bonny lad.'

Fran said, 'Remind me to skelp yer for yer cheek when we get home.' But Stan was staring at Sarah and Beth, who were taking their tea trays from table to table. Which one was he looking at? wondered Fran.

Sid shoved Stan from behind. 'Then pay up, get out me way, and let me at 'em.'

The boys were washed and in their best bib and tucker, their hair shining, though tiredness dragged at their faces. When she looked around, though, Fran realised that everyone was tired. 'But we're all alive,' she murmured aloud.

'Hey, Franny,' called Stan, 'are you just going to talk to yoursel', lass, or will you take our money?'

She held out her hand. They each paid their sixpence and Stan, Sid and Norm went onto the floor, while Davey stood beside her. As always, she felt complete when he was there and she repeated silently, 'Alive, all of us.' She put the money in the tin cashbox, and her hands were less yellow, because they had been moved on to the detonators, but the rash was worse. She grinned to herself: best not to be thinking about hands; they were the bits you were most likely to lose on the detonators.

In a lull, while the band was playing 'It Had to Be You', Davey slipped his arm around her and she leaned into him; he kissed the top of her head. 'Your hair's getting towards its proper colour, bonny lass, and look at Sarah's – not bad at all.'

Fran wanted to say that they'd escaped the yellow for a while, but of course she couldn't. Then another thought caught at her. 'Is Ralph coming, d'you reckon?' she asked, straightening up.

Davey shook his head, pulling her back. 'He said nowt, and we were careful not to an' all. I reckon he's hunkered down at the Hall. Why would he trip the light fantastic amongst the 'common folk' unless his da laid down the law? Unless he's about to start up his haunting of us, that is, and I reckon he's found better things to do with his time. It's been a few days now since the bus shelter's seen him. By, it's like Christmas without him.'

Just then the soldiers from the nearby training camp entered, their khaki spotted with rain, their boots clattering on the hall floor and so polished you could see your face in them, Fran reckoned. They paid, then tossed their berets onto a couple of chairs lined up against the wall to the right of the door and headed for the group of girls chatting by the stage. Soon they were dancing as the band seemed to come alive. Fran left the door and she and Davey waltzed to the music, humming along as they did so. Fran rested her head on Davey's shoulder, and he kissed her hair.

'Oh, bonny, bonny Fran, I don't half love you.'

'Aye, I do you an' all,' she murmured, and on and on they danced, she on feet that ached from standing at the detonator bench, but it didn't matter a jot when she was in his arms.

Sarah was dancing with a lance corporal from the camp. His uniform was prickly but his smile kind. He said, 'I'm from Worcester, and I miss me girl some'at chronic.' Sarah looked up at him just as he trod on her foot. She hoped she hadn't winced too obviously.

'She'll be missing you. I expect she's written?' she said.

'Oh yes, almost daily, but it's not the same.'

Sarah nodded, wishing she had someone who ached for her, as this lad did for his lass, as she did for—No, none of that, though the thought made her look around for Beth, but she couldn't see her amongst the swirling dancers. The music ended, and the soldier left to return to his friends. She swung round, banging into Stan. 'Look where you're going, you daft whatnot,' she laughed, sidestepping him, but he did the same. She went back the other way, and he copied. Finally, as the band began 'A Nightingale Sang in Berkeley Square', she grabbed hold of his arms. 'Right, lad, you stay still and I'll go t'right.'

She went right, but again Stan moved to his left. She laughed up at him. 'Pin back your lugs, lad.'

But he wasn't laughing, he was looking at her, just her. For a moment it was the same as it had been in the beck, deep down in the water, and though people were bumping into them, the room seemed to have faded into quiet. At last he said, 'Dance with me, bonny Sarah.'

She did, and it was a foxtrot, and then a waltz. Neither of them spoke, and slowly Sarah found herself leaning into him. He spoke quietly now, his breath rustling her hair, which she had looped up for the evening. 'You need to cut this hair, Sarah.'

He was touching it, then her cheek, gently. She felt the shock and the warmth as he ran his finger down and onto her neck, and she stared up at him. She struggled to find words, but when she did, they sounded strange – hesitant, reluctant – because all she wanted was to stay in his arms. 'The music's good.' He said nothing, just looked at her. She felt as she had done when he led the gang – safe, happy, complete, but there was love too, an all encompassing love and it was as though she'd waited for this moment all her life . . .

But what about Beth? The thought stopped the rush of feelings. They still danced, but she kept air between them and said, 'I like me hair, so keep yer opinions to yourself, our Stan. You might be leader of the gang, but—'

She couldn't go on because he was tilting her head. She tried to pull away. He whispered, 'You see, I couldn't bear it to catch in the machinery and you to be hurt in any way. I think I've known that all me life, but only just seen that all I really want is right here: you, and me family, but most of all, you.'

She stared up at him, unable to speak. She watched his lips and felt his breath, beer-tinged, on her face as he said, 'Something happened to me at the beck, in the water. I looked at you and knew I loved you properly, deeply. That's all I'm saying. There's no need for you to love me, but there is a need for you to stay safe.'

The music stopped. He dropped his arms and walked away. She walked after him, but before she could reach him, she saw Beth turn to talk to a young soldier and bump into Stan. He reached out to stop her from falling and she looked up at him, laughing. Sarah felt sick. What the hell was Stan playing at with his fine words? Was he really still holding a candle for Beth and just making do with little Sarah Bedley? The music began again, but Stan walked on with Beth towards the hatch, without a backward glance.

But Beth was called back to take someone's cup, and before she could stop herself, Sarah was half running across the floor. She snatched the cup from Beth and half shouted, 'You've got a husband. Stan's just said he loves me. Give us a chance, for God's sake, Beth. Just leave him be.'

Beth stared at her and tried to snatch the cup back, but Sarah hung on to it. Beth struggled to be heard against the music. 'You don't understand, Sarah. I canna remember what Bob looks like, but I've never forgotten what Stan looks, and feels, like. His kisses, his words. He's back, and why d'you think he's back? It's got to be for me, it's got to be.'

They were both almost crying, and although people danced around them, they stayed still, each with a hand on the cup and the anguish in Beth's voice was reflected in her pale blue eyes. Sarah recoiled, shocked, half wanting to hold the girl, half wanting to slap her.

It was then that the hall door opened. Behind Beth, Sarah saw a sailor in his naval uniform walk in on crutches. His white rollneck sweater was smudged with grime and he stood there watching the dancers before he was lost from view.

Amelia passed, carrying a cup of tea and one of Mrs Hatfield's biscuits. 'Hey, best get off the dance floor, you two, you'll get jostled. I'm sitting this one out. These squaddies aren't quite the thing, are they? Shame there are no officers.' She jerked her head towards the door. 'Someone should get the matelot to pay. We've no time for gatecrashers.'

Feeling as though she'd been whacked back into the real world, Sarah let go of the cup. Matelot? Oh, the sailor. But a gatecrasher? She shouted after Amelia, 'Every serviceman is entitled to come in here, and a matelot is as good as an officer any day. They're all fighting for you and me and everyone here.' She turned to Beth who was stalking off, heading for the kitchen.

Amelia had hesitated, and now came back. 'I'm sorry. I had a sip from the saxophonist's flask, it's made me silly.'

She walked on, Sarah looking after her. She knew that Amelia didn't think of herself as a factory girl but for goodness' sake . . . If she ever did get into the office, what a treat the others had in store. The music was getting louder, and Sarah threaded her way through the dancers, heading for the sailor to see if he wanted a cup of tea.

She was almost there when she saw Fran approaching from the stage area, Davey in her wake. But before any of them could reach the sailor, Stan materialised from the centre of the room and tossed the servicemen's caps off the nearest chair onto a vacant one. He gripped the matelot's arm and guided him towards it.

Sarah arrived. 'What . . . ?'

The lad lifted his head, 'Ta, Stan. Could do with a sit-down, man.'

It was Bob Jones, Beth's husband. But he was drawn, tired, old. Stan rested the crutches against the wall. 'First things first, lad.'

He turned to Sarah and his voice grew softer. 'Bonny lass, find Beth, eh? But wait one—' It was love she heard in his voice, and saw in his eyes, and it held Sarah breathless. But was it really for her?

Then Stan asked Bob, 'Beer, Beth or tea?' and the two men smiled at one another.

'Aye, a beer'd be grand,' Bob nodded. 'But Beth first, lad, and I'm right sorry about all that . . .'

Before she left to find Beth, Sarah saw Stan shaking Bob's hand, and heard him say, 'By, lad, all in the past. I'm sorted at last, if our Sarah'll have me.'

The music had stopped and the dancers made their way to the tables. Sarah's legs felt weak as she headed towards the stage, where Beth was talking to the vicar. 'Beth, our Beth,' she called. 'You have a canny visitor.'

Her shout caused people to turn at the same time Beth did, and they all followed Sarah's waving arm. Then Beth let out a cry and ran full pelt across the length of the hall to Bob, falling to her knees and holding him. He laid his head on hers and Stan rose, patting Bob on the shoulder before heading across the hall, straight to Sarah. He took her in his arms in front of everyone, then stepped back, grabbed her hand and led her outside.

Once out in the cool darkness, with only the smouldering slag heaps giving light as clouds covered the moon, they stood together.

'This isn't a game, is it, our Stan?' she asked.

He edged closer, holding both her hands now. 'I'm not playing at anything. I'm right serious, Sarah. I don't know how I didn't see you properly before, but now . . . I could an' all after the beck, but I didn't know what to do. All I know is I can't sleep, eat or any damn thing, and I've kept me distance, because though I said I don't need you to love me back and just want for you to be safe, I bliddy do. I need you.' He looked furious with himself and dragged his hand through his hair. 'No, not just need, but love you. No, not that. What I'm trying to say is, I bliddy need your love.'

She could only see the outline of his face in the gloom, and she smiled. Their gang leader could be as confused by love as her, and was as desperate as she realised she had been since he'd arrived home. She pulled her hands free of his grip and now that her eyes had become accustomed to the lack of light, she saw the shadow of pain pass cross his face as he nodded to himself and muttered, 'Still friends, though?'

She shook her head and he swallowed, stepped back, his shoulders braced, nodding. She followed though, reaching up and holding his face, love making her braver than she'd ever been. Standing on tiptoes, she kissed his mouth and said against his lips, 'More than friends. I love you too, so much. I didn't rightly know . . . I just knew you made me feel safe, but like you, all the time it were love.'

In the hall, Davey brought across a tray with a few teacups full to the brim with the beer the marrers had donated for the lad, trying not to spill it, or give the game away to the ladies in the kitchen. Beth thanked him as Bob sipped, his hand trembling, so she took hold of the cup and held it for him. He drained it and she replaced it on the tray and reached for another. 'Nay, lass,' Bob said, 'that be enough.'

She sat next to him as the band began again and the dancers whirled, though not Fran and Davey. Instead, they sat nearby, should they be needed. Just as her friends always did, as she had only lately come to realise; even Sarah, just now who, though she had been so fearful and hurt, had wanted to reach out to her when she, Beth Jones, had wailed like a bairn in her misery. As Beth took her hold of her husband's hand, she felt ashamed of her own fickleness, her weakness, and her thoughtlessness.

Beth and Bob sat shoulder to shoulder, her hand held in his, and she could feel him still trembling. He leaned back against the wall as the dancers whirled and the band played louder. Fran gave Beth a look as the band called for her and the girls to sing with them. Beth shook her head, but Bob wasn't sleeping and he murmured, 'Please, I want to hear you.' Beth said, 'No, I want to stay by your side.'

Bob smiled, raised her hand to his mouth. 'Go,' he said. 'Let me hear you sing again.'

Only then would she leave him to join Fran, though Davey remained on guard.

Fran started to sing, 'I've Got You Under My Skin' and Beth joined in, and from the look Davey gave Fran, he knew it was for him.

Beth looked over at Bob, who was still leaning back. He had dark circles under his eyes, and his cheeks were hollow. His right foot started to tap as they sang and he picked up on the lyrics as Beth made up her own words: '. . . each time that I do just the thought of Bob . . .'

Bob sang then, in his powerful tenor: 'Beautiful, and yellow, my Beth . . . I love you, darling lass.'

She was too moved to sing, so Fran continued while Beth smiled at her Bob, for he was hers, and she wanted to be with him, holding him. How could she ever have forgotten his hazel eyes, his kind mouth, his strong body, his kindness. She left the stage to Fran then, unable to be away from him for a moment longer, all thoughts of Stan or any such nonsense quite gone. She sat with him, holding his hand, leaning against his shoulder. 'What happened to you, bonny lad?'

'Ah, what happened was me job, that's all. In a place you canna know, doing things yer don't want to know. Then I got a bath in freezing water when one of the mines we was sweeping for bit back and aimed a damned great splinter of shrapnel into me leg. Gave me a knock on me bonce into t'bargain. I have sick leave for a week, lass, and made it this far, but I'm not sure I can manage to make it to the house.' He groaned as he leaned forward. 'I need to get to me bed, with you, in our house, and then when I get back on duty I want to think of you with your mam in Massingham, with yer friends.'

Beth looked around. Friends? Had she ruined all this? Stan and Sarah had returned and his arm was tight around her. Sarah had the sort of smile that twisted Beth's heart because it was so young, so unsullied, so pure, but she shook her head at herself. Her man was back, alive, and that's all that mattered.

She beckoned towards Stan. They both came – she'd have to become used to that – and she explained that Bob needed help to get to the house. Stan whistled, cutting the music dead. 'A couple of strong blokes needed,' he shouted. 'The lad's gone about as far as he can. He's only a sailor, not a pongo or a pitman.'

The hall was filled with laughter. All the men started towards them and Stan picked a couple of the soldiers, which made Bob grunt, 'A couple of pongo lads giving me a lift – I'll bloody never live it down.'

The youngest of the soldiers muttered, as he dragged Bob to his feet, 'It's always the pongos who get you lot out of trouble, mate.'

His mate took the other side and they set off into the darkness, followed by Stan with the kitbag and Davey carrying the crutches. The marrers carried the remaining teacups still with the beer, while the girls walked behind, each with a plate of pickle sandwiches. They all watched as Stan talked quietly to Bob until the soldiers edged him through the front door and helped him gently into the house. 'Thanks, lads,' Bob muttered. 'I owe you a pint.'

'That you do,' said the boy from Worcester. 'We'll collect it, don't you worry. And any time you sailor boys need us to save your arse, just whistle, eh?'

They left and the girls watched while the pitmen helped

Bob up the stairs. Fran slipped her arms around her friends. 'Are you both all right?'

The two girls looked at one another. Beth reached out a hand to Sarah.

'I'm sorry.'

'Aye, me an' all.'

Fran looked confused, but the other two merely smiled at one another, and Sarah said, 'Aye, Fran, we're all right.'

The next day they were bleary-eyed, but all ready for the bus at four in the morning, though the grumbles were loud. Once there, Amelia was directed to the office, rushing back into the changing room once the girls had stripped, been searched and were dressed again in their clothes, overalls and turbans.

'I say, I've been asked to move to Administration, forthwith. Someone is leaving soon, so I am to shadow them for the next three weeks and take over properly then. Daddy and Mummy will be so pleased. I expect the powers that be felt it more my thing.'

Mrs Oborne said, in that voice of hers which said more than her words, 'Quite likely they did. Well, I reckon we just need to say good luck.'

Amelia was already edging to the door, where the accompanying security officer was waiting to escort her to her new workplace. Amelia smiled. 'So nice to get to know you all. I've learned a lot about how the common – well, what a factory girl is.'

Fran almost gasped, but stopped herself. Not Valerie, though, who said, 'Can you still bear to live in a factory girl's house, Amelia?'

But she had gone, the door slamming in her wake. There were murmurings, but not many since people were glad to be rid of her. It was then that Beth spoke to Miss Ellington about whether she could take leave for a week while Bob was here? Miss Ellington got back to her at the end of the shift. She had arranged for Amelia's transfer to be postponed in order to keep the numbers up while Beth had the week off. While they were waiting to clamber onto the bus, Amelia stormed up to them.

'That takes the damned biscuit. Your bloke comes home with a bit of a bad leg, so you get leave and I have to fiddle about with bloody detonators or the yellow again. Honestly, it's not fair because they'll offer the position to someone else, I just know they will.'

Mrs Oborne came up behind her. 'Steady the buffs, lass. I've just been checking and they're going to try to keep the office job for you, and if it were your man you'd want to be with him, eh? Best not to make a bliddy fool of yourself. People don't forget spite.'

Amelia's mouth twisted, and she clambered on board, sitting down on her seat with a thump. She flashed a glare at the three girls as they filed past.

Fran said, 'We're sorry, but things are what they are.'

They found seats and Sarah hoped that Stan would be with Davey at the bus shelter, while Fran hoped that Ralph wouldn't be. Beth hoped that Bob was a little better, and was glad her mam had come over to care for him, bringing her rug to work on too. She'd said that if there was any nonsense, he'd be progged through the hessian. Bob, holding up his hands as he lay back on the pillow, had surrendered.

As they travelled, they scratched their itching skin and checked their arms against one another, for they had been switched into stemming, probably just for the day. Soon, they'd been promised, they would be transferred to the sewing sector, but there was a war on and supplies were needed, Mr Swinton had said, looking supremely happy at their discomfort.

Chapter Thirteen

Beth hurried from the bus to her home in Sledgeford, hoping to be back by four to see her mam, only to find she had left tea ready, and a note to say she'd been offered a drive back in the postman's van a bit earlier and had grabbed it because Da needed her. Beth and Bob ate her mam's hotpot of gravy and vegetables, and had a cuppa, while she told him she had leave, though Amelia wasn't best pleased. But she'd try and do her a favour in return, one day. Bob eased himself to his feet, saying, 'Best news I've heard in a long, long time. Days for you and me to just be together. But first things first, let's collect your bike from the hall, lass.'

He led the way, swinging himself on his crutches as she dragged her mac back on and followed, shutting the door behind them. They saw their way by the light of the moon and although progress was slow, they reached the hall, then Beth pushed her bike past the blacked-out cottages while Bob smiled as he listened to the owls, a cock pheasant, and in the distance the colliery train. He said, 'Strange to be landlocked again, but good to get away from the wind and the waves.'

She said, 'I can't imagine being lurched about day after day.'

'Aye, well, you get used to anything, so they say.' He stopped and drew breath. 'By, I bliddy hope me armpits get used to these beggars.' They laughed together, and then set off again while he said, 'But listen, hinny, yer mam and me've been talking, and it's time you went home to Massingham. I know she's asked before, and I know I've said it's what I want for you, but it really is time, Beth. What is there to stop you, eh, when she needs support?'

She stroked his back because she knew she really did love him, and what was more, Stan had Sarah and really didn't want her, so . . . She drew in a deep breath, so Stan wouldn't be sneaking over to see her, as she had hoped – once hoped, yes, that was better. As they walked along, Bob talked of the salt-heavy sea air, the tumbling clouds and waves higher than the houses they were passing. Another owl hooted. She turned to Bob, just as he stumbled. She reached out, but the bike caught her, and his crutches were in the way, and she didn't know how to help.

'What should I do when this happens?' she asked. 'Choose you or the bike?'

He looked at her, roared with laughter, steadied himself and swung himself forward. 'Just be by my side, Beth. That's all I want, now and for ever.'

She replied quietly, 'Then that's where I will be.'

They walked slowly home, and she opened the front door of their terraced house, owned by Mr Massingham's tenant farmer. He nodded. 'You'll give in your notice to Farmer Martin then?'

'Oh, aye, I'll be doing that, never fear.'

Bob laughed. 'With your mam on the case I reckon that's a given.' He eased himself through the doorway and stared at the stairs. 'I reckon I can get up there on me bum, and won't need the lads to help this time.'

She flicked on the light and he hopped and swung his way to the foot of the stairs, staring upwards, then turned and sat with a thump on the third step. She rushed forward, her hands out. He pulled her on to him, leaning back, his crutches falling to the side. He held her close, and it was as though they fitted. This is what she had missed. But did they fit as well as she and Stan had? She closed her eyes and kissed him fiercely, wanting her mind to stop, needing it to give her some peace.

He said, holding her as fiercely as she had kissed him, 'By, lass, it's a lifesaver to be here, even for a few days.'

'Aye, it is, sweet Bob.' For it had to be for her too.

They clung together for a minute longer, and then he pushed free of her. 'You wait here, pet. I don't want to slither down and take you out like a skittle. Fat lot of good we'll be to one another if we both break a leg.'

Once on the landing, he called down: 'I'll be getting meself into bed, but a cuppa would be right good, our Beth. But I'll need me crutches up here. Would yer mind?'

She gathered them up and delivered them to him with a kiss, then hurried down and into the kitchen to test the kettle, which she'd left on the range after their tea. It was hot, but not boiling. She threw her mackintosh onto the back of her chair and shoved wood and fresh coal into the firebox, watching it roar into flames, shutting the door, opening the vent, hearing the draught whip the coals into a frenzy, and it echoed her heart. She reached up for their wedding photograph, perched on the mantelpiece.

Since this was taken he'd become thin and drawn, but so had she. She pressed the photo to her heart, feeling for the armchair and sinking into it as her legs gave way. Sarah with Stan, it would take a bit of getting used to; but Bob was back and it would give her time to get her head sorted and she'd go home where she was needed to help with her da. That would stop the loneliness, which must have led to the mischief of her heart, and—The kettle was whistling.

She made tea and paced as she waited for it to mash, picking up the wedding picture again, and now, as she traced the pair of them with her finger, she remembered how it was that day ... Bob's family at the church, hers,

201

some Massingham families, and just before the doors closed, when she and Bob were standing before Vicar Walters, the gang had entered, all of them, including Stan, and afterwards they'd thrown confetti. They had kissed her, and wished her well, and Stan had done that too, but had not quite met her eyes. He had shaken Bob's hand, but not quite met his eyes either.

She replaced the photo and poured the tea, putting her ration of sugar in her husband's. She had her man again, and the gang were there for her, the girls either side of her as they travelled on the bus and worked at whatever bench they were designated by that beggar Swinton, who chose them for transfer, every time. So the war had taken her man, but brought the girls together again, so how dare she be lonely? How could she have even thought of causing mischief again? She reached up to the mantelpiece and touched the image of Bob.

'I canna wait much longer, lass,' he called.

She picked up the two cups of tea and called back, 'On my way.' And she was – on her way to being who she should be.

She heard a dot dot dot from Bob's crutch, followed by a scrape scrape, then another dot dot dot, and hurried to the bottom of the stairs and called up, 'SOS yourself, bonny lad, I said any minute now.' His laugh reached her.

She carried the two cups upstairs. There he was, sitting up in their bed, his bare chest bruised and cut, adding to his blue pitman scars.

He had thrown the blanket off his broken leg which was plastered to above the knee. He held out his arms and she placed the tea on the side table and went to him, her heart thudding, her mouth dry. Holding her gently as she sat on the side of the bed, he said, 'I love you so much. I'm glad I saw Stan. I hadn't said I were sorry, but he divint want to hear.'

'He's happy with Sarah,' she said as he stroked her hair. 'It's well over, lovely boy.'

They said nothing while the tea cooled, then against her hair he said, 'I love you, but not your hair. That strange streaking don't become you.'

They laughed together. 'Well, I canna care for black and blue, lad,' she replied.

They drank their tea, she undressed and, for the first time in far too long, they lay in bed together, the covers pulled over. That was all, for his pain was sharp and his tiredness overwhelming, and she lay there, glad that he was back and relieved that they had not made love, for it seemed as though a stranger lay beside her.

On Sunday afternoon, Ralph Massingham stood absolutely still in the hall as six young boys erupted onto the landing at the top of the stairs, leaning on the bannisters and shouting, 'Oy, yous. Shift yer arse, we're coming full pelt across the 'all at t'bottom.'

His father was insane to have allowed his stepmother to take in evacuees. 'No, you stop right there or you'll feel the back of my hand. I am crossing my own hallway in my own time and you mind your damned manners,' he yelled.

The boys had not been evacuated during the Newcastle Blitz of 1940, but had been after the particularly bad bombing on 1 September, when the New Bridge Street goods-station area had been plastered, and so many made homeless. The boys now roared down the stairs as though he had not spoken, and barged across the hall, running either side and thumbing their noses at him as he strutted to the door of his father's study.

He opened the door, entered, and almost slammed it shut. His father looked up from his desk.

'Good morning, Ralph. How strange I didn't hear you knock. Going deaf, am I?'

'For heaven's sake, Father, couldn't the billeting officer find anywhere else for the dirty little tykes?'

'Probably, but your mother and I suggested they send us six lads. They are not dirty, merely high-spirited, and, indeed, perhaps need to learn some manners. But that's something several others not a million miles away could also consider. One is tempted to say, put your chin down, keep your mouth closed and put up with it, Ralph. After all, we are at war and there are many who need help, so if we can, we do, because we are fortunate not to need such aid. Or do you? Is that why you're here?'

As his father waved him to a chair, Ralph thought that the bags under his father's eyes could take a few pounds of bliddy spuds. Then he realised he had absorbed too much of the working-class way of thinking, and that wouldn't do.

Ralph took the chair, easing his back and looking up at the portrait of his great-grandfather hanging on the wood-panelled wall behind his father. The other walls were lined with bookcases full of tomes his father had been ploughing through ever since Ralph could remember.

'Your mother and I were sorry not to see you at St Oswald's morning service, Ralph. It's good to meet people and keep in touch with their concerns, as well as saying a prayer or two.' He placed his pen on the blotter and now leaned forward and waited.

Ralph felt the stirrings of anger. There were no blue scars on his father's hands, so who was he to talk? He examined his own, wondering how he could remove the coal already ingrained in his cuts. Bleach, perhaps.

He muttered, 'I believe you mean my stepmother, and I

wasn't at church because I've had a busy week, scrabbling about shifting coal into tubs and shoving them along to the roadway.'

'Ah.' That was all his father said as he sat upright, resting his elbows on the arms of his chair, his hands steepled, waiting. Ralph glanced up at the portrait again. His great-grandfather had begun by manufacturing something for steam engines, which had led to the development of his several collieries – after all, why not feed the engines with his own coal? It was the engine factory that his father had taken over first, after working as an apprentice at his parents' insistence. In due course he had also inherited Sledgeford, Minton and Massingham collieries. These would one day be his.

'So, tell me why you're here, Ralph. What can I do for you?' his father asked.

Ralph had memorised his proposal and began: 'As you know, I've been working in Auld Hilda with Stan, Sid and Norm. And also Davey Bedley.'

At the mention of Davey's name Mr Massingham tilted his head, his eyes showing a glimmer of amusement. 'Ah yes, Tom Bedley's boy, the one who bet on you striking the centre of the goal, the one whose ball you destr—'

Ralph interrupted, shaking his head. 'Father, I was an idiot, but don't forget he stabbed my ball, the one mother gave me which could also be called an act of destruction.'

His father put up his hand. 'Hardly, for I seem to remember the gardener was easily able to make it good.'

Ralph ground his teeth, wanting to lash out, but instead said, 'As I said, I was an idiot, but I wasn't much bigger than those evacuee ragamuffins you make excuses for, so can't we let it rest?'

His father sighed. 'But they haven't had your advantages.'

'Father, for goodness—' Ralph almost spat.

Mr Massingham held up his hand. 'I'm tired, Ralph, forgive me. Go on, but I hope not to complain about Davey Bedley. As you say, we've all grown up, or should have. Incidentally, why aren't you on the overtime aft-shift?'

Ralph sat on his fury, wondering why he'd had to come back to work here, why he had to put up with these idiots. But of course he knew why, there was a war on, an unnecessary one, for they should have come to an agreement with Hitler, course they should. He calmed down. 'The overman said someone else really needed the money.' This was the truth, and he'd been relieved. A rest would do him good. He continued, 'The thing is, Father, Davey Bedley is wasted here. He's got a bloody good brain.'

Now his father was listening closely. 'Yes, I know that, as it happens,' he said.

'Well, Father, your chum Professor Smythe thinks Bedley's brilliant at crosswords and the sort of coded clues he sets. I know because I heard him tell various people as I walked behind them. And I can't help but think that would be of use to the war effort, more so than hewing out coal. Anyone can do that, after all, and that's partly why I'm glad to be here, because I can take his place.'

He paused, thinking of Fran, because he wanted to take her from Davey bloody Bedley and so far she wouldn't play ball. He half laughed, play ball eh? Well, he'd teach the whole bloody lot of them that you didn't turn against him, take what was his. He found himself glaring at his father, who hadn't saved his wife from TB and had instead taken Ralph's nanny for himself.

His father was looking down at his blotting pad, which was a sure sign he was giving the idea some serious thought, but he said nothing. Inside, there was just the ticking of the clock, but outside Ralph could hear the evacuees running riot in the garden where he had played cricket with his cousins. Did these boys even know what cricket was? No, they probably kicked the same sort of paper ball in their mean streets, and bet on anything that came their way.

His father looked towards the windows and walked over to open one, calling out, 'Abraham, move everyone across to the back lawn, there's a good chap. There's a football in the summer house. Kick it around a bit out there and you won't hurt the flowers.'

'Abraham – ah yes, I'd forgotten he was one of those.' Ralph looked at the boys hobnobbing on the lawn and then traipsing off.

'I thought all that Blackshirt nonsense was behind you?' said his father.

Ralph sighed. When would these people realise who was going to win—He stopped, and knew he needed to gain more control of his thoughts, because thoughts could so easily turn into words.

'I went to a couple of meetings, as I am sick, sore and tired of saying, but I also went to a Commie one, and so did lots of people. But that's not what I want to talk about. I just feel Davey's wasted, and only you can sort something out with the Prof.'

His father was standing in front of the portrait. Oh Lord, thought Ralph, not a homily about the great and the good and the advantages of hard work. Instead, his father said, as though he was deep in thought, 'That's a very sensible suggestion, Ralph, and I'm pleased to hear that you are looking out for the lad – burying the hatchet, if you like. But fuel is a bit like gold dust at the moment and we need our best men on it. Davey Bedley *is* one of our best men, so no, I don't want him leaving the pit. Besides, he's got that feisty Hall girl on his arm, which makes him a steady worker. I agree that Professor Smythe admires the lad, he has said so several times, but accept my verdict, for now at least. Damned good pitman, one who sets crosswords. Wants to start a magazine, I gather. Maybe that is something to think of investing in?'

The tea gong sounded, thank heavens, or Ralph would have exploded. Invest? Over his dead body. He fought for control as they both rose and he thought instead of the miserable slices of bread that awaited them. He wished his father wouldn't subscribe to wartime rationing, as he and his wife insisted on doing. Had his mother's TB been a result of starvation? He followed his father from the room, laughing harshly, and Mr Massingham turned. 'Just thinking of something funny, Father,' Ralph said.

They continued across the hall to the drawing room. Ralph wished he could remember his mother, but he couldn't, only the loss, like a big, dark hole. He could remember his nanny, though. He had wept on leaving her when he was sent straight back to boarding school after his mother's funeral. When he'd returned for the holidays, Nanny had become his stepmother and that had spoilt everything. She was no longer his alone, and if that was the case, then he didn't want her at all.

At five o'clock, Mrs Hall, Mrs Oborne and Mrs Bedley were first on the train to Newcastle, with the girls following in their wake. With their men on Sunday overtime in the pit, Fran and Sarah had agreed there was no point in lolling about at home. It took barely twenty minutes to reach Newcastle and head for the discreet restaurant that the Briddlestone's buyer had suggested for an early supper.

They wore their best coats, hats and scarves, but as usual no stockings. Mrs Hall hesitated at the doorway, then looked at the windows, with their paper reinforcement against bomb blasts. 'There, you see, no better than the rest of us,' she tutted. She lifted the sneck and led the way inside, stopping at the head waiter's lectern.

'Blimey, it's so quiet, and him just standing there,' Sarah whispered. 'It's like being in church. Should we sing "Abide with Me"?'

'Shhh,' her mother hissed.

Fran nudged her. 'Behave,' she whispered, on the edge of giggles. The restaurant décor was dark red, the lighting dim. 'All the better for us,' she murmured to Sarah. 'We'll look quite normal, not yellow beacons with strange hair, and won't put anyone off their food.'

It was Sarah's turn to snigger.

The tables were set into alcoves and the head waiter led them towards the back, where a large round table was set up on the right-hand side of the room. Two men were already there, sipping whiskey and rose to greet them. They all shook hands, then the waiters took their coats before ushering them to their seats.

Fran and Sarah sat together as the small talk continued over a supper of pigeon pie. Fran crunched on a piece of shot and pushed it around her mouth, wondering quite what to do with it. The middle-aged man who had been introduced as Bill Witherspoon, the managing director and owner of Briddlestone's, winked at her.

'Spit it out if I were you. Lead's as bad for you as the chemicals I daresay you've come into contact with.'

Fran merely said, 'I don't know what you mean,' but she let the piece of shot drop with a ping onto the plate.

Mr Witherspoon nodded and said quietly, 'Quite right too, sorry. Foolish of me.'

The small talk resumed. They spoke of families, rationing and the weather, and Fran wondered where they'd all be without the weather to moan about and also wondered when they'd get down to business. She looked across at her mam, filled with admiration because there she was, Mrs Annie Hall, talking as though she met businessmen every day of her life.

Finally, the meal was finished and her mother sat back while their plates were removed.

Mr Witherspoon was looking from one to the other and said, as the waiter brought a glass of brandy for each of them, 'Please, a drop of rather nice brandy for us all. It's the least I can do. I want to put a proposition to your cooperative, ladies.'

Fran picked up her own balloon glass, sniffed and sipped, just like Stan had said he did in the university at the special dinners they had. It felt raw in her throat, but she listened as Mr Witherspoon talked of a charity he ran for those who were bombed out and needed rehoming here, there and everywhere. He explained that he had matched financial backing from Mr Massingham, but that the rooms needed something homely. 'Which brings me to your rugs.' He waited.

Fran, thinking how Mr Massingham got everywhere with his good works, watched her mam put down her glass. She saw it was empty. Heaven's, Mam, thought Fran, you got a wriggle on.

'I hope you're not suggesting we work for nothing, young man – what did you say your name was?' asked Mrs Hall.

'Ah, I'm Mr Witherspoon.'

Fran smiled, because he wasn't young but it rather established the hierarchy, and it wasn't in his favour. Well, well, clever Mam.

'Mr Witherspoon, we have families to feed. And I reckon you need to hear that, an' all, Mr Danvers,' her mam said.

Mr Danvers, who was the Briddlestone's buyer, hid a smile. Fran sipped her brandy, proud of her mother.

Mr Witherspoon shook his head. 'Oh no, not at all, not for nothing. Briddlestone's and the London store that buy some of our goods, including your rugs, are willing to donate ten per cent of every rug sold on the open market, but out of courtesy we felt we must discuss this with you. It doesn't in any way affect your wholesale price, since the stores are absorbing the loss, unless, of course, there is a middle ground . . . ?'

He waited.

Fran and Sarah continued to drink their brandies as their mothers and Mrs Oborne whispered together. Finally, Mrs Bedley took over the negotiations, and Fran realised that the co-op wouldn't be taking any prisoners.

'So, let's get this clear, the retailers will be donating ten per cent of the price per item sold?' asked Mrs Bedley.

Goodness, thought Fran, you mothers sound as though you've been at this for years. Well, perhaps they had. It was all that haggling housewives did with stallholders in the market.

'Well, we feel that our members will also be eager to donate, to the extent of two per cent of each item delivered to you, Mr Danvers, but only if you pay the cost of delivery, which so far we have borne. But we would need proof that this charitable gesture is indeed the case, and not some sharp practice.'

This time it was Mr Witherspoon who hid his smile, for he knew damn well that the delivery costs would be at least half a per cent of the two per cent.

'However –' this time it was Mrs Oborne speaking '– we would expect a label on each rug saying: "The Massingham Rug Co-operative have kindly donated a percentage of the cost towards the . . ." What did you say your charity was called?'

Mr Witherspoon, beginning to look rather harassed, told them.

The three older women sat back, their brandies finished, their cheeks rather pink.

'This would have to be in writing,' said Fran.

'The co-op members will have to agree, but we feel that this would be acceptable to them,' her mother added.

Sarah nodded wisely. 'Of course, and in addition we will each require another brandy.'

Both men laughed and stood to shake everyone's hand. Then Mr Danvers sat down again and ordered another round of brandies.

The air was cooler when they left at seven o'clock. They used their torches, even though it was remarkably light, given such a clear sky and a good moon. The three older women followed Fran and Sarah, who were the only ones who could remember the way to the station. The mothers were laughing together, their arms linked and excitement in their voices. Sarah and Fran linked arms too, looking carefully before herding their wobbly mothers across the road.

'Well, I hope Beth's having a grand time with Bob,' muttered Sarah, 'because she's missing a good day out. By, I'm missing her, and I have to say, I'm surprised.'

'So am I – missing and surprised,' said Fran. 'It doesn't feel quite right to be somewhere without her.'

They set off again, and slowly the realisation that they were going to help those in the North-East who had lost so much, sobered them. Fran's mam called, 'I'm right glad to be helping. Aye, we lose our men in the pit, but not our wee bairns these days. But it's wee bairns who've died under these bliddy bombs. I reckon I'll put a bit of me own money into the charity every time I sell them a rug.'

The others thought they would too, and celebrated more quietly now, glad to be going home to their families. Fran's mam said as they drew near the station, 'By, it's been a good day, but me head's beginning to split, so it is. It'll be the cool evening, and nothing to do with the brandies.'

This set them off laughing again as they crossed yet another road, as a bus ground towards them. It caught them in its slit headlights as it pulled to a stop. Some women piled off, heading towards them, their torches playing on them, shining in Fran's eyes. One roared ahead of her friends, barring their way, her finger wagging at them. Fran couldn't understand what was happening until the woman shouted, 'Warmongers, that's what you are, with your yellow faces, making those bullets. Murderers, just as much as the men who fire the buggers. Murderers. Look at you, stained with the shadow of death.'

Fran's mouth dried but she stepped forward. The woman was raising her hand, as though to strike her, when Mrs Hall stormed round the girls and stood between them.

'Murderers, you call them? Murder, and you with your fist in the air. Get away with you, and hope to God these lovely girls, who risk their lives every day, soldier on, because if Hitler gets over here, heaven help us all, you stupid, silly woman. You'll know death then, right enough.'

Mrs Oborne and Mrs Bedley were with her now, forcing their way past the woman, whose friends were standing helplessly to one side, muttering, 'So sorry.'

Chastened, they headed towards the station, which was just a few hundred yards away. Fran was shaking, but soon she was laughing again, and Sarah too. They held on to one another as they followed in the wake of those majestic women. 'Trojans, the three of them. They frighten me to death,' Fran gasped as they finally reached the station. The train was already at the platform, so they ran, the beams of their torches jogging ahead of them, until finally they stopped, opened a door, and slumped into their seats just as the guard's whistle blew.

But then her mam wagged a finger at her. 'That bliddy well does it. Tomorrow when you start your week of nights, you tell that supervisor person you need a transfer to the clean room, sewing bliddy overalls or knickers, or whatever the hell you do. You still look like ruddy canaries. Beth is resting up with her Bob, so it's time you lot did too, do you hear me?'

How could they not? The whole compartment were agog.

On the Monday the night shift saw them in the sewing room with many others from the stemming shop, including Amelia, so there had been no need to make a fuss, thought Fran, with relief. Amelia's face was still down to her armpits because of her delayed office transfer but like everyone else, she was relieved to be in a clean sector. Well, everyone but the girls they were replacing who were off to work with detonators, pellets or pouring the stemming powder into thingumybobs.

The girls cut out the patterns for the blue overalls on the wide tables though Amelia refused to sit with Fran and Sarah because she blamed them as well as Beth. In the end, they stopped smiling and just ignored her, realising there was nothing they could say or do that would make a difference. Instead, Fran let herself enjoy the crunch of scissors through cotton.

All around them, the ticketty-tick of the sewing machines made a soothing sound, and suddenly, for no reason other than she was happy to be away from the powder, Fran started to sing 'Blue moon, you saw me standing alone . . .' Within a few bars all the others were joining in. Sarah sang harmony, and the only thing missing was Beth's contralto. Amelia could have made up for her, for she was a contralto too, but she chose to work on, silently.

The singing continued most of the night. Some of the older women nodded off over their machines, but here they could, for there was no danger of causing an explosion. As they left the next morning at six o'clock, Mrs Brown, the supervisor and an ex-seamstress, pulled Fran to one side.

'I'm not sure if you have heard that the wireless show *Workers' Playtime* might well come our way, or so a little bird has told me? Even though they've their own comedians, and singers, they like to feature budding talent and Miss Ellington is going to try to get a choir ready just in case they do come. Her idea is to get all of the various departments to put up a group of singers, and she'll then hold a competition to find the winner. She says we should be prepared for possible opportunities, like the Scouts.'

The two of them laughed. Mrs Brown went on, 'You and your friends'd be right canny, and I reckon you should be putting together some singers. Have a think, and I daresay Miss Ellington'll say more, if it's likely to happen.'

Fran watched the others disappearing into the changing rooms. The tannoy was giving out a message for the next shift, which was already at work throughout the Factory. Why not? Just think, they could be on the wireless. What would Davey say, and her mam? Thrilled, they'd be.

Mrs Brown raised an eyebrow. 'Well, are you too jiggered to answer?'

'Too excited, I reckon,' Fran said. 'Just think, *Workers' Playtime* might be here.'

Mrs Brown shook her head, and walked along with her. 'Might be, that's all, pet.'

They smiled at each other. As they reached the changing room, a lass hurried out, scampering towards the sewing shop followed by a security officer, and calling to Mrs Brown, 'I'm late for me shift, lost me purse, and it were in the safe box all along. Daft I am, up with the bairns most of the night. Who's on, missus? Will I get a bollocking?'

'Fore shift is Mrs Easton, so aye, reckon you will. Tell her I had it, and forgot to tell yer, eh?'

The girl grinned. 'You're a pal.'

'I'm not,' said Mrs Brown. 'I'm your supervisor, not your pal, so don't you forget it.'

But the girl had wrenched open the door and disappeared, with the security officer on her heels. Fran said, as she was reaching for the changing-room door.'It'll be grand, Mrs Brown, and aye, we've lots of good voices. There's Beth, when she's back, Sarah, and Amelia, if she feels she can join in, and then Mary and Sylv.'

Mrs Brown nodded. 'That's sorted then, so get some songs sorted, Fran, and it won't hurt to start rehearsing, just in case. We can have the competition in the canteen at dinner times should we get good news. After all, why shouldn't our lasses cheer up the nation, as well as get ill for it, eh? I daresay if it seems likely to happen Miss Ellington will find you one dinner time, with some music, so be ready to push the others to think it a good idea. You can read music, can't you? We hear you, Sarah and Beth were in St Oswald's choir.' With that, she whooshed off, probably in search of further prey, Fran thought.

After Fran had changed in the now nearly empty room and gathered up her belongings while a security officer waited to accompany her to the gates, she caught up with Mrs Oborne, who was trailing the rest, and in the moonlight she suddenly remembered the fury on the face of the woman in Newcastle. Well, if Fran Hall was a warmonger, so be it. They were going to win this war if it was the last thing she did, and she'd be singing all the way.

At the siding, Robert, the night-shift driver, was idling the engine. He flashed his lights, leaned out of the window and yelled, 'On yer hop, our Franny, and you too, Mrs Oborne. You won't hear anything above the snores.'

She clambered on board and he was right. Most were asleep, their chins on their chests. He drew away gently. She edged up the aisle as Sarah waved, and slumped down next to her. Across the way sat Valerie and Amelia. Amelia was asleep, her mouth hanging open. Soon all would lose their yellow, the sheets would be white in the morning, and everyone would be fit for the harder sectors. And in time, they could all go back to being normal.

'What did Mrs Brown want?' Sarah whispered.

Fran whispered the news and Sarah said, 'By, that'd be a bit of fun, and just imagine being heard by so many. We could wear a big badge that says "We're famous, bow to us".'

The two girls laughed softly as their lids grew heavy, and then they slept and Fran dreamed of being the singer she'd always wanted to be. Singing while Davey worked on his magazine, both of them safe.

Chapter Fourteen

One week later

Davey watched Stan piling out of his backyard on the heels of his da and called out, "Ow do.'

They both turned and Mr Hall replied, 'You lads be safe, or I'll tan yer backsides.'

Beside Davey, Sid laughed. 'You too, Mr Hall,' Norm called.

Joe Hall clattered on, catching up with Tom Bedley, but he shouted back, 'Yer keep yer hands off me backside, lad, or I'll be 'aving yer.'

Davey grinned and tugged down his cap in the keen wind, Fran's kiss still light on his lips. Stan joined them, and they carried along in the clomping stream.

'I had to sort out the hens, so I missed Sarah at the bus stop,' Stan grumbled.

Davey nodded. 'Aye, and if you think she didn't notice, you've a shock coming, bonny lad. It will be discussed good and proper, and a pound of your flesh will be paid.'

Ahead of them, Norm was walking backwards. 'Such a frown there were on that pretty young face, Stan, lad. Bit of a grovel needed, I reckon.'

Davey winked at Stan as Norm spun on his heels and waited for them, then they all marched along to the pithead. 'I reckon we could outmarch them army lads who came t'village hall, and we'd all be made up to corporal in no time,' Sid muttered.

'Aye, 'appen you're right,' Norm laughed, winking at Davey and Stan. 'You tell 'em that when they come to the next dance. It's to collect extra for yer mams' co-op charity, in't it? I hear the girls will be singing. Be grand if they get asked to do a few more bookings, cos they're as good as them you hear on the wireless, and I reckon they love doing it. Nice of the Sledgeford lot to ask 'em. Word's bound to get around?'

Davey said, 'Aye, they're the best, and I reckon we could put a bucket for change on the stage. It's for furniture for them that's been bombed out, me mam says. Crikey, them women 'ave the wind in their sails, right enough. Rugs, wall thingies and now helping them poor buggers.'

The noise of the pithead closed in on them and they joined the slow-moving queue heading for the gates, with no sign of Ralph yet.

'I heard tell Massingham has taken in some bairns?' yelled Sid.

'Bet that didn't bring a smile to you-know-who,' Davey muttered to Stan.

'Still a no-show, so where the hell is he?' he replied. 'He can't be late again.'

Davey gave a quick look around, for Ralph had a way of sliding up when you least expected it. It was the same with the tubs when he shoved them to the main seam and then took for ever to come back. Sid reckoned he got himself in a funk down the seams and had to keep doing a piddle out of fright, which was why it took him so long.

The wind was whipping at their scarves. It was still dark, but the slag heap smouldered as always, and sulphur was heavy on the air as the miners dragged on the last of their Woodbines. They stamped slowly up the incline and into the yard, past the gateman, calling their numbers to the overman.

Amongst the scrabble to stub out cigarettes, they heard the calls of those on bikes telling them to 'shift yer arses out t'way'. One of them was Ralph, who slammed his bike into the hut with the others and joined them. He now wore boots and old trousers, and had tied string below his knees, but only after a mouse had dashed up his leg when he was shoving a full tub. The men had laughed as he bellowed, until he let go the tub, so it nearly crashed into the Galloway pony hauling the tub train.

The hewers had sworn at him, so the story went, and the lad on the pony 'train' had yelled, 'If it'd hit us or gone faster you'd have a bloody accident on yer hands, cos it've jumped the bleedin' rails, and I'm not having Blossom hurt, not for you, nor no one, and I don't care if your da's the Queen of bleedin' Sheba.'

Davey smiled at the memory and Ralph tipped his cap, which looked like it had last been worn while shooting grouse, but at least he was trying to fit in.

"Ow do,' Davey called, the others murmuring the same, not breaking stride as they headed for the lamp room.

'Good morning to you all.'

Stan groaned. 'That's all we damned well need, someone chipper in this bliddy wind, at this bliddy time of day.'

The laughter was kind towards Ralph, but not yet familiar. Davey wondered if it ever would be. The boss's son was always the boss's son, and although he'd stopped the bus-shelter nonsense, it had not been forgotten. They picked up their lamps and tokens, and with their bait tins hanging from their belts, they nodded to the banksman and entered the cage.

Davey thought about Fran and Sarah and felt more relaxed. They were in the sewing section now and were not just safe, but would also feel better right soon. He looked across at Stan, who was squashed between Ralph and

Norm. Stan raised his eyebrows, shaking his head slightly as the cage whooshed down. There was a look about the lad, Davey thought, an 'all's right with the world' look, and he knew he carried that same one with him.

Steve Oborne's lad, Colin, was humming next to him. He always did or else he'd say again and again, 'I hate this bliddy cage', or stot and jig and end up stomping on someone's feet. The humming was preferable. Now, thought Davey, preferable's a good word for three across. He needed a clue before Monday, when his setting was to go to the magazine.

They were slowing, then jerked to a stop. The chain was released and they headed down the roadway, which as always was damned noisy, but then main seams were. Ralph walked in front and kicked up dust for those following, as usual. Did he do it deliberately? Well, none of them were about to give him the satisfaction of asking.

The men were peeling off down half-worked seams, which the manager was opening up willy-bliddy-nilly because of the need for more coal, but nonetheless Elliott was a good one and wouldn't take chances. Davey knew he sent in the old hands first to check the props and make sure there was nothing wrong. If there was, then they or the night shift would set up new props and roof planks. Davey's da was one of the old hands, Stan's too. They were also the ones who'd be first in if there was a fall, directing everyone and remaining calm.

They walked on to their own seam, the Mary Lou, which was a way ahead. Lord knew why it was called that. He listened to the crash and screech of tubs, the whack of picks, and the shouts of the men from the off seams. On they went, coughing in the dust and settling with their own thoughts. Davey would have sworn he could feel the squeezing of the coal against the pit props, hear the sighing of the roof and the scuttle of the rats. But of course it was his imagination, because he couldn't possibly hear anything above the noise.

The heat was rising, his sweat was falling and still he fiddled in his bonce for a clue to set this crossword. Maybe a numbered word clue, superimposing numbers instead of letters? He stooped as the ceiling lowered and the jagged coal caught his shoulder, ripping his jacket. Pretty soon there'd be no jacket, just a few threads. He felt the dampness of blood. Bugger. He moved on, able to straighten as they neared the face.

Aye, there'd have to be a key in the clue, he thought. Yes, that's what Professor Smythe had written in that little book he'd sent up with Stan. Find the key to a code, and then you'd break it. You needed to look for a letter or cipher that repeated, and that's what he had to create for his readers. Most often, the Prof said, you could find it in a short word, for example 'for'. If you gave the 'o' a number such as 6 when you superimposed numbers on the letters of your clue, you could track the 6 to see the short words. So 'to' or 'for' would have a 6 for the 'o'. Once you had one letter in your head, the rest happened. The repeater was your key. Always the repeater, and you couldn't work anything out without the key. Though as the Prof said, this was the simple version. Well, he'd leave his brain to work something out. It usually did, and Halford, the editor, always liked the coded clues.

'Wake up, for the love of Mike,' shouted Stan, stumbling alongside, then catching himself. He whacked Davey's back. 'Howay, lad, listen up, cos I was asking yer if Sarah was really down on me.'

Davey grinned, holding up his lamp as the seam grew darker. 'Right steamin' she were.'

'Bliddy hell.' Stan held up his lamp towards the roof. 'Did you hear that?'

Davey laughed. 'Stop changing the subject. I can hear nowt but the bloody tubs crackin' along the rails.'

Stan shrugged. 'Aye, well, she means the world to me, Davey. I reckon she always has, but I didn't know it. Bloody blind, deaf—'

'And stupid,' Davey interrupted as they reached the face at last. 'Aye, well, I were only yanking your leg. She's a pitman's daughter, for heaven's sake, and she knew you'd make it if you could, but messing around with hens, bonny lad? Better bring her an egg at least when you meet the bus.' He lowered his voice at the end, because he didn't want the whelp hearing, just in case it got the lad going again.

Davey threw his pick to the ground, shook off most of his clothes and set to work in his drawers, just as Stan shouted at Ralph, 'We're to take it turn and turn about as your minder, Ralph, so says the deputy manager. Good practice for us all. Davey's your minder today, lad. All right with that, Davey?'

Ralph grabbed the empty tub and heaved it to where he'd fill it with their coal, shouting back, 'I understand.'

He was streaming with sweat but wouldn't take off his trousers. He just tied the string good and tight because he'd said he wasn't having any more damned rodents taking liberties, ever again. At ten o'clock, they sat for a cold tea with their backs against the props and Stan looked around. 'Ralph should be back with the tub by now,' he said.

Davey struggled to hear him against the background noise that carried along the seam and yelled, 'Did he take another break? He needs to get his waterworks looked at.'

Sid dragged his hand across his mouth, then hung his head, sweat dripping onto the ground. 'He was shoving the tub up the slope to the roadway last I saws of him. So aye, I reckon he's doing another Jimmy Riddle on the way to the main seam, but he better hurry himself if he does want a drink, or a bit of bait.'

Stan groaned. 'Best you go and see if he's all right, Davey, and before you moan, that's been my job since he started.'

Davey eased his cut shoulder. 'Aye, right you are. Another mouse might have gone up his leg, chewed through the string, and is playing merry hell with his crown jewels and he's having a right hop and skip.'

They laughed. Davey limped off into the darkness, his old injury aching today, for whatever reason, and headed along the uphill slope. He cursed himself for leaving his lamp with his bait tin. It was so dark that his eyes wouldn't get accustomed, so he just kept to one side of the tub rails. He guessed where the roof would lower and ducked. He was right and then he limped on.

He bent lower still, thanking whoever was up above this world that he wasn't a putter any longer, for it was no joke shoving the tub along.

He cupped his hands and called, 'Ralph, Ralph Massingham.' Nothing. On he trudged, hating the pit when he was alone; not like Stan, who seemed to think the pit talked to him with its sighs and creaks. How he could hear it, he didn't know. He laughed slightly, and called, 'Ralph, come on, lad. Pull your drawers up and get to work.'

There was no reply and now he was worried. What if the bugger was hurt, and on his watch an' all? But just then, in the distance, he thought he saw a lamp glowing low, jiggling as someone walked, but then it disappeared – how, when there was no bend up there? He yelled over the noise: 'That you, Ralph? Get a wriggle on with your tub onto the roadway and come back, or if 'tis empty, get yer arse back here and tek a drink and some bait with us, cos there'll be coal piling up.'

He wasn't sure the lad could hear him, but he listened as

he walked and it was then that he heard the rumble of the tub. Well, he was on his way then. He stood still, shading his eyes, calling the lad, but no answer. Was the bliddy thing loose? He touched the rails and they were vibrating. The rumble got louder and he knew it was the tub and it was too fast for a putter to be with it. 'Loose tub,' he called in warning to the marrers at the coalface. But was it empty or full? He tried to hear from the rumble, but there was too much noise. If it was empty it would build up a sway and could come off either side. If it was full, he reckoned it would go off right or even hold its course and head straight through. But where was Ralph? Hurt? Had it knocked him sideways?

'Tub loose,' he yelled again to the others. 'Bliddy tub loose, Ralph, wherever the hell you are. Stand aside. Tub loose. Yell if you're all right?' Had they all heard and where the hell was Ralph? He turned to run, but why? It was too late, because he could hear it good and proper now. He had to guess where was safe. He listened, his mouth dry. Aye, it was empty. Or was it? 'For Pete's sake, decide, yer bliddy fool,' he shouted at himself, and jumped left, cramming himself against the side and screaming, 'Tub loose. Stand aside. Ralph, stand aside, lads.'

But would any of them hear? At least it would slow off the incline before it got to the face. 'Ralph, Ralph, you all right?' he yelled.

The rumble grew louder, but at least it was a rumble, so the tub hadn't jumped the rails, yet, perhaps pinning the lad down. Closer and closer it drew. The air was rushing. He pressed himself back hard. Aye, the bugger would pass soon, he thought. He breathed out, only then realising he'd been holding his breath. Had it gone over Ralph? They'd have to rush to get help and—

The tub was closer, like a steam train. It was so damned

near, but then there was nothing. Just a big silent space for a second as the tub flew in the air. He froze. Where was the beggar? The tub screeched as it landed, and the ground shuddered. Davey shut his eyes and prayed, but he felt the blow before he heard it as the tub hit the pit prop at his side, which cracked and buckled into him, throwing him across the rails. The tub spun and flew backwards. The wall blew out, jagged, cruel and heavy, taking his air away. 'Fran,' he groaned. Then nothing.

Stan was at work, hacking at the face. He could neither hear nor see anything but the thud of the pick on the gleaming coal, the thud of Sid's and Norm's, the splinter of the bloody great slab, the crash as it came down, the flying dust and the flash of the pick, the sweat as it dropped on his hands as he heaved more of the coal down. Sid and Norm heaved too, dug and delved alongside him. The coal was piling up, so Davey had better get the pillock to get a move on. He rested his pick and only then felt the shudder through his feet and up the handle, into his hands, then heard the rumble, the crash.

He stood stock-still, just as Sid and Norm were doing. Listening. Fearing. Their mouths souring because they knew it was a fall. Where? The air whooshed from the narrow roadway. Close, then.

Davey? Stan moved, snatching up his lamp and dragging his pick, hurtling along with Sid and Norm behind him into the billowing coal dust. The shadows leapt as they battled through the dust, crunched over fine debris, bent low as the roof dictated, clambered closer, calling into the hush that had fallen in the pit. For when a fall resonated, men paused, listened and judged. Stan yelled as he ran, hunched over, heedless of the coal ripping his back. 'Davey? Ralph?'

'Davey, talk to me, lad,' Sid yelled.

'Davey. Howay, Davey?' Norm called.

He hadn't called back. So they knew, and they weren't having it. Not their Davey, not again.

The dust was too thick. Stan coughed, but still he ran. 'Davey, Ralph,' he called, choking, struggling for breath. There was no answer and their lamps picked out the gleam of heaped coal through the dust. Heaped coal where there should be none. Coal that was still tumbling from the roof and slithering like a filthy stream onto the rails and along towards them. But not right across. Not across at least, so it hadn't trapped them, but Davey . . . ?

Stan held up his hand. Sid and Norm pressed close, panting. 'Can we get past? Is the whole bloody lot on its way down?'

'Where the hell is Davey?'

'Ralph?'

They edged to one side, stepping through, their eyes and ears on the roof. They reached the other side to see Ralph stumbling down the slope, calling, 'It got away, the damned thing got away. But only after I heard the roof come down.' He was holding up his lamp and pointing to the empty tub, which had been thrown at an odd angle, where it appeared to have hit the heaped coal.

Sid yelled, 'Where's Davey? Were he near you?'

Ralph was shaking his head. 'He was with you.'

Stan was tearing at the coal now, screaming, 'Davey.'

Sid shouted into Ralph's face, 'You must have heard him call you. For he would have done, cos he were looking for you.'

Norm grabbed Sid's arm. 'Help, for God's sake. Just help.'

They all began digging gently with their picks, and then threw those aside in frustration and used their hands. Where was their Davey? Stan worked as the dust stung his eyes and his hands were shredded, his back screaming as others came. Then there was Mr Bedley beside him, but still he tore at the coal, until a stronger hand was pulling him away, forcing him back. It was his da. 'Stand back, lad. We've props and planks coming. Got to shore up the roof, the walls, make 'em safe.'

Stan threw him off. 'It's our Davey under that lot. So we get him out, now.'

His da shook him. 'We shore the bastard up – look, they're here. Stand back, and let us do our jobs.'

Sid grabbed Stan, and Norm gestured to Ralph, who was standing uncertainly in the quiet of the pit, for it was quiet, as though waiting. Stan stared at Sid and said, 'But it's our lad, our Davey.'

He was panting, as though he'd run a mile, but his marrer was under that lot. His marrer, his best marrer, his Davey. And what about Fran? Oh God. His da and Mr Bedley were heaving in the props as close to the fall as they could make it, and banging in the roof planks. Never had he seen men work so hard, so fast and so silently, as they were joined by the deputy manager and two others from the rescue team. Together they worked, but his Davey was under that jagged heap.

His da turned to him, mallet in hand. 'Now, you get in there and dig for his life, lads.'

Norm was already scrabbling at the coal, and now Stan, Sid and Ralph were there with the rest of the pitmen and the rescuers. They pulled away the small stuff, getting their picks at the large slabs that had sheared off from the walls.

Stan was calling through the dust, 'Come on, Davey, lad. Come on, let's get you out. Yes, we'll get you out. Your lass will want you out. We want you out.'

Tom Bedley was tearing at the coal too. 'Da's here, bonny lad. Don't yer fret, Da's here.' Tom Bedley repeated it the whole time they worked, and Stan began sobbing like a bairn, the tears running down into his mouth, until he crunched salt and coal. Sid cursed Auld Hilda and Norm cursed God, the war, Ralph, everything and everyone.

It was then that Stan stopped and looked for Ralph. There he was, still working as hard as the rest, as he should. But why had he taken so long with the tub, so Davey had to go looking? And why was the tub at that crazy angle if it had hit the heap? It would have tipped, of course it would . . . But like that? Nothing made sense, for why had the wall and roof fallen? It'd all been checked overnight, it always was, and it weren't creaking when they came on shift. Had something hit it? But Ralph had only let the tub go when he heard the fall . . .

Davey was under there. Davey, laughing; Davey, singing; Davey who should have fought him for the scholarship, but who was happy to be with Fran and build his crosswords. 'So come on, bonny lad. Come on, Davey, lots of crosswords to set. Come on, lad. Fran's waiting. She's always waiting for yer because you're the air she breathes.'

He heard his own da then, shouting, 'Come on, lad, us'll get you out of there, you keep going till we get to you. I told yer I'd tan yer backside for yer, but instead I'll buy you a pint, and then the canaries need more chickweed, so how about it, lad? You feed 'em the chickweed, eh?'

And Mr Bedley worked like he'd never worked before. He probably didn't know that his coal-dust-clad face was scored with tear tracks, and his whole body was wracked with silent sobs.

Davey couldn't breathe. Not properly, just a bit, and the pain washed over him like the beck in full flood. He heard his da and Mr Hall, so everything would be all right. They were there, and so was Stan. He could hear Stan, and Mr Hall, and Sid and Norm. Everyone was there, but Fran. He felt tired, so tired, and he hurt. All he wanted was to sleep. He wished they'd just stop shouting. Just so he could sleep, but then he heard Stan again: '. . . crosswords. Come on, Davey. You must be setting one in your head, cos you always are. Come on, keep thinking.'

Stan's voice was strange, sort of choked, but he was right. What was that word he'd had in his head? Ah, that's right, preferable, or preferably. But what was the clue? How far had he got? The key? He was looking for the key. Then it all went, and he just rested, rested, and perhaps he slept. But then the word nagged again. The coded clue. That was it. A letter that repeated; turned into a number that repeated. He needed a phrase, a key to the code . . . 6, something about a 6. He drifted again, the pain . . . The dust was in his mouth, and the coal too, wet coal. But was it his blood that made it wet? Blood and coal.

His da was calling, faintly, and he could hear the clatter as they grappled and tossed coal. They'd be clearing a path to him, like he'd done many a time before now. They were working hard, like they'd worked on Stan and him when their legs were busted. Like he and Stan had worked when Norm got caught. But that was mining. No one promised a rose garden. It was cuts, aches, pints, canaries, ponies, and love . . .

What had Ralph been doing to let go of the tub? Why hadn't he answered when he'd called? Why didn't he shout when the tub ran free like Da was shouting now? 'We're nearer, bonny lad. Getting to yer. Call if'n you can, eh? Keep on breathing, that's me bairn.'

He tried to call, but he had no breath, or maybe there was just a whisper of a breath, which hurt. The coal was jagged and heavy, pressing on him like it pressed the roof planks and made them creak. He just wanted to sleep, but Stan was yelling and it was tiring to hear them. He wanted them to hush, just hush, but then Stan said, 'Fran'll be the one giving you a leathering, lad, if you're not back and talking to her when she's off shift. Got to get to the bus shelter. It has to be *you*.'

Ralph called then: 'Don't worry, I'll fetch her to you.'

Davey breathed a little bit deeper then. Fran and he were one, so they were. That Ralph wasn't going to fetch her anywhere. She didn't want it. He was coming out from under this lot, of course he was. *He* had to fetch her. Not Ralph.

He drifted, but then the pain caught, cutting into his mind, and there was a sudden question. What was the key? He needed the key. The reader must be able to find the first repeater letter in the gobbledygook of letters. A vowel, eh? A repeater like Ralph, always there when something went wrong.

The coal was heavier, and it was getting harder to fight. He just wanted to rest. Just rest. But if he did then Ralph would be going for his Fran, and she *was* his, like he was hers. And no bloody Ralph was coming between them. Yes, the key was Ralph. There with the football, there with Fran at the bus, there with the lamp that went dark up the seam, and letting go the tub. Yes, he was the key, because it was him—

Stan yelled, 'You got that crossword finished yet? The magazine will be waiting, so stop being so bloody idle. Shout – tell me. Come on, call. You've got to call. Got to know you're putting up a fight.'

But the coal and blood were in his mouth and if he shouted, the blood and coal would go down his throat and he'd drown. Could you drown in the pit? You could in the beck, but that was cool and fresh and he went to the beck with his Fran. He felt the water, the coolness, and then he was calm. He knew Stan and his da were right. He must breathe, he must set the crossword and sort his magazine if he was to keep the lass comfortable. He wanted her life to be easier than his mam's. So he lay there as the coal dust showered down, and into his mouth, more and more of it into his mouth, but not his nose, not yet because his head was tilted, just a bit, but enough, but if it built up, layer on layer he'd die and he mustn't because he needed to meet Fran. He thought of 'preferable' and if the clue was in code then it would need a key. Come on, a phrase. 'Choose the best'? But the 'e' could be the repeater. The 'e' was a 6. But was the clue good enough?

Crash, noise and a crushing weight, heavier and heavier, which whooshed away the crossword as his da yelled, 'The bugger's coming down again.'

It'd be the roof, of course it was, and it was pressing him worse. It was jagged and cutting as it squeezed and pinched. The coal was on his face, his head, his everything. He thought of Ralph. How he was always in the way, always causing trouble. The shredded ball. Fran and the bus shelter. The tub whacking into the pit prop – just like a key, repeating. Just like his mind, repeating, bliddy repeating. There was a code there somewhere, a code in what Ralph was up to . . . Ralph destroying things, like a bliddy war zone. He moaned. The coal and blood slipped from his mouth to his throat.

But he couldn't think, nor breathe, any more.

Chapter Fifteen

Fran, Sarah and the rest of their group were really beginning to feel better, for here in the clean room there was good air, the soothing sound of the sewing machines and the scissors cutting through layers of blue cotton. And here they could actually bring in their bottles of water to flush out the chemicals throughout the shift, and nip to the lavatory, which was attached so you didn't need a guard. Did flushing their bodies with water work? Who knew, but it made them feel as though they were doing something for themselves.

As their break was called, they filed into the canteen and saw there were still jugs of water on the table. Perhaps there always would be. Good for you, Mam, Fran thought. 'By, you could lead a revolution.'

She must have spoken aloud, for Beth, who had returned today, the very day Bob left said, 'Aye, she could that.'

They queued for food, taking both mains and pudding, and headed for their table, gobbling it all down with little said now their appetites were back. As the pudding bowls were being scraped clean of sugarless rice, and the spoons licked back and front, Fran saw Miss Ellington heading towards their table. She was waving sheets of music at Fran, who shouted above the din, 'Howay, ladies, heads up. Remember I said something about the *Workers' Playtime* competition? Well, looks like we're about to hear more.'

The women looked up while Valerie licked her finger,

which she'd wiped around her bowl, and the tannoy played music quietly. They waited as Miss Ellington wound her way through the tables, carrying sheet music beneath her arm. Mrs Oborne leaned forward. 'What the devil are you talking about, Franny Hall?'

Maisie groaned. 'She were in the next shop, remember, and missed t'news. Then I forgot to tell her later, Fran.'

Miss Ellington distributed a copy of 'All or Nothing at All' to each of them, typed up on the back of a list of last year's food lists. She raised her voice to be heard above the tannoy's music and the chatter of the other workers while they ate. Mrs Oborne, Valerie and the others read the lyrics, chatting and laughing, ignoring Miss Ellington. Fran wondered if they simply hadn't heard?

In exasperation, Miss Ellington, standing beside Fran, reached over, snatched up Sarah's pudding spoon and banged it like a gavel on the Formica-topped table, yelling for silence. Remnants of Sarah's rice pudding flicked through the air, landing on Mrs Oborne's bust. She brushed it off and it lay to rest in her smeared pudding bowl. The whole table called, 'Goal.'

The security officer banged the spoon again and everyone ducked, but then sat up, grinning. They were ready to listen, but Miss Ellington still had to raise her voice against the tinny music and chatter from all around. 'One sheet for each of you. All the others, whatever shift they're on, will have, or have had, the same song given to them too. The carbon paper is quite done in, I have to tell you. I also have to let you know that in a couple of weeks we'll be holding a sort of song play-off over a series of lunchtimes, with the winners decided by the majority of workers' votes.'

'So, is the wireless coming, Miss Ellington?' Beth asked.

'Ah well, as you know, *Workers' Playtime* is announced as coming from a factory somewhere in Britain.' Miss Ellington held up her finger, paused, then said, 'Well, that somewhere might be here, or will even probably be here.'

Mrs Oborne stood up, the smear from the rice still visible. 'Does probably mean actually, pet?'

Fran grinned at Beth and Sarah. Miss Ellington tapped her nose. 'If it becomes actually, that's for me to know, and you to be told.'

The table of women groaned, and Sarah muttered, 'You're power-mad, Miss Ellington, so you are.'

'You make sure you believe that, Sarah Bedley.' Miss Ellington wagged her finger, grinning.

Valerie called, 'So what you're taking so long to tell us is that the winning group will sing on the wireless for *Workers' Playtime*, and will Arthur Askey be with them? If so, me mam will sign up to work here just so she can sing with 'im, and she's got a voice like a bleedin' foghorn.'

'Like mam, like daughter,' Mrs Oborne shouted.

The whole table laughed until Miss Ellington, with a look at the clock, conducted them, one-handed as always, to a halt. 'But Valerie, of course your mam won't know where we are, will she? You must remember that, for there must be no one outside wanting anyone's autograph. Say no more than the winner will be on the wireless. You may tell them what time the programme is, but not who else will be on. So button your mouths shut – don't let them run away with you.' She paused, stood straight, and sniggered a bit before saying, 'But you will need to make sure your mouths open and shut while you practise.'

The table groaned and someone called, 'Howay, that just isn't funny.'

Again, Miss Ellington smiled. 'Open and shut them on the bus, or in the hall you have your dances in, or the privacy of the netty, but only concerning the song, and a competition. I repeat, if you win you may tell them what time on the wireless. That's all. Is that quite clear? I don't want to come and visit you in prison, and if I do, I assure you I won't be bringing you a hacksaw.' The women groaned again.

Miss Ellington shook her head. 'I know it's boring, but it's essential. Sabotage is an increasing worry . . .' She trailed off, as though thinking of something in particular, but then perked up. 'Look, let me tell you that what I've just said is quite true, sabotage *is* an increasing worry, so you really must be careful about what you say and, as always, keep alert to anything that isn't quite normal. But back to business. Learn your words, and the music, because I want the girls under my umbrella to do well, and so does Mrs Brown in sewing, and so do Mrs Raydon and Mr Swinton, and all the other Security Officers and foremen, is that quite clear?'

She laughed as they saluted. Mrs Oborne and Valerie handed their music back, protesting they would ruin it with their voices, and the whole table agreed. Valerie grimaced and grabbed Maisie's sheet, making a paper dart that she aimed at Fran and let fly. 'Bullseye,' she crowed as it hit Fran's turban.

Fran aimed it at Maisie, who laughed and ducked, catching it before throwing it to someone else, while Miss Ellington raised her voice even higher. 'Learn it thoroughly, and then let's show the *Workers' Playtime* team just what a bunch of three-year-olds – in other words, you lot – can do. Of course, you might be wiped out by one of these other tables . . . And do remember, that there *is* competition from the other sectors.' She touched her nose. 'I say no more, for who knows what other sectors do here? You have a task before you, girls. Do your best, and try not to be wiped out, eh?'

Beth had the dart, and this time aimed it at Miss Ellington, yelling, 'Wiped out, in this place? Bad choice of words, Miss Ellington.'

Miss Ellington dipped a curtsy, grabbed the dart and stuffed it in her pocket, shaking her head as she smiled.

Fran sat back, aching with laughter and relief because after a week with Bob, Beth was rosy and contented, which meant Amelia had taken what she considered her rightful place in the office and was no longer glowering.

As she listened to the excitement of the others, Sarah muttered, 'I do wonder if Miss Ellington worked some magic to get Amelia transferred, because I'd heard her position had gone to someone else. Perhaps she's wedged in a corner counting paper clips, but whatever it is, she'll be happy and at least we won't have her bellyaching around us all.'

Beth leaned against Sarah. 'Sorry. It's because I had leave.'

Fran shook her head. 'It's a good thing really because it just alerted us to what she's really like. By, Beth, it's good to have someone as common as the rest of us in our midst again.'

Sarah and Beth burst out laughing and it was good to hear, and it was as if something in Beth settled. And thank the Lord for that, Fran thought.

As Miss Ellington headed for the door, Beth grinned at the bus 'team' sitting round the table. 'Now Bob's gone back on duty, even if it's only something on shore until his leg is quite better, I've all the time in the world to learn and practise, so, let's go all out, shall we? I reckon I fancy being part of a right grand choir.'

'Hang about, perhaps they'll just think we're a load of grubby factory girls, not worth the candle,' Valerie warned, winking at Fran. 'They might choose the office workers. Our Amelia is doing their solo.'

As the outrage began, Valerie waved them down. 'Oh, you're just so easy to rile, that you are. I reckon you just need to buff yourselves and your voices to a shine, and then Mrs Oborne and me can slip in the back to mime and add to the glow, pets.'

Beth muttered, 'No one but me Bob's going to buff me to a shine, let me tell you.'

Mrs Oborne laughed long and hard, then said, 'You'd best wash yer mouth out with soap, our Beth.'

There was another twenty minutes till break was over, and Fran eased her shoulders, thinking that she could have eaten another bowl of rice pudding, she felt so much better, and then Beth reached for her hand as Sarah went for another cup of tea.

'Is everything really all right with you and Bob?' Fran asked.

'Aye, pet, I was a daft idiot, snappy and picky. I got lonely, and was thinking all sorts, especially when I heard your Stan were back.' Beth's turban was slipping and she dragged it off, her auburn hair falling to her shoulders without a blemish to spoil it. 'Bob said I should have this lot cut in case I caught it in machinery or it flopped over me eyes at a critical moment.'

Fran nodded. 'Aye, they keep on about it, so maybe we should. There just doesn't seem time. I reckon they should do it here. Get us all in a bit earlier, line us up, cut it after we've stripped, then we won't itch from the bitty bits of hair for the rest of the shift. And let the bliddy government pay for it.'

Mrs Oborne was leaning across the table, resting on her elbows. 'Good idea. Will you ask about it, or shall I?'

Fran could do nothing other than say she'd have a go, and curse her big mouth for opening and shutting it too often. Sarah brought a tray of tea for them all, and Beth whispered, 'She's a good lass. Some would only have brought one for theirselves.'

Fran smiled. 'So are you, pet.'

'Are what?' asked Sarah.

'A good 'un,' Fran answered.

Beth put an arm around her. 'Not really. I got too wrapped up in meself. Mam says I should know better.'

Fran grinned. 'Oh, that's what mams say all the time.'

Beth sighed. 'Aye, but this time she were right. I don't half wish Bob weren't back on duty. But at least he'll be safe for a while. Be better if he'd been discharged though, and safe. War's such a damned worry.'

Mrs Oborne nudged Maisie. 'Lass'll be saying next he could have joined the rug co-op, but with your mam in charge, our Fran, safe isn't the word. A tyrant she is, as she progs the strips into the mat as though they were the enemy themselves, checking the rest of us all the time with them eyes that miss not a thing. Lost her calling, she has. Should have been a bleedin' general. That'd sort the buggers.'

Sarah was laughing as Fran sniggered, running her finger round her pudding bowl, like everyone seemed to be doing now their appetites were back. Her mam would have a fit.

Mrs Oborne raised her eyebrows at Sarah and said, 'You can wipe that smile off your face an' all. Your mam is her partner in crime – yours too, Beth. But we've raised a fair bit for them that's been bombed out, so bless the three of them.'

They were all smiling when Fran saw Mr Swinton enter with Miss Ellington. Fran checked the clock and sighed. Ten minutes to go, then back to work, but Davey said he'd be at the bus shelter, and so would Stan for Sarah. He'd better have a good grovel ready, she thought, then they could all walk or cycle to the beck for fresh air. Maybe take some scones, or so Davey had promised, because he'd talked the corner shop into letting him have a couple. She felt her whole body relaxing at the thought.

It was a cold but sunny day, her itching had stopped and her hair was going back to dark brown. It would just be the four of them. But then she looked at Beth. If she wanted to stay on the bus and come, it'd be good for her.

She saw Miss Ellington speaking urgently to Mr Swinton, who shook his head, and held up one finger. 'Just the sister, as next of kin,' Fran saw him mouth.

She turned to tell the other two that someone was in for bad news, but as she did so she saw Miss Ellington shake her head and point to their table. By now the whole table had seen and had fallen silent. Steadily, the canteen quietened and all eyes were on the small group. It was only the tannoy that continued as before, playing music.

Mrs Oborne had a brother in the mine, as well as a husband. Valerie and Maisie had brothers too, but it couldn't possibly be Maisie because her husband had already died, and lightning didn't strike twice. No, not Maisie, life couldn't be that cruel, or so Fran prayed. The canteen doors swung open, and Amelia came in, her brown hair gleaming. She stood with Miss Ellington, listening, and looked doubtful. Miss Ellington gripped her arm and spoke at length. It was then that Amelia could be seen nodding.

Both women turned to Mr Swinton, talking at once, but Mr Swinton brushed them aside and strutted towards the bus team's table, his overalls flapping. No one spoke on the tables he passed, they just looked. The bus table saw that Miss Ellington was following in his wake, and behind her came Amelia, a file under one arm and a piece of paper in her other hand.

Mr Swinton reached their table and he eyed each and every one of them, and it was at that moment that Fran realised he was enjoying this, and knew that it was Stan, for it was only her family Swinton hated enough to toy with like this. She stood, but he waved her down. Her legs felt weak with relief, but then he pointed to Sarah. 'A bit of an accident at Massingham Colliery. Your brother is in the Newcastle Royal Victoria Infirmary. Mr Massingham has sent his car for you. Best hurry, or he might not—'

Miss Ellington spun round. 'Enough, Mr Swinton.'

She turned back to Sarah, who had already risen, pale as a ghost, gripping her hands together. Amelia stepped forward, tugging on Mr Swinton's arm, then pointing to Fran and whispering urgently. He shook her off. 'Relatives only. There's a war on, and targets to be met. Get changed, Miss Bedley. There is Mr Massingham's car waiting for you. The rest of you, press on at due time.'

Fran stared at Sarah, then Mr Swinton, then Miss Ellington. She stood. 'I must go. I'm to marry my Davey.'

Sarah reached out to her. They clasped hands as though they were drowning and the only safety was in one another. Fran pushed back her chair, which screeched on the concrete floor. The tannoy still played, and over it Mr Swinton said, 'Family only, I said. There is work to be done, and that starts in –' he checked the clock '– five and a half minutes.'

Miss Ellington swung round to stand in front of him. 'If Fran goes I'm sure the other girls will work harder and the target will be reached. And that, Mr Swinton, is the right thing to do.'

Mr Swinton started to push Miss Ellington to one side, but she pushed back. He snarled, 'You'll tell the men at the front this, will you?'

Fran dropped Sarah's hand and started round the table, but Beth caught and pulled her back. 'Hold her,' she urged Maisie, who came and did so, whispering, 'Wait, let Beth . . .'

She petered out because Beth had reached Miss Ellington and Mr Swinton.

'The men at the front don't make bloody overalls, do they, or wear them, you half-arsed idiot,' Beth said grimly.

Mr Swinton paled at that, and stepped back into Amelia, who pushed him off. It was only now that she spoke so the table could hear. 'Bugger the office. I'll take Fran's place, and then we can keep up.'

Mr Swinton stared wildly from one to the other, but all Fran could think was, Davey . . . a bit of an accident. You didn't send for the family for a bit of an accident. She couldn't breathe, and Sarah was white and panting, but Mrs Oborne had hold of her, shaking her by the shoulders. 'Stop that, Sarah, you need to be strong for your brother, and your parents.'

The rest of the room were watching. Some rose and drew near. Mr Swinton roared, 'Relatives only, I said.'

Miss Ellington spoke to Amelia. 'You meant it?'

'Of course I damn well did. These are my friends, and I didn't know they were until I wasn't amongst them. Of course I meant it.'

She was closer to Swinton now, along with Miss Ellington, who said to him, 'Then the shift is covered. We can sort the office. I'm sure you agree – for the sake of morale?'

'Sod morale,' shouted Beth, and by now all the women at the tables were standing, staring. 'Any more of your bliddy nonsense, Mr Swinton, and I'm not working, not today, not ever. I'm on strike. Anyone with me?'

Everyone who wasn't already standing, stood up, and a chorus of 'Ayes' resonated over the endless music. Then there was a long pause, or so it seemed to Fran, but it was only twelve seconds, or so the clock said. Now thirteen, as the second hand clicked round. Was Davey alive? Was he hurt badly? Oh Davey . . . Was it only Fran who heard Miss

Ellington whisper, 'Recover some moral high ground, Mr Swinton, for the love of God?'

'I'll have the lot of them for treason.'

Miss Ellington whispered again. 'Act your age, and dig yourself out of this damned great hole you've created for your idiotic arse before we see who actually is charged with treason. How's your son, by the way?'

At those words Mr Swinton flushed and, after a pause, nodded. Mrs Oborne let go of Sarah, who started to rush towards the door, then stopped, calling frantically, 'Fran, Fran, hurry.'

Fran moved then, feeling strange, as though she was floating miles above the world, but then Maisie came after her. 'Go. Just knowing you are there will seep into him, as it would have done my Derek if I had been with him on that beach.'

Maisie shoved her, and Fran sped past Amelia, who called, 'God speed.'

Again Fran stopped. 'How can I thank—' she said to Amelia.

'Friends don't have to,' Amelia said. 'I've only just realised that. Go.'

Beth went with them to the door. 'I'll come later, somehow.'

Again Fran said, 'How can we tha—'

'Don't.' Beth was fierce. 'Don't you dare thank me. We're all together, we three, and no one can mess us about. I won't have it.'

Fran and Sarah changed, full of fear and groping for gumption. They ran to the gates alongside Mrs Raydon, who had appeared as they left the changing rooms. They fumbled for their passes, showed them, and were waved through. They ran towards Massingham's great big Rolls. The front and back doors were open. 'Take the front,' Sarah shouted. 'I can't bear to have to talk, even to the chauffeur.'

Fran did, and shut the door, smelling . . . What? She turned but instead of Alfie Biggins it was Ralph. Of course, his cologne. She reached for the door, for today of all days she would not be near this man who had haunted her since his return. But she was too late, for Ralph was starting the car and driving off as Sarah slammed her door shut. All Fran could think was that Ralph was never going to leave her alone, never, and was using even this accident to stand between her and Davey. But he said, 'The chauffeur was off, and Father said I should take the car and drive you both. Where the hell have you been? We have to hurry.'

He was behaving normally, like any other man who wanted to help. She leaned back in the seat, too terrified at the thought of Davey and too grieved to even reply. So much for gumption, she thought.

In the back seat Sarah was silent, and that's how they travelled as they drove away from the Factory.

Back in the sewing room, Amelia took over Fran's machine and all the girls tucked their chins in and worked, ticketty-tick, crunch, crunch of the scissors. Finally, as two o'clock chimed, they reached their target. Amelia and Beth changed and walked to the bus with Valerie, Maisie and Mrs Oborne. Bert had heard the news and drove with a determination and speed the likes of which no one had experienced with him. As Beth got off at Sledgeford, he called after her, 'Tom Bedley were me marrer till I buggered me back. I've a grand liking for his lad. Fair breaks me heart, for yer know they don't send for relatives till it's right bad.' As the engine idled and the last of the Sledgeford passengers alighted, he looked at Beth. 'You'll be going to the station on yer bike?'

Beth nodded. 'Course I am, they're my friends. Just off to get it now.'

Bert nodded. 'Your marrers, yer mean. So go on, fetch yer bike. I'll drop you near the station at Massingham. They'll need yer, like as not. But you watch that Swinton. I heard you girls have had your tussles with him afore, and this might be one time too many. Like his boy, he be. Nasty when riled. Howay now, we'll wait.'

Beth ran all the way, hearing footsteps behind her, but she was heedless. She flew into her backyard, and it was then that Amelia arrived, helping her to haul the bike into the back lane. Just before she mounted, Amelia dug into her bag and drew out some money, stuffing it into Beth's pocket, 'For the train, and whatever you need.' She then brushed Beth's face with the ends of her scarf. 'Try not to cry, Beth. Come on.'

She ran alongside as Beth cycled back to the bus. She pushed while Beth hauled the bike up the steps, and Amelia called, 'I won't come, I'm not one of your marrers, as Bert called you, but anything I can do . . .'

Beth reached down as Mrs Oborne grabbed the bike and hauled it into the aisle, and held Amelia's hand. 'You have done so much. He'd never have let Fran off without you. They'll remember, I'll remember.'

Bert roared off, and Beth sat with a thump in the aisle. She said to Mrs Oborne, who still held the bike, 'You'll tell me mam for me when you get to Massingham? Tell her I'll be as long as it takes, but will need to bed down in me old room tonight.'

'Aye, lass, now wipe yer face, get rid of them tears and make 'em stop, cos that won't help the lasses.'

Beth hadn't known she was still crying.

Chapter Sixteen

Ralph drove in silence and in his presence Fran wouldn't cry. She wouldn't picture Davey as he and Stan had looked when they'd reached the hospital in the last accident. She wouldn't think, or feel, so she stared out at the scenery, if slag heaps could be scenery. But yes, they could, for Stan had said, 'They are the living embodiment of the land we live on.'

Her da had replied, 'Shut yer noise and eat yer tea.'

That had been when Stan started in the pit. Sixteen, like Davey, because they did a couple of extra years at school. She looked down at her hands, clenched into fists. No, she was thinking. No.

She looked at the road ahead, the distant pitheads, the church towers, the weathered old trees that were so lucky to make old bones ... Davey, her beloved Davey ... And then she felt a hand on hers. Ralph. She snatched hers away.

'I need to apologise. Davey came looking for me – he was my mentor for the day – and I was scrabbling to get a load of blacklocks out of my hair. Can't stand the devils, and they'd just dropped from the roof. When I heard the rock fall I was startled, and ran down with the tub, but was going so fast I tripped and it whacked off the rails, just before it reached the fall,' Ralph said.

'So why apologise?' Sarah said from the back seat. Fran just kept looking ahead. She mustn't open her mouth or a wail would be all that came out. A wail for her love, her Davey. What did she care about Ralph's blacklocks, his tub?

'You need to understand – he was looking for me because I was pithering about and he was my mentor for the day.' Ralph changed gear for the hill.

Sarah said quietly, 'He was doing his job, that's all. No one's fault. Can't you drive any faster?'

But Ralph was turning left into Massingham. Fran almost screamed, but controlled her voice and said, 'He's not here. He's in Newcastle, and to be in the Royal Victoria Infirmary means he's dead, or just hanging in. Where the bliddy hell are you taking us?'

Sarah reached forward and gripped Fran's shoulder. 'Hush, wee bairn. Hush.' But her voice was tight, and sick with grief. Fran reached up and held on to Sarah's hand as though she was drowning.

Ralph replied, 'I'm picking up Mrs Bedley. My father suggested we should gather the whole family, but your father went in the ambulance with Stan.'

Sarah breathed, 'Oh Stan, thank God.'

They turned down another left, and then a right, until Sarah yelled, 'Stop here.' Then added, 'Please.'

She flew from the car and beat on the front door, screaming, 'Mam, Mam, hurry.'

The door opened, and Sarah fell into her mam's arms. Behind Mrs Bedley was Fran's mam, who urged them towards the car and snapped at Sarah, 'Pull yourself together, pet. This isn't helping anyone, or anything. You're a pitman's daughter, and one who works in the midst of danger and laughs in its face. You remember that.'

Listening to her, Fran sat up straight, opened her door and stepped out. She hurried round and led Sarah and her mother to the car, passing neighbours who had gathered to help, and squashed into the back with them. This was where she belonged.

Her eyes met Ralph's in the mirror. 'If you would hurry

on now, please, Ralph. And thank you. Please believe that accidents happen and you didn't cause it. It was Davey's job to check on you.' Had she already said that? She didn't know, or care. Ralph must put his foot down, because who knew how long Davey would live, if he would live at all?

Sarah, Mrs Bedley and Fran all held hands, their chins in the air. They were strong and did indeed laugh in the face of danger, as did their pitmen fathers and husbands.

They arrived as the afternoon was ending.

At the red brick Victorian hospital, Fran, Mrs Bedley and Sarah clambered from the car.

'I'll wait,' said Ralph.

'No need, lad,' replied Mrs Bedley. 'We'll find a taxi or walk to the station.'

'No, I'll park and see how things are. My father will want to know.' His eyes flickered from Mrs Bedley to Fran, who merely nodded because what else could she do? He was the boss's son, and the boss wanted to know how her Davey was doing. It was what Mr Massingham always did, because he was a good owner. He even gave people time to find a different house if their man was killed or couldn't work, and paid the first month's rent. That's if a replacement pitman needed the house, otherwise you could stay on. It was only when you'd done wrong, like stealing or poaching his stock or birds, that you could sing for kindness from the big house. Seemed fair; the man had a mine to run.

The three women entered the hospital, stopped at the desk and then found their way to the ward where Davey had been taken. Was it the same one as before, when Stan had been in the next bed? Fran couldn't remember. They entered. A nurse who was sitting at a table in the centre of the room came to them, and Mrs Bedley explained who they were. 'Ah,' the nursing sister said. 'Yes, indeed. Well, I'm Sister Newsome, and now you are here I need to shoo his father and friend away, and then I can let two of you in behind the curtain, but only two.'

Fran suddenly felt unutterably weary as she traipsed out into the corridor to sit and wait. Within a minute Mr Bedley and Stan were waiting with her, as black as any pitmen who had come straight from the pit, but their faces were smeared. Stan took her hand. 'If he makes it, he'll never work in a pit again, bonny lass. His bad leg is pretty buggered again. The rest of him . . . Well, there's a limit . . .' He shrugged.

She leaned against his shoulder while Mr Bedley sat on the other side of her, thinking of things that only he could see. She whispered, for Stan's ears only, 'Will he live? That's all I need to know.'

'Oh God, I hope so. He's too much of a bliddy bugger to let a thing like a few tons of coal shut him up. He were talking about a key, a repeater, on and off in t'ambulance. Couldn't make head nor tail of it.'

Mr Bedley nudged her. 'Here comes Sarah. 'Tis your turn, lass.'

Fran rose, her heart thumping. Her Davey was in there, and now Sarah looked even paler, if that was possible. Mrs Bedley followed, her blue hat askew, her coat undone, showing her apron. She'd hate that she'd forgotten to remove it, but who would mention it, even if they noticed? Sarah leaned for a moment into Fran's open arms. 'The sister says he'll live, probably. He'll walk, probably, but the leg won't ever be strong, not enough it won't be, and I don't know what he'll do, and I don't bliddy care, for he'll live, probably.'

Mrs Bedley patted her hat. 'Enough of that. Our Davey's not going to leave us, cos he wouldn't dare, and mebbe his *leg* won't be strong, but our Davey always will be, you know that, you girls. And stand up straight, Sarah.'

She guided a weeping Sarah to a seat, and Fran set off into the ward, but as she was about to enter, something clicked in her mind and she turned. 'I expect "key" was to do with his latest crossword. He was trying to fiddle about with a coded one and was looking for the key.'

Everyone looked up and Stan nodded. 'Ah well, if he can't remember, he'll produce another.'

In the ward of about fourteen beds, Sister Newsome smiled as she stood in front of a curtained cubicle. 'If you're Fran, you'll do him the world of good.' The sister lifted the curtain. Fran entered and there he was, lying against a pillow, his face almost as white as the pillowcase, his grin a shadow of its normal self. He lifted his hand, and then let it drop. His leg was plastered to his thigh, and held up by a winch.

'Fran.' That was all.

She came to sit with him, taking his hand, lifting and kissing it. She said, 'By, lad, they've scrubbed you cleaner than you've ever been.'

'Aye.' His voice was little more than a whisper. 'And made me almost as good as new. It were Stan, you know. He stopped the bleeding in me thigh. Summat about an artery, so he'll never stop going on that I owe him me life. It'll be "Your round, Davey," not once but a million times.'

They smiled at one another. Fran murmured, 'Talking of keeping on, what's all this about a key?'

'Blowed if I knows, bonny lass. Our da asked an' all, and Stan.'

She leaned close and kissed his lips, whispering, 'I reckon it was about a coded clue you were probably working on.'

'Maybe.' He seemed to drift, then returned, concentrating on her. 'I meant to ask Sarah . . . how you got away from t'Factory?' His voice was little more than a sigh.

'Ah, Beth threatened a strike, and Amelia took my place.'

At this he raised his eyebrows and grinned for a moment, looking more like himself. Then it was gone. In the ward, someone called, 'Nurse, bedpan, please. Quick.'

'Better make that bliddy quick, Sister Newsome,' called another voice, 'or it'll be clean sheets needed an' all.'

Davey winced. Again, that sigh and a half-smile. 'The joys to come. Ah, so Beth is showing her mettle . . . at last. Knew it were there, somewhere. But how did you get here so quick . . . for it were quick, weren't it? Lose track here, I do.'

Just then they both heard Ralph's voice from the other side of the curtain. 'Knock, knock.'

Sister Newsome let him in and Davey stared as Ralph came to stand behind Fran. Then Davey looked at her. His voice was just the merest whisper, the light in his eyes fading until they seemed almost dead and it scared Fran, but he spoke: 'I see.'

He pulled his blue-scarred, and now black and blue hand away, but Fran recaptured it, gently, but firmly. 'Mr Massingham sent Ralph to pick up Sarah from the Factory and your mam from the house. I hitched a ride because if they could see you, I had to.'

Ralph laughed slightly. 'Well, not quite like that. You leapt into the front seat, if I remember rightly. Talking of memory, young Davey, do you remember anything of what happened? I hear it was a close-run thing, but even if . . . Well, of course, there's no doubt you'll survive, but there will be a weakness, and perhaps the pit is a lost cause. There are surface jobs, I suppose, but other war work's always an option.'

Fran turned, looked up at him and said, 'We told you we could get a taxi home, so do please feel free to leave, and if you remember, I sat in the back with Sarah and Mrs Bedley once I'd collected my wits. But I do want you to thank your da, since it was he who asked you to help out. And now Davey is tired, Ralph, and these two visitors are one too many, because he's real ill and he must get better, for he's me life.'

Ralph looked as though he'd been slapped, and for some reason she felt sorry for him. He had been there, after all, and blamed himself. She said, looking back at Davey, 'Davey, Ralph apologised for the fact that you had to come and find him, and were then caught in the roof fall.'

Davey frowned, shaking his head slightly. 'I don't remember, but it's me job to do that, or were.'

Ralph said, 'You really don't remember?'

'Nothing.'

A doctor entered with his stethoscope draped round his neck, his white coat as tired and creased as his middle-aged face. 'Evening, all. I heard the last bit of your conversation, and it's quite common to have memory loss. You will probably never remember. The brain is kind and wipes us free of trauma. I overheard you saying that his pit days are probably over?'

It was a question directed at Ralph, who muttered, 'That's what his father said, Doctor . . . ?'

'Wilson, Doctor Wilson. Listen, it's too early to say, but that could well be the case. First we have to stabilise him, because he's not out of the woods yet. But he's a strong young man with, Sister Newsome tells me, everything to live for.' He looked at Fran and smiled, then turned back to Davey. 'Did you know your jacket came with you, young man, rescued by your friend Stanhope? Or was it Sid? In the pocket is my favourite crossword magazine, and I know your column well. I daresay you can find a way to earn a few pennies, once you are on your feet, for my bet is that you will be, and will put this behind you. Any takers for a few bob on it?' He looked at Fran, who shook her head.

'I don't bet on certainties, Doctor.'

Dr Wilson muttered, 'Very wise.' Fran realised that he wasn't as old as she had first thought, just weary. 'We'll know more as time goes by,' he continued. 'Talking of time, it's time you went, sir.' He nodded to Mr Massingham. 'Let these two have a bit of peace and quiet together, eh.'

He held the curtain back, and Ralph could do nothing but leave, followed by the doctor, who winked at the pair of them.

Davey lay with his eyes closed, then murmured, 'What good is a couple of quid from a magazine? I couldn't even pay for a bliddy taxi for you, let alone drive you about in a bliddy great Rolls, ever.' Then he slept.

Fran sat with him, letting her eyes wander to his leg and back to his poor, cut face, his arms, blue scars crossed with red gashes, and bruises wherever you cared to look, and that was just the outside. But he must survive, and out of the pit he'd be safe, that was the main thing. She could go on working at the Factory, and when the war was over she'd work somewhere else. Anything, anything at all to keep him safe, with no more of these bliddy slashes. No more pain. Now the tears were silently falling.

Finally Sister Newsome came to shoo her away so that Davey could be checked. Sarah was in the corridor, waiting with Beth. The others had left to find some food and a beer. The three girls waited and for a while Fran found peace and comfort, Sarah too. At length they caught the last train home, but before they did, Sister Newsome weakened and allowed the three of them to wait by Davey's bed, whispering that the doctors were more than hopeful that he'd pull through, practically certain in fact. She left, and somehow the girls' presence roused him.

He didn't move, but he watched them stand around his bed. In that sigh of a voice he called them the three witches, and they called him the cauldron. His smile was slight, but his eyes were blank. It was as though something had gone out of him as he glanced at Fran, and then away.

While Fran talked quietly, speaking of the village, the beck, times gone by, Davey knew that something in him had changed. It wasn't the roof fall, it was Ralph, and all that Davey had seen in Ralph that he himself couldn't provide. And it was also Fran, because she had chosen to sit in the front with the whelp, not the back with Sarah, and hadn't told him. It was more than he could bear.

The girls had to leave to get the train, and he knew they would be up and ready to catch the bus to work at 4 a.m. He longed to hold her when they said farewell, but he had no strength. She slipped from him and from his bedside, then through the curtain, and it was as though his life and courage, and the will to fight, left with her.

He lay there, his eyes closed, and when his parents came to sit through the night with him, he pretended to sleep.

Chapter Seventeen

The next day Fran and Sarah were back at the bus shelter for the early shift, their minds and hearts full of Davey. They waited as the queue of women mounted the steps into the bus, Sarah hoping to see Stan before he went on shift.

'Wait up, Sarah.'

There was the sound of running and Stan's whistle rent the air. Sarah looked for him, and she and Fran heard Sid and Norm yelling at her to wait or they'd have to put a sock in Stan's mouth to stop the wailing. The other pitmen were streaming towards the pithead as usual, calling their "Ow do,' and one said, 'Sorry about your Davey, lasses.'

Another said, 'Howay, he's a grand lad, and'll get on his feet soon.'

Another, 'Aye that he will, or find a way through if he can't.'

But none stopped striding towards the pithead.

Stan weaved in between them, running up and pulling Sarah to one side so that others could mount the bus. Fran waited on the pavement, of course she did, because Stan looked strange, all of a dither, a bit . . . weak? Yes, that was it, and Stan never looked weak.

He was pulling Sarah to him, his voice desperate, his words hurried, his breathing rapid. 'You be safe, bonny Sarah. You hear me? Be safe, don't you be careless, cos I love you and we'll marry when this lot is over – if you'll have me – and then we'll never be apart.'

There it was, thought Fran, the weakness, the desperation. Sarah leaned back in his arms, the circles under her eyes deep, and the vestiges of her skin's yellow tinge visible in the early-morning moonlight. 'What?' she gasped.

As Fran watched, she suspected that after a night of pacing and worrying about his marrer, Stan had realised what life would be like if Sarah, his love, was ever hurt or killed. She had heard him rattling about in the kitchen at two in the morning. Slipping on her old dressing gown, she had joined him by the range and he had said, 'I don't know how you can bear it?'

And she'd replied, 'I'll take whatever I can have of him as long as he's alive because I've always loved him, I always will. I'll scrub every bliddy floor in Massingham to keep us and not count the cost.'

He'd stood there, his Woodbine between his lips. 'You sound like a bleedin' play.'

'Aye, well, that's as maybe, but I mean it, you beggar.' They'd laughed together and he held her as the range spluttered on its slack and they gave one another what comfort they could.

She watched now as Stan pulled Sarah close again. 'Life's too damned short to mither on. I love you, lass, and want you for my girl, for ever. Say you will.'

Sarah looked from him to Fran just as Bert called, 'Say aye, for the love of God, lass, or we'll be late.' The bus exhaust was cloudy in the freezing predawn.

The whole bus yelled then. 'Aye, course she will, our Stan.'

Mrs Oborne's voice reached them. 'Get on with it, do.'

Maisie's followed. 'Got a bottom drawer?'

Laughing, Fran added her own voice. 'Do you love my daft great brother, our Sarah, or not? That's the question.'

Sarah flung her arms around Stan's neck. 'Course I do, and course I will.' She kissed his mouth, and he lifted her up, spinning her round, then putting her down as Sid and Norm, who had been waiting near the shelter, banged their bait tins together.

'At bliddy last. Come on, lad, or we'll be running, and we've got Davey's load to make up today.'

Sid called to Fran, 'T'manager said yer lad'll get his pay if we meet the target. 'Twas what Massingham woulda done afore it were under government war management. Though I reckon he's had something to do wi' it.'

Fran smiled. 'That's right good of you, lads.' She squeezed past Sarah and Stan, winking at her brother and grinning, but the smile wouldn't mean anything until she knew Davey was really going to live.

Sarah was climbing up behind her and the women on the bus were cheering. Mrs Oborne grabbed Sarah's mac belt as she passed. 'That Stan's a good 'un.'

'But it's Davey we need to know about,' called Maisie.

The two girls took a seat behind her. No one spoke while Bert drove past the Hanging Tree, but afterwards, in the quiet, Sarah left it to Fran to tell the women.

'Doing as well as expected, so they said. Too early to tell if his perfection is blemished, but probably not.' She put on a posh voice because no one must know how close she was to screaming.

The women laughed along with Fran, which was what she had intended. Sarah laughed too, and then sat quietly as the bus eased over a beck bridge and on towards Sledgeford. At last, she whispered, 'It seems bad to be happy when Davey's so hurt.'

'It's never bad to be happy,' said Fran, 'and he'll be right glad, you know he will. We'll all be together, the gang, and we'll let Bob in too, when he's home. Think of the beck, and how we'll swim, and then our bairns too, after the war.'

Everything was 'after the war'.

Maisie turned. 'You just hang on to that. Bairns are a good thought, just don't work with any powder that's nasty while you're heavy with the babe, eh?' She laughed, but Fran recognised the pain in her laugh. Poor Derek, poor Maisie, poor babe. They were driving through the ford, the water swishing up either side, and then pulling into Sledge-ford, where Beth clambered on, waving at the applause.

'Here's our striking firebrand,' Mrs Oborne called.

Beth's eyes looked deep-set from tiredness too. She'd left her bike at Fran's and the taxi had taken her on to her house because she'd wanted to sleep in the sheets she and Bob had slept in rather than at her mam's. After the shift today they'd all cycle to the station and on into Newcastle. She bowed. 'Aye, and you lot stood behind me an' all, so we'll all go to clink together.'

Amelia clambered on the bus after her, and was greeted by more applause. Surprised, she grinned.

'You're one of us,' called Mrs Oborne, 'after you stood tall yesterday and then worked so bliddy hard alongside us.'

As Bert drove on, Amelia said, 'I rather think I will really be back with you all after Mr Swinton's vented his spleen about me to the office administrator, but that's all right. I know my place – it's with the girls.'

There were more cheers, and Beth made room for her on her seat. Looking across at Fran, Amelia asked, 'You all right, our Fran?'

'Oh aye, we're always all right, aren't we.' It wasn't a question.

As they arrived, the dawn was promising to break. Well, of course it was, Fran told herself, just as it always would. Huddled in their macs, their hats pulled down and their scarves up, they passed through the security gate and into their building, heading for the clean-room changing rooms, only to find Miss Ellington waiting for them in the corridor, pointing to the changing rooms on the other side. Mrs Oborne stopped, looked, then understood, just as they all did. 'Our Mr Swinton's getting his own back, I reckon?'

Miss Ellington nodded, her expression grim. 'I tried. I failed.'

'Ah well, pellets?'

'Bullets.'

'Huh,' Maisie sighed.

Miss Ellington sighed along with her. 'Indeed.'

'There's a special place for people like Swinton. And it's not up there,' Amelia said as she pointed to the heavens.

Miss Ellington shook her head. 'Don't worry, you're for the office, Amelia.'

Everyone stopped. Amelia shook her head. 'That's not fair. I was part of the strike, or threatened strike.'

Miss Ellington nodded. 'Which hurts more, moving with your friends or being different?'

Amelia paused, then nodded. 'Devious fecking bastard.'

Miss Ellington, as surprised as the rest of them, murmured again, 'Indeed.'

'Can't we do something, Miss Ellington?' Fran called.

'No. It would need to come from the office administrator, so all you can do, Amelia, is try and wheedle a transfer. But, on the bright side, and to keep our spirits up, don't forget the rehearsal at lunchtime. I have checked with the office manager and you can work it so that you have the same break.'

Amelia merely nodded. 'Received and understood, off to wheedle. See you later, girls.'

They traipsed to the changing rooms with their bottles and stripped. The security officers checked them as Fran said to the others, 'I'm right sorry.'

Sarah came to stand beside her after they'd been told they could dress again. 'Me too, everyone. It was our problem and you don't deserve this.'

Mrs Oborne hitched her large bosom, then dressed again, and slipped into her overalls. 'What's deserving got to do with the price of eggs, daft girls? We knew the little rat—'

'Mouse, Mrs Oborne,' interrupted Valerie. 'He's not big enough for a rat.'

The women drank half a bottle of water each and were laughing by the time they headed into the bullet workshop anteroom, where lo and behold, Mr Swinton was on foreman duties. 'Of course he bliddy is,' muttered Maisie.

They were read the security warnings by Mr Swinton, who actually smiled this morning. He ended, looked around, then barked, 'Follow me.'

They did and Fran comforted herself that at least the day would end. Mr Swinton must have suspected that gestures were being made behind his back but at least they made the women feel better as they took the places of the departing night shift at the benches. Hour after hour they worked, putting the detonators into the bullets brought by conveyor belt. The noise built, the belts creaked and rumbled, and Fran knew that she must not think of Davey, and that neither must Sarah. Instead they must concentrate, that's all, concentrate.

After the first hour they were so familiar with it all, that concentration was only a part of it. Fran found herself singing 'All or Nothing at All', and then again, until they were all singing, even Mrs Oborne and Valerie, so that the others sang louder to drown them out. 'You two are our secret weapon,' Fran called. As time went on, Fran suggested the contraltos should add harmony. It sounded good, but at this point a security officer stepped into the room and placed her hand on Fran's shoulder.

Fran stepped away from the bench and the security

officer checked her for illicit hairgrips and so on, a precaution which happened more frequently these days. All the while the bus team were repeating the second verse, as they pushed in the detonators, carefully, carefully, but as they did so the conveyor juddered to a halt.

Mr Swinton yelled, 'What have you done?'

'Nothing at all,' sang Fran.

The women laughed. Mr Swinton did not. 'You, Miss Hall, should know your place.'

A mechanic was called. While they waited, they had to step away from the belt and bullets while the security officer checked other workers at random. They still sang and this time Fran wondered if a staccato deep bass would give the idea of drums. It was just a question of seeing who could go low enough.

Without a doubt, Mrs Oborne would be perfect, and Valerie too. Mrs Oborne blamed her large bosom, but Valerie couldn't claim that. For the third drum they were joined by a new lass from Massingham, Marjorie, who was young and big-boned. They tried it again as they watched the clock. They'd have to stay and do overtime to meet the target if the ruddy belt held them up for long and then when could they visit Davey, oh when?

After an hour the belt was working, and as the mechanic left he tipped his cap, which he had not removed, even for a moment, and said, 'Right nice that were. I've set it to break down again tomorrow, just so's I can hear it.'

Their boos followed him out of the section and all the women there, not just the bus team, laughed, until Mr Swinton strutted along from the end and again wanted to know who'd buggered the belt? It took the security officer, who had finished her checks, to stop by Mr Swinton and assure him that it was overworked machinery, not overworked women. Swinton huffed off on his rounds again.

As they returned to work, Fran found herself drawn back to Davey, though she'd never been far from him, and to her horror started weeping silently at his pain, his despair—

'Concentrate, concentrate,' Sarah snapped next to her. She jerked upright. Of course she must.

They broke for lunch and ate cottage pie, with a lot of potato and just a little mince. Fran pushed hers away. Maisie raised an eyebrow and Fran nodded. Maisie gobbled it down, but said, as she ate Fran's rice pudding too, 'You'll feel hungry again soon. I promise, lass.'

They rose, following Miss Ellington to the side room as she wanted to hear their rendition. This time they followed the sheet music exactly. It was uncertain and flat as though they'd run out of energy. After the first run-through, Amelia rushed in, panting. 'Am I in time?'

Mrs Oborne laughed. 'We'll always make time for you from now on,' she said, and Amelia smiled, embarrassed.

Mrs Raydon put her head through the door. 'I heard, the whole canteen heard, and it's messy. You need a leader to conduct, and I reckon on Fran, since I gather you had some good ideas in the bullet section, or so the security officer told me. What do you say, girls? She needs something to think about, Sarah too, so why not have them share it between the pair of them? Before you mither, Fran Hall, I've just heard from one of the other groups that you were the Angel Gabriel in the Nativity at St Oswald's, singing "Silent Night". What more of a reference do you need?'

Everyone laughed as Mrs Raydon disappeared again. Miss Ellington waved her truncated arm. 'Come along now, Fran, you can't ask me to embarrass myself by waving this about in the air for the rehearsals. What's more, I have money riding on you lot to win. I want to hear you singing for the wireless *when* they come.'

The women gasped.

'*When*, she said,' shouted Maisie.

'And she's got a bet on us,' added Valerie.

The mood lifted, though more because of the bet, Fran thought. Suddenly she was nervous at the idea of the whole country hearing them. Fran shook her head at their security officer. 'That's blackmail.'

Beth stepped forward and turned to the women, who were grouped together as a choir would be. 'Come along, we look the part, or would do if a choir with a banana tinge were needed, so let's win this damned thing, or we'll never hear the end of it and we'll be frisked every hour of the shift by an angry Miss Ellington.'

Mrs Oborne replied, 'Aye, and I'm not having that lot out in the canteen calling us a mess.'

Miss Ellington coughed. 'I rather thought you and Valerie had decided not to be included . . . Foghorns were mentioned.'

Mrs Oborne put her hands on her hips. 'We're to be the drums, I'll have you know, along with Marjorie, the new girl, and that's that. Cos if our mates can say they've been on the wireless, we want to say we've been on too. Anyone got a problem with that?'

No one dared say a word.

Miss Ellington grinned and made for the door, calling over her shoulder, 'Your dinner break runs for another twenty minutes. I expect great things from my girls. Don't let me down. Can't have Swinton's favourites winning – the choir from the artillery-shell sector.'

She shut the door behind her. Fran looked down at the music, shaking her head. 'I was five when I was the Angel Gabriel.'

The women burst out laughing. 'You should see your sulky face, lass,' called Maisie.

'Never mind her face,' said Mrs Oborne. 'I'm not having

Swinton getting his lot on the wireless, so come along, get serious.'

At 2 p.m., the girls streamed onto the bus, but not Amelia. She had to wait until the end of the working day at five. Neither would she be on the morning bus again, now she was permanently in the office. Beth stayed on with them past Sledgeford, and at four they hurried from the bus to find Ralph there, in his roadster. He tipped what looked like a new Harris tweed cap at Fran. 'Your carriage awaits.'

Sarah pinched Fran's arm, her indrawn breath an indication of her fury. 'We've our bikes, Mr Massingham,' she said.

'Well, as Fran is Davey's special friend, I expect she'd rather have a ride.' Ralph's voice was as cold as his expression.

Beth said, 'Aye, but Sarah's his sister, so I reckon if it's anyone—'

Ralph put up his hand, as though to stop her. Beth was not about to take any notice and began again, but Fran took over. 'We can all squash in, two of us in the dicky seat. Stan told me the luggage-rack can lift up like magic to make a couple of seats. What do you say, girls – we'll take turns with the dicky for as long as Ralph gives us lifts? And thank you kindly for the offer, Mr Massingham.'

Her gaze was calm as he stared at her with that look he had given Sarah. She stared back without expression, hiding her rage at his attempt to muscle into her life, and even having the bloody cheek to use Davey's hospital stay to do so.

She became aware that most of the women were off the bus, standing around waiting, the wind lifting their hats or tugging at their headscarves. Their pallid, sallow faces were pinched with tiredness, and no one said a word. They just looked, and it was like having an army behind her. She stood straighter.

Finally Ralph broke his gaze and smiled round at everyone. 'Why not? I'm sure Davey will be pleased to see us – all. After all, anything I can do for him, I will. I feel so very annoyed with myself for being so tardy on his watch.'

On Ralph's return from the hospital, he saw through the open study door that his father was back from London and was once again sitting at his desk.

Ralph's heart sank. The open door meant 'A word with you, Ralph.' He put his coat as quietly as possible on the coat stand, along with his scarf, and walked across the hall on his toes. His father heard him nonetheless and called, 'A word with you, Ralph.'

At least, Ralph thought as he changed direction, he sounded mellow. He allowed his heels to click on the black and white marble floor, his cigarette smoke trailing behind him. No sound from the boys, thank God, because the weekend had been bedlam. If it wasn't bad enough having those ghastly children, the mothers had appeared, invited by his stepmother, who should damned well know her place.

His father had moved from the desk and was waiting by the fireplace, in which blazed a roaring fire. At least it would be warm while Ralph received what would no doubt be some parental homily. And presumably it would be something to do with the accident in the mine, again.

He crossed the study carpet soundlessly, making for his father's desk, and stubbed out his cigarette in the crystal ashtray which already held several stubs. 'Good evening, Father. Satisfactory trip, I hope? London's surviving its travails?'

His father smiled. 'Good enough, but tiring. I suppose

265

we all feel that, in the midst of this wretched war. There's so much for us all to do and perhaps to worry about, including London, which is, as you say, surviving its travails.'

Ralph drew out his cigarette case and offered it to his father, who took a Player's. Ralph took another as well, not really wanting it, but it gave his hands something to do. He lit both with his gold lighter and stood by the fire too. It was good to feel the heat. 'Where are the boys?' he asked.

'At Cubs in Sledgeford. Sophia has taken them, thought it might be a good idea to meet the other evacuees. I gather they collect jam jars, or pans, or some such, for the war effort, or . . .' His father stopped, and ran his hand over his forehead. 'No, they dig about in the rubbish tip for them, then they are washed and so on and taken to the Women's Institute for jam or some such.'

Ralph knew his father was preoccupied; the endless repetition of 'some such' was the clue. Thinking about clues, he wondered if his father wanted to see him because of the call Ralph had made to Professor Smythe between the end of his shift at the mine and collecting the girls? His excitement rose.

His father was holding up his cigarette and staring at the glowing end. 'I had a call while you were out. I gather you contacted Professor Smythe following the Bedley boy's accident with an update on his condition and to suggest that the lad's crossword facility could surely be put to better use than making a few column inches in a magazine. Smythe was able to relay to me that in all likelihood the Bedley lad's days as a pitman are over, which comes as no surprise, given what the doctor at the hospital told me about the severity of his injuries. Though, thankfully, he is out of danger.'

His father paused, the eyes that examined Ralph carefully expressionless. 'I did wonder, shall we say, after our recent discussion about the lad and his feisty lass, whether the accident was a tad convenient—'

That was all, but it was enough. Ralph felt himself grow cold, and his cigarette smoke trembled as much as his hand as he cut in. 'Father, how could you? Indeed, how dare you? How could a mine accident be convenient?'

'How indeed? But you didn't allow me to finish, Ralph. That was indeed my initial thought, but Smythe tells me you admitted being slow, causing Davey to have to check on your well-being. This, of course, had already been reported to me by Elliott. As you explained to Smythe, your guilt is why you feel the need to make reparations and, er, explore some way of finding an alternative to the less-than-satisfactory surface job that might be all that is on offer.'

Ralph did wish his father didn't talk as though he'd swallowed a dictionary.

He leaned forward and flicked his ash onto the flames, muttering, 'It was the blacklocks. The beggars fell down my neck. I hate the things. It held me up, and I didn't hear him call over the noise of the mine. I just heard the falling coal and let go of the tub as I rushed to have a look-see. It almost whacked into the coal, but sort of spun off the rails before then.

'D'you know, Father, I think one of the pit props was in need of replacement – you could see where it broke, so it's no wonder the roof caved in. Perhaps Elliott should have a word with the security team? That's Bedley's father and Stan's old man, isn't it? Not that one would wish to cast aspersions on their actions, or lack of them.' He inhaled deeply on his cigarette. If his father could come up with long words, so could he.

His father looked up sharply. 'Indeed not. You speak of two of Massingham Colliery's best men, and don't you forget it. It's more likely that the movement of the coal increased for some unaccountable reason. A possible explanation that was considered was that the tub was released beforehand, hit the prop and snapped it, but there also seemed to be another cut on that particular prop, which made a fall inevitable when the coal squeezed against it. Poor Davey – how sad that he was there at that particular time. And good for your peace of mind that you let go of the tub *after* the fall, for it isn't hard to see that an empty one would crash off at that particular point. However, who can say what happened, for the accident has muddied . . .'

His father's eyes were sharp as he trailed into silence, just staring at Ralph, who grew cold again, unable to breathe for he had indeed cut the prop after speaking to someone – he knew not who, for it was on the telephone, but someone within the group – to establish that a tub would career off just as had actually happened. He forced a breath, then another. Thank God these things were 'muddied'. He threw his cigarette in the fire, watching it, not his father.

'Ah well, mines are damnable things,' his father continued. 'There's a creak, a groan and the whole lot comes down. It doesn't necessarily need help to do that.' He looked at his son, his eyes hard, but worried. 'You look relieved – why?'

'Relieved? Oh, because it was nothing to do with the two families. They've had enough with the accident.'

Ralph drew out his cigarette case for something to do, waved it at his father who shook his head. Ralph didn't want yet another, but lit up anyway as the front door banged open and the boys barged across the hall. Sophia, her voice full of laughter, called after them, 'Is that really wiping your feet, boys? I think not. Return and do it properly.'

Ralph watched the joy light up his father's face, and

knew he had to be quick if he was to sort Davey Bedley's future. 'So, Father, back to Davey? I can't cope with thinking that I contributed to the accident in any way. After all, if he hadn't been there, it wouldn't have happened . . . That's why I attempted to see if Smythe knew of some way of using the lad's skills for the war effort, or of simply admitting him to Oxford once he's fit enough. He has a good brain; he drew with Stan on the scholarship, after all.'

His father strode across the room as Sophia entered. She raised her head for his kiss. She was elegant, her dark hair up in a French pleat, and her deep brown eyes danced as Fran's did when she looked at Davey, and how one day they might when Fran, Davey's most precious possession, looked at Ralph. Then he could unpin her hair and it would fall as Sophia's had when she had calmed his childhood nightmares and told him everything would be all right, even though his mother had died. It was the only time he had not felt alone, during that period of time.

'Father?' Ralph called.

'Yes, you're right,' his father said as he hugged Sophia. 'And as it happens, I'm off to see the lad soon with a few ideas of my own. I'll add yours to my fevered brain so I have something coherent . . . Thank you, Ralph, for your concern. It cheers me immensely. Now, let's all three retire to the drawing room for a drink. Sophia, darling, slip out of your coat, and join us.'

Sophia waved to Ralph as she left the study, saying over her shoulder, 'Ralph, dear. I hope you had a good day and managed to see the Bedley boy? I also hope he's a bit better, at the very least.'

The boys rushed past her, up the stairs. 'That's better,' she called after them. 'Now Nanny will give you hot milk and biscuits in the nursery and I will be up to kiss you goodnight.'

The pang that cut through Ralph was sharp and long-lasting, because once that had been the two of them. He watched as she graced both men with her smile, which was beautiful and kind in a way his mother had not been. But again, that was enough. First Davey and Fran. Then the war, to help bring about Hitler's victory.

Chapter Eighteen

At the start of the following week, Annie Hall put more coal on the range and then poured the co-op ladies' tea. She smiled at Madge, whose eyepatch today was green for Monday. Madge had told them a few years ago how she'd been pedalling like a wild thing over Minton's beck bridge as a new bride when 'crash, bang wallop'. The hospital had done what they could, but she had arrived in Massingham with Rob, now her ex-husband, and an eyepatch. Annie stopped her train of thought. Not hospitals, anything but that.

She cleared her throat. 'We must send our twenty wall coverings to Briddlestone's tomorrow, but we only have eighteen. Mrs Oborne is working the afternoon shift at the moment at you-know-where, so she says she'll try and work into the night on her return to finish hers, and in the morning too, if need be. We, ladies, must finish Mrs Bedley's.'

Just then, Audrey Smith, Beth's mam, knocked on the back door and hurtled in. 'Sorry to be late. I travelled with Maud Bedley to the hospital this afternoon, and sat a while. Fran and Sarah nipped in this morning with Mr Bedley as them're all on aft-shift, but you'll know that.'

She stripped off her coat and unwrapped a wall hanging. It was a Christmas scene. 'I picked this up from the Bedleys' old pigeon house. Maud left it for us, God bless her, so I'll work on it now, as she's told me what colours go where. She says her Sarah and Fran cut up strips before they went to work yesterday.'

She settled on a spare chair while Annie poured another cup of tea. 'Here you are, lass.'

Audrey slurped it down, quick as a flash. She was about to set to work, but then dug in her handbag, bringing out some coins. 'The Miners' Club had a collection for the bus and train fares to the hospital. Who's going with Maud tomorrow?'

Madge said, 'I'm on the rota for it, I reckon?' It was a question and Annie snatched a look at the names on the wall, which she had listed on the back of a piece of wallpaper the corner shop had donated. When Annie had left the shop with it, Mrs Adams, Maisie's mam, had called, 'Wait on, Annie.' She'd dipped into the broken-biscuit tin on the counter and bagged up several handfuls. 'To be taken to the hospital for the lad.'

There it was: *Tuesday – Madge*.

Annie smiled. 'That'll be the navy blue eyepatch, then, Madge?'

Madge laughed. 'It will an' all, poor bairn.'

The women settled and worked solidly for the next hour or two. Only when Mrs Bedley's was finished did they call it a night.

Madge stayed on to help Annie wash the pots and whilst they were busy they talked about Davey, and mithered about the future. 'I worry about those girls too,' Annie said. 'They hadn't lost the colour before they were sent back where . . . Oh well, never mind, and then there's this Davey business, and . . . By, I don't know, pet. It's all a bit of a do.'

'There's nowt we can do about any of it, is there? All a bit of a mishmash, isn't it.' Madge put the last of the cups on the shelf. 'What'd do those two some good would be for Sarah to have her brother back, and Fran to have her man home. Or, let's face it, a bliddy good piece of right red meat.'

The two of them laughed, and Annie said, 'Aye, that's what most need and won't get, but it's good to dream.'

After their shift at the mine, Tom Bedley and Joe Hall sat in the canaries' shed. Tom eased his back, his strong fingers sorting through the seed, listening as their latest cock warbled, his neck stretched and his throat throbbing. 'A beauty,' Tom whispered, as though he didn't want to disturb the song.

Joe Hall listened with him, finally murmuring, 'Reckon he's not a patch on them three girls. Did you hear the lasses singing in the backyard? Word-perfect, they are. Mind, it helps having Beth back staying with her mam at Langton Terrace. And it's company for Audrey, with Tubby reet poorly. Saves the pennies, too.'

'Aye, the lasses could teach the old bird a few tricks, right enough. D'you remember poor auld Tubby's voice? He were a great tenor, he were. Bloody black lung,' Tom said, coughing. The two men looked at one another and laughed.

'Have a fag,' Joe muttered, throwing him a pack of Woodbines.

'Not in wi' the birds, what's the matter wi' yer?'

Joe nodded. 'Aye, yer right, so chuck 'em back then.'

He caught the pack and pushed it into his pocket as Tom said, 'I canna get that prop out me 'ead.'

Joe rose and stuffed chickweed in the wire of the cages. 'Aye, so you've said, lad, more'n once.'

'But it's that cut, it divint make sense. The gouge would if it had been hit by a tub, but there weren't a tub near, so 'tis said. The whelp had hold, and it were let go with the sound of the fall. But that still leaves the cut . . .'

Joe took more chickweed from the bucket and did the top tier of cages. 'So what're you saying?'

Tom joined him, sighing again. 'I don't rightly know, our Joe. It just divint feel right.'

'Ah, but is that because it's your lad in the hospital? The coal can squeeze something powerful, lad, and just snap the buggers, yer know it. And the cut could have been done when t'prop were put up.'

Neither of them spoke as they continued prodding in the chickweed, then Joe started laughing. Tom put up with it for as long as he could, then said, 'For the love of God, what's the matter wi' ye?'

'I'm thinking that we're getting so good at prodding in the weed we could be part of the co-op our lasses have put together. If the mine ever folds, anyways.'

Simon Parrot spoke from the doorway. 'Fat chance of that, lads. I just heard in the club they're opening up all the really old seams, the ones that are more'n half used up, not just about half used up. The government management want every spare bit of coal found, so you two'll be too bliddy busy checking them out to be prodding strips through hessian. Sorted the seed, 'ave ye?'

'Ah, so you've come, eh. Been reading the newspapers at the club, no doubt, instead o' pulling your weight here. Tell us then what's happening, and then happen we'll tell yer what we've been up to.'

The three of them sat down again and Simon rabbited on about the Russians and their war, and the Royal Navy's first successful Arctic convoy. All the while, Joe thought about his lad in the mine, his lass in the Factory and his boy at school, and Tom chased his thoughts about the gouged and cut pit prop and his poor bairn of a boy in his hospital bed. And worried about what the hell Davey was going to do to earn some bliddy money for his future.

On Wednesday Mr Massingham finally arrived at the Royal Victoria Infirmary and waited in the corridor to see Dr Wilson, who had been caring for the Bedley lad. The chairs were lined up hard against the green-tiled wall. He'd sat on chairs like this at school when he'd waited for the cane for kicking the football and breaking the large glass-house window. He'd been made to pick up the pieces and then report for punishment.

At the memory he worried again about his son. Should he, as his father, have insisted Ralph went to help pick up the shredded papier-mâché football with the other lads all those years ago? Might it have created some common ground, and drawn a line under the incident, which seemed to have left such a seething fury in the boy? Massingham shifted on the chair. But he hadn't, what he'd done was to try to explain to Ralph that the Bedley boy had been within his rights to damage the football in retaliation. It was easily repaired after all. But Ralph had just seen it as his father taking sides against him.

Reginald Massingham eased his arse again. Lord above, he needed to put on a bit of weight, or the hospital needed to provide cushions. Mark you, he thought that every time he came to visit his injured pitmen, so it was about time he did something about it. He found his pen and made a note in his diary to offer the funds and was checking his watch for the third time when he heard a bevy of voices. Wilson was leading a phalanx of doctors and nurses along the corridor towards the ward. He hesitated when he saw Mr Massingham, then had a quick word with the white-coated doctor on his right, who nodded and carried on.

Dr Wilson stopped and held out his hand. Massingham shook it. 'Good to see you again, and equally good of you to spare me a moment,' Massingham said, only then remembering his homburg, whipping it off and throwing it on the chair on which he'd just been sitting.

Dr Wilson smiled. 'It will be only a moment, I'm afraid,

but I'm relieved to talk about the Bedley boy. Walk with me?'

Massingham left his hat where it was; he couldn't be up and down like a jack-in-the-box. They walked towards the ward, but just before they reached it, Wilson turned right into his office, shutting the door behind them. He pointed to a chair in front of his desk, whilst he took his place behind it, drawing a file from a pile and scanning it quickly. He tapped it and, with his eyes on Massingham, said: 'There's a slight chance Bedley'll be back in the mine, but only slight, and not for quite a while.' Wilson placed his hands flat on the desk. 'I was in two minds whether to put in a telephone call to you, Mr Massingham, so I'm pleased you beat me to it.'

Massingham looked at the doctor, interested. Suddenly he was not in such a hurry and hoped the doc wasn't either. He found himself feeling relieved just to be sitting here, on the other side of someone's desk, and not having to think about his factories or his family or various wartime concerns that were landing on his lap, courtesy of Professor Smythe who seemed to be tinkering about here and there, but mainly in intelligence. He sighed, half smiling, for Professor Smythe was a force of nature and impossible to dodge.

'Carry on,' Massingham said, crossing his legs.

Wilson withdrew a crossword magazine from his pocket and placed it on the desk between them. 'Please look at page six.'

Massingham did so, and saw that the page was given over to D. Bedley's crosswords. He nodded, for this wasn't new to him. He looked at the doctor with renewed interest.

'That lad is wasted here,' said Wilson. 'I happen to know you—' He stopped. 'Well, how can I put this—'

Massingham interrupted. 'You think I might have a contact?'

Wilson looked surprised. 'Contact? Er, no. I was talking to Davey's friend, Stan, who tells me there was an examination for a scholarship . . . ?'

Massingham nodded. Stanhope Hall, of course. He smiled. He liked loyalty between friends, and those two boys had been competitors as well as friends. They had stayed marrers, in spite of one of them taking the prize and the other forfeiting it. He smiled again. Ah, forfeiting for the sake of the feisty young Frances Hall . . . he admired that too.

Massingham stood. Wilson looked surprised, then embarrassed. 'Ah, I've overstepped the mark.'

Massingham shook his head. 'On the contrary. I applaud your care for the whole person, Dr Wilson. Leave it with me. Let's see what can be done for the lad, eh? I can slip in and see him, I presume?'

Dr Wilson was up and dashing to the door to usher Mr Massingham out. 'By all means. Sister Newsome will be happy to show you to his bed, though you can't miss him as he's the one with his leg in the air, with a plaster covered with rude messages from his friends. You might like to add one yourself. I daresay you'll have to beard Sister Newsome's wrath if you don't. She's quite a tartar, in her own way.' For a moment Dr Wilson looked preoccupied, and murmured, 'And she has the most amazing eyes and cheekbones.'

Reginald Massingham found himself roaring with laughter as he shook the doctor's hand. 'Ah, so obedience is the order of the day, eh? And I suggest you discuss Sister Newsome's eyes and cheekbones with her personally. You never know, she might admire your stethoscope in return.' It was the doctor's turn to laugh and, indeed, blush.

As they approached the ward, the phalanx of doctors and nurses burst back through the swing doors. Wilson swerved, took up his place at their head and led his ducklings off at a cracking pace. Left on his own, Reginald Massingham entered the ward, only to be accosted by a slim, dark-haired sister who held out her arms as though daring him to pass. 'These are not visiting hours,' she snapped.

'Dr Wilson gave me permission. I have just been speaking with him. I need to see young Davey Bedley you see,' Reginald said meekly.

Sister Newsome flashed a look at the ward clock. 'Ten minutes. We've just had the chaos of doctors' rounds, and we have bedpans to do, and those wait for no man, trust me. Better in the pan than the bed.'

Reginald blanched, and promised. 'Ten minutes only.'

He spied the raised leg in plaster and headed in that direction, settling himself down on the chair beside the bed as Davey tried to heave himself upright from the stacked pillows. 'Steady, no need to sit to attention, though I can see why you feel you might have to,' Reginald muttered, nodding towards Sister Newsome. He and Davey shared a grin. 'We have ten minutes before the bedpans are produced, and I have no intention of being here when they are.'

Davey smiled. 'Good of you to come, sir.'

Reginald shook his head. 'I usually pop in to see how my men are doing.' He paused, not quite sure how to go on. 'Er, I've been wondering . . .' Someone shouted out and there was a kerfuffle with Sister Newsome and a nurse striding down the ward, sweeping past Davey's bed, towards the patient in question.

Yes, Massingham thought, he had indeed been wondering – even before the accident – about young Bedley, and had actually spoken to the owners of the publishing house that produced the magazine, after a conversation about intelligence gathering at one of his, or rather Smythe's, meetings in Whitehall. Upon hearing of the respect in which Bedley was held by the owner of the magazine, Smythe and he had spoken further at their club about a place called Bletchley Park and were on the point of pursuing the matter with Bedley, when the accident had occurred.

Now he talked to Davey of the need to gather information in a war, information that was of course in another language, and in code which did not make it a simple matter to understand but progress was being made. He was, as Smythe had insisted, careful not to mention the names of places or people. He ended: 'Your days in the mine are over for now, but your country needs you in other ways, *perhaps*.' He emphasised 'perhaps'. 'I have a suggestion, therefore. As you have been here a week or some such, and have made rapid progress, I feel that you are no doubt champing at the bit to be out, and busy.'

Davey nodded, looking puzzled. 'Aye, sir, you could say that. Gets a—'

Reginald raised his hand. 'If I may continue.' It wasn't a question. 'I can say little more because of the Official Secrets Act, but I am in fact driving down to London in two days' time as I have a meeting, and I have had the temerity to arrange an appointment for you to have a chat about this and that at the Foreign Office. You will accompany me, if you so wish, and if I may say so, I do feel you should.'

Davey was looking downright confused now. 'An appointment for what?'

'Ah, well, that's the question, isn't it? Let us just say it will be to discuss your language skills, for I happen to have heard that you were learning German whilst swotting for the scholarship, and more to the point, it will include a chat about your crossword expertise.'

Davey was shaking his head slightly. 'Language skills? I don't think skill is involved. My German is rudimentary.'

'But good enough to use as clues in an international crossword competition – before the war, of course?'

'How did you—'

Reginald pointed to the clock at the head of the ward. 'Let's just say I did, and now I must continue as the clatter of bedpans draws nigh. The country could well need you, and if so, your work would be more valuable than working on the screens or other such surface work. After the war, Oxford awaits.'

'But I don't want to leave Fran.'

Reginald saw the longing in the lad's face, and thought of his own dear Sophia, and how he would drive back through the night to take breakfast with her rather than be absent for longer than he had to. He was indeed fortunate to have married such a wonderful woman after the rather fraught—No, one mustn't speak ill of the dead. He sighed, wondering if he and Sophia should have waited longer, but the boy had had no need of a nanny once he was at school—

He cut off the thought, looking at the blue scars and the healing red ones on the hands and face of the lad before him. 'In war there are many things we don't want to do, but at least you will be in this country, not fighting abroad. Know, however, that the work you do, should you prove suitable, would make the lives of those who are fighting safer and the end of Hitler more likely, with less bloodshed all round. David Bedley, it is up to you. Is it to be the lives of others or your own needs?'

Davey stared at him. 'Howay, man, I see why you run a bliddy good ship.'

Reginald smiled, wanting to reach out and shake this lad's hand, for he liked him more with every second that passed. A son to cherish indeed. The Bedleys were fortunate, or perhaps just better parents than he. He felt the weight of his failure with Ralph lie heavily on his shoulders.

They talked for a little longer, with Reginald creasing the spotless bed as he leaned on his elbows and listened to Davey. Davey listened to him in return and the more they talked, the more Massingham admired the quickness of the lad's mind, and his endurance, for clearly the pain still beset him. Finally, Sister Newsome stood at the foot of the bed, brandishing a bedpan and saying, 'Quite twenty minutes have gone by, Mr Massingham, not ten.'

Reginald laughed and ended their conversation by saying to Davey, 'One round peg, your friend Stanhope, has arrived back to a round hole, and another should depart – you. Dr Wilson will receive your decision, and he will convey it to me.' He looked at Sister Newsome. 'That is, if you would be kind enough to inform Dr Wilson, as he is completely au fait with all this.'

'Which is a damn sight more than I am,' grumbled Davey.

Mr Massingham rose, reached out his hand, and shook Davey's, careful of his cuts and bruises. 'Your Fran will wait for you, you know, for the Hall family has a true core. You should respect that in her, and she is doing her bit too, of course. By the way, say nothing to her, to the family or anyone else about where we will be going. Well, if you agree, of course. Perhaps it could be put that you are seeing a specialist – yes, I feel that is less than a lie. I will talk to Dr Wilson when I hear from him. I hope the pain improves soon. I have much enjoyed our meeting.'

He walked past Sister Newsome, saying, 'Thank you for your indulgence.'

'Not so fast, Mr Massingham.' She took a pen from her top pocket. 'You need to sign the plaster. Everyone else has. Preferably something that doesn't aspire to the heights of vulgarity or rudeness. Or if it must, that it is not a repeat of the many such things already inscribed.'

Reginald grinned, enjoying his farewell. He scribbled something, returned the pen and walked from the ward.

Davey watched him go, knowing he had been offered a chance to do something important, though in what way he couldn't quite fathom. But how could he leave Fran with that idiot Ralph sniffing around?

Sister Newsome was reading Mr Massingham's message.

'Well,' asked Davey, 'what does it say?'

' "It's best to be fiddling about above, rather than being banged about below", which I feel is probably very rude and suggestive.'

Davey grinned, and he realised that his boss – after all, he still owned the mine, their cottages, and perhaps their souls – was just a man like the rest of them, and a rather fine one.

In spite of himself, he felt hope stirring, because if whatever it was that was in him could really help the war effort, he and Fran could be together, in a peaceful world, sooner.

Chapter Nineteen

That evening, Fran and the other two girls cycled to the train and thence to the hospital, but it was late and they could only stay for an hour, which was entirely at Sister Newsome's discretion since it was after visiting hours. The time seemed to fly, but each day Davey was looking so much better that the trip was no burden to them, not even to Beth, who insisted that if the other two were going, there was no way she wasn't.

As always, Sarah and Beth sat in the corridor for the last fifteen minutes while Fran and Davey said their goodbyes. Fran held his hand, 'Reet, out with it, lad. Why's that look in your eyes? You're sitting on something good, I can tell.'

Davey laughed. 'I shouldn't tell you anything, but you told me a bit about where you are working. I promised secrecy, though, so you must do the same.' He waited. She did. He said, 'Mr Massingham came to see me. He wants me to have an interview in London for some sort of job, a safe one, where I use me noddle. Something that'll help the war, and to do with me crosswords, though I expect I'll be a clerk somewhere.'

He sat back against the pillows and Fran reached forward to stroke back his blond hair, then ran her fingers down to his lips. He kissed them. She gripped his hand with both of hers then, looking at the blue scars. London? Well, it wasn't a trawler, or a beach where he'd be blown to smithereens. 'Then you must go,' she said. 'Find out about it. As long as you don't forget me.' Though she was smiling,

she'd never been more serious, because her heart was sinking. Davey gone from Massingham, leaving her alone. No,
not alone, with her family and her marrers. She sat up
straight and repeated, 'Yes, you must go.'

She was glad when Sister Newsome called, 'Off you go
now, Fran. Don't fret, I'll look after him.'

But when she tried to release Davey's hand, he held her
tight, and his voice was firm as he said, 'Forget you? Never.
If the earth froze over, I'd fight to find you, daft lass. This
way I might be able to help end the war and get back to you
quicker. And there are telephones, trains, leave. But I
haven't got a job yet. Let's wait, eh. I'm supposed to be going
down in a couple of days' time.'

She kissed his lips and walked away.

Two days later, in the evening, Davey was sitting by his
bed, his leg stretched out before him. His cigarettes had
just been confiscated for the umpteenth time and Sister
Newsome was not amused. She'd said they would be
flushed down the lavatory, and if she caught him out on the
fire-escape platform once more, now October was waning
and the weather cooling, he would not live long enough to
regret it.

Fred, in with a broken arm after a fall at Sledgeford Pit,
cackled from his chair and called after her, 'So you say, but
they're in your top drawer, lass. With our names written on
them and we know how many were in each.'

Sister Newsome continued on her rounds, but not before
calling back, 'That's quite enough from you, young man, or
it'll be an enema before bedtime, you mark my words.' Fred
laughed more at the 'young man' than the enema, since he
was fifty if he was a day.

Sister Newsome reached the end of the ward, and her
clarion call made everyone jerk to attention. 'Now, lads,

listen up. Remember, if there's a raid the doctors will come and help us shove you under the beds.'

Tobias, a youngster who had lost a leg in the bombing of the New Bridge Street goods station, called, 'Aye, that'll be grand if you tuck in with me, Sister.'

Sister Newsome surveyed her charges. 'Right, that's two for my enema list. Any more for any more?'

The laughter did them all good and stopped Davey's mind from playing with all that would happen at the interview that the 'powers that be' had arranged for tomorrow rather than today. It was at the Foreign Office, which sounded a bit bliddy grand. In spite of Mr Massingham being in London today, he had suggested the car should turn about and take Davey all the way to London the next morning. Davey had refused, for he wasn't a babe and, after all, he had his painkillers and was steady on his pins. But Mr Massingham was insistant that at least his car should drop him at Newcastle station for the train to London, and pick him up on his return, and this Davey had accepted.

Sister Newsome walked back now and stopped at the foot of his bed, lifting his clipboard and checking it. She hung it on the bed frame again and smiled at him. 'I hear you are to go to a specialist appointment tomorrow, young man, at the crack of dawn and deposited back here again, late in the day, by Mr Massingham's driver. Her voice dropped. 'Such has been your improvement, a little bird tells me that you should be going home very soon after that.' She winked.

Davey knew that Sister Newsome and Dr Wilson had become engaged yesterday, so presumably shared this, that and the other. He smiled. She checked the clock. 'Your three admirers will be allowed in now. You know, Davey, that fiancée of yours needs a break. Would a day in London be a good idea? I suggested the same to Mr Massingham, and I believe he is taking a hand in acquiring permission for a leave of absence. Only for Fran, though. The trio will have to be a duo for a day.'

Davey stared, astonished. The two of them together, for a day? 'But . . . it was supposed to be a secret?'

Sister Newsome came to the side of the bed, her voice low. 'Her place of work has been advised that you need an attendant to accompany you to London for a possible medical procedure. This has also been conveyed to Miss Hall. I hasten to add I am using the language used by the esteemed Mr Massingham. Of course, bonny lad, what you care to tell her, or have already told her about the reason for your journey, is between you and her, but if Dr Wilson kept anything from me, I would strangle him with his own stethoscope.'

Davey laughed and asked, 'But he'd escape an enema, at least?'

'Oh no, that would be administered first.'

He whispered, 'She reads me like a book and knew something was up right away, so I told her what I knew, which is diddly-squat.'

She laughed and swept off to open the double swing doors, and in came the three canaries, as the lads in the ward had nicknamed them, for they were back in stemming. But Fran had told him that if he repeated that, she'd have to kill him.

The girls kissed him and sat on his bed to tell him about their progress with the choir, for the women were practising in one another's homes – the sopranos in one, the contraltos in another. Mrs Oborne was now not a drum but the conductor, and it was chaos. They were all laughing so much that they were shouted at by Sister Newsome: 'A, get off the bed and B, less of the noise.' They stood instead and giggled quietly and a couple of the patients brought chairs across, earning the girls' profuse thanks.

Finally, Davey and Fran sat close together, hand in hand,

while the other two girls talked of the canaries, which were sitting on eggs, and Tubby Smith, who wasn't at all well so Beth was glad she was home to help. They moved on to the specialist Davey was to see, and how devastated London might look after the bombing, and then on to the wall hanging and rug cooperative. There was a new girl, June Archibald, and Sylv's mam was teaching her to use a hook to get a looped finish, and a longer run of colour.

Meanwhile, Davey and Fran spoke in whispers of nothing in particular except love, and finally he whispered, 'I'll bring you up to scratch on the train about what's really going on, bonny lass.'

Fran looked so tired that his growing guilt at lolling about when the pain was improving, nagged at him. In fact, all three looked tired. The other two leaned forward, berating him for only needing one nurse on the journey to the specialist. They wondered if they could break his other leg so he would need more help.

Sister Newsome returned and handed a folded piece of paper to him. He opened it. It was a note from Dr Wilson, saying that the two return train fares were booked and paid for courtesy of Mr Massingham.

Fran returned home on the train with the others. She listened to their chatter as they dug and delved into Davey's improvement and the puzzle of why he had need of a London specialist, fearing that he was keeping the truth from them. Sarah, sitting one side of Fran, said, 'By, lass, I hope to goodness it means that they can work miracles and make his leg perfect. But at least he's got his one good leg, so I suppose that's something.'

They leaned against the back of the seat, listening to the engine, feeling the wheels rumbling over the points. Outside it was dark with no lights showing, and Fran said, 'It's going to be so strange to see lights on again. If that ever happens,' she muttered.

Beth nudged her. 'Enough of that. Just take the music with you. It's getting so complicated with Miss Ellington wanting us three as a front-line group, while the choir hums like a sort of low-key orchestra, breaking into song from time to time, and she loves Marjorie and Valerie as drums. And it's best Amelia is singing with the office choir. Our rehearsal times never mashed with hers.'

Fran was laughing. 'And what about the other passengers, while I rehearse?'

Sarah was laughing so hard she could hardly speak. 'They'll be so in awe they'll fall at your feet.'

'In horror,' crowed Beth. 'But seriously, you must try and squeeze in some rehearsing, because we'll be hard at it. The competition's only a week or so away and you can't miss a whole day.'

The train whistle blew as they came into Massingham station. They buttoned their mackintoshes and wound their mufflers round their necks as the train stopped. Once on the platform, they hurried to find their bikes in the corrugated-iron shed, and were wheeling them out of the side gate when they heard the roar of a car, and the roadster swept up to the entrance of the station.

'Guess who?' groaned Sarah.

'Quick, he hasn't seen us,' Beth whispered, getting onto her saddle.

The roadster was idling, its exhaust billowing into the air. They stood on their pedals and pumped clear of the station yard, their laughter catching in their throats as they tore along the road, listening for the car on their heels, but it never came. Beth said, as they neared their homes, 'I don't know if he's being kind, or after you again, Fran?'

'Who knows?' Fran replied. 'So best just to thank him if he catches us. Come on, keep pedalling.'

The next day the Rolls picked up Fran from her house in the early-morning darkness. After checking it was Mr Massingham's driver, Alfie, the hewer Fred Biggins's lad, Fran clambered into the front of the car, her sandwiches tucked in her bag. She was wearing her best coat, which was from the Salvation Army shop, and a newly knitted scarf, with another for Davey from the co-op ladies.

Alfie chatted as they drove to Newcastle station via the hospital, where Davey was waiting on the doorstep. He made her stay in the front, so he could use the back seat as a sofa, sitting sideways and resting his plastered leg along the seat, but only after Alfie tutted, and put down a newspaper. As they drove the short distance, Davey issued orders to them both until Alfie and Fran threatened him with death and disaster, which he ignored. It took a reference to Sister Newsome having a good cure for such silliness to bring stifled laughter and then silence.

When they arrived, Alfie tugged him out, and walked with them to the platform as Davey swung along on his crutches. Finally, huffing and puffing, the train arrived, just as Alfie finished writing a message on Davey's plaster. Fran and Alfie helped Davey into the carriage and as the train hurtled towards London, the pair of them sat next to one another, and at last Fran felt herself relax. She was away from the chemicals, and from the explosion that had happened in the detonator sector yesterday on the night shift, while she was with Davey.

Even now she couldn't quite believe what had happened when one of the girls, who was on the Minton singing team, had dropped a tray of detonators, and lost both feet. She'd sung in the ambulance, in her shock. Her rendition of 'All or Nothing at All' had filled the vehicle, so it was whispered, until she'd suddenly fallen silent, and died.

The Minton bus team had withdrawn from the competition that very night, until the rest of the night shift convinced them that their choir must sing in memory of their star and the other two girls who'd been injured.

Fran shut her eyes and Davey held her hand, knowing something had happened but not what. He did not ask, for it was war, and war got into every damned crack in their lives. His arm slipped around her and she rested her head on his shoulder. For two hours they slept, his head on hers, and it was the first time both had slept so deeply for what seemed like months.

They woke when more passengers embarked at another station and had to clamber over Davey's outstretched and plastered leg, Davey apologising as they said, 'No, lad, it's nothing. What happened?'

He told them and they wrote on the plaster – polite messages – and Fran and he hoped they wouldn't read all the others, but most of them did, and laughed. As they travelled, everyone talked to everyone else, and it was as though they'd all been let out of a cage, just for a day. Fran handed him a breakfast of jam sandwiches and cold tea. 'By, just like Auld Hilda,' he said.

It was the first time he'd mentioned the pit and she examined him closely, but he kissed her cheek. 'I'm canny about it, pet. It happened, it's over, life goes on. Accidents can give opportunities, you know.' His voice and expression were calm, accepting, and she wondered about the details of the interview for he had not expanded on what he had already told her. But he had secrets, and she had too. That's just the way it was.

She remembered her 'homework' and drew out the music, humming the first three lines as the other passengers talked.

As she finished she realised the compartment was silent and a woman across the way said, 'I love "All or Nothing at All".'

The woman joined in, and soon the whole of the compartment was singing. Fran explained that their choir was competing in a competiton in their factory.

'What do you make?' asked one.

She shook her head. 'That'd be telling, but let's just say, something useful.' She pointed to the posters above the seats. BE LIKE DAD, KEEP MUM. 'Perhaps it's pots and pans,' she murmured.

The woman winked. 'Ah well, now the day has broken and we can see your skin, there's not much of a secret to it.'

Fran braced herself, remembering being called a warmonger. The other passengers just shook their heads and an elderly man murmured, 'We all have to do what we can to help.'

Davey hugged her and whispered, 'Aye, that we have, bonny lass.'

As they approached London they began to see war as it was in the capital, the damage and debris more extensive than in any of the other towns they'd passed. As they reached King's Cross, the passengers heaved themselves into their coats and one gave Davey a couple of biscuits made by her mother with her sugar ration. He refused; the woman insisted. 'One each,' she whispered. 'The lass needs feeding up. And best move her to another sector for a while. It's what we did in the last war. Rotated, they called it.'

Fran smiled, tired again now, because it brought Mr Swinton to mind. He was still rotating their sector, but she and her marrers kept finding themselves back amongst the chemicals. Perhaps by the time Fran returned Miss Ellington would have had better luck talking to the deputy manager, who had been off sick.

They took an Underground train to the 'specialist', as they continued to call the interview. As Davey swung along on his crutches they passed by the debris of house after house, building after building, and breathed in the smell of destruction. She said, 'I didn't know.'

Davey gripped her hand when they paused for him to rest. There was a bench beside a blasted tree. They sat. He gripped her hand again and, only now told her more of what Massingham had said. About crosswords, about codes, about a big place quite near London, but he couldn't say what or where, about the German he'd learned for the scholarship. Finally he reminded her that, like her Factory, this really must be secret, 'But I have to help defeat Hitler.'

They sat side by side as tired people passed by or queued at nearby shops. It was all because some madman and his nation had decided they wanted more than they were entitled to, Fran thought, and the British were right to do what they could. It seemed she was for ever telling herself this, as the hours they worked were increasing, with Sunday working becoming more frequent.

'What are you thinking?' Davey asked.

A red double-decker bus full of passengers passed them, weaving round a deep bomb crater that had a sort of fencing around it. She kissed his hand. 'We live in strange times. Who would have thought we'd be in this pickle, all of us? Who'd have thought a Hitler would spring up and make life so sad and painful?'

They set off again towards Whitehall. While Davey walked around the sandbags, and showed his letter to the guards on the door, and entered the Foreign Office, Fran walked to St James's Park and sat on a bench. The summer was well and truly over, the leaves changing, falling and scudding in the wind. She found herself sobbing because life was so different to how anyone had thought it would be, and her Davey was leaving her.

Davey stood for a moment, in awe at the sight of the vaulted ceiling and the paintings on the walls. He was surprised his crutches didn't echo as he stotted and jigged across the marble floor to the reception desk, where he gave his name and the time of his interview.

The man in the peaked cap and dark uniform made a telephone call. 'Sit yourself down, lad. Rest your plaster, eh?' He pointed to a row of chairs against the wall, but they seemed a mile away, and Davey's armpits were sore from the crutches. Davey nodded and set off, but a woman caught up with him, her footsteps out of time with his hop-along gait, and gestured for him to follow. Past the main desk and along a corridor they went at such a speed that Davey swore silently with each step. She swept before him into an office where files were piled in columns on a desk. The room was no more than a cupboard, he thought, with no window. Bit like the pit. He grinned to himself. She indicated a chair in front of her desk.

He settled down, laying his crutches across his legs, feeling that somehow this woman, with her stern bun and dark-rimmed spectacles, wouldn't be signing his plaster. She asked him in German if he was fluent. He replied, also in German, that clearly he was not. She didn't laugh, or even smile. She nodded, then introduced herself as Miss Downes.

She talked about his crosswords and in particular the coded clues he had introduced. He explained then about the need to allow the crossword puzzler to access the key ... He paused. The key ... He remembered, quite

suddenly, that beneath the coal he was thinking of a key . . .
He was staring at her, a key . . . to . . . Damn, a key to what?
Ralph came into his mind. How ridiculous. He shook his
head as Miss Downes asked, 'Mr Bedley, are you quite all
right? Would you care for a glass of water?'

He concentrated then – on her. 'No, I'm all reet, just
remembering . . . Or sort of . . .'

'Ah.' Her expression was one of sympathy. 'Yes, I see,
Professor Smythe did apprise us of your recent situation.'

Before he could recover from his shock at the mention of
Professor Smythe, who had written to him about his crosswords and sent the notebook, she was off again, talking of
his scholarship examination and more about his crosswords and his choice to remain in the colliery. He said
nothing, just nodded. They were facts and therefore irrefut-
able, so there was no need for further discussion, surely.

Miss Downes shuffled some papers on her desk before
looking up. 'We are looking primarily for graduates to
intercept and help decode messages being sent between the
enemy's army, navy and air force. This will enhance our
knowledge of their movements and intentions. You are not
a graduate but come highly recommended, as your recent
crossword settings support.' She fumbled in a drawer on
the right side of her desk and brought out several copies of
the crossword magazine. 'The question is, are you interested in working at our newly established nerve centre,
which is much further south than Massingham? I will
remind you now that this conversation is covered by the
Official Secrets Act.'

There it was, the chance of a lifetime. The chance to help,
to use his brain, to play with codes. But Fran? Darling,
bonny Fran.

He found himself nodding. Miss Downes continued.
'Ah, good. You will be quite near London. It's a pleasant

area, and considered by many to be the countryside, to the extent that even evacuees find themselves there.'

That was all, for she was rising and walking towards the door. She stopped, turned and beckoned. 'Come along then, Mr Bedley.'

He gathered up his crutches, wincing as they settled into his armpits, and swung himself after her along the corridor to a room with maps on the walls. There was a large table in the centre, with several army officers sitting around it while another stood. Miss Downes ignored them, just as, after their brief examination of Davey, they ignored Miss Downes and him. Instead, she picked up a document from a side table and explained how signing it would mean he would be breaching the Official Secrets Act if he disclosed any information about his work, his place of work, or anything about his work.

Because it had sounded like a prayer, Davey said, 'In the name of the Father, the Son and the Holy Ghost, amen. Me fiancée can't talk about hers, either.'

At this the officers swung round, then looked at one another, raised their eyebrows and grinned. They got back to murmuring quietly, staring at the maps as they did so. 'Ah, so you fully comprehend?' Miss Downes insisted.

'Oh aye.'

The door swung open and in strode a civilian. 'Ah, at it again, Miss Downes. She means, dear heart, "so you understand", but you know that because you, Davey Bedley, are a bright young lad, with a bit of a clipped wing at present, but your loss is our gain. Professor Smythe, at your service, dear heart. Know and admire young Stanhope Hall. Hear you have a penchant for his sister. Good stock, should work well, eh? From what I know she'll understand, and what's more she's no wilting violet herself. Likes to give a belt or two when needed. Swinton's a case in point. And that lad of his who . . . well, who knows. And let's not even mention the whelp. I tend to say about that young man that the apple fell far from the tree. Like his mother, of course. Funny woman, mean of spirit. Best she popped her clogs, but I suppose one shouldn't say that.'

Professor Smythe smiled, but his eyes were busy. He carried on: 'Young Swinton and the whelp, quite a pair, oh . . . Still waters, dear boy. Find him a pen, Miss Downes. The sooner we win this war the better.'

He disappeared again and Miss Downes handed Davey a pen. He felt he was signing his life away, but that's what Fran had also done. And she was mixing bloody chemicals and God knew what, with explosions likely at any time.

The officer who was standing said, as Davey followed Miss Downes out of the room, 'I'd sign your plaster, but I'd have to kill you if you knew my name.' He laughed.

Davey stopped and said over his shoulder, 'Not before I broke your neck, sir. Pongos are no match for pitmen.'

The men laughed and one of them rose and walked across to hold the door for him. 'Good luck, pitman.'

Fran was waiting. Davey had said an hour, because that's what Mr Massingham had told him. It was an hour exactly. They made their way back to the station, but stopped for a late lunch at the restaurant Mr Massingham had booked for them. There was lamb and she hadn't tasted it for so long, and though it was only one slice, it was a thick one. They whispered together as Davey told her a bit, just as she had told him, but no one else, ever.

'I don't want to leave you,' he said, 'but I will be back when I can. I've been thinking that I could telephone the call box at the same time on certain evenings. If you're on nights we can make it another time?'

'Aye, sounds grand, Davey.'

She felt as though they were two lovers who trusted one another enough to share more than they should, and could never be parted, not really. They finished, and for a moment Fran felt a bit recovered, and her stomach rather more settled. It would improve once they were in the sewing sector again, but when would that be?

Mr Massingham had an account so there was nothing to pay. 'I'd have ordered the meal twice for us both if I'd known that,' Davey said to the maître d'.

The maître d' smiled, but didn't reply. Fran poked Davey in the back, and outside they laughed together.

They made the train and as the darkness fell they slept, their arms around one another. As they drew into Newcastle, Davey woke with a start, knowing he'd understood the key that would break the secret of his accident in the pit – but ... No, it had gone again. All he could think of were Professor Smythe's words about that whelp of Massingham's and also Swinton's lad, and it had jogged Davey's memory of passing the Blackshirt meetings on the bus, and seeing the pair of them together. But who hadn't gone to a meeting or two, out of curiosity? First the Commies, then the Blackshirts ...

But what about the accident? He closed his eyes. *Think*, he urged himself. But no, he still had no memory of it. The train screeched to a stop and Fran woke. 'I love you,' she murmured.

When they left the station, Mr Massingham's Rolls was waiting. Davey pulled her to a stop. 'The two of us are bound never to talk of what we're doing – for ever. So, we're bound together for ever, aren't we?' The Rolls had made him anxious. What if Ralph was driving? What if the whelp kept on chasing Fran?

She stood in front of him. 'For ever,' she said. 'For ever

and ever, Davey Bedley, or I'll come down and pull your lugs off and any girl's an' all, if she dares to tempt you from me, all reet.'

He laughed. 'It's not me I'm thinking of, bonny lass.' He nodded at the Rolls.

She sighed. 'Ralph is a right menace, but not a danger. I don't even get the snidey comments from the women any more, but that were the chemicals making them poky, and aye, it does make us strange, right enough, and sort of tight in the head, and soul. That Ralph's a daft lad who needs to grow up, so don't let's even think on him.'

The Rolls's horn sounded. They set off again, with Alfie driving and muttering about wanting to get to his rooms over the Massingham garages for his supper. The world was light under the bombers' moon, and Davey thought of London, Newcastle, Hull and all the other towns, and was glad he and those he knew were doing their best.

Chapter Twenty

Davey was discharged from hospital a few days later, plaster-free but well bandaged, and for Fran it was bitter-sweet for they were both on tenterhooks, waiting for the letter or telegram that would summon him away. After his return, Davey used two walking sticks rather than the crutches. As he said to Fran and Sarah when he met them from the bus on the day he arrived back, 'Me armpits have said, any more of them things and they'll go on strike.'

A day later the three girls supported him on the way back from the bus at four o'clock, two of them holding one arm, Fran taking the other, until he stopped and shouted, 'One of you daffodils let go, or I'll fall flat on me face. And time you were out of the whatever-it-is.'

Sarah shrieked with laughter. 'The real Davey is back, eh, our Fran?'

Beth called, 'I have to get back anyway to keep an eye on me da as Mam is at your place, Sarah. Just hope Mam's already wrapped his chest in brown paper and goose grease. He's such an old mitherer when I do it. See you later.' She walked down the back lane of Langton Terrace with Sarah calling after her, 'Come to our place if he's asleep. Mam will have tea mashing and we can do yet another run-through of our three-person solo.'

Stan called out then, hurrying along, washed and buffed, his scarf streaming, and Sarah spun round, knocking one of Davey's sticks. Fran steadied him, calling after her, 'Well, just leave your brother to fall in the street, eh?'

Stan yelled as he caught Sarah and lifted her off the ground. 'Aye, as though you can't sort out Davey with one hand tied behind your back, Fran, before moving on to the rest of the world.'

Stan and Sarah caught up with them, and all four walked on. Fran thought she could never be happier, but yes, she could, once they could trust their tomorrows. They headed for the Bedleys' and the co-op's laughter and chat reached them as they crossed the backyard. The boys shook off their boots, and the girls theirs, and they entered into the light and warmth. It would make their itching worse, but Fran could almost forget it until she lay in bed wanting to scratch herself raw. And it was what it was, so aye, if they weren't iching and yellow from the pellets, they were yellow and itching from the stemming, and she half smiled. What a game it all was, like a revolving door, one day pellets, one day stemming, and ending up itching wherever they were. But at least they still had both feet, and were alive.

Mrs Bedley turned. 'Sit yourselves down. The wounded warrior must have his da's chair. Fran, you take the arm. Sarah and Stan, sort yourselves out a seat.'

Fran exchanged a look with her mam, who had fallen silent, as indeed had everyone around the table. Her mam glanced meaningfully at the mantelpiece, where a telegram was propped against the clock. Mrs Bedley said, 'Your orders, lad, I reckon.'

The women, their hooks and proggy sticks poised, looked at Davey, who had already settled himself in the chair, his leg out straight, but plaster-free.

Davey looked at Stan and Fran thought it was like a game, everyone looking at everyone else. Stan sighed. 'I suppose you want your servant to hand it to you?'

'Aye, that about sums it up, lad.'

Stan, who had been leaning on the back of Sarah's arm-chair, did so. Now the co-op had stopped all pretence of work and watched as Davey opened the buff envelope. Fran read the telegram with him, her heart sinking. Davey folded it carefully. 'Well, Monday it is.' His mam nodded, Sarah too, though she held Stan's hand as his grip tightened on her shoulder. Davey said, 'There it is, ladies, I leave to do an administrative job in London, which, let's face it, is better than on the screens, and what's more, I won't have to rub shoulders with these bliddy hewers for a while.'

Stan laughed. 'And we won't have to put up with your mithering, so always a silver lining.'

The women all nodded, but it was clear that no one believed his story of an administrative job.

Mrs Bedley nodded too. 'I reckon our Sarah and Stan could trot on down to Simon Parrot's shed and let Da know.'

Sarah smiled at her mam, but her voice was sad as she said, 'Aye, we'll do that right now.'

But Davey was struggling to his feet. 'Fran and me'll come too. Exercise is good for me leg, and we could do with some fresh air.'

Madge, adjusting her eyepatch, shoved her hook through the hessian and almost sang, 'And a bit of a cuddle on the way, eh?'

Audrey Smith was wrapping up her rug. 'If you're picking up Beth, tell her I'll be along in a minute. But no cuddles around me, or I'll blush, eh?'

The women were laughing as the four of them left, but Mrs Bedley called, 'And no more language, if you please, our Davey. Bliddy hewers, indeed.' The laughter grew and only faded slowly for they kept to Davey's pace. They turned into Beth's back alley and collected her. She should hear the news too.

It was gone five in the afternoon and the darkness was

deepening as the early November frost settled, but they'd run through these alleys for enough years to find their way blindfolded. At the allotment shed they tapped and entered. Davey had thrust the telegram into his pocket and just told the men that he was off to London, to push a pen. His da nodded. 'Aye, well, we'll miss you hard, our lad, but at least if you stay out of the way of them bliddy bombers, you'll be safe.'

Fran's da came to shake Davey's hand. 'Aye, 'tis best you use your noddle, lad, instead of fiddling about on them screens.' Joe's voice was gruff.

Mr Parrot said much the same, but instead of shaking Davey's hand he gave him chickweed. 'Best you feed them for one last time, eh?'

The others all sat on old tubs, chairs and boxes, and watched. An oil lamp burned behind the blacked-out windows and Fran felt that this image would remain with her for as long as it had to: all of them here, with the birds, the cock singing his heart out.

On Sunday, the three families set off for the beck as Davey was to take the train to London early the next day. The parents walked whilst the young cycled ahead, even Davey, who sat on Stan's handlebars, his leg stuck out before him. Ben rode Davey's bike, bequeathed to him for the duration, though it was on its last legs, as Ben muttered repeatedly, until Stan told him to put a sock in it or walk with the old 'uns. Ben put a sock in it.

They rode into the wind, which held a hint of sleet. Fran cycled alongside, watching the two boys, now men, and realised from the set of Stan's face that she would not be the only one to feel the loss.

She listened to the low murmur from both of them, the talk of the future and of the past, the scrumping they had

302

done, the minnows they had caught, and the swimming lessons their fathers had given them, after which they had taught the girls. They spoke of their first day at the pit: the blacklocks, the rats, the mice, the bait, the sweat streaming down their bodies and the blue 'buttons' they had from scraping their backs on the jagged coal as the roof lowered, narrowed and compressed. Stan said, 'The buttons and scars are a sort of code, aren't they? To the past, to something shared. The minute you see 'em on someone, you know the key to them – they're pitmen.'

'By,' Davey laughed, 'we'll have you –' he paused '– setting crosswords any day now, lad.' He snatched a look at Fran and she guessed he'd been about to say 'breaking codes any day now'. Secrecy, deceit, pretence didn't come easily. She wondered how many there were about the place who were doing the same, and what those secrets were? The thought was unsettling.

They stood on the pedals, crested the bridge and then freewheeled down, lifting their legs. With the wind in their faces, they all cried, 'Yay, yay.' The seagulls flew overhead as though leading the way, and the cyclists followed along the road, heads down, the lads whistling. On either side ploughed fields glistened, and ice lay in the furrows. Sarah and Beth drew up alongside Fran. 'It'll be like Stan has lost an arm,' Sarah muttered.

Just then a voice whooped from behind, and Sid and then Norm swept past them. 'Thought you'd leave us out, did you?'

They carried rucksacks on their backs, and Beth, cycling to Fran's right, panted, 'I heard the clink of beer bottles. I reckon they'll all be walking back. Either that or wobbling all over the road.'

They freewheeled down the next hill too, and turned off onto the lane, bumping in and over the tractor's ruts, arriving at the beck at last. Propping their bikes against the hawthorn hedge the girls joined the men, who were already collecting sticks for a fire. They built it and Davey held the match to the newspaper they'd brought. The fire caught, driven by the wind; the flames licked and soon roared.

Fran grabbed the rugs rolled up tightly in the saddle-bags and baskets and then they all sat in the shelter of the hedge and talked of the times they'd had. In particular, they remembered Miss Stephens, the headmistress of their small school, who had brought cocoa so that in the winter they all had a hot milky drink, which she maintained built healthy bones and able brains.

Sid nudged Davey, who was sitting with Fran. 'Reckon she were right. Either that or you and Stan pinched our share, for you're a good few inches taller, as well as having brains a couple of pounds heavier.' They laughed and while the girls drank tea the lads drank beer, and then they played ducks and drakes on the beck pool by the bridge. They watched the rope swinging as the wind caught it, and remembered so much. They fell silent suddenly, all of them, for the past had been good and the future unknown.

Then the parents arrived, the mothers with baskets of food and even some ham in the sandwiches, and biscuits made with honey. Best of all was the remains of a bottle of sweet sherry, which had been hoarded for cooking. 'Aye, but I reckon we should slurp it down as there're no cherries to soak in it, anyhows,' Mrs Bedley said.

She poured an inch in the bottom of the women's tin mugs, and they all bunched up on the blankets. The boys, young and old, kept with the beer and gave Ben half a mug. The girls sipped their sherry, feeling its warmth in their throats. They listened to the parents, whose turn it was to reminisce over *their* years at school, when they'd all been together until Beth's grandda had taken off for Darlington.

Today, Beth's da had stayed at home by the kitchen range to help his cough, but they all knew nothing could. It was the last stages of black lung and that was that, and a neighbour would pop in and out to check on him.

They moved on to their singing, but as always tried to keep the details of the competition to the minimum, unless they won, in which case they would tell the date, time and that it was the Home Service.

Mr Bedley smiled at Davey. 'Reckon we should all hear it, lad?'

Davey raised his beer bottle. 'Oh aye, then we'll know that if they don't get chosen for whatever it is, that it were fixed. If we have to stuff our fingers in our lugs, the girls'll know they have more work to do.'

The three girls and the mothers shook their fists, Audrey Smith whispering, 'Sing up, lasses. Show these clodhoppers what's what, eh. Them talk as though they're the experts, but nay, they couldn't sing in tune if their lives depended on it.'

Though Audrey was smiling, her eyes were as sad as Beth's had become over the last few days as her da slipped downhill. Somewhere a pheasant called. Davey kissed the top of Fran's head and her neck, nuzzling her while her da looked away, embarrassed. Davey whispered, 'You sing out, Fran. Give me something more to remember, as though all this isn't enough.' He waved at everyone sitting around the fire.

Fran scrambled to her feet, pointing to each of her friends. 'Come on, bonny lasses, time this rabble was taught some manners and had their eyes opened.'

Fran's mam called, 'Never mind their eyes, open their lugs, eh?'

The girls were all word-perfect and had been working hard on harmonising while the 'select choir', as the others had elected to be called, supported them under the waving arms of Mrs Oborne. Two 'drums' were enough, it seemed and Mrs Oborne was not to be budged.

Fran counted them in. 'One, two, three . . .' They were off. 'All or nothing at all, half a love, never appealed to me . . .'

On they went, soaring over the heightening wind and the crackling of the fire as sleet fell, and the mothers looked at one another, smiling, and then gazed into the flames while the men stared at the girls. Fran sang for Davey, whose face showed his love. Sarah nudged her as Stan moved closer to Davey, gripping his shoulder, whispering something. Davey nodded, his mouth set firmly. The girls slowed, lowered their voices, and sang the finale they had devised for their choir. 'So you see, I've got to say no, no, all or nothing at all. Nothing, absolutely nothing at all.'

They repeated the last line and fell silent. No one moved for a moment, but then, after applauding along with the men, the three mothers began to sing, lifting their faces to the sleet, which was lessening, 'When they begin the beguine, it brings back the sound of music so tender'. They sat on their blanket and swayed as they sang, and the daughters, taking their places on the blankets, joined in, repeating the final lines: 'And we suddenly know, what heaven we're in, When they begin the beguine.'

There was no time for applause for Mr Bedley began, 'It's a long way to Tipperary, it's a long way to go.' The other men joined in. 'It's a long way to Tipperary, to the sweetest girl I know.' Mr Bedley looked at his wife all the time he sang.

Fran listened to their singing, and it was so strange to think that such a short time ago these men had been in a different war – a war to end all wars. How awful it must be for them to know their daughters and sons were involved in another one, and their efforts had failed. At last she really understood her father's fury when she had signed up for the Factory. She left Davey then, and sat beside her da. He slipped his arm around her as he sang with his old friend, his mug full of beer, and now the girls joined in. As the fire died so did their singing, but it left peace of a sort.

The next day, Monday, Fran, Sarah and Beth clambered on board the bus for the fore-shift, having been rotated away from the night shift, in order to replace workers hit by the influenza which was sweeping the Factory. Stan had been at the bus shelter and he'd hugged them each, then passed on with Sid and Norm. For the first time, there was no Davey. Fran watched the three marrers walk towards the back alley, and the tightness in her chest grew. Her love would be on the train by now, trundling down to Buckinghamshire, for he had shared that much with her. As they left Massingham and she watched the countryside unwinding, she was bereft, but in another way she felt that yesterday she had at last grown up.

The day ran much as it always did, with their full concentration on the pellets, which was where they were today. They pasted the paper around the fuse pellets, their fingers already tinged with yellow and sticky from the chemicals, and laid them gently in their trays, and then another, and another. After they had bolted down their dinner of tasteless grey mince and mash, which stung Fran's and Sarah's pellet-induced mouth ulcers, they had their final rehearsal for *Workers' Playtime* in the side room.

Mrs Oborne's conducting had become more and more controlled over the last few days, with her downward stroke exactly on the beat. She brought in the sopranos, hushing them like a professional before bringing in Fran, Beth and Sarah to sing their lines to the quiet humming of the choir and the bursts of repeated staccato drumbeats from Valerie and Marjorie. The song ran through Fran's head as they returned to the fuse pellets, pasting fluted paper with a paintbrush, wrapping the pellet, then placing it in the tray, even when there was a great bang at one thirty from somewhere in the Factory grounds. On they pasted, hundreds of the little beggars, Fran thought, hating the stickiness of her fingers, so coated with the paste that she could almost feel her rash spread, and her hair become more obviously streaked.

Fran worked on, as did the others, just like machines: collecting the pot of paste if more was needed, dipping in the brush, pasting the paper, wrapping it around the pellet as though it was a sweet. It was ironic, because where were sweets in wartime? Pasting, papering, wrapping and placing in the trays until Sarah began to hum, and then sing, and the whole of the bus team joined in – sopranos, contraltos, drums. Every run-through was close to perfect, but still they pasted, still they sang, until finally, the clock showed 2 p.m.

They moved away from the workbench, allowing the next shift to take over before they trailed to the changing rooms, talking about the progress they'd made. But were they ready enough? 'Who knows,' said Mrs Oborne. 'We'll do our best, and that's all we can do.'

Once they had closed the changing-room door behind them, Miss Ellington appeared, along with a new security officer, Mrs Costello, to check that there were no pellets being taken from the Factory. Why would anyone? Fran wondered, as she always did, but this time she also wondered where Davey was.

As they slipped into their tatty shoes and shabby macs, the door opened again and in slipped Amelia. They seldom saw her these days, though it seemed she was still practising hard with the office choir, or so she mentioned as she flitted about with her clipboard, delivering messages to foremen or security staff, or passing on bad news from home. Now, the women stood still, wondering why, who, what? All looked on as Amelia spoke to Miss Ellington and nodded towards Beth, who was tying her headscarf under her chin. Fran and Sarah instinctively moved towards their friend, Sarah whispering to Fran, 'I wonder if he's gone right down. Mam said it looked as though he wouldn't last more'n a couple of days.'

Miss Ellington made her way over and gently took Beth aside. Her da had been taken proper poorly, so Bert would get his foot down. Miss Ellington raised her voice. 'Beth needs to get back quick as possible, ladies, so . . .' She had no need to say more, because the women left the sector, their scarves still in their hands, accompanied by Mrs Costello, and ran out through the gates, only to be called back to be checked and counted out.

Mrs Oborne yelled to the guard, 'Get a bliddy move on, you auld fool, someone's dying.'

Frank Winslow just nodded. 'Aye, we heard, ducks. You know we have to do this, but see, quick as a wink we are today.'

He was and they rushed on towards the bus, Mrs Costello calling, 'I hope . . . Well, take care, Beth.'

The women shoved Beth on first. The journey was quiet, and those dropped en route were up and ready by the door before the bus had stopped and hurried off, with Bert leaving almost before the last woman was out. When they arrived at Massingham, Fran and Sarah ran with Beth to her home and waited in the kitchen for hours. They made tea and left it to mash in case it was needed. The doctor came, bustled through the kitchen and up the stairs, then back down. They'd poured him a cup and he slurped it down before rushing out, shaking his head and whispering, 'It's not good.'

Again it was quiet except for the awful coughing from upstairs. Sarah whispered, 'Me da said Mr Smith has paid into the sickness fund, so the doctor is sorted.'

Fran saw quite clearly the account book her da wedged onto the mantelpiece. She remembered her da's cough and couldn't bear it, so dragged into her mind the image of Davey instead, out of the pit for now. But where?

They poured more boiling water onto the mashed tea leaves, for the caddy was empty. Sarah looked at her. 'There's a war on.' They grinned wryly, picturing the ration cards.

'Aye, well, Mrs Smith'll have some drying from yesterday.' They found them at the back of the range and tipped them into the caddy, then sat round the table where Mrs Smith's proggy frame lay. It was cool away from the range but they couldn't bring themselves to sit in Mr Smith's armchair. Mrs Smith came down the stairs and poured tea for Mrs Heath, who acted as midwife, nurse and the woman who laid out the bodies.

'You and Beth must have some tea too,' Fran said.

As though she was in a dream, Mrs Smith poured two more. Sarah fetched a tray and Fran placed the three cups and saucers on it, the best bone china, as befitted a death. Mrs Smith stared at the tea and the rising steam, smiling a little at something only she could remember. She said, touching the rim of one, 'That was me bottom drawer – not summat sensible like sheets, but bone china. By, it's kept us going, just seeing it. You remember that, pets. Get yourselves summat beautiful that brings you joy. It'll see you through a lot, you ken?'

They did. Mrs Smith continued, 'You get on home now, pets, you have work in the morning and need your rest. Nothing will happen for a while.'

As they left, one co-op lady after another filed in through the backyard with food and their frames. Mrs Smith and Beth would not be alone through the long night. Fran caught hold of her mam. 'Mam, they've no tea leaves left, so we put the dried and used ones in the caddy. Shall I bring some of ours over?'

Mrs Hall said, 'Aye, if you would. Get a paper twist from us, and one from Sarah's. I'll tell Mrs Bedley. Hurry now.'

They did, and returned, each with a twist of tea, and they waited in the kitchen with the other women until four in the morning, when it was time for Sarah and Fran to head for the bus, with Fran scratching Sarah's back where the rash had spread. Bert drove at his usual calm pace, which was a relief because their heads throbbed and their eyes were dry and sore. Their friends were quiet as they travelled, waiting, knowing that as the darkness lifted, Mr Smith's spirit was likely to fly free. Dawn finally rose, and as one they closed their eyes and wished Tubby Smith Godspeed. Sarah whispered, 'He'll not hear his Beth on the wireless if we win.'

Mrs Oborne turned round. 'Oh aye, he'll hear, never you fret.'

All morning they worked, with Mr Swinton pacing and looking over them while they tried not to think of the competition which Miss Ellington had announced would be held today over the dinner time, and during the meal breaks of the other shifts. Neither did they think of Tubby Smith, because they couldn't afford to be distracted, or slowed down as they had to make up for Beth's absence and finish more pellets to meet their target. Fran felt dead on her feet, and beside her Sarah sighed and said, 'By, I can hardly keep me eyes open. How are we going to be any good at singing feeling like this? And what's more, it'll be a duo, not a trio, so it'll sound as thin as powdered milk.'

Fran pasted the paper and wrapped it around the pellet, remembering the twist of paper filled with tea leaves, and she smiled to herself. She did the same with another pellet, and thought about the packet of mischief she held in her fingers that worked with the detonator to activate explosives such as TNT to make a shell go 'pop goes the weasel'. How did people learn to invent these things? Through wars, she supposed.

'Did you hear me, Fran?'

'Aye, we'll just have to sing up because we've got to do it, everyone's worked so hard.' She pasted another fluted paper.

When their break was called they gulped their dinner because the performances would begin any minute, though Fran left most of hers because her mouth ulcers were so bad. After pudding, it was time for the start of this sector's programme of performers and they listened to the groups, all of whom sounded too good, too professional. They all wondered if they should sing it just like an ordinary choir, no humming, no drums, but it was too late and they were called forward a mere ten minutes before they all had to return to work. They trooped up on stage and Fran and Sarah stood at the front of the choir, gazing out over the workers, still sitting, some smoking, some still eating.

Fran and Sarah exchanged looks, acute tiredness dragging at them. Fran thought of a twist of tea, a twist of pellet – what the hell was it all about? For Beth should have been here and suddenly it seemed silly and pointless. Were Beth and her mam alone in the house, just the two of them now? Had Tubby really gone with the dawn?

Mrs Oborne bustled to stand in front of the choir. She had wanted a pencil to use as a baton but had no way of obtaining one. She had wondered about a knife from their canteen table but had been shouted down. She said quietly,

'Reet, we are one short, so we will sing, though our hearts are full to bursting, for Beth and her family.'

Fran straightened, pushed her shoulders back, and next to her, and behind her, all the women did the same. Miss Ellington asked, 'What are you calling yourselves?' No one said a word, and then Sarah nudged Fran, for Amelia had entered with the office girls' choir, all smart, all in suits and high heels. Fran straightened her shoulders even more and answered, 'The Factory Girls, Miss Ellington.'

Miss Ellington wrote this down, grinning to herself. Mrs Oborne's eyes gleamed, she smiled, then asked to borrow Miss Ellington's pencil. Miss Ellington reached up to the stage from the canteen floor. 'I'll have it back immediately, you know the rules. You can't take it back with you to pellets.'

Mrs Oborne held up the pencil, nodded at Fran and only then did she count them in, conducting with crisp moves, dead on the beat. The choir hummed and then the sopranos came in, and then the contraltos, and then Mrs Oborne stabbing her pencil towards Valerie and Marjorie, and in they came as drums. It should all have been ridiculous – from the pencil baton through to the humming and the drumbeats – but it was grand. Mrs Oborne stabbed the pencil at Fran and Sarah, and they stepped forward and sang for their friend Beth, and for Mr Smith, and for all those in peril.

On they sang, until Mrs Oborne drew in everyone, including the drums, and then swept them to a clean stop, dropping her hand to her side. The choir stood, unmoving, watching the tears running down Mrs Oborne's cheeks. There was silence and the choir didn't care if no one thought they were worth even a clap, for they all knew they'd done their bliddy best for one of their team.

The applause began then, long, loud, and some of the

women stood and cheered as Mrs Oborne dragged her sleeve across her eyes, turned to face the audience and bowed, as did the choir. They traipsed off, and suddenly everything was all right. They *had* done their best for Beth and it didn't matter if they didn't win. Over by the wall, Amelia forced a smile and a wave. Miss Oborne murmured, 'Well, I didn't like to say before, but I heard tell she was offered a return to the floor, but she said no, and were a mite rude about us an' all, or so I'm told. But on t'other hand, she were good when needed. Strange old world.'

Miss Ellington was running after them. 'Pencil.' It was an order.

They headed from the canteen back to the workshop. They talked, feeling excited and pleased with themselves, pasting, wrapping, heedless of the yellow and the itching, and Fran and Sarah no longer felt tired, but could have danced around the workroom. They reached their target by two and stepped away so the new shift could take over. Mrs Oborne led their team out, past Miss Ellington, who was cursorily checking them for pellets, as it was deemed more sensible than in the changing rooms.

'It makes one wonder just how much work Miss Smith does, if the target is reached so easily. Perhaps we have no need of her,' muttered Mr Swinton.

The shift didn't have time to respond because Miss Ellington snapped, 'Don't be absurd, Mr Swinton, or would you like me to go now and relay your opinion to management that we should operate with an inadequate number of personnel? And it's time you stopped using this team to fill in here and there all over the ruddy place. I see you've marked them for stemming next week, and it isn't right.'

Mr Swinton waved the women on. 'Hurry up, the next shift is already operating.'

Miss Ellington, who was gripping her clipboard under her handless arm, looked as though she wanted to use it to belt him around his lugs, thought Fran. She called down the corridor after the girls, 'The votes of the supervisors and security staff will be cast and added to the workers' and you will all hear the results tomorrow. And please convey my regards to Beth and her family. And just to let you know, we hope for more workers soon.'

So had Mr Smith really passed and yes, new workers might happen, but might not and what could they do about that? What could they do about anything? the women wondered in the changing rooms. In the car park, Bert was revving the bus and everyone clambered on. Amelia sat across the aisle from Sarah and Fran. 'I've the afternoon off,' she said. 'I thought I'd like to see if I could help at Beth's in case Mr Smith died today.' Those who had heard nodded, confused because they didn't know where they were with this girl, for they too had heard the recent rumours of her latest views of the shop floor girls. But Fran and Sarah were too tired and at last slept.

When Bert pulled in at Massingham, Ralph was waiting. Fran and Sarah walked firmly past him, even though he called after Fran. Maisie and Mrs Oborne followed, and it was Mrs Oborne who said, 'Mr Smith will have passed today, but thank you for your concern.'

She too swept on and he called after them, 'I was bringing the news, so how did you know?'

Mrs Oborne called back, 'He will have gone with the ending of the night, reet enough, or the coming of dawn, whichever way you want to put it.'

Amelia hurried after Fran and Sarah.

At Mrs Smith's they almost tiptoed across the yard, and tapped on the door. Beth opened it, shutting it behind her, and came to them. She hugged Fran and Sarah, and nodded to Amelia. 'He went with the dawn, and it were best. He can breathe easy at last. I put brown paper and goose grease round his chest last night, and he didn't grumble. He just lay back and smiled, and said, "Thank ye, lass. I does love you, and always will. Take care of your mam, and she'll take care of ye."'

'Shall we stay?' asked Sarah.

'No, go home, but be with me for the funeral, eh? We'll have it on the Sunday. You come too, Amelia. If you wish.'

The girls left, and walked Amelia to the bus shelter; there was a regular bus, not a works one, due soon for Sledgeford. They waited with her, and as the wind grew fierce their headaches worsened and no one said anything, for what was there to say. They waved her off, and returned to their homes. Fran lifted the sneck, opened the gate and clumped across the yard, into the kitchen, too tired to remove her shoes. She tried to pull the chair out from the table but felt the air leaving her body, and the floor lift to meet her. The last thing she heard was her mam calling, 'Fran? Oh, Fran.'

Chapter Twenty-One

Fran lay on the floor. She knew she must go to bed, but her head was heavy and she just wanted to sleep where she was. But the itching from the paste wouldn't stop, and her head was pounding. She heard the back door slam and Ben's panicked 'Mam?'

'It's all right, she's tired and had a tumble. Help me get her to her feet.'

Fran lifted her head. 'I'm better. I just felt a bit odd. I'm better.'

'You look a bliddy sight,' Ben said. 'A bit yellow, and that rash's back on yer hands. Time you was where they put you to get you right. It's that bugger Swinton, in't it?' He grabbed her under her right arm, her mam under her left, and as they got her to her feet she thought, how does he know about Swinton? Well, the beggar lives local, so of course it's known. The back door opened, letting in the cold.

'What the hell?' shouted Da.

It's like a game, Fran thought, but she was thinking that a lot as her thoughts chased one another around, day after day. Doors, revolving doors. Pellets, stemming. Stemming, pellets detonators, bullets. Ben. Da. Poor Mr Smith, and Davey, her lovely Davey, and strange Amelia.

Mam said, 'She's worn out. I expect it's the same with Sarah. Give us a hand up with her, Joe.'

Fran shook herself free and sat with a thump on her kitchen chair. 'I tripped, that's all. Thought I'd take a minute to check the dust under the table. By, Mam, you should do summat about it.'

Ben laughed; her parents didn't. Her mam snapped at no one in particular, 'She could do with a good supper, that she could, but I've only a piece of cheese, and your veggies, Joe. Thank heavens for those. I'll get cooking. She can have it on a tray like Lady Muck, and a cuppa, so I'll get a pan on while your da gets you up them stairs, eh?'

'Oh, Mam, don't fuss.' Fran stood, her legs like water. She remembered then that she had barely bothered to eat at the Factory because her mouth was sore, but at least her itching wasn't worse. Poor Sarah's was right bad on her back.

Fran reached the door to the hall, realised her da was behind her and turned. His hands were either side of her in case she fell. It comforted her as she climbed the stairs. He stood helplessly as she reached the bed, and said, 'I don't want you to be working like this, on a wee piece of cheese. Why the hell couldn't you work in the bliddy office, like I wanted?'

Fran turned and grasped one of his hands in both of hers. 'Oh Da, because I want to help win this war. You might not like it, but I'm not going to stop, and I eat the same as you an' all, probably better what with the canteen, so stop with your mithering. Me money helps Mam with the laundry, and makes life easier for Madge too. Sarah gives hers to her mam for the savings jar, because who knows what might happen in the future, and Beth's done it too. It's only what we're all doing.'

Her da took hold of her hands now. 'But you need a break from it. Get back into the sewing, eh, pet?'

Fran fought against her tiredness. 'We are just needed as cover for the moment, that's all. The flu is a beggar, and some have been transferred to other factories to cover there. We'll be getting more workers soon, Miss Ellington told us, and then we can rotate to a clean place, but you know I can't talk about it.'

Her mam came in then. 'Off you go, Joe. Keep an eye on the vegetables. I'll be down in a minute. You, Frances Hall, get into that bed.'

Fran undressed, and her mam saw her hives. 'I didn't know,' she murmured. She hurried downstairs and came back with her lavender mixture, which she created from marinating the crushed flower spikes and leaves in goose grease. She rubbed it on gently. 'You silly girl,' her mam said. 'Silly girl, you should have told me. I think this will be better than the moss, but we can move on to that when this improves. What about your hands? Moss or lavender? I'll do a mouthwash of hot salt water for your ulcers, eh?'

They decided on lavender for her hands, which would help Fran sleep too. Her mam smiled. 'Lavender is the cure for all diseases.' Fran thought, no, that's death, but knew she must shake herself free of such meanderings.

'Mam, don't fret,' said Fran. 'I don't notice after a while.' She pulled her nightgown down and settled back against her raised pillows. She wondered where Davey was, and the longing tore at her.

There was clumping on the stairs and Ben came in with a tray on which were piled vegetables, chopped cheese, a bit of spam and dripping, a cup of tea, a mug of salted water for afterwards, and a spit bowl. He set it on her knees. 'Eat it, our da says, and you'd better, because you've our share of cheese. I had some when I was at Farmer Newton's with the evacuee, Bobby, doing the bliddy great pile of crosswords that Davey left us. He's going to send us others.'

Her mam sighed. 'Language, Ben, if you don't mind. Once your sister's eaten she'll sleep, so don't go on for hours.'

Fran laughed and began to eat. 'Sit down, Ben, talk a bit,

then I want to sleep for weeks, but a night will be grand, and let's not forget Mam was up all night too.'

Her mam stood by the door. 'Aye, maybe, but I had a snooze in t'day and I'm not doing heaven knows what with that little Hitler, Swinton, breathing down me neck.'

'Mam, you shouldn't say that. You know better than to name names.'

'Oh, aye, walls have ears. It's only in here we say anything about it, so rest easy.'

She shut the door gently while Ben threw himself onto the bed, jogging the tray and slopping the tea. 'Tell me about London. I know you can't tell me about his job, but what's London like, our Fran?'

She told him about the pigeons that still settled on Trafalgar Square, about Piccadilly Circus with Eros all boarded up, and the bomb damage, and the meal that Mr Massingham had paid for. 'It was a thick slice of lamb,' she said. 'With potatoes roasted in dripping, and vegetables and gravy, and it was brought to us all posh like, along with mint sauce.'

Ben just stared. 'A whole slice each? Was it really a thick one?'

She nodded. She could taste it now. Would Davey be settling in? Were there girls there? Would it change his love for her?

She looked at the plate, no longer hungry and her ulcers hurting. Ben smacked her legs, jogging the tray again. 'You best eat it or our mam'll be up the stairs, and Stan right after her when he gets in. I bet right now he's fussing round at Sarah's. He's soft over her, the lad is.'

Fran burst out laughing. 'Oh, the lad is, is he, old man?'

'Aye,' Ben said, as she pushed her tray towards him. 'Help me out, I don't want a lathering for being a bad girl.'

He winked and gobbled the plate clean, picking up the

tray and looking down at her. 'And Mam said you needn't wash tonight, or do your teeth, because they won't rot missing just one night. Go to sleep, and stop being so soft, eh?'

He headed for the door, calling to her, but not looking round. 'You be safe, our Fran. We does love you, daft lass.'

He balanced the tray with one hand and opened the door, calling back, 'And don't you fret, cos our Davey's soft about you too, always has been, and always will be, daft buggers the lot of you.'

He shut the door as she shouted, 'Language.'

As she slid down the bed she heard his laugh. She was alive and Ben was right, she and Davey had one another, for ever. It was only then she thought of the singing competition, and went to sleep hearing their choir, and seeing Mrs Oborne's tears and knew she'd be better in the morning.

At her home, Mrs Oborne tucked herself into bed beside her old bugger, feeling the pencil in her hand, seeing the choir, her choir, again, hearing them singing their hearts out, sending their words up to poor old Tubby, and she didn't know if her tears were for Tubby, the beauty of the choir, or because her rash was so bad it was driving her right barmy. She too slept.

Joe Hall poked at his tiny bit of chopped cheese and finally finished it. He rose from the table, snatched up his cap and headed out of the door, stopping to kiss the top of Annie's head. 'Going to check on me birds, bonny lass.'

'Aye, you do that.' As Joe left he heard his Annie say to Ben, 'You get on with your homework. If Stan can get a scholarship, and your sister can pass her typing exams, you can do well too. I'm not having you with black lung after a lifetime in t'pit, and that's that. Just think on, young Ben, we've a funeral on Sunday.'

Joe stifled a cough as he tied up the laces on his boots out in the dark of the yard. Poor old Tubby. Not that he was tubby by the end. He moved the brick off the lid of the hen feed and threw seed to supplement the cabbage leaves. Fifty wasn't old, but Tubby'd wanted to go when he couldn't get his breath proper any more. Could you will yourself to die? He bloody well hoped so. Joe slammed the yard gate behind him.

He passed Stan on his way back from Sarah's. "Ow do, lad. Sarah all reet?'

'She's about all in, sallow, itching, not herself, had a bit of a tumble.'

'Same as your sister. Mam's sent her to bed. I reckon she had a faint. But the pair of them were up all night, your Sarah and our Fran.'

Stan sank his hands deep into his pockets. 'Aye, and Mam an' all. They're just weary, but they're not bothered cos it's the same for 'em all. I reckon they're proud of themselves. Sarah's da's gone to check the canaries. Simon's got beer on the go, so Tom said. Not sure if it's his own or a jug from the club.'

Joe nodded, and walked on. Course Si had beer, he always had, using the pennies in the divvy pot they held at the shed. Not that the beer at the club was up to much, bit thin it seemed, but rations were rations. It wasn't anyone's business that they brewed their own as well. He didn't ask where Simon got the yeast, but it could be true that once yeast started brewing it just went on growing like a plant if you fed it. He supposed Si used honey, not the sugar ration, or his missus would skelp him.

In the shed the oil lamp was lit, the boards were up at the window, and the smell of birds and feed was soft and comforting. He took his place beside the other two, already perched on upturned barrels, and nodded his thanks to

Simon for the tin mug he'd pressed into his hand. Simon said, 'Us'll get a jug of the beer from the club tomorrow, eh? Manage wi' our own tonight to set our Tubby on his way.'

They raised their mugs and muttered, 'Tubby, God rest his soul.'

Simon added, 'Lord, let me go under a pile of rock, or when I'm eighty in me sleep, but, for the love of Mike, not coughing me lungs up till I canna breathe no more.'

'Aye, to that,' Tom Bedley agreed, as Joe nodded. They sat in silence, watching the birds, then working out which to sell for there was a market coming up, near the Town Moor in Newcastle.

Si murmured, 'Wars may come and go, but birds go on for ever.'

Tom Bedley smiled, sipping his beer. 'Could do with a bit of extra money, so we could find an ounce or two of meat being offered by some toerag for the women. Don't hold with it normal, but I don't give a damn if it's off the back of a bliddy lorry. Our Sarah's reet pasty. Them damned chemicals turn 'em to tired old women, yellow, itchy an' all. And I'm her da, and it's up to me, but I canna do owt.'

Joe nodded. 'I heard Fran tell our Ben that Massingham stood Davey and her a lunch in London.'

Simon and Tom stared. 'What, the whelp?' Tom asked.

Joe shook his head. 'Don't be daft, they'd know better than to tek it from him. He'd want his pound of flesh as a thanks – if not now, sometime, and they've had enough of that sort of thing with his hanging about. No, 'twas the old man. Fran told Ben she had a slice of lamb, a whole thick slice. She were right gobsmacked. Yet, before the war she'd not have thought anything to a slice of lamb to herself.'

Tom shook his head. 'Think on, lad. You're forgetting when times were bad we'd have t'choose between lamb or just gravy on a Sunday, or any damned day, come to that.'

Simon stood and pressed close to the birds' cage, studying one whose crop was looking too full.

'Leave the lad,' Tom called.

Joe lifted his beer, waving it at Simon. 'Aye, Si, if'n you get that close it'll keel over from beer fumes, you daft pillock.'

Simon laughed; the bird fluffed its feathers and hopped along the perch. Joe called, 'It's intoxicated, you daft beggar. It's dancing.'

Tom, head down, was swilling his beer. Joe asked, 'Reading the tea leaves, lad? What's our future then?'

Tom replied, 'Best we don't know, our Joe. Nay, just wondering how the girls will do in this competition of theirs. Would do 'em good to win the beggar, and Lordy, they can sing. I was fair gobsmacked at the beck. Do Beth good an' all, cheer her on a bit. Our Sarah said they performed today, just when they were all fair whacked, and it went down a treat, but Beth were missed.'

Sarah ran for the bus the next morning, glad of the long sleep. Snow had fallen in the night and was already a few inches thick, but crunchy, so not a lot of slip sliding. She was even more pleased to see Stan waiting with Fran at the bus shelter, his shoulders hunched against the wind, his muffler tied tight, snow settling on his cap. She looked, and there, as she'd known they would be, were Sid and Norm sheltering in the lee, cupping their hands round a match as they tried to light their cigarettes, but the matches kept being doused by the falling snow.

Stan hugged her tight, then held her away, studying her closely. 'Right, you two lasses, you make sure you've won the singing and then you can take us all to London, where you'll be stars and keep us in the lap of luxury. Failin' that, get moved somewhere to give your bodies a break.'

More women were arriving, chatting, scratching, and

wrapping their scarves tightly round their throats and faces. Mrs Oborne called, 'Mek way for the workers, lad.'

Stan called, 'Mitherers, you mean.'

He kissed Sarah, ducking Mrs Oborne's hand, which missed him deliberately, but caught his cap. She tossed it to Maisie, who threw it to Fran, who whirled it above her head, then turned and tossed it to Sid, shouting, 'Go, fetch, Stan, and put Sarah down or you'll be late for your shift.'

He laughed as Bert drove the bus in from Hawton, stopping it with a pumping of the screeching brakes, though it still slid a fraction. Stan cocked a head at the cab. 'Them brake linings sound in need of a look-see, Bert, and your nearside tyre's looking a bit worn. Yer need chains if this snow gets worse.'

Bert leaned out of his cab. 'There's a war on, laddie, or hadn't you noticed down in t'pit? Where do the depot get new tyres before the webbing's showing? And Gawd knows where the chains are. Come on, ladies, get in, the snow's getting heavier.'

Stan waved, kissed Sarah once more and headed off after Sid and Norm, and the three of them jostled one another as the girls watched them take the short cut they usually bypassed because the dogs peed down it, but there was never hide nor hair of them when the snow was falling. Beth came running now, slithering. Sarah watched, her heart going out to her, seeing that she couldn't have slept from the darkness of her eyes, but, aye, here she was, coming to work. She and Fran waited and they boarded together, Fran sitting with Marjorie, leaving Sarah and Beth to sit together.

As Bert drew away, Sarah listened to Beth talking of the funeral tea her mam was worrying about, and interrupted. 'Don't let her. The co-op ladies are bustling, and not with rugs. They're pooling their rations and making all sorts.'

Fran called across the aisle, 'Aye, me mam's going round to yer mam to sort it out. She was on her way as I left, then she'll go on to her ARP thing.'

Mrs Oborne called then. 'Aye, don't let her fret. It's all taken care of, you can bank on that. I've baked a few honey biscuits and added me last capful of sherry to the mix. Fair broke me heart, I can tell you, but I had a good sniff before it went in.'

Even Beth laughed, and soon she was chatting just as much as before. As they reached the Factory, she shared with Sarah that she'd actually slept really well. Her da's coughing and choking for weeks before had kept them awake, and she reckoned her mam had slept too.

They showed their passes at the gates, and moved on to the changing rooms, past the rows of huts, including those underground where the shells were filled. Sarah shuddered.

In the changing rooms they saw chairs against the wall, and in came two security officers as usual, but they had another six women with them, in flowered overalls. The girls looked at them, but then were distracted as they were checked for contraband by the security officers while the six women waited by the chairs. Then Miss Ellington stuck her head round the door. 'I've said until I'm sick, sore and tired that you should get your hair cut, and have you? No. Today, you will. But in recompense you will no longer have to undress. You'll merely be checked as usual. It's time-wasting and undignified and I won't have it.'

The bus team looked at one another, then at the chairs, which the women were pulling away from the walls, before drawing out scissors from their pockets, then grinned at Miss Ellington's news. Mrs Oborne called, 'We can say no to the hair?'

'Oh, aye,' Miss Ellington said. 'I just thought it would save you all a couple of pennies for it's free.'

At that, no one objected, and indeed, they were pleased.

'So,' Miss Ellington continued, 'you will sit here, wearing these overalls.' One of the security officers, a Mrs Gains, held up flowered overalls and a towel, while the other security officer, Mrs Raydon, grinned like the Cheshire cat.

Miss Ellington went on. 'Mrs Raydon, over to you. I have others to beard in their changing rooms. Hurry, please. Work to be done, but I will have my girls safe, and if you won't do it yourselves ... By the way, stemming today. Wellingtons please.'

The cutting was quick: the bits of cut hair which fell down their necks to their backs prickled, but what was another itch on top of those already existing, for heaven's sake? Once finished, they all fluffed out their hair. Sarah thought it felt good, free somehow. In no time at all they were in their proper overalls, their turbans on, their belts tied tight, and wearing Wellingtons. Amelia caught up to them as they filed out.

Amelia said, 'I am available to sing in Beth's place, should it all be too much. I thought to tell you when I accompanied you to see how Beth was, but I felt perhaps it was inappropriate.'

'Is that reet? Well thank you kindly,' Mrs Oborne called. 'But Beth is here, so you go on enjoying the office, and its choir, pet, eh?'

They were all being hustled along by Miss Ellington, who had reappeared, and who told each one of them that from next week they'd be in the sewing shop for a good long break. But they'd been promised that before, so they all just smiled.

At lunch Sarah, Beth and Fran sat together, eating their omelettes, which seemed as rubbery as the thingummybobs they filled with the 'something' powder that puffed up into their faces and filled the air. Mrs Oborne was telling them about the wall hanging she was making, going for the looped finish, not the proggy shaggy. As the clock ticked towards the end of their dinner hour, they noticed that the office choir had entered and was standing near the stage. They were followed by Miss Ellington, with her clipboard.

Mrs Raydon stood by Fran's table and reached for her pudding spoon to bang on the table. Maisie yelled, 'Take cover, the flak's about to fly.'

Fran grabbed her spoon and licked the rice pudding off it, realising that her ulcers seemed better. Thank you, lavender, she thought. Mrs Raydon took the spoon back, and whacked the table three times. Silence fell. Maisie called out again, this time saying, 'I'd check that for dents, our Fran.' The table burst out laughing, but Mrs Raydon shouted, 'Silence, for Pete's sake.'

Amelia was standing close to Miss Ellington, her face set. The light dawned, for of course Amelia would in all likelihood have typed it up, so she already knew. So had The Factory Girls won? Is that why she had made the offer this morning? But no, all the other choirs were so good, so Amelia was just being kind.

Ellington said, 'We should have a drum roll. Perhaps Marjorie and Valerie would like to give us one?' Their table looked at one another, and laughed.

The canteen laughed, and even the catering team were out from behind their hatch now. Miss Ellington cleared her throat. 'The judging was difficult, as always, because we wanted you all to win, but nonetheless we collected all the votes from this sector, then collated the figures with the other sectors' votes. We noted the greatest percentage of votes for any one performance. We then added our own votes and reasons. Just now we mentioned drums. Well, the winners included many ingredients within just the one performance. Music, singing, humming, harmony, and even a pencil.'

Miss Ellington held up the clipboard. These tables were looking round at one another, then at The Factory Girls. Mrs Oborne muttered, 'Does she mean what I think she does?'

Maisie yelled, 'Who the bliddy hell won, then?'

Above the laughter, Miss Ellington called out, 'The Factory Girls.'

The whole canteen was laughing, cheering and whistling and perhaps it was only Fran and Sarah, and possibly Beth, who noticed Amelia storm from the hall as Maisie put her fingers in her mouth and added a piercing whistle. Mavis from the next table down yelled, 'Howay, grand drumming, Val and Marjorie, reckon that tipped it.'

Mrs Oborne called, 'No, 'twas me waving me pencil about like a a demented canary, so put a sock where it belongs, our Mavis.'

Everyone was laughing, everyone was proud, the whole damned canteen, it seemed. Finally Miss Ellington waved for silence. 'Now we wait to see if the wireless is really coming.'

Mavis pretended to pull a sock out of her mouth and shouted, 'I reckon we should have a concert even if they don't, with all, or at least some, of the choirs.'

Sarah yelled, 'Aye, and it should be for Christmas, to raise funds for those bombed out. We'll be working over Christmas anyway, so let's have some fun. Miss Ellington, can we use the canteen?'

There were wild cheers as Miss Ellington said she'd try, and then the cheers subsided to chatter. Some of The Factory Girls choir started humming the song, while at other tables they talked of other songs to learn if there was to be a concert. Fran, Beth and Sarah thought it should be carols, and suddenly it was as though life had lifted itself up off the floor again.

As they wound their way back to the stemming section, Mrs Oborne looked at them all. 'If the wireless comes, we'll sing for Mr Smith, and all them miners who haven't made it through this year, eh?'

Beth whispered to Sarah, 'Did you see Amelia leave, and her face?'

Mrs Oborne heard. 'Well, she made her bed in the office, so she must lie in it. Beth's back, so she mustn't try to muscle in. We can't be dodging about, can we, and you three make a grand sound? I had hopes for the lass, tis a shame, if she goes back to the way she was.'

Fran, Beth and Sarah looked at one another. 'Can't be dodging about, eh? You can if you're in someone's bad books.'

The rest of them shouted, 'And we always are.' The laughter carried on along the corridor as they passed posters that beseeched them to keep mum.

'Not a chance, pet,' yelled Maisie.

Somehow the rest of the shift flew by, and the journey home with Bert seemed fast too. They dropped Valerie and the others off at Sledgeford, and continued to Massingham, piling off the bus, still singing, and Maisie almost fell into the arms of Ralph. Sarah closed her eyes and pulled Fran on, but Ralph stepped in front of them. 'I can walk you home, Fran.'

Sarah started to say, 'No—' but Fran overrode her.

'No, I'm walking with me marrers.'

Ralph stood his ground. 'I'm only offering to walk you home.'

Fran doggedly continued, walking around him and saying, 'And I'm only telling you I'm walking with me friends.'

Ralph came alongside Fran. Sarah and Beth snatched

looks at one another and Beth slipped behind and eased in between Ralph and Fran. The girls carried on walking and Fran heard Ralph mutter, 'Davey's gone, he's left you here alone. The least I can do is walk you home in his place, since I feel guilty he was hurt because of me. And where's your lovely hair?'

Fran just kept walking as she said, 'Me hair's gone to keep me safe. Thank you, Mr Massingham, but as I keep saying, there is no need for guilt or the need to make amends, it's not just having me hair cut that makes me safe. I make meself safe, and as I say, I am to marry Davey, and there is no need for anyone to take his place.'

Even to her the words sounded like they should be spouted by an actress on a stage. The girls turned down the back lane. Ralph was left standing, while Beth whispered, 'Guilty, my arse. He just wants to get into yer knickers.'

The other two laughed. But Sarah said, 'We ought to tell Stan he's still trying.'

Fran walked even more quickly. 'That's exactly who we mustn't tell, because he'll do something that can't be undone and then Mr Massingham will have to choose his son above us, and we'll be out of our house. Ralph's just being a bliddy nuisance because he thinks Davey's not here, and that I'll fall at his feet.'

Beth said, as though deep in thought, 'When you think of it, he's been right snotty since his mam died and his da married the nanny. He's more'n a bit twisted me da reckoned, a one for holding a grudge . . .' She fell silent.

'Well, he'll not get me,' Fran muttered, and Sarah was glad it was Davey who'd taken his ball and Fran who was copping it, for Fran was strong enough to stand her ground, whereas she, Davey's sister, was a little mouse, and she hated herself for it.

Chapter Twenty-Two

Davey looked out of his attic-room window, relieved to be there at last. The train had broken down near the station, and had been shunted into a siding until repairs could be carried out. He'd walked along the tracks to the station they'd recently passed through to make a phone call to Mr Massingham, because he didn't know who else to tell about his delayed arrival at Bletchley Park. He explained to him about the pig's ear of a journey, and the old boy had said he'd sort it with those expecting him.

It was only last night that Davey had finally arrived at his village digs, in time to crash into bed in a room shared with another Bletchley worker who had left early for work, it seemed. He looked to the right, down the street, and there, just a few hundred yards away, was a bombed building. So even here they had not escaped.

He ate breakfast with his landlady's young children staring at him from behind their mother's skirts. He said, 'Off to school?'

The boy of about seven said, 'What'd he say, Mum?'

The mother, tired, with grey in her hair, was apologetic. 'Could you speak slowly, Mr Bedley. We're not used to . . . Well, the way you speak.'

He did so. The lad said 'Yes.' That was all. Davey finished his toast, drank his tea with no milk. There had been no range spluttering in the kitchen when he'd knocked on the door, but he'd seen a cooker, gas he'd thought, as he was directed by his landlady to the dining room. He checked his watch and said slowly, 'Aye, I must be off.'

The woman nodded, looking almost scared, as though he was from another planet. The boy came running after him. 'Why've you got them marks on your hands and face?' He was pointing to Davey's blue scars.

'I got them digging for coal,' he said, again slowly.

'Coal? Where'd you dig for coal?'

'In the ground.'

'You're stupid, it comes on a lorry.'

Davey gave up, put on his cap and said, 'Not sure when I'll be back, Mrs Siddely.' When no answer came and the boy ran back down the hall, Davey called slowly, 'Not sure when I'll be back.'

Mrs Siddely came to the kitchen door, wiping her hands on a towel. 'Right you are.'

Davey caught the staff bus outside the pub. It would return him, and pick up others for a different shift. He smiled to himself as the thought of Fran doing the same came to him, but the picture tugged at his heart too much, and he turned away from it.

The bus trundled along the lanes, picking up more people, including a great many women, who moved along the aisle looking for seats that were all taken. He rose, taking his weight on his good leg, and gestured a woman to his seat. She smiled her thanks. He didn't speak because he couldn't face the incomprehension. The bus stopped near the gates of Bletchley Park and they all disembarked and made their way up to the guards, showing their passes, and the pole was raised. The drive was concrete to begin with, then turned to gravel. He used his stick because his leg hurt too much to be trusted to take his weight. There were others alongside, and one lad, from Lancashire, said,

'Haven't a bloody clue what to do, and where to go. Oxford, were you?'

Davey grinned. 'Nay, lad. Massingham.'

The young man said, 'Oh, I don't know that university. Where do you think we go?'

There was an old man standing in front of the grand house, pointing to the right, where there were a number of large huts with concrete walls alongside the hut walls. Perhaps for protection if attacked? Who knew, because Davey certainly didn't. The lad said, 'Oh, well, that's a shame. I thought we'd be swanning about in a stately home, but we'll just have to get used to it. Would have been nice to be posh for a bit. My mum would have been impressed.'

Davey smiled at him as he limped along. 'Aye, but you'd not be able to tell her.'

The young man laughed. 'Too right. Daniel's the name, and you're . . . ?'

'Davey, Davey Bedley.'

Daniel walked on, as though he was thinking. 'I say, not the Bedley who sets the crosswords?'

'Not sure if I'd have to kill you if I said yes?'

Daniel laughed again. 'Ah yes, indeed.'

They were waved into one of the huts that smelled of fresh paint. With each step, the hut seemed to shake. It was large, with a door at the end of the corridor, and other doors off either side. They opened the door at the end, peering in because they didn't know if they should. It was a large room, with drawn curtains, even though it was daytime.

To stop peepers? Davey wondered. There were a few men and many women in the room working at strange typing machines housed in heavy wooden boxes, or that's what they looked like at first sight. The racket was appalling, as keys were pressed relentlessly and things whirred, and clicked. Daniel and he were waved in by an elderly woman standing just inside the door. No one looked up.

The elderly woman, who seemed to be in charge, pointed to two chairs set at a long table, at which women and a few men were already hard at work on the machines. 'Yours, lads. Put your things there, next to your machines, but don't get settled. We'll be on the move in a moment.'

Davey set his pencil case and notebook down next to his machine, not sure what he should have brought, and fascinated by the machine, which had several rows of strange typing keys and what looked like rotar wheels at the top. It reminded him of a shop till, mixed with a typewriter. He thought of Fran tapping away in the office she had worked in, then shut off the thought, because he missed her too much.

A few women came in, some in uniform, some not, and were given places at the table too. 'I'm Norah,' the elderly woman said finally. 'Newcomers, follow me.' They were taken through a door at the back into a much smaller room where they were given a talk about secrecy, and the honour of working there, and about the fact that they were graduates.

'I'm not,' Davey said.

'Maybe, but you must have skills, so pipe down,' Norah said.

Davey grinned, and Daniel elbowed him in the ribs. She continued. 'You will be handling enemy communications so sensitive that it could lose us the war if you speak of them, and now may I remind you that you have signed the Official Secrets Act. Therefore, if you do speak of anything you see or hear at Bletchley Park, you will be dismissed and probably marched straight to prison, whether or not you are a graduate, young man.' Her gimlet eyes peered at Davey.

She explained that the British had listening stations all

over Britain and were able to intercept enemy communications between the enemy's forces, not to mention the secret services. These intercepts were couriered here, thousands a day, to be decoded.

'Your machines are copies of the German Enigma coding machine. We are now able to break the settings the Germans use to encipher – don't ask me how – though what I will tell you is that finer minds than ours have devised a way. It seems the German settings change every twenty-four hours. So every twenty-four hours we adjust *our* settings to theirs.

Norah was pacing up and down in front of them now, talking as though by rote. 'You will read the instructions someone will be placing by your machines as we speak . . .' she checked her watch. 'Now. You will adjust your machines according to the daily setting. You will receive endless coded messages. You will punch these into your machine and you will place the decoded messages on a pile, which will go for translation. It is not for you to wonder where. It is not for you to wonder about anything.' Norah smiled round at them all. 'However, you might find that you recognise a certain operator's "signature". Perhaps he always starts his message in the same way, or ends it thus. It is now that you take note and tell us, but no need to wonder why.'

As she talked, something clicked in Davey's brain, and he knew that he had found his home, amongst work such as this for he understood why tracing a particular operator was important. Someone, somewhere at Bletchely could track his movements, and those of the outfits he is messaging, and perhaps get an idea of what the troop movements might be.

Eventually Norah stopped pacing, and stood quite still, smiling at them all. 'Finally, I repeat: none of you will talk of your work, or stray into other huts, or ask questions. This hut is your world, this hut will drive you to aspirin, such is the noise, click click clickety click. Make sure you have some upon your person. Take advantage of the clubs within this world, the grounds are pretty, the lake might freeze if you fancy some skating, there are chess groups, music, start one if there's not one you wish to join. Remember that intelligence is comprised of bricks, which can create a wonderful structure. Each brick is crucial. You are crucial. But keep your mouths shut.'

Norah stopped, and Davey knew that Fran would love her, because though this woman looked like a granny she had the power of a pitman's wife.

Norah checked her watch. Motes danced in the air as she rushed on. 'Now basic housekeeping. You are on the eight to four o'clock shift. Next week it will be four to midnight. The week after, midnight to eight in the morning. There will be a meal break in the canteen. The toilets are outside.'

Just like the netty at home, Davey thought, as Daniel and most of them looked appalled. This was his life now – work, sleep, and remember to speak slowly so people could understand and try and get your bliddy head to stop whirling as you try to understand what the hell she's talking about. But the thrill of it was, he already did understand.

Fran tied up the belt of her overalls in the changing rooms thinking the dog-end of November was showing itself to be cruel. The snow was already standing in high drifts against walls, but at least Mr Smith's funeral had taken place before the bitter cold struck and life was back in its routine. Well, she was thinking that, but here was Miss Ellington just telling The Factory Girls that the wireless crew had arrived, as she had warned them they would only a couple of days before, because the later they knew about it, the less chance of idle talk.

Apparently, The Factory Girls would be summoned to the canteen an hour before lunchtime, which was when the half-hour show would be broadcast. Fran's mam had thought they should use 'the Co-op Girls' instead, because their mams were the co-op women. 'Too late,' Fran had laughed. 'It's decided. You'd best start your own choir, eh?'

Now, here in the canteen, The Factory Girls' nerves were fraying as the men from the Home Service huddled together, referring to their clipboards while the choir hummed to warm up at the end of the room. They watched as microphones were slung over the steel girders above the stage and left to dangle. The Factory Girls pulled off their turbans, having set their short hair overnight in what rollers they had, patting and fluffing it, but nothing seemed to make anyone's hair look anything other than a mess, so they replaced the turbans and tried to forget what they looked like.

Miss Ellington came up, waving a sheet of paper. 'Right, it seems I have drawn the short straw, as apparently the administrative department are far too busy to fiddle about with something as silly as this, though they'll be here for the performance, or so they say. So, as I'm in charge, and as the kitchen is agreeable, it seems sensible that all of those who can be here as the audience will eat lunch early, after which the canteen will be cleared of cutlery, plates and anything that rattles. *Workers' Playtime* will then be broadcast, and I have been told by those tinpot gods over yonder that you, the choir, must be standing over there, by that table.'

She turned and pointed. 'Oh,' she said, sounding surprised, for Amelia was handing round a tray of tea to the 'gods', who seemed to own the table. She wore lippy, her long hair was freshly curled and brushed, her smile was broad and her heels high.

Valerie muttered, 'She was washing her hair last night,

and look, she's wearing stockings with those high heels. She weren't wearing them on the bus, were she, which she got this morning with us. I wondered what she was up to catching it with me, as she weren't on till nine, like the rest of the Administration Office.'

Miss Ellington clapped her hands. 'Come on, pets, let's try and ignore anything that grates.'

Valerie pursed her lips. 'Aye, I will in a minute, but I've got to tell you all that she said last evening that she'd be more in tune with the wireless people because she's from the south, and more their sort.'

Mrs Oborne grinned. 'Aye, don't fret, she probably doesn't mean anything by it. It stands to reason they can probably understand her, whereas we're Geordies from the wild lands of the North, so we probably scare them out of what wits they have.'

The choir laughed. The huddle of clipboards turned and frowned. Amelia tottered over to the serving hatch with the tray of drained cups and saucers. A man with his spectacles on a leather string around his neck clapped his hands, beckoning The Factory Girls to him. Sarah nudged Fran. 'Reckon we should be in step and salute when we get there, eh?'

The laughter was relaxed as they made their way across in their overalls, still wearing turbans even though they were on sewing machines now. The clean room was putting paid to the itches and hives, but the yellow was taking longer. They stood before the man, whose pot belly was hanging over his trousers. He coughed a small pretend cough as he looked them over, and suddenly Fran was furious. She had listened to her da heading back from the pit yesterday, coughing his lungs up, and they'd only buried Mr Smith ten days ago, and here was this white-collared clipboard king sizing them up.

She turned away, unable to look at him, and saw Amelia making her way over, her smile eager. Mr Pot Belly, whose real name Fran couldn't remember, explained that once lunch was over there was not to be any crashing and banging.

He hesitated as the women burst out laughing. Mrs Oborne said, 'Aye, we hope there's not neither. Who knows which of us'd have our heads blown off if there were.'

Mr Pot Belly looked blank and Fran wondered if the men still huddled together knew what sort of factory this was? It was supposed to be secret after all, but if a bang happened, all would be revealed soon enough. As she thought of secrets, she saw Davey, as clear as day. She had spoken to him on the public telephone yesterday evening and he'd seemed grand, but not too grand, or any happier than she was.

Mr Pot Belly said, 'I want the four lead singers over here, please.'

Sarah looked from Beth to Fran. 'Four?'

Amelia reached them. 'I told Mr Fraser that Beth had been unable to sing for the competition, and he agreed it would be wise to have four of us, just in case Beth was overcome.'

Fran looked at Beth. 'And are you overcome, Beth?'

Beth shook her head. 'Never felt more undercome, our Fran.'

The three of them, and the choir, just looked at Amelia. Fran wondered yet again who was the real Amelia? The one who had supported them against Swinton, and worked to reach the target, or this one? Sarah said quietly, 'If you wanted to be one of the lead singers, Amelia, why didn't you say? We could all have rehearsed together.'

Amelia shook her head; her hair bounced and gleamed. 'I didn't want to intrude, and all I did was mention that

Beth had had a recent loss, and he said I should sing too, to support you just in case.'

'In case what?' Beth asked quietly.

'Oh, I don't know,' Amelia snapped. 'It's just what he said.'

At that moment the leader of the band called to them. 'Best have a run-through, girls. The clock's ticking. Come on over. I'll count you in, on three. You all right with that?'

Mrs Oborne called, 'Oh aye, we know our numbers to ten.'

Mr Pot Belly tutted, along with Amelia, but the band roared with laughter as The Factory Girls hurried across. Amelia followed in her high heels, which added two inches, so that she towered over the three lead singers. 'So, am I to sing with you?' she asked, tossing her hair.

'Perhaps she should,' murmured Beth to Fran and Sarah. 'She's obviously practised in Valerie's mam's mirror with all this tossing of the locks, so she's probably practised the song too. Let me check.' With a voice like ice, she called across to Valerie, who answered that there had been singing from Amelia's room, and her voice was all right.

The choir had been getting itself together all the time this was going on, and now Mrs Oborne came to stand in front of them near the band – on the floor, not the stage, because there was still so much microphone slinging and stage adjustment going on. She made sure that the contraltos were to the left, the sopranos to the right behind the three, no, four, lead singers.

When she turned to check that the band was ready, the leader was nodding, impressed. 'Well done. Let's hope that you sing as well as your Miss Ellington seems to think you do. I'm Stan, by the way.'

'Like me brother,' Fran called.

He replied, grinning, his bald head shining, 'Then I'm

Stan Two. I know my place.' The choir laughed, liking this middle-aged man who seemed to have a wealth of common sense and experience under his belt. Stan 2 called to the band. 'Ready.'

The saxophonist waved his instrument, the pianist rushed to the piano and waved, the drummer did a rattle on his drums.

'Howay, drums?' Mrs Oborne asked.

'We go on as we've rehearsed, Mrs Oborne, with our own too,' said Fran.

'On three then,' Stan 2 said, looking confused at their conversation, so confused clearly that he stopped. 'What drums?'

Mrs Oborne said, 'You'll see, and it's nothing for you to worry about.' Stan 2 just nodded. Mrs Oborne put up her finger. 'Wait one.'

She hurried over to Pot Belly and snatched his pen from his hand. 'Ta,' she said, and hurried back. 'Got me baton,' she said. The choir grinned and Stan 2 laughed, then counted them in. They were late and petered out while the band played on. Fran felt the sweat break out on her forehead. She braced herself as she looked across at Stan 2, who waved the band to silence.

'Not a problem, Mrs Oborne. Maybe this time?'

The girls could see that the men in the huddle were shaking their heads and their hearts sank. What if they weren't on the wireless, with their mams listening, and all their friends too, for of course they had given them the time, said it was the Home Service, and suggested they might hear something interesting. And, Fran thought, when he'd phoned Davey had said he'd get to a wireless too.

The music began again, and this time The Factory Girls were off perfectly: 'All or nothing at all . . .'

The choir harmonised like a dream, swaying to the music and following Mrs Oborne, then the quartet came in, and the staccato drums, at which Stan 2 looked around, nodding and grinning, the pianist too. Across the hall, Mr Pot Belly had his hand up, quietening his team while he listened. It was then Fran heard that Amelia was just a beat behind, though not too noticeably. Mrs Oborne gestured the choir in for the second verse, and now they changed from humming to singing, giving it their all. As Fran, Sarah and Beth sang, they could hear the glorious harmonisation, and with a swoop of her arm and Pot Belly's pen, Mrs Oborne brought them to the quiet penultimate 'No, no,' before building to a slow, tender crescendo: 'All or nothing at all.'

At the end there was silence, and Fran breathed deeply as the band members just looked at one another, then over at Mr Pot Belly. The stars had come to the door of the huge store cupboard that was acting as a dressing room. All right, Fran thought in the silence, they'd just do it again until they got it right, and make sure, somehow, that Amelia was actually on the beat.

But then the band applauded, well, everyone did, except the huddle of men, and Mr Pot Belly. Stan 2 grinned. 'Bit of work's gone into that, I reckon, and on the replay whoever was a beat behind might just scramble to get on top of it, though with the rest of you so accurate most wouldn't notice. Also, seems to me that whoever was supposed to be overwhelmed in the lead-singer group was anything but. May I offer my condolences to Beth, who is, I think, the lass who suffered the loss? So, I repeat, Amelia, just get on the beat.' As he said this he winked at Mrs Oborne.

Amelia blushed and the others relaxed. Stan 2 turned his back, spoke quietly to his band, and they moved on to sort out the rest of their music. As the stars were gathering for their own run-throughs, Amelia drifted back to Mr Pot Belly and his team, a notepad in her hand. The clatter of lunch preparations began, and the choir queued to get theirs first, though they were so nervous they barely ate, each running through the song, repeating it again and again. Amelia, happy to go without food, stuck to Pot Belly like glue.

As the lunch was being cleared away, the choir stood about at the side of the hall. They were ignored by Mr Pot Belly who, it transpired, was the producer or something like that, and was busy virtually stroking the performers. 'Do they purr, d'you think?' muttered Maisie.

Amelia was smiling at the group of men from London who still clustered around Pot Belly, all southerners from the sounds of them, all like her. She was making notes on a clipboard she had found somewhere. But, thought Fran, who could blame her? Just as she, Sarah and Beth were amongst their own, so was Amelia at this moment.

As she watched Fran understood the loneliness of those sent away from home to do something they would ordinarily never have thought of doing. Like Amelia, like Stan once, and now like Davey, her darling Davey, amongst the graduates. But he was a smart alec too, so he *was* in the right place. But he wouldn't sound like a smarty-pants, would he? She shared her thoughts with the others as the canteen started to fill up, and Mrs Oborne nodded.

'Aye, lass, we live and die here, don't we, Beth? Your da and my other brother Perce, here, amongst their own, and there's a fair bit to be said for that.'

They stood quietly at first, then ferreted out chairs and set them up against the wall, staking their claim by sitting there, firm and immovable until Miss Ellington panted up, a bag hung over her shoulder. 'Follow me. I'm not having you up at the front with your turbans, no indeed I'm not.'

They followed like ducklings, but instead of quacking they were quaking in her wake, because the moment was getting nearer. Once in the rehearsal room, Miss Ellington dragged out several hairbrushes. 'Right, off with those and get brushing. I got these off numerous women, so ignore the hairs in them, we haven't time for niceties.'

She then dragged out lipsticks she'd taken from the contraband locker. 'No idea whose these are, so go lightly, if you please, then I'll put 'em back with no one any the wiser. Quick as a wink, come along. Everyone fluff your neighbour's hair. You're my girls, and you'll go out there in your overalls, without stockings or high heels, just your own court shoes, which Mrs Raydon has brought in.' She pointed to the pile of shoes. 'Find your own, and today, my lovelies, you will look like the princesses you are, is that clear? Once you've got them on, report to the producer.'

They did, and were sent to their chairs to wait until they saw him beckon to them. Outside the snow was still falling. As they stared out through the canteen window, Beth said, 'I'm singing for me da.'

Sarah smiled, and Fran knew she would be singing for Stan, whilst for her it was Davey.

The hall had filled up with people from all over the site, most of them women. Some even stood at the sides. The audience smiled at their bouncing hair and lipstick, several waved, the producer beckoned. Fran led the way along the front of the hall, below the stage, to the producer. As she drew near, she heard Amelia saying, 'Oh no, I'm certainly not really one of these girls. I've been transferred from the South, and am definitely not a factory worker, dear me, no. I am administration, as I said, and my education opens me to all sorts of opportunities. I mean, look at their short hair, their voices – just like a badge, isn't it? Makes visible the stark difference between us.'

He handed her a card. 'Take this. Call me if you decide to pursue singing. We'll be needing entertainers for the troops, and why not you? What about The Factory Girls' lead singers while we're at it?'

Fran waited and heard the answer. 'No no, they wouldn't leave here. Once a factory girl always a factory girl, clinging to their mothers' apron strings.'

Fran coughed. Amelia turned. Fran said, 'The Factory Girls are ready, Mr Producer.' Her voice was like ice. Later, when Stan 2 was whispering their timings, he said to the four of them, 'There'll be troops to entertain. Take my card.' Fran beat Amelia to it, pocketing it in her overalls and saying to Beth and Sarah, 'One day, eh?'

As they moved into position, she felt that one day she'd forgive Amelia, who was a girl far from home, but she'd always distrust her.

Davey sat in the canteen, having arranged with the catering manager to turn the wireless to the Home Service, which had been done, so he was listening as Fran's choir was introduced. It was on good and loud, so he could hear it over the clatter of people eating an early lunch all around him, and was thrilled to hear the name, The Factory Girls. It was like magic, and he could see the three of them, and Mrs Oborne getting ready to wave her pencil about. Fran had said they'd be singing 'All or Nothing at All', and that she'd be thinking of him the whole time.

Daisy from the huts came and sat down next to him just as they began to sing. 'And how's our lad from the deep and dark North, Davey? Dreaming of your pit?'

He shouted, his hand raised, 'Howay, not now. I need to listen – it's me girl singing.'

At that, the whole table fell quiet and listened too, and Davey's throat was so full with pride and longing that he lowered his head and looked at the table. When the choir had finished, Daisy Leonard, said, 'Ah, I see why you were so rude. The Factory Girls, eh? Your girl's one of them?'

Davey turned to look at her, studying her ginger hair, her freckles, her green eyes and thin lips. He said, 'Are yer saying I'm rude because me girl's a factory girl and I know no better? Or because I'm just rude? Well, pet, that weren't me being rude. That's me not wanting to miss a second. Worry not, you'll know right well when I'm rude, Miss Daisy Leonard.'

There was a silence, and Daniel poked him, but Davey hadn't come all this way to be put down by someone with a plum in her mouth when Fran was having her moment.

'Hard to tell what you're saying anyway, with that accent, and they'll be the same,' said Daisy.

Davey shrugged, eating his meal, wondering where the brown sauce was. It'd been promised, but apparently, the cook said, no one else asked for it so it wasn't a priority. Perhaps they couldn't find any off ration. As he ate, he longed for the sulphur in the air, the clump of pitmen's boots, his marrers and Fran. Most of all he longed for her, and now, sneaking a look round the table, he saw again how out of place he was when he was anywhere but the pit. Down here, people couldn't understand him; not his speech or his ways. He was different also because he had no degree, and there surely wouldn't be time to get one at war's end. He had to get tough enough again to go back down the pit to make money for him and Fran, to try and build up his own magazine. How else would he keep his head up, and expect her to stay with him for ever?

The bell went and they rose. Daniel walked beside him. 'Your Fran must be a grand girl.'

'Aye, she's the best, and the air I breathe.'

Daisy walked ahead, kicking at the gravel, and snapped at Daniel when he called, 'Walk with us.'

347

'I've better things to do.'

Daniel whispered, 'Oooh, someone didn't like your contretemps. She's obviously taken a shine to you.'

Davey heard, but took no notice, because his mind was so full of Fran and the letter he'd write that evening.

Chapter Twenty-Three

On Monday of the next week Fran and Beth got on the bus at midday for the aft-shift, leaving Sarah on the pavement with Stan. Mrs Oborne and Maisie clambered on, with Maisie calling back, 'Put Stan down and let him get to work.'

'Aye,' Stan called, 'can't wait to get below, out of this cold, but she won't let me go.'

The women laughed as Bert, who was doing the morning and afternoon shifts while Cecil got over his pneumonia, hooted the horn. Fran's mam in her ARP uniform crossed over the road. 'Are you hooting to attract the Luftwaffe, our Bert? If so, stop. And you, our Stan, Sid and Norm are waiting.'

Bert leaned out of the window. 'That ARP hat makes yer bossy, our Annie.'

'Aye, maybe, and it's a grand feeling.'

Fran looked out of the window and waved. Her mam waved back, then they all heard her say to Bert, 'Keep your eyes open, and you too, our Stan. Everyone's in a bit of a do about sabotage. They're suspicious of a fall in a pit t'other side of the valley, and summat about a railway line not far from here, so we're all to keep alert. Though I doubt they'll have a sign round their necks saying "Spy" or "Saboteur". But mind what I say, Bert, and our Stan, and you and Norm too, our Sid. Eyes open, gobs shut.'

Sid and Norm were yelling from the bus shelter, 'Except for you, Mrs H.'

She laughed. 'No details, were there, daft lads.'

Sid laughed. 'You tell our Stan, Mrs H, to get a move on an' all. This wind's fair biting, so it is, and he'll see the lass when the bus comes in later.'

Bert called to Sarah, 'Going, ready or not.' Annie Hall stepped back onto the pavement, and Sarah leapt aboard. 'About bliddy time,' Bert said, as Mrs Oborne started to sing and the others joined in: 'Don't know why there's no sun up in the sky, stormy weather . . .'

Fran and Beth looked at one another, smiling. Stan 2, the band leader, had left them a long note about how it was important to keep the troops' morale up, and that they should extend their repertoire as the band would be touring with something called ENSA and could do with a three-girl group if they ever got sick of factory work, or even if just one of them did.

Sarah came along the aisle and slumped in the seat next to Maisie, across from Beth and Fran. She was humming along as she still couldn't remember all the words, but then few could, yet.

'Still think it's grand he said a three-girl group,' Beth said, breaking off for a sip of water from her bottle.

Fran shrugged. 'Well, he knew Amelia was an extra, and we were the three old 'uns.'

Mrs Oborne turned round. 'Aye, more likely because she were often slipping off the beat, even though I were fixing my beady eye on her and stabbing at her with me pen.'

Beth and Sarah laughed. Beth tutted. 'Whose pen? And I hope you gave it back.'

'Couldn't do owt else, he were after me like a policeman.'

They were laughing as Sarah leaned across the aisle. 'I reckon it was because she'd cosied up to Mr Pot Belly, who were rude to Stan Two every time he spoke. Not rude rude, but as though Stan Two were summat less than him.'

Fran frowned. 'Well, Pot Belly spoke to every one of us

like that, and where'd he get all that food to build up that great pudding of a belly is what I want to know?'

'Probably ate his underlings,' Maisie grumped. The laughter grew louder. The women took turns guessing what else he might be eating, or who, and they were soon licking their lips at the thought of pork belly, or roast lamb and spuds roasted in dripping.

They were still at it as snow began to fall again, just as it had much of the night, growing heavier with each turn of the bus's wheels. Mrs Oborne groaned. 'We'll be late and have our pay docked and me old mam needs the doc for her chest.'

One of the new girls, Beryl, who was sitting next to her, said, 'No, if it's weather, they're taking a better line on it. They want us there with all limbs working, instead of skidding off the road and ending up squashed as jam.'

Maisie groaned. 'Steady, Beryl. Don't want that picture to stick in our minds when we're fiddling with—Well, the you-know-whats.'

The bus passengers broke off from listing food and shouted, 'Aye, the thingummybobs.' Raucous laughter rolled around the bus as it gradually slowed to a crawl, then the women grew quiet, staring out of the windows, hearing the laboured swish of the wipers in the hush. Mrs Oborne called, 'You go steady an' all, Bert. Last thing we wants is to end up on t'verge and have to get out and shove the damn great thing back on the bliddy road.'

Beth began to laugh. 'Well, if we end up pushing it out of a slip t'other side of Sledgeford, I reckon Amelia's high heels'll take a bashing.'

Though the others laughed, Fran said nothing, for no one else had heard what Amelia had said about factory girls and she was still furious, though she had no intention of repeating it. Why upset them? She slumped back in the seat, fed up because they were back in stemming again, and what really gripped her knickers was that Swinton had smiled when he told them yesterday, adding, 'What would I do without my "filling in the gaps" team?'

Mrs Oborne had muttered that she knew what she'd fill him in with, in a dark alley.

Fran sat back in her seat, sipping water like a woman possessed, wanting a reservoir inside her so she could nip to the loo and flush herself through after an hour or two. 'Once this war is over,' she said, 'I am never ever going to mess about with powder again – unless it's face powder.'

Sylv called across the aisle, 'Aye, I'll second that. Wouldn't be so bad if I didn't itch all the time.'

Maisie turned to face Fran. 'You and everyone else on this bus, not to mention washing the sheets with it all soaked into them.'

Madge had tried boiling them up twice, each time in soda, she'd told Fran when Fran had taken another load to her and collected the clean ones. 'But it's still there. Try and use the same ones for the yellow, lass, then at least you've some white for afters. Once the war is over, it'll fade from the cotton, I dare say.'

She'd pocketed Fran's money as Fran had asked, 'Are you sure it's not too much for you, Madge?'

Madge had said, shaking her head, 'I only get a few hours at Mrs Adams' corner shop, and this helps feed the bairn. Me mam comes and sits with the little soul while I do my ARP shift, and there's the rugs, of course. What I'd do without the co-op, I don't know. A laugh and some dibs when we sell 'em – what could be better?'

Mrs Oborne had been there and asked, 'Still not heard from your Rob, then? Weren't he supposed to send you something for the lad, Madge?'

Madge had smiled. 'Nay, and hope we never will. He's

long gone now and we're the better for it. He'll be selling something off the back of a lorry, or worse, and I don't want a bar of it. Mr Massingham's said the house is ours for as long as we need it. He's good with – well, you know. Just as well he didn't know the beggar poached pheasant from his land while he were here, or we'd have been out like a dose of salts.'

Bert was calling, 'Okey-doke, lasses, that long uphill corner into Sledgeford is coming up, so lift yourselves and whack your arses down on the seat when I tell yer, to get a bit of traction. Need to get up it in one. If we stop, we're done for, and I've still got that ruddy bald tyre an' all.'

He jammed the gear into second, for first would cause a skid; the engine growled and the bus slid. The women each gripped the back of the seat in front and stood, then whacked down again, and again. Mrs Oborne panted, 'It's lucky for you lot I'm a big-boned lass, I'll tell yer that for nothing, our Bert, for I've some padding to absorb the shock.'

They were driving alongside Massingham's grazing land, steadily climbing. They couldn't see the fields or the drystone wall through the snow, but on the bend there was the blare of a horn and the slit beam of car lights approaching on the wrong side of the road. The lights danced off the falling snow and tree branches in the afternoon gloom.

Bert swung the steering wheel. 'You bliddy bugger,' he yelled. The back of the bus swung round, the car blasted past, keeping its course, but the bus didn't. It slewed round, then back, and then tipped as the front caught the verge. The women screamed and fell against one another. Sarah slid from her seat, across the aisle and onto Fran, and then knocked into Beth. The bus teetered, and Fran whacked against the seat, falling into the aisle, with Beth now on top of her. The bus tipped once more, then settled back on all four wheels. Sarah fell on them both, knocking the air from all their lungs. There was silence and into it came the sound of groans and shouts.

'Get off me.'

'Help.'

'We'll lose our pay.'

'Better'n our lives. Anyone hurt?' It was Mrs Oborne. The slit beams of the bus still cut through the falling snow as the women struggled to their feet. Fran shoved Sarah off, while Beth pulled herself up and onto her seat so that Fran could do the same. Fran tasted blood; it was running into her mouth. She snatched out her handkerchief and held it tight to her nose.

Beth was wincing. 'Bliddy hell,' she whispered. 'You stood on me hand, you great daft thing. Look at it.'

Fran did, but her head was throbbing where Beth had kicked her. She took the handkerchief away, but blood still pumped. Beth gripped Fran's hand and pressed it against her nose again. 'Stop fannying about. Keep your hanky there till it clots, while I pinch the bridge of your nose.'

Fran yelled, 'No, don't do that, it bliddy hurts.'

'Then press the hanky against the nostrils.'

Mrs Oborne was hauling her way to the front of the bus. 'Are you hurt, or just making a bliddy fuss, Bert?'

Bert groaned and pushed himself off the steering wheel, growling. 'Go and sit your great arse down, you auld bisom, and get whacking up and down, for the love of God.'

Fran started to laugh, Beth too, and soon the whole of the bus was. There were bruises, cuts and bangs everywhere, but nothing bad. And still the snow fell, and seemed to dance.

Bert started the engine again, calling, 'All set for another go?'

Fran, her nose still pumping, asked, 'Did the car stop?'

'Did it hell,' said Bert. 'Now shut up and get whacking, while I drive off slow and see what happens.'

What happened was that the wheels spun and the bus skidded. There were a few screams, and Mrs Oborne snapped, 'That's enough of that. Where's your gumption?'

Once the bus came to rest, Bert kept it idling and turned around to say, 'I have a load of sacks under me seat, but I need a few to go and ram 'em up against the front of all the wheels. I need half of you in here, whacking up and down, and the rest out there to give it a bloody good shove up the arse.'

'You're obsessed with that word, Bert,' called Mrs Oborne.

The women sniggered as they tied on their headscarves and made sure their mufflers were tight. They were not surprised at any of this because they were used to snow; it came every year for heaven's sake, but it didn't make it any less of a nuisance. Fran tested her nose bleed and it was only dribbling as she followed along after Mrs Oborne, Beryl, Sylv, Sarah and Beth, who was explaining to Fran that her nose had stopped because of Miss Smith's very wonderful, healing hands.

Bert handed out the sacks from under his driving seat as the women filed into the cold. The snow fell as Fran and Beth rammed a sack up to the nearside front tyre. Sarah hunkered down to give them a hand. 'This cold'll stop your nose completely, anyways.'

Beth muttered, 'Howay, it was all down to me, if yer don't mind.'

They were all three laughing as they trudged to the back of the bus, tapping Mrs Oborne on the shoulder. 'Come on, give us the benefit of your—'

Mrs Oborne said, 'Not another word. Sick I am of the word arse.'

355

They were roaring with laughter as the four of them made their way to where Sylv and Beryl were already braced with their backs against the rear of the bus, their heels dug in. Two more came from the bus to help as Bert leaned out of his window and shouted, 'On three.'

As Fran shoved back, her heels slipping and the exhaust billowing, she saw clouds of white moving on the verge, almost hidden by the falling snow and heard the baaing of sheep. Massingham's wall must be down.

Mrs Oborne had seen them too, and called to Bert. 'Howay, lad, the sheep are through. We'd best get the beggars back first.'

'That's just bliddy lovely,' shouted Bert. The engine cut out, and they heard the driver's door slam. Then they heard Bert say, 'What the hell?'

Mrs Oborne called, 'What's the matter, lad?'

'Nowt's the matter, let's get the beasts back.' There was the slam of what sounded like the luggage door set in the side. Mrs Oborne called, 'What was that?'

'Just me, losing me feet and what, whacking into the side of the bus.'

He came around to the back while he sent Fran and Beth to find the gap in the wall.

Fran dragged her torch from her pocket, wading through snow that chilled her legs and slipped down the tops of her boots, but her toes were so numb it didn't matter. She shone her torch, but the snow was so heavy the light just bounced back. She shouted, 'We'll have to find it almost by touch.' They waded alongside the wall, Beth moving in the opposite direction. It was Beth who found the gap, and the others then herded the sheep through it while Bert shouted behind them, 'In yer get, yer bliddy idiot beasts.'

The girls then scrabbled about in the snow, their fingers numb as they and Bert rebuilt the wall, with Mrs Oborne muttering that Mr Massingham owed them a bob or two for saving his sheep.

Finally they were finished and Bert clambered back into the driving seat, the women pushing and shoving the bus while the inside 'crew' bounced on the seats. The wheels slipped, the wind howled, and Beth muttered, 'I could bliddy howl wi' it.'

Together, as a team – well, what else? Fran thought – they dug in their heels, pushing, pushing, their boots beginning to slip. Suddenly the bus was moving back onto the road; the women were on their backsides and scrambling up, Mrs Oborne muttering, 'I'll bliddy murder him, so I will, cos my big arse is a freezing wet one, and I'm bliddy sick of this bliddy war.'

They were all screaming with laughter as they collected up the sacks, now matted with clumps of freezing snow. They could taste the fast-falling snowflakes as they scrambled after the slow-moving vehicle, with Bert hanging out of the window and yelling against the wind, 'I canna stop, catch up.'

They panted as finally they piled on board. Bert picked up speed steadily and the bus seemed to claw its way up and into Sledgeford as the women dragged off their headscarves, caked solid with snow, and shook them onto the aisle. Mrs Oborne yelled, 'If yer don't get yer heater going full pelt, Bert, I'll bliddy strangle yer.'

'Tis on, lass. It'll warm soon,' he called back.

Fran muttered, as her nose began to bleed again, 'It'd better do an' all.'

The women at the Sledgeford Village bus shelter were full of complaints as they boarded, but Bert stood up and roared, 'Shut the hell up. The lasses've had to push the bus back onto the road and get it up the hill, and you, Amelia what's-your-name, would be no damn good in them silly shoes. Wear boots in the winter, for pity's sake, whether you bliddy want to show us all you're a cut above us or not. Now all go and sit down, and I don't want to hear a peep out of you lot, and neither do any of these lasses who bliddy got us 'ere.'

It was then that all the women saw the gash on his forehead, and the blood that was still dribbling on his cheek.

They were silent as the bus crawled to the Factory, an hour late. But would they get back?

'Farmer Watson will bring out his tractor, never you fear,' shouted Bert. 'I'm not slogging through this lot on me own with a load of bliddy hooligans roaring about on the roads, or mithering cos they've had to bliddy wait.'

In the changing rooms, Mrs Raydon checked them quickly. Mr Swinton entered, flapping his clipboard towards them as he pointed to the clock. Fran, so cold she couldn't feel her fingers, toes, legs or hands, her nose so sore it throbbed, opened her mouth, but Mrs Oborne was there before her. 'You put that clipboard down, Mr Swinton, or it'll end up in a dark place and you'll know the pain of childbirth. We're here because we pushed the bus back onto the road, but only after herding Mr Massingham's blithering sheep into their pasture, and we're sick, sore and tired, so we'd best not find our pay's been cut an' all.'

She rammed her turban on her head and swept past him out into the corridor, followed by them all, barging along the corridor towards their other enemy, the yellow.

Late that night Bert knocked on the Canary Club's shed door, after he'd tried to find Joe, Tom and Simon at the Miners' Club. He slipped inside when Joe opened it, not wanting one of the ARPs to yell at him about the light.

He told them he'd discovered he'd whacked one of

Massingham's sheep with the front of the bus when he slid off the road. 'The stone wall were down, yer see, and they got out. We put them back, so I reckon we've paid for the little beggar, else Massingham'd lost the lot. It were already a goner, so I stacked it in the luggage bay. Reckon we could all do with a bit of a feed, and it were dead so it's not poaching.' He pointed at Simon. 'You did a bit of butchering in the thirties when us miners were laid off, didn't you, lad?'

'Whether a beast be dead or not is a moot point where poaching's concerned,' Simon muttered. 'Not sure Massingham would agree.'

Joe shook his head, and turned to him. 'Don't be so bliddy silly, Si. Our lasses need the food, and it wouldn't hurt any of the rest of 'em women, neither, or the bairns. It were running free, and 'twere an accident.'

Tom was nodding, watching Simon who studied his Woodbine, took a drag and stood up. 'What we waiting for then?' he muttered. They followed him out into the freezing cold and the snow, which was a good foot high and still falling.

Simon fetched the wheelbarrow and they trundled to the bus garage and into the darkness of the old shed where Bert had hidden the sheep. They lugged it through Massingham, grateful for once for the blackout, then headed to the back of Simon's brother's butcher shop. They stepped inside the jointing room, and only then did they speak. Bert said he'd have a couple of chops for him and the missus, and they could sort the rest as they pleased. 'Sooner the better, though, in case word gets around. By then we'll have eaten the evidence, eh?'

Simon nodded. 'Yer'll have it by tomorrow. And not a word to me brother. I don't want him involved. I'll divvy it up for those with Massingham women at the Factory, and get someone to deliver it around, no questions asked. That suit you?'

Tom muttered, 'Will they all keep their mouths shut?'

'They won't know whose it is,' said Joe. 'It could just have come off the back of a lorry, and anyway they'd rather have their tongues cut out than split. We all would, eh. No point in getting Bert into trouble, not at his age.'

'Not at any age, nor any of us,' Simon said. 'I don't want to end up in clink, or chucked out of me house by Massingham, and I wouldn't do it, but that the lasses are looking proper done in. And if I thought the truth will out, I'd be burying the woolly bastard now.'

The next day, when the bus arrived back at ten after their shift, the three girls peered from the window, grateful that Ralph was not there. They'd thought he'd keep turning up like a bad penny once Davey went but he hadn't, not after the first day. They hurried home, Fran waving to the other two when they reached their back lanes. She then slid and slipped home, for her mam had promised something special for a late tea, a treat. She'd said nothing to the others because her mam had said not to.

Fran had feared for a moment that her da had poached a Massingham pheasant or two, as he sometimes threatened to do, but he wouldn't dare, for her mam would have his guts for garters. She must have got something on ration from the shop, but what?

She rushed across the yard, which had been cleared by Ben. He'd also thrown down ash to stop anyone skidding which was always a bugger to sweep clean. But better than breaking a leg, or a nose, she thought, touching her own. By, it had hurt when Stan straightened it. She kicked off the snow and ash from her boots, eased open the kitchen door, and when she was met by the smell of lamb she thought she'd gone to heaven.

Her mam stood at the scullery doorway, grinning and wearing her Christmas apron.

'Lamb?' Fran breathed, her mouth actually watering.

'Aye, lass. Your da said it were from a man with a lorry, and to say nothing, and just enjoy it. Sit yourself down.'

Ben was already there, his knife and fork at the ready, along with Stan, who called out, 'Come on, Fran, for goodness' sake.'

Her da was at the head of the table. 'Sit, eat, don't worry to wash yer hands. Wipe yer boots, and get this down yer, eh?'

She hung up her mac on the back door and slid into her seat, dropping her bag to the floor, forgetting that it contained the empty water bottles. Luckily they fell on the rug and didn't break. She lifted the lid on the vegetable pot and saw sprouts, leeks and carrots from the allotment, there was gravy in the jug, and was suddenly ravenous, when she'd thought she'd never want to eat again after Swinton sent them back into the stemming shop. He still had workers down with flu, or sickness of some sort, so they'd be moved round again, unless they got it too.

The lamb was set before them, and now her mam sat and said, 'Begin, and eat hearty.' They did, no one having the time to speak, and it was better than the lamb at the restaurant in London because her family were enjoying it with her too. She hoped that Davey was eating heartily as well. As she ate she even forgot about her black eyes, her nose and her mouth ulcers, she just savoured every mouthful. She had just finished, and had laid down her knife and fork like the others, when they heard a knocking at the front door. The *front* door. They looked at one another. Her da stood. 'Best get the dishes out in t'scullery, quick. It were off back of a lorry, remember, so there could be questions.'

Her mam rose too, turning on him. 'You said Simon bought it off a friend with a lorry, and every Massingham lass from the factory's had some, so it'll likely only be one of 'em coming to – well, I don't know what?'

The knock came again. Joe gripped Annie's arm. 'Coming to bliddy what? They'd use the back door, woman.'

Fran and Stan stared at their da, then at one another. Their da had shaken his wife, and he looked terrified. Annie said, 'Who was this bloke with a lorry?'

Stan answered, 'If Si knew him, that's enough for us. So we keep quiet, just as everyone will. But I suppose that's still the black market. God almighty. Could it be the police?'

Her mam was rushing with the plates to the scullery. 'Ben, get the vegetables.'

'Who's getting the door?' Fran asked.

Stan said, 'Ben can go. They won't be tough with him. Anyway, we're probably just showing a light and it'll be the ARP. Who's on tonight, Mam?'

They were all standing around and her father had broken into a sweat; it was dripping down his face. Her mam said, 'I don't know. If it were Madge she'd come in the back. Ben, let 'em in if they show you a warrant. Not a word about Simon. We bought it off a man, all right. In fact, me, nowt a body else. I'll have it laid at my door, I bought it, you all hear me.'

Fran shook her head, her mind racing. The knock came again. Stan murmured, 'Mam, bring back the vegetables and the gravy. If it's someone who's heard a whisper, we can just say we had a bit of scrag end on ration, and made gravy, eh?'

Fran pushed Ben back in his chair. 'Just sit down everyone. We've got a story, we stick to it. A bit of scrag end, and that's that.' Fran looked past Ben to her da, and now it was her mam gripping his arm and muttering, 'You wouldn't be so daft, Joe. Not to poach a sheep?'

He pulled away from her, staring into the range.

Fran stepped into the corridor. She shut the kitchen door on the family, feeling sick, the lamb tasting sour in her mouth. Had Da thought of poaching after she told him about rounding up Massingham's sheep? No, he couldn't be so stupid. Any farmer'd have their guts for garters. But no, if he had it wouldn't be Massingham's for that was the one thing that'd ruin them, make them homeless, jobless . . . She hurried as the knock came again.

She opened the door a crack, and peered out. Ralph stood there, smiling. 'I wanted to check on you, because I thought I'd meet the bus again, just to walk you back, keep you safe. But I was called home because the sheep were brought in by old Hughes and we're one short. So I had to double-check them with him, in this bloody weather. He was right. Bloody poachers.'

He pushed on the door, banging it open. Fran stepped out, pulling the door to behind her. Ralph said, pushing the door open again, 'No, don't get cold. I'll step in with you because I heard Stan say you had a broken nose and a couple of shiners and perhaps there's something I can do.' He stopped as the smell of lamb wafted from the hall out into the night.

'My word,' he muttered. 'Oh my word, Miss Frances Hall. What would my father say and do, eh? Rather a stickler where poachers are concerned, and there is the slight problem of breaking the ration too. What can we do about this, do you think? Too much of a coincidence, for us to be one sheep down and for little old me to be greeted by the rich smell of roast lamb issuing forth from your front door?'

They stood in silence, Fran on the step and Ralph still

outside, both in darkness. All Fran could smell was his cologne and all she could see was his shape looming there, with the bright, starlit sky as silent as they were. She put out her hand, feeling the door behind her. Her family's door, no, Mr Massingham's door, and over to the right, in the distance, the smouldering slag heap, the only thing not snow-covered, also owned by Mr Massingham. She breathed in to the count of four, and smelled the sulphur; it felt as though the air was owned by him. The cold wind whipped at her. She said nothing.

Ralph said nothing either, but she could still smell his cologne. A pitman smelled of honest graft: sweat and coal. This bastard was no pitman. Oh no, he was fit only for the dungheap.

'Well, we find ourselves in a situation, dear Frances, that seems to me to require a little bit of friendliness and understanding on both our parts. Heavens, we don't want Davey's family without a roof either, do we? Because a whole sheep for one family? I don't think so. So, probably much of Massingham . . .'

She stared from him to the slag heap, watching it brighten as the wind got up. He leaned closer. She stood her ground. He said, his breath wine-tinged, 'Have you nothing to say to someone who is eager and willing to help the Hall family? Of course, as well as tucking in, this could not have been poached by your father alone, so there could be many looking for a roof over their family's heads, and a pit that will take them without a reference, eh?'

Again there was silence. Fran knew Tom Bedley would be in it up to his neck, and Lord knew how many others, because if a sheep had been poached, Ralph was right, it would be shared.

Ralph's teeth seemed to gleam in the light from the crescent moon, like a bliddy wolf's. The wind whined in the winding gear of the pithead. Somewhere a train whistle blew, and nearer an owl hooted. Perhaps it had just flown over the house.

'So, shall we toddle on up to the Hall, and perhaps take your father, maybe Stan as well?'

'There will be no need for that, Mr Massingham.'

Chapter Twenty-Four

Fran sat quietly on the bus returning from the morning shift at the Factory a few days after Ralph's visit. The gloom was already descending as they entered Minton, where they stopped briefly to offload two of the passengers, and then off they went again to Sledgeford. Beth was telling Sarah how Bob had got through on the public telephone box, as arranged, and he had talked endlessly about the sinking of the *Ark Royal* by a U-boat. 'By, it were only at the end he talked of love. But then, lass, the lines were hot.'

Fran heard them from across the aisle and tried to join in once more, as she had always done, until ... Well, until Ralph had called and sniffed the air, and smelled the lamb before November was out and the very next day had been at the bus shelter, and she had left her friends to walk home with him as he'd grabbed her hand and tucked it under his arm.

Beth looked at her now, her eyes as they were that day when she and Sarah had just stared, along with the rest of the bus, and called after her, shocked. Ralph had said, 'We'll ignore them, don't you think.' It wasn't a question.

They had run after her, but Fran had said, 'Best you leave it, you two. Ralph is walking me back from now on.' They had tried to talk to her on the bus the next morning, and during dinner break, but she had just said, 'Things change.' For they did. Everyone could only be safe if she played the whelp's game and what's more, said nothing, or her da would confess and ...

Her friends, all of them, and Stan, and Ben, her mam and da, had all tried, but all she could do was repeat, 'Things change, so leave me alone. I have a right to my own life and feelings.'

Since then, her friends' eyes had been as cold and confused and hurt as they were today. Sarah, whose profile was so like Davey's that Fran wanted to weep, looked anywhere but at her old friend.

Valerie spoke loudly now from across the aisle: 'You've chosen your side, Fran, and how bliddy could you? I've said it before: you were one of us, an' that makes it worse, but I'm not saying it again. I'm not saying anything at all to you ever again. Bad enough when it's that Amelia strutting about being too good for us. But you taking up with the whelp the minute Davey's back's turned . . . Surprised you don't get swept to the Factory for your shift in comfort, the chauffeur tipping his bliddy hat at yer.' There was hurt as well as anger in her eyes too.

Maisie, sitting in front of Fran, swung round. 'Shame on you, Fran Hall, that's all I've got to say.'

'So you keep saying, Maisie,' said Fran because Maisie's eyes were full of tears.

Now Sarah looked at Fran, her voice shaky. 'Just tell us what's changed, Fran. Then we might understand.'

'I need to do it, that's all,' Fran said. It wasn't a lie and she longed to tell them all, but then they'd protect her, fight for her, and they'd all be in the same position, all struggling for work, for a roof, all . . . Oh well.

Sarah and Beth just stared. It was what she had said before, but it meant nothing to them. 'Need? Why? For the money? Has the concert gone to your head?' It was Beth, but there was nothing more Fran could tell them, however much they'd all asked over the preceding days.

The one thing Fran knew was that no one would tell

Davey, not for her sake, but for his. How could they, anyway, for no one knew where he was, not even her. He'd said he'd send a P.O. address, but hadn't, yet. So there were some things to be thankful for.

She sat back, wanting to quiet her mind, but she couldn't because rage with her da vied with her fury at Ralph, and her terrible pain at the price she was paying so that no one else would have to. How could this ever end? How could she clear her head, how could she stop itching, stop feeling sick, stop having mouth ulcers, feeling giddy?

Ralph didn't care for her, she was sure, he only wanted to hurt Davey, to hurt the pitmen, to hurt all of them, as though it was all a game. Why? Why was he so full of hate, or something else she didn't recognise? But then her family and friends no longer recognised her either but what did that matter? They must be safe for Ralph was cruel, capable of— What? She didn't know, and had no intention of her family having to find out.

She closed her mind. There was nothing to be done until something happened. Perhaps the bugger would be killed by a bomb, or in the pit, and then, only then, could she explain.

They were approaching Sledgeford now, on reasonably clear roads, because the wind had blasted most of the snow off the road and verges, and built up great drifts by the stone walls. Yet again she wondered if she should explain to Davey, but then he would come back and challenge Ralph, and the same with Stan, and that would be the end. Wiping her hand across her mouth, she recalled the feel of Ralph's lips on hers yesterday, until she'd struggled free, telling him he didn't want her mouth ulcers. He'd recoiled, but then smiled. 'Ah, but they'll be gone one day, my dear Frances.'

She looked out of the window. At least he didn't call her Fran; that remained hers. That and her telephone conversations with Davey, because they still spoke at their arranged time, using the public telephone box. All he talked about was love, and she did too, though her words didn't sound right. They both knew it, but all he said was, 'You're working too hard again, sweet lass. Seven days a week is too bliddy much.'

Would Ralph be there today, at the bus shelter, with that look on his face as though he owned her? Perhaps not, because it was Sunday and the miners' day off and he'd be at home with the Massinghams. She was so glad they were having to go in to the Factory every day now, because otherwise she might tell her family the truth and her da would march to Massingham Hall and confess, while she and her mam packed up the house.

No, that mustn't happen, ever.

They left Sledgeford, and the bus ground along towards Massingham, but still no one spoke to Fran and no one sang with her, though she knew they rehearsed. She bit down hard on her lip and dared tears to form, concentrating instead on the itching of her body, which was worse. She couldn't bear her mam to bind it with sphagnum moss, for that was when she tried to talk to Fran about loyalty towards someone working away. Of course the family had asked who had called, and she had explained it was Ralph, just checking up on her in Davey's absence, and said how kind he'd been.

As the bus passed the Massingham pastures she cursed her da and Mr Bedley yet again. Had those two stupid men crept out at night, sacks over their shoulders, and grabbed and killed the poor wretched animal? Shame on them, bloody old fools. She cursed Stan for not understanding. He should, he was her brother, he should be able to read her mind and trust her. Ben too, and her mam most of all, and, of course, her marrers.

The worst had been yesterday when Amelia, carrying her clipboard, had whispered in the canteen: 'Is it true what I'm hearing? Davey's gone and you're in the Massingham boy's pocket? Well, and you thought I was snooty when you overheard that remark about factory girls. Not so smug now, are we? Because that Ralph won't let you sing in a band, you know, or entertain troops, which leaves a place for me. That's why I'm going to ask to rehearse with Beth and Sarah from next week. What do you think about that?'

Fran hadn't answered, just felt a further stab in the heart as she watched the girl trot off down the corridor. Nor had Fran answered when Beryl came up behind her and said, 'Having a go, was she? Well, Fran, what *are* you doing? What must your mam and da think? What if Davey hears about it? Ralph doesn't want you – he's just playing with Davey. He knows someone will tell the lad, and I wouldn't put it past the whelp to tell him himself.'

Now, as the bus trundled along, she knew that at least he couldn't do that, and she repeated that no one had his address, and for a moment her headache eased, but as they drove up towards Massingham her head was aching again because she hadn't slept for days and all she wanted was some peace and the world as it had been before the war. Did you really know nothing if you died, or was there a kind God who understood and made it all better? Perhaps you just slept for ever?

They were passing St Oswald's church. Its spire shone dark against the failing day. It was a beautiful church, outside and in, calm, peaceful and closer to God up there on the hill. Once it had been a beacon for the faithful across the area when darkness fell, but it was war now and no lights showed, though it still drew those who knew that Vicar Walters always kept it open.

Suddenly, she stood up. Yes, it was open, and it would be

quiet and she could rest, at last. She walked down the aisle of the moving bus.

'Fran?' called Sarah.

She didn't stop and as she passed the seats on which sat all those others she had thought of as her friends, they fell silent, then whispered together. But who could blame them? Once she was next to the driver's seat, she said, 'Please stop, Bert. I'm meeting someone.'

Bert grunted, and slowed. He knew about Ralph too. Perhaps he'd been one of the poachers, so it was his fault and all.

The bus stopped and she left, her head up and her exhaustion building as she kept on walking through the snow, which filled her boots and dragged at her. She couldn't find the path beneath the snow, but what did it matter? She just had to head uphill. She leaned forward as the incline grew steeper. The wind covered the sound of the bus pulling away. She didn't look back, just ploughed ahead, heading step by step for the darkness of the church, with its scent of used candles and the memories of past services and thousands of prayers said. She just wanted to sit and 'be'.

The wind howled, and more snow came. She stared through the snow to the church, which came and went as the flurries gusted and died; on and on she plodded, her bag with the empty bottles over one shoulder, her gas mask on the other. She just needed to let her body go, let her mind ease, and not have to pretend that she didn't care that her life was swirling in and out and round everyone's shock.

Her feet were so cold she couldn't feel them, nor her hands. She pulled up her scarf, the one her mam had knitted, and she wanted to wrench it off, leave it in the snow, leave all thoughts of them. It. Leave it all. Her teeth were chattering, and at least she could feel that.

She was at the top, walking along the path that the vicar kept clear of weeds all summer, but which was now snow covered. Her itch seemed to grow worse now with every step, the pain of her mouth ulcers seemed sharper, her stomach hurt more. She didn't know why it hurt all the time, perhaps it was the yellow? Her head thudded, but what did any of this matter? She passed snow-covered gravestones, looking to the left where little Betty rested, though with no headstone yet. One day they would have enough if they all kept their jobs, but if her da lost his, and the house, they would have to leave her behind. She'd be lonely because her mam couldn't come to see her.

Fran stopped for a moment. She said, 'I should come, our Betty, but it makes me cry.' She walked on until she reached the porch and suddenly it was quiet. She tried to lift the latch but her hands were so cold that she couldn't. She tried again, and then felt someone alongside her, then another person on her other side.

'Meeting someone, my Aunt Fanny,' said Beth.

'Let's get inside,' said Sarah, 'and get to the bliddy bottom of it all, in the quiet. We've all decided there's something else going on.'

They had to shout against the weather. It was Beth who was finally able to open the door and they almost fell into the tiny church, which smelled of the huge candles that had burned for Morning Service. As the door slammed behind them, Beth and Sarah jumped, but Fran barely noticed as she walked to the altar, then the side table, her boots clumping on the stone floor, leaving impacted snow in her wake.

She used a taper to light a candle, and set it alongside the others. She'd give money when she was next here. The other two followed. Sarah stood behind her and whispered, 'If the vicar came in now he'd think that angels had left their footprints, and his sister would tell him to pull himself together.'

The spell was broken. The other two walked around Fran and stood in front of the candles. Beth reached out and touched Fran's cheek. 'I always knew the lass was soft in the head, and she's proved it, walking in this weather.'

Sarah laughed, then slid her arm through Fran's and dragged her to the front pew and all three of them sat. Fran fixed her eyes on the window above the altar. She couldn't see the colours of the stained glass, only the faint flickering of reflected light from the candles.

'What's going on, our Fran?' Sarah finally asked. 'We've had enough of not knowing, and more than enough of the gossip and the whispers, and much more than enough of you glowering through life, and us being horrid, so very, very horrid, to you. We've behaved badly – we all have.'

'Not to mention Amelia talking of taking your place in our line-up, stupid cow,' added Beth.

Deep sobs now wrenched Fran's body. Sarah and Beth sat either side of her, patting her gently, Sarah whispering, 'There, there. It's not right when you're like this.'

Beth murmured, 'There bliddy there,' and began crying too. 'We've all been so mean, so upset but it was only when you went out into the snow that we all really talked. We none of us understands, and it's made us angry, and scared, and worried, because you've always been so strong, so right.'

'There, there,' Sarah said again, and now she was crying as well. 'Come on, tell us,' she sobbed. 'We're not bliddy leaving without you, because we're marrers, and we've got to sort it. And what's more, you're driving us to swearing in church, and Walters wouldn't like it.'

Then suddenly they were laughing, all three of them, great gulping laughs as the wind battered the church and the crucifix shone. Fran told them then and they just sat and listened, and then sat some more. No one knew what to say, or what to do, except, as Sarah said, 'Kick my bliddy father down the bliddy hill till his arse rings.' Which was what Beth wanted to do to Ralph too.

'We all ate the lamb,' said Beth. 'So you're protecting us all, aren't you, pet. So you're still the strong one.' It wasn't a question and there was relief in her voice.

Meanwhile, the snow on their gloves and headscarves was thawing and water was pooling at their feet. 'We should find a mop,' said Fran.

Sarah pointed to the door of the little office. 'Feel free.'

They laughed again, but it was only Fran who rose to find the mop, and only she who swabbed the floor, because the other two were deep in conversation. Fran wrung out the mop in the bucket, returned it, and then made her way back to them.

Sarah stood up, and together they all walked out into the cold again. They stood in the porch staring at the snow, and glimpsed the slit headlights of the bus down the hill. 'They're waiting for us. You didn't think any of us'd let you just disappear? Meeting someone, you said. We knew better, but you didn't tell us, and you should have done. We're your marrers, and they're your friends.'

Fran shook her head. 'I couldn't for his da must never hear and the more who know, the more the secret can be broken.'

Before Beth led the way out into the face of the storm, she said, 'We'll sort it all together, Fran, just us women, because the blokes will do something right crazy. But I could still bliddy knock 'em poachers on the head, daft buggers. We'll have to box clever with the whelp, and we can do that. Aye, we can indeed.'

They headed for the path, but Fran stopped. 'I need to see Betty.'

The other two followed as Fran led the way, making fresh footprints in the untouched snow. She headed for the yew tree on the edge of the cemetery and checked for her great-grandmother's headstone, knowing that they had buried Betty to the right of her. Her da said they could have slipped her into Mrs Henson's coffin to be buried with her, unmarked, as her son had offered, for then it would have cost nothing, but this was their lass and Grandmother Nancy would take care of her.

They had finished paying off the funeral within six months, for her da had made, and carried the coffin himself, and dug the grave too. Fran stopped by her sister's resting place and whispered, 'You'll have your headstone, bonny lass. We're putting money aside, and it will be done, and I'll come again next month. I wish I'd come before, but I couldn't bear it. Sleep well, little hinny.'

They slipped and slid down the hill, then clambered back on the bus.

'Girl trouble,' Sarah said to Bert.

Beth muttered, 'Not for your ears, bonny lad.'

'Grateful for small mercies, I am,' said Bert, his cut almost healed, just as Fran's broken nose was.

As they walked down the length of the bus, the women rose and followed them. Bert drove slowly to Massingham. The truth came out, and as all her friends squeezed or patted Fran's hand, they whispered and came up with a plan. They would always be there as support, and she would never be alone with the whelp, but nothing would be said until somehow someone came up with a way out of this hole.

All of them wanted to kick the arses of the men who had poached the sheep, because they would rather have gone hungry, but they still loved them for it, and it was only

Ralph they couldn't forgive. 'He's a right bastard,' Mrs Oborne said, then added, 'But aye, you're right, we can know but not the rest of the cooperative, or the parents or relatives, for they might do something stupid.'

'We must just soldier on,' said Maisie, 'and we'll be there, Fran, every step of the way. You are not alone.'

That night Fran slept for the first time in days, because the anger and fear had seeped away.

In Sledgeford, Amelia was writing to Davey. She would send it to his mother, who would know where to forward it.

Mrs Bedley sat by the range, reading Davey's letter, in which he'd sent the P.O. Box address, which would find him. He'd send the same, he said, to Fran of course. Mrs Bedley smiled. 'Of course,' she murmured.

Chapter Twenty-Five

Davey sat in the dining room of his digs a few days later, staring out at the bairns – evacuees and village children – who were walking to school. He smiled to himself, for the school operated a shift system like the pit, but then homesickness swept over him.

Two years ago, he couldn't have imagined any of the scenarios he was now a part of: handing a ration card over to a landlady, making do with a small bit of bacon if he was lucky. Home-grown vegetables if you were fortunate, and heaven help you if not. And what about the lodgers being given a vote on when to have fresh tea leaves, and when to make do with reused? He stared down at the dregs. Some tea leaves had escaped the tea strainer and remained stranded in a broken line leading to the handle. What did that mean? Was it perhaps that he'd travel, because coming down here had been a bit of a leg, and going back would be too, but it was what he wanted more than heaven itself.

He grinned across the table at Daniel, who, it transpired, was his room mate. They didn't usually have time to sit and ponder over breakfast. Daniel had folded *The Times* newspaper and was reading the editorial. Daniel knew everything because he had the memory of an elephant – once seen, never forgotten.

Daniel looked up from the newspaper. 'What?'

'Aye, lad, while you're sorting out the problems of the world, I'm looking at me tea leaves. That says it all, doesn't it? The brainbox and the want-to-be brainbox.'

Daniel reached out, taking the cup while Davey finished his toast, dry because it was a non-butter or -margarine day. 'Ah,' he said, handing it back.

It was Davey's turn to say 'What?' A crumb escaped from his mouth onto his plate.

'Serves you right for speaking with your mouth full,' Daniel said.

'Stop with your nagging. You sound like me mam.'

Daniel grinned, then waggled his own cup at Davey. 'I saw an article about reading tea leaves—'

Davey laughed. 'Of course you did, and you can quote it verbatim.'

Daniel drained his own tea and peered into the cup. 'Not quite, old duck,' he joked, 'and besides, the tea strainer has allowed no tea leaves to escape into my cup, so I seem to have no future.' He shook his head. 'Whereas you, my lad, have a broken line towards the handle, which means, allegedly, that you'll return home.' He held up a finger. 'But the voyage will not be without effort, or perhaps hiccups.'

Davey checked the clock. 'Come on, you might have set the alarm wrong, giving us an extra twenty minutes, oh mighty brain, but time's caught up with us. We're going to be running for the bus again.'

Daniel checked his watch, then shoved back his chair. Davey called to Colin and Morris, who as usual were deep in discussion at a small table by the fireplace. 'Get your coats, bonny lads. Beer at the pub at seven?'

In the hall, Davey took the mac that Daniel threw at him, then the hat, ramming it on. Daniel called down the hall, 'Thanks for brekkie, Mrs Siddely. See you later.'

Mrs Siddely called from the kitchen, 'Don't do anything I wouldn't, boys.'

All four of them laughed as they hustled themselves out of the door, down the path and into the stream of bairns. If there was a smouldering slag heap and pitmen, it'd be like home, Davey thought, weaving through the youngsters, one of whom called, 'Any spare change, gents?'

Another ran up and leapt, his hand reaching for Davey's hat and knocking it sideways. Davey laughed, catching it. Morris sniffed. 'Ratbags, the lot of them.'

'That's as maybe, but sometimes I feel like doing that, Morris. Not necessarily to you, but usually,' Daniel said.

All four of them burst out laughing, with Colin calling, as he hurried ahead, 'There's the damned bus. If he buggers off again just as we reach him, I'll . . . Well . . .'

They were running and Davey shouted across to Colin, 'What, let his tyres down? Howay, man, just throw yourself in front of him and do us all a favour.'

Colin flicked a rude sign, yelling, 'In this coat, I rather think not. But your old mac shouldn't stop you.'

They clambered on the bus and clattered down the aisle, buying their tickets from the conductress, Sylvia, who pulled them out of her ticket holder. She'd come along later to clip them, which Davey thought was a ridiculous waste of energy, but which Daniel liked because he thought Sylvia a bit of a looker. There were others on the bus heading to Bletchley, but what they all did, Davey had no idea. What's more, Colin and Morris had no more idea of what Davey and Daniel did than they knew about them.

Daniel dragged *The Times* from under his arm, while Davey thought of Fran and how he'd give her his digs address, when he called, and tell her how much better his leg was getting, though not that he thought it might be because he wasn't dragging himself on his belly along two-foot-high seams any more. He didn't want her to think he was getting too posh to be a pitman, or to come home.

But would he want to go back to it when his mind was expanding so much here? He stared out of the window, and knew that of course he would. It was what he knew, it was his world; his marrers, his family. He could start his magazine at last when he was off shift, and build it to give his noddle something to do, and what's more, he could give Fran and their bairns a good life. Perhaps best of all, he wouldn't have to speak slowly so people could understand.

He stared out of the window at the school they were passing. How would the bairns fare when they returned to London? How were they faring here, in the country? Country? It was only fifty miles from London. When would they return? The Blitz might be done and dusted, but Hitler would have factories making more bombs, some of which were smashing Malta to smithereens right now.

It made him think of Fran again. She would be—He stopped. No, he shouldn't know, any more than she should know what he was doing.

He laughed to himself, because he wasn't sure *he* knew what he was doing either. Well, he did – he was decoding messages, and looking for signatures, which was a bit like his magazine readers trying to find the 'key' he had set in his crossword clues. As always when he was thinking about a key, the mine accident nagged at him. He'd been thinking then about a key to the crossword, but there had been another key ... He shook his head. It couldn't be important or he'd remember, but ...

They were driving alongside the camouflaged factory where Mrs Siddley's husband worked and which used to make railway carriages and now made ... But Davey was schooling his mind to turn away from knowledge – it was safer. It wasn't until starting here that he'd understood just how little anyone knew about anything, and if you did know, how careful you had to be; how vital intelligence was, how precarious people's safety. It wasn't just the obvious enemy that threatened. He understood now that there were people in Britain whose allegiance was not to Britain. How could you turn against your own past and present to work for a different future, and do harm to all you knew?

Davey pondered this conundrum and not for the first time, because it fascinated him. Of course those people felt that *his* enemy was where their 'home' was, and believed that they were working for the greater good, just as he did. But understanding a traitor didn't mean he wouldn't want to stop them, or even strangle them, for the very thought of it made his blood boil. This country was his, these people were his. He watched as the bus passed railway cottages that looked much like Massingham's pit terraces.

In one he could see paper chains looped across the window. Christmas? Lord above, he kept forgetting they were in December. Would there be leave? For some lucky few, he supposed, but not him. They arrived at the gates, showed their passes and trooped off, walking up the drive, the gravel crunching beneath their feet.

Colin and Morris headed for their hut, while he and Daniel walked to theirs. There was the low hum of the shift changing, but soon the racket of the machines would begin again as they settled into work. He and Daniel hung up their coats, and took chairs that were still warm from the night shift. He smiled at Phil, who was grabbing up his pencils and could barely keep his eyes open. 'Have fun,' Phil grimaced.

'Oh aye, always do,' Davey muttered, as Phil laughed.

Davey worked until he felt his eyes were hanging out of their sockets but he was getting used to sitting on his arse, fiddling about, as he thought of it. More and more intercepts arrived, which he decoded with the day's setting and always he looked for any repetitive patterns. He'd picked up one which had apparently proved helpful. It was a basic mistake by the German operator, who started each and every message with the same phrase.

On he worked, and his pile for the translation room grew, and his pile of intercepts for decoding too. With each day, as he decoded, his knowledge of German was growing so he had more of a sense of the war. He eased his shoulders, stretched out his legs, and the pain in his bad leg caught him. He winced, and then, for a moment he stopped breathing, because he could smell coal dust, the seam, the mine, and a key.

Then it was gone and he was back at Bletchley, with some of the finest minds in Britain, not in an accident which had left the trace of a pattern. But only the merest trace. He sighed, shrugged, and worked on until half of them stopped for lunch and traipsed off to the catering hut, searching out their usual tables, while the other half covered the shift.

Davey and Daniel sat with Daisy, with whom they had managed to establish some sort of friendship, even though she was difficult, oversensitive and neurotic. She worked in another hut, but they didn't know which. They hadn't asked, any more than she had asked them. She was eating her stew with one hand and with the other was distributing coloured strips to everyone who came past. 'Take these home,' she ordered. 'Lick the ends, and we'll have paper chains in this canteen if it damned well kills me. I'm sick, sick of the blandness. It'll be Christmas soon, and we'll likely be stuck here.'

Colin and Morris joined them. 'Hello, the three Ds,' Morris boomed. He loved food, and perked up no end at mealtimes, though would endlessly extoll the misery and measliness of rationing, in which reused tea leaves at breakfast loomed large and were the bane of his life.

Daniel winked at Davey. 'Oh, and who cast the final vote for reused tea leaves for brekkie?'

Morris grumbled. 'That's as maybe, and I wasn't listening. It was Colin's fault, he shoved my arm up, but what a bloody war that even our tea is a pig's ear.' He stuffed the paper chains in his pocket.

'Don't crease them,' shrieked Daisy.

Morris continued cramming food into his mouth, speaking at the same time so that they could see it churning around. 'I thought ironing was a girl's job. If I lick and stick, you can iron them when I return them.'

He was joking, but Daisy flushed with rage – or was it laughter? Davey never knew with her, but nor did he really care.

That evening the staff bus took them home, which was better because they didn't have to pay, but it also meant that Daniel missed seeing the bus conductress. The cold was biting, but Davey knew it was snowing up North, and would be ten times bleaker.

'Morris, you're coming to the pub?'

'Most certainly, especially after working such overtime. What's happened to our shifts, eh? It's getting to be a habit, staying on hour after hour. One needs sustenance, and I do hope that lovely landlady might just have some of the batter scratchings she keeps in the kitchen.'

'Do you think of anything other than your belly?' Daniel asked.

'Should I, dear boy?' drawled Morris, like some fat-arsed old politician, as Davey's da, and Fran's, would say.

As they stood to return to work, Morris stopped, dug into his breast pocket. 'Letter for you, Davey. It was in your pigeon hole, so I grabbed it for you.'

They had their own keys to the Siddley house, but out of courtesy always rang the bell first. This time Mrs Siddley opened the door, taking off her headscarf as she did so. 'I've just got in myself. It's the WI today.'

Davey smiled as Mrs Siddley dragged off her boots and

said,'Oh, Daniel, if you are sharing a room you should put your socks in the linen basket provided. If I'd whistled they'd have joined me in the kitchen, and it can't be pleasant for Davey. As a penance perhaps you'd bring in a few logs for the dining room fire?'

Davey removed his shoes, winked at Daniel who followed Mrs Siddley, his shoulders slumped. Davey mounted the stairs two at a time, calling after him, 'I don't know, you with smelly socks, me sewing the waistband of my drawers up tight, because the elastic's gone.'

Daniel laughed up at him. 'I know, I was wondering how you were going to get out of them tonight, or when needed.'

'Ah, give 'em a good yank and the stitching'll snap. I'll have to get some elastic, but where from, that's the problem? It's in short supply, like everything else.'

As he hurried along the landing he heard Mrs Siddley saying, 'You lads, sewing up your drawers, whatever next. I'll see what I can find in my sewing box.'

Davey closed the bedroom door behind him, desperate to read his letter, for there was no privacy at the Park as they called it. By, his mam had been quick to reply, or was it Da? He crossed the linoleum-covered bedroom floor and sat on his bed. His night-time glass of water was still there on his bedside table, and he swallowed down a couple of aspirin for his leg which bothered him something chronic in the cold weather, and his headache which Norah had warned them all about. He tore open the buff envelope.

The writing on the enclosed envelope was that of a stranger's and 'please forward' in his mother's hand had been written in the corner, and his P.O. Box address too, with her own crossed out. His disappointment was deep. Oh mam, he could have done to hear from her, and reminded himself to give his P.O. address to Fran when he phoned at— He checked his watch. He just had time to read this, though first he examined the envelope. No, he really didn't recognise the looped writing. He opened the envelope and withdrew the letter, checking the signature. There was none.

Davey,

You should know that Fran seems to be accepting Ralph Massingham's advances now that you have left, with every evidence of pleasure. They walk home together arm and arm and she has accepted lifts in his car. I don't know where they go, but she seems very keen, quite swooning really and listens to no one's advice.

He read it again, then threw it into the empty grate as though it had burned his hand. Daniel entered at just that moment and asked, 'What is it? Bad news?'

Davey muttered, feeling sick, 'You could say that.' He checked his watch again. 'I have to make my telephone call.'

He ran down the stairs, ramming his feet into his boots, his heart hammering, his mouth dry because he must ask his Fran what was going on? Yes, he'd ask her for this was nonsense, it had to be. Fran wouldn't.

He started to run down the village street, but his legs were unsteady. He checked his watch again, and walked, his mind racing. There was someone in the phone box. He waited, smoked, waited. Finally the elderly woman replaced the receiver, pushed open the door, smiled. He couldn't smile back. He just grabbed the door, and entered. He asked to be connected and could hardly breathe. Would she pick up? How late was he? He checked. He wasn't late. He slotted in the money when she, Fran, his love, answered. 'Hello, Fran, it's me.'

'Hello, me.' She sounded tired.

Usually his heart leapt when he heard her voice, but now he paused. So what on earth was he to say? He pictured the letter, blue ink on white paper, unsigned. Those words that must be absurd. 'How's work?' he asked.

'Oh, you know, same as usual,' she said. Then, after a moment's pause, she went on, 'Davey, I'm sorry, but I have something I need to tell you—' She hesitated. He pictured the letter, and no. No. No. He wouldn't listen. He would not listen to those words, for he knew now what she was going to say. What his Fran was going to say. His. Fran. He mustn't actually know. If he didn't know then there was time for her to change her mind.

She started to say, 'You see—'

He said, 'I have to go, Fran. I have a queue. I'll phone next week.' There was no queue. In a week things could change. In a week she might not need to tell him anything. If he didn't know, it hadn't happened, wasn't happening. Whatever 'it' was. But why would anyone write that, if it wasn't true? Why would Fran say she was sorry? Why would she want to tell him something she was sorry about? Why?

He started to replace the receiver, but heard her say, 'But Davey, I need you to know—'

He slammed the receiver to his ear, then. 'Well, I don't bliddy want to know,' he shouted. 'I'm working my balls off here and I don't . . . Oh never mind. I'm just tired. Tired, that's all, Fran.'

'But Davey, I have to tell you that Ralph has—'

He slammed down the receiver, gripping it so tightly that his knuckles whitened. He stared at the information board explaining how to call the police. How to keep mum, how to—

He punched it, but then someone knocked on the glass. An elderly woman in a headscarf pressed against it. It made her look like a gargoyle and her breath smeared the pane. She shouted, 'Bad news, lad? Sorry, but I need the telephone.'

He dragged his arm over his eyes and then stamped out, not apologising as he normally would.

Later that evening he downed yet another pint when Edward held a lock-in with beer that must have come off the back of a lorry. The pub was festooned with paper chains. He remembered the ones he had in his jacket pocket and drew them out. Daisy and Megan, who were sitting with them, looked aghast.

'Don't you tell me to iron them too,' snapped Daisy. 'I spent time on those.'

For a moment she sounded and looked like Fran. He reached for her hand, only to feel Daniel nudge him and whisper, 'What the hell? Surely you know how she feels about you?'

Davey shoved him away. He'd had enough. Of Daniel, Daisy, of bliddy paper chains, of Fran, of the letter, of bloody Ralph. Fran had wanted to tell him something, needed to . . .

He slammed out of the pub, limping, his leg hurt so much, and suddenly he wished he'd brought his stick, which he hadn't used all week. The rain began then, heavy, cold, soaking him. He felt sick. He'd sunk a few beers on very little food and breathed in everyone's smoke, as well as puffing on a few fags himself. He laughed bitterly. Breathed in smoke? God, how could he moan about that when his da was breathing in coal dust? Just as he had, up there, at home.

He leaned against a wall, sheltering under the eaves, and dragged out his Woodbines, flicking the packet open. He pressed one into his mouth, his pain growing as he recalled

Fran's voice, her words. She had sounded so different, so strange, and—He should never bloody well have left.

Suddenly a match was struck and held at the end of his cigarette. He ducked, inhaled, the end glowed and the match died.

'Oh, Davey, what's the matter?' said Daisy. 'Come on, let's get you back.' She slipped her arm around his waist. 'Come on, lad.'

He inhaled again as they started walking and shook his head, then wished he hadn't because he still felt sick and his head was swimming. 'I don't want to go back. Daniel, he'll . . .' He stopped.

She said, 'Snore? Yes I can imagine.'

No, he'd ask what was the matter, and how could he tell anyone. He said, 'I just need to think, to have some quiet. I'll have a sit-down.'

They were walking along the dark street. Of course there were no lights. Not with this war. Fran wouldn't be walking, for Ralph took her for drives, and he'd give her more than David bliddy Bedley ever could. A nice house, a car, an easy life, and it would be a life where a bet over a football would just be a memory.

He was crying. How bloody silly, and thank God it was raining, for the tears wouldn't show. But he was so far away, and she'd wanted to talk to him, and had said, 'Ralph has—'

What? Asked her to marry him? Of course. Why wouldn't he? His Fran was the best thing in Massingham, but she wasn't a thing, she was a lass. His head was swimming; he'd drunk too much. He shouldn't, not when he'd taken the hospital's painkillers on top of aspirin, and now his head was spinning, and his legs felt as though they weren't his, and still his bad one bliddy hurt. He staggered.

'I've got you, Davey. I've always got you,' said Daisy.

It's what he'd thought about Fran, and she about him. For

years they'd had one another, had held each other up. He could have screamed because he wanted to kill Ralph, and her, his Fran, because she was his home, his life, his everything.

Now it was Daisy holding him up, and they staggered up the stairs to the little bedsit, her billet. She whispered, 'The landlady's asleep.' The lavatory was down the corridor, not in the yard. In Ralph's house there'd be a bath too, so who could blame the lass? Well, he bliddy could because she'd promised she'd wait.

She propped him against the corridor wall after he came back from doing a pee, then unlocked her door, and helped him into her room, hushing him all the time.

'I'll drip rain on your floor,' he said.

'You can take your mac off.'

And that was where he found himself in the morning – on the bed. He lay there, wondering where he was, his head bursting. Then he remembered it all. He checked to make sure he was on it, not in it, but it was only the other side that was ruffled. And he had his vest on, and his drawers – he remembered he'd sewn himself into them, and felt ashamed. Had Daisy seen? Well, he was a right sight, even if he'd had his good drawers on, with scars all over his body. He shook his head, but his brain seemed to knock against the sides of his skull as though he'd had a skinful in the Miners' Club on a Friday night.

He dragged himself into a sitting position. Daisy was dressed, and turned from the basin in the corner of her room. In the other corner was a small hotplate on which a pan of water was bubbling. 'Tea in a moment, sweetheart,' she said.

He registered her voice, the words, and scrambled to his feet, stumbling, his head swimming, nausea catching him. Oh God, what had he done? 'I don't . . . I'm not . . .'

She came to him. 'You will be.'

'It's all a terrible mistake. Really.'

'Hush,' she said.

He ran his fingers through his hair, fighting to clear his head, to beat down the sickness. He said at last, 'You don't remember – I have a sweetheart.' He was dragging his trousers off the back of a chair set at the small kitchen table and clambering into them, then his shirt, his tie but it wouldn't bliddy knot, his fingers were shaking. He swallowed, and thrust his arms into his jacket, and then his mac, both of which were hanging on a hook on the back of the door.

'You said she had someone else, that you'd had a letter. You said, as you lay on the bed you'd telephoned her, she'd said—'

'No,' he said. 'Don't.' The pain came flooding back, and he took a cup of tea from her because he didn't know what else to do. It was too hot and burned his mouth.

Daisy took it from him and kissed his lips. 'You told me all about it. Let me make it better.'

He backed away. 'So sorry, really sorry, but I can't. You've been very kind, but I must get to work. Yes, that's it, I have work. And Fran's someone I will always love. I'm so sorry about . . . Your paper chains, I'll straighten them. Your bed . . . In my clothes. Well, some of them. So bliddy rude. So sorry.'

She repeated, 'But you said she has someone else.' Her pale freckled skin was flushed now.

He couldn't think. His head was going to burst. He reached for his scarf, which lay on the sofa. His mam had knitted it, his Fran had touched it. But the letter . . . the telephone call . . . And what had she been going to say on the telephone? 'Ralph has . . .' Yes, he remembered. 'No, I can't believe, not in here.' He banged his chest, knowing he sounded like a bloody fool, but it was how he felt.

Daisy was crying and beating at his chest too. 'You led me on, then, and I don't believe you. Anyway, it's too late, because we . . . you know, did it. And that was because I'm here and she's not.'

He fled down the stairs, his leg hurting like buggery, and out of the front door. He wanted to run to Fran, but she wasn't here. Was she with Ralph? Had he wooed her away because he thought Davey had once stabbed his stupid ball? He'd said he'd take everything from him but they were bairns, for pity's sake. Was the world mad? And of course he hadn't done anything with Daisy. He couldn't have, he'd been too bliddy drunk, and still had his drawers on, and couldn't get the beggars off without breaking the thread. What the hell was she talking about? But he shouldn't have been there at all . . .

He stopped. Davey bloody Bedley, what the hell are you playing at, half undressed in a girl's bedroom? And it was all because he didn't know what Fran had been about to say, not for certain. Oh God. He checked his watch and ran for the bus. At the bus stop he ignored Daniel's raised eyebrows and his whispered 'No show last night, and the same shirt . . .'

Chapter Twenty-Six

The next morning, in the basement kitchen, with the clock showing 3 o'clock, Ralph drank tea and breakfasted on cheese on toast, made by his own fair hands, because the cook was still in bed. But at least he was spared the evacuees rampaging through the house and bursting into the dining room as they had on Sunday. What the hell were they going to do now that the nursery maid had left to work in a factory? Not just because the pay was better, but also because she 'couldn't put up with the bed-wetting no more'. The very idea of it had made him feel sick. What the boys needed was discipline.

He made his way up the stairs, his bait tin in his hand and was crossing the hall when his father called from the landing. 'Wait one, Ralph.'

Ralph looked up to see his father standing there in his carpet slippers and tartan dressing gown, no spectacles and his hair awry. It made him look quite different. Ralph wondered if the old boy would actually see if he ignored him and slipped out of the house.

'Father, it's almost three thirty in the morning. What on earth are you doing awake?'

His father sighed. 'Steven, one of the boys, had a nightmare, so your mother has been up and down to the nursery all night. One simply can't get back to sleep.'

Ralph continued to look up at his father, but all he could see was his nanny soothing his nightmares while he cried for his mother. His nanny had always smelled of roses – did she still? He shut his eyes, not wanting to think of how he had been sent to school and when he returned he found his father had taken her away from him. Fran had hair like Sophia's, or had until it had been cut. But what did he really care about that factory girl? He paused for a moment, seeing only Fran, which wasn't the idea at all.

'Ralph?' his father called.

'What can I do for you, Father?'

'Just a word, Ralph. Sabotage it seems is encroaching on this area. There have been several incidents or so I have been informed. We must be on our guard in every establishment and workplace, including the mines. If production can be curtailed, it is more than a nuisance, it is treasonable. Quite frankly, security can only do so much, so it is up to us all. Please do emphasise this to everyone you work with, and be careful yourself. Sorry to go on, but—'

The man looked absurd, Ralph thought, standing there in his dressing gown, handing down his warnings. Was he finished? But no. On his father went.

'Look, my boy, I do hope that ghastly little tyke Tim Swinton you used to spend time with isn't back in the area? It's his sort whose beliefs might not have changed, who are likely to cause damage.' His father hesitated. 'Or am I flinching at shadows? Perhaps so, one hears so much in London. One—'

Ralph straightened. What exactly was his father driving at? 'Are you back on the same old roundabout, Father? What Swinton does is no business of mine. We aren't, and never were, bosom friends who dress up in Nazi uniforms and secretly march in our bedrooms. Why not go and ask every last bloody miner in every bloody pit if he's laid any fuses recently in support of Stalin, or Hitler, and leave me be.'

There was a pause, and his father said, 'Fuses? Who said anything about fuses?'

393

Ralph reached for the front-door knob. 'You never said anything about the British Union of Fascists either, but one assumes they weren't far from your mind. I wasn't a member, not of them or of the Communist Party. I just found some of Mosley's ideas . . . Well, you know, having experts to run government departments, having some order in things . . . Anyway, may I go to work? Who knows, it might be me caught under a collapse one day and that might prove I'm as sound as the next man.'

He stormed out, slamming the door as his father called out, 'Ralph, my boy—'

Stan followed his da and Tom Bedley and several other pitmen into the pit yard while Sid and Norm played the fools as always, but they stopped when they saw Elliott the manager in the lamp hut. They all looked at one another, but no one said anything. Once the current cageload had started to descend, Elliott said to those waiting, 'I'm saying this only once because there's another lot coming hot on yer heels, and I'm sick, sore and tired of having to say it to each cageload. Me throat's as raspy as the bottom of a budgie's cage.'

'Or a canary's,' Sid said to Joe, 'for them's not smooth buggers neither, are they, with all the seed husks and you-know-whats?'

'And that's enough from you, lad,' Elliott said. 'Thing is, there's been a bit of a fall at Sledgeford overnight in a half-worked out seam that was about to be opened. Happened as the safety crew was doing its rounds. Bang it went, like a bliddy pack o' cards.'

'Owt hurt?' called Tom Bedley.

'Not this time, Tom, but once they clear it, they'll check for a charge. There's been talk racking up, as yer know, of sabotage and I had a message from Mr Massingham last night giving me the same warning going round all the pits. So I want you all to be right careful. Now get in the cage and off to work. Tom and Joe, stay back with me, please.'

Stan looked at his da. 'Please?' he mouthed.

His da smiled, and shrugged. 'Ah well, we go back a ways.'

Stan looked around for Ralph as they filed into the cage. The banksman said, 'You lost your bait, lad, or just your wits, you're looking so gormless?' He closed the doors behind them.

Stan shook his head. 'Only the boss's son. Late again it seems.'

'Howay with you. Turned over a new leaf, I reckon. He was here, what, twenty, thirty minutes ago, so he's tramping out to t'face, though he knows he's ahead of you, so he might wait.'

'Well, that's a bit of a treat if the beggar's way ahead of us,' said Sid, 'so's we've a few minutes' peace, and just for once I won't have to eat his bliddy dust. The beggar won't pick up his precious feet, he won't.'

Someone squashed at the back of the cage called, 'Howay, he's trying, got to give the whelp that. Not many o' his ilk'd come down and get dirty like he do.'

'You after a raise, then, Timmo?' Norm called as the lift accelerated.

'Aye, lad. Course I am. That Ralph's got such big lugs on him he'll no doubt hear me kind words.'

Stan stared into the darkness, knowing he'd not care a wit if he never saw the bugger again, after all his panting after Fran. She was his sister, and his best marrer's girl, and because of a poxy football the lad had held a payback grudge, or that's what they had all come to think. He was behaving like a devil, and for two pins he'd knock his bliddy block off, thought Stan. But last night he'd promised

Sarah, yet again, that he wouldn't. Why, when his fists had itched?

He still didn't know if he'd been right, but Sarah had told him Fran wasn't encouraging him, not like people thought, and it had been sorted between all the lasses. She said that Ralph really was just trying to do a kindness, and added that his sort thought they knew best. He wasn't exactly soft on Fran, but thought Fran would be sad because she missed Davey.

Now, in the cold light of a bitter morning, Stan knew such a story didn't made sense, but Sarah had pulled him to her, kissed him and muttered. 'Best leave it be, why make a mountain out of a molehill, eh? He'll likely find someone more his own sort. We girls can handle it, so let us.'

Stan could still feel the power of her kisses, her almost frantic voice as she'd said, 'Just be glad we're still together, lad. Everyone's in turmoil, everyone's worrying about someone or something. Beth doesn't know where Bob is, we know Davey's safe but not what he's doing, but whatever it is, he's not here. The whole thing's a ruddy mess, so you stay safe, and trust us girls to sort ourselves, eh? Trust us.'

She'd even made him cross his heart, like they used to when they were bairns, and he had, because she'd offered him another kiss if he did. He smiled as the cage slowed and jolted and the gate was hauled open.

Norm led the way, his bait tin banging on his lamp. The deputy in his office to the right of the lifts bellowed, 'You three, over here.'

They went as the cage clanged shut and rose again taking the night shift up, and all around the banging resonated against the screeching of the tubs. In the dimly lit roadway, Albright said, 'Yon Ralph's gone on a while ago. Says he were keen to get started. But listen, Stan, your da's having to nose down a couple of half-used seams to the left of the roadway, just before the Mary Lou. He's got auld Bedley with him, and they may not be out with you at shift end, so don't go fretting. Depends how they do, how many props need replacing, and so on. We need to produce more coal, and t'boss reckons they're worth opening up, as they're a good grade.'

Stan shifted his weight on to his better leg. Get on with it, man, he wanted to say, as restless as Sid and Norm. Albright said, 'So, to get to the point, if they're looking fair for a good few tons, but the props are mangy, Elliott says I'm to get Ralph to take your da replacements. It'll get him off the face, cos your loads are down since he's been on the pick. If you get the message that he's needed, tell him to find your da and Bedley in the left-hand seams, not the bliddy right. In the meantime, you could move him back to putting, just get him out of the way, eh.'

Norm laughed. 'Aye, your da will be right thrilled to have him bring him props, Stan, but he'll only be able in between his tiddle walkabouts. Says he doesn't like to take a pee in public, and even less a pooh.'

Albright shut his eyes. 'Listen, lad, there's some things I want to hear, and t'others I don't. Get along now, but I'll send down a message if yer da needs him, but best warn "Sir", eh.'

Stan tipped his cap and they set off, joining the miners streaming from the cage which had just rattled to a stop. On they walked, passing the openings to the two seams where the planks across the entrance had been removed. Stan listened but couldn't hear his da or Tom Bedley. No doubt they'd be down by the face of one or t'other, having chalked the props for replacement.

He looked ahead, and there was no putter shoving Ralph's tub out along the roadway to hitch up to the pony's chain, so clearly not a lot of pick work had been done. What was the whelp doing, studying his navel and thinking of Oxford? What was the putter lad doing? Driving himself mad with time wasted because of the lazy dolt of a boss's son? Stan raised his eyebrows, coughing in the heat and dust. It wasn't just that Ralph was inexperienced, it was that he wasn't used to work of any sort.

Perhaps he'd be better in a smart and shiny uniform leading a hopeless charge of poor bloody men into the face of the enemy, like they did in the old days. Something with a bit of a flourish.

They turned off down the Mary Lou, bending and then crouching lower, the jagged coal catching their backs, the heat building and the sweat running. Gradually the ache in their backs eased as they rose with the roof, but they were still not able to straighten, and wouldn't until they were nearer the face. Soon they'd need Stan's da and Tom to lever in more props to take the roof planks, as they moved the face forwards. There was no one better than his da and Tom Bedley. They'd look at a roof and walls and know what they were telling them from the sighs and creaks.

Stan could too, and Davey, but not as well as their das. The marrers heard no sound of Ralph's pick from the face and Sid muttered, 'Bet the bugger's sitting on his arse. His pick work is a load of bloody rubbish.'

Stan shook his head. 'Give him a chance, at least he got here early.'

At that moment they heard the whack of a pick, the slither of coal to the ground, another whack, but Stan could tell from the crack it had hit slate. Norm murmured, 'Bet that went right up his arm into his head, ricocheting around the empty space and giving the lad a headache cos there's no brain to absorb it.'

Stan hushed him as they reached the face and saw that

the bottom of the tub was barely covered, though Ralph was stripped of trousers and top and working in his drawers. The putter was hunkered with his shovel, waiting for more coal to be hewed. The boy shook his head at them. Norm called, 'Oh, so you've done a bit of work, then, Ralph? Long pee was it? You need to get yer willy sorted, lad. Yer need to get yer arm behind the pick, and into a flaw, eh.' He and Sid were tearing off their clothes and laying their bait tins on top of their piles.

Ralph nodded in the light from his lamp. 'Oh yes, helps you get rid of a load of buggerance, doesn't it?'

Sid shrugged and, bare-chested, levered his pick into a split in the coal. 'What does, peeing, or pick work? Listen, lad, don't whack it. Find the weakness and sort of splice it, see?'

Ralph grinned, his face smeared with coal dust, his teeth white. 'Pick work, I meant. And yes, finding a weakness is a good idea.' He tracked a split and did the same, heaving out the coal, which fell in bits.

Stan said to the putter, 'Off you go, lad. Talk to the deputy, he'll find you a better face, eh? Ralph, you take back the putting cos we've time to make up. We'll have more seams later in t'week if—'

'That's the two off to the left, and there're more to the right?'

Stan was wielding his pick. 'How'd you know that?'

'Oh . . .' Ralph paused, then shovelled up some of Sid's coal. 'The planks were down on the left, and as I was here good and early I had time to take a peek.'

Stan coughed as the coal came down, again in bits. It was better this way because when it came in a great bloody slab, they had to smash it. As Ralph shovelled, Stan said, 'You mustn't go down them seams, you know, before they've been checked, else we could be taking you back in the tub, in as many bits as this lot.' They worked on, until the tub was filled. Stan looked at Ralph. 'What are you waiting for? Off you go with it, it's as near full as damn it. Fred'll be passing with the pony and linkage and you'll bliddy miss him. Oh, aye, and the deputy will be sending a message if you're needed to bring props to the two seams being checked today. I should have told you earlier.'

Ralph got his shoulder behind the tub and said, 'What? Today? I thought they were checked on the night shift.'

'Usually are but there's a war on, lad. Coal is needed, all hands to the pump, as they say.'

'But—'

Stan was hacking at the face again. 'Howay with you, man, what's yer problem wi' it? Tek the tub to the pony, then get on back, we've coal to shift, same as always.' He was wiping the sweat from his eyes before he dug his pick into the face again, when they all felt the ground shudder, heard . . . ? A charge? No, there was no charge work today, they'd have been warned. It'd be – holy Mother, a crash, a fall, and now the air had changed, was moving. All four had stopped dead still, listening, and knew it was coming from one of the turn-offs back along the line, one of the old—

'God almighty.'

They were running, grabbing lamps and picks, Stan elbowing Ralph to one side. 'Out the way, for God's sake, you heard the fall. It could be me da.'

Sid was keeping up with Stan, yelling, 'Get a bliddy move on, Norm.'

Ralph followed as Stan shouted, his voice muffled against the rumbling of more coal falling and men shouting. 'You too, Ralph.'

Ralph's groan was loud enough for them all to hear. 'I thought the seams were checked at night. I thought—'

They were too busy rushing along the narrowed seam,

bending double, banging their backs, heading for the open roadway.

'Hurry,' Stan bellowed.

'Steady, lad,' yelled Sid. 'It might not be yer da.'

Chapter Twenty-Seven

Joe Hall and Tom Bedley had started the fore shift by checking the Bell Seam – the first one on Albright's list and the first on the left of the roadway. Joe hated slogging down closed seams and tearing spiderwebs draped thick as sheets. He hated how they clung to his hands, his head, even to his lamp, which he held high as he led the way. Every few feet he hawked out what seemed like inch-thick webs.

'Good for healing,' Tom muttered over his shoulder, hawking out some himself.

Joe laughed. 'Then we won't have sore mouths, or lugs, or any damn thing.'

Tom had stopped at a prop, and could tell just by looking at it and feeling it that it would stand firm. But he gave it a knock with his pick end anyway. It was firm. 'Whoever worked this did a right grand job.'

Joe laughed. 'Mebbe us, lad.'

'Oh aye, course it were.'

They moved on, dragging aside the next of the web drapes, and as they did so an army of blacklocks cascaded down. The two of them forced themselves not to shudder, but instead just knocked them from their hair, for they'd stuffed their caps in their pockets. Joe grinned at the thought of Annie's shudder at the tenacious webs, and then the force of her shoulder swinging his clothes against the back wall, dadding 'em good and proper to loosen the web's grip. As they walked and talked, the two men were checking the planks, the props, chalking some, but the seam was a good few hundred yards long, so it would take them until bait time to finish this seam. Still, there were worse ways to fill the day.

Joe called, 'I were just thinkin' there are worse ways to fill the day.'

Tom grunted. 'Well, you're a ruddy maniac then. Give us one worse way, man.'

'You'll have to give me a minute, or buy me a pint and I'll come up with one.'

'Money on it, is there?'

They both laughed and clumped on, the dust getting in their throats, and they seemed to be taking turns to cough. A blacklock had gone down Joe's neck, and he could feel it working its way down his back. He scrubbed it dead against the wall, or so he hoped. Every so often they stopped and listened to the creaking, the squeezing of the coal. One prop was falling forward, but it had just been squeezed a bit too hard. 'Best to get rid,' Tom said, chalking it.

They moved on, checking, listening and coughing. 'Ah,' Tom muttered, 'it's a grand life, if yer don't weaken. All the sun and fresh air, and a beer at every prop.'

They were laughing as they walked on, looking, looking, holding up their lamps, double-checking when needed. Tom called, 'This 'un's fallen out something cruel. Seems recent, look, there's summat here, at t'base, behind the bugger. Come and hold yer lamp, lad. Let me get a better look.' It was dislodged coal. Joe chalked it. On they went, feeling the cool draught. 'Vents are working, anyway.'

'Aye, Albright said they were checked a week ago. Too bloody right, or we'd not be here now, lad. Need a bit of air, we do. Here's another fallen out. Summat behind this an' all. Hang on.'

Joe stepped forward, just as hot air smacked into him, lifting and flinging him against the wall, his lamp flying past Tom. It all happened so slowly, so silently. He felt more heat, and then came the noise. A blast, but not a large one. That's what he saw; that's what he thought. 'Tom?' he called. But it was a soundless call as the planks splintered above him, as he was spun and flung, crash, smack down onto the rails. Tom? Where was the lad? The rail dug hard into his thigh. Was it doing the same to Tom?

His mind wasn't working, right. He wasn't seeing Tom, right, for his lamp was upright not two yards from him? How? It should be in his hand. But now he was seeing the coal swelling instead, hearing it groan, and he knew that . . . Yes, now he could see and hear the props bursting free, pushed forward by the coal. He couldn't move. Only watch as the coal crushed Tom's lamp, and then his. It was dark and heavy, and the dust was chronic. He felt the prop fall hard on him, and the coal hard on top of that. It was a big wedge, one that was driving the prop into his hip. This wasn't the first time, though. It was the way of the pit. And now the pain, like a black, bloody punch. Always the pain was last.

Tom called, his voice strange, weary, full of pain. 'It's got me good, our Joe.'

It was quiet now. Good and quiet. Joe could breathe, but the dust were so thick. The wedge was taking most of the weight, but the prop was deep into both hips now. The wedge was just above him, close, so close he could feel his own breath bouncing back from it. He lifted his head a fraction. Yes, it was there, not that he could see it, but he banged his forehead on it, and it was just a tidy inch away.

Tom's voice was muffled. 'But you're right, lad. There's a worse day, when you think o' Tubby. Poor bugger.'

Joe thought Tom's voice sounded a bit queer, but it might be his own lugs. It had been noisy enough to bring a rescue. His boy was down the roadway. He'd come.

The coal continued to rumble, falling and tumbling, but

not on them, not yet. Had the charge been laid long since? For it was a charge, a small one, a fused charge – he knew the sound. Bloody careless for the buggers to leave it. Well, at least Tom and he had found it, not some wet-behind-the-ears youngster who'd panic and not know to stay still and wait. They'd not know their marrers'd come; they always came and lifted the great weight and hauled them out, and quickly – maybe. The pain was leaping and bounding now, but there was none when it first hit you. Strange, how it did that. 'Hey, Tom, lad, you got the wedge an' all?'

'Aye, if they're quick they'll get us out, but there's more to come on top, I reckon, lad.'

Joe felt tired, really tired. Tom muttered, 'Glad our girls have one another, eh?'

'Aye,' Joe said, feeling better again, and the pain leaving. 'Aye, and glad we gave 'em the lamb. They needed food. Made me feel like a da again, proud I'd looked after me own.'

Tom coughed, then groaned. Joe wanted to reach out, but he couldn't because the coal was too heavy, of course it was, and the pain were back and he asked, 'You hurting, our Tom?'

'Not a lot. They'll come soon. And aye, they liked the lamb, our lasses did. And our Davey's out of it, and there's him and Fran who'll stride out together and toss that Ralph's silly buggering about.'

'Aye, there is the two of them, and Stan for your lass. They'll tek care of Ben, but maybe they won't need to, we've the wedge to give us time for the blokes to get here.' The dust was in Joe's throat, the dark was as dark as the pit. He laughed to himself. Dark as the pit, eh? Daft . . . But no matter for he felt like he was flying.

Tom said, his voice fading, 'I reckon I'm going, our lad. But not like . . . Tubby, and I'm . . . pleased about that. I'm right pleased about . . . a lot of things.'

'We got our . . . canaries,' Joe said, his mouth not saying his words proper, the coal dust filling him. 'Simon will . . .'

'Aye, Joe . . . he will.'

The wedge was shifting, Joe could hear it; grating and wheezing, pressing down on them. It would only take one more fall of coal, but it wasn't all bad. He'd be with the bairn. He'd told wee Betty, as he held her, so white and still, 'I'll come and find you.' He'd said, 'I'll come when the time is right, don't you fret, our lass.'

He laughed out loud now, his pain, his aches, his cough fading. He wouldn't be white like her, he'd be as black as the pitman he was but she'd know who he was. He tried to call to Tom but it didn't matter. The lad would be waiting, and they'd go on together. The houses were safe, for the boss let the houses stay with the families.

He was drifting and saw his Fran. He knew she was good and strong, and she'd give Ralph a bit of rope, because he was the boss's son, but know when to cut it, clean and sharp. Soon he was drifting higher, but then things were clear again and he called out long and strong, 'Tom, Tom, our lasses were right. They're earning good money, so Annie and Maud are set up grand. Our lasses were right all along because they'll keep themselves safe, and everyone else. And our Stan too, he's a good bairn.' He couldn't hear his words. He could in his head, but his lips hadn't moved, his mouth was too full of dust, which was seeping on down, choking him. He was just too tired to cough.

Stan ran on, crouching where he had to, edging beneath the low roof and cursing the jagged coal of the Mary Lou as they headed for main seam. He could hear the others, but it was his dust they were cursing as well. He slowed, but Sid yelled, 'Don't slow, man.'

Stan screamed, 'I don't know which seams me da were checking, Sid. I don't bliddy know if it's him.'

Sid pushed him on. 'We'll see the dust billow, so get a grip and shove on, you daft idiot.'

But Stan didn't want to because he didn't want to see if it was his da. It mustn't be, not him. Not his da. Nor Tom, for where Joe was, Tom was too. But if it were . . . He pumped his legs, faster and faster, and no longer felt the knock and cut of the coal. He went until they reached the main seam roadway and headed in the direction of the noise they had heard, and finally saw the dust thrusting from Bell Seam.

They picked up speed and tore on down it, the breath snatching in their throats and chests, coughing. They only slowed as a figure emerged from the dust, heading towards them. It was Fred Saunders and Stan grabbed him. 'Are we needed? Anyone down here? Anyone I know?'

'Aye, we reckon someone's down there, as we found a lamp on the edge of the fall. I'm on me way to Albright to check the number. He'll know who were checking which side seam and to get the rescue team to help. T'others are busy at it. It's a bloody mess, man, the whole roof came down. A bloody prop must have failed an' all.'

Ralph asked, panting from the run, 'Why?'

'Why what?' Fred called over his shoulder as he set off again.

'Why did it come down?' Ralph shouted after him as Stan grabbed his arm, pulling him along.

'That's for later, for God's sake. Get a bliddy move on.'

'We investigate later, if we can clear it at all,' called Fred.

Stan called after him, backing down the seam, 'Course we'll bloody clear it, we leave no one under the bliddy stuff.'

Stan and the others ran, their pickaxes in one hand, their lamps in the other, carefully carefully. Pit props could be like dominoes – one crashed down, and another would find a way to do the same. This time, the figure emerging from the dust was Theodore Phynes. He was walking, not running, and when he saw Stan he shook his head. 'Sorry, lad, it were Tom's lamp. I know his number, but Fred'll bring back help.'

Stan ran on, his marrers close behind. They all slowed when they saw the huge fall, the gleaming coal, the wedges of the bloody stuff, and Stan found himself panting, sweating, trembling. Eddie Corbitt was there, and turned. He held up his lamp, shaking his head.

Ralph was about to speak when Albright came running along the seam, his lamp held up, calling to Stan, 'It'll be your da with Tom. Rescue's on its way.'

He brushed past Stan, who just watched Eddie, who was holding up his lamp, looking at the roof, listening, and then he shouted, flinging out his arm to stop Albright, backing away, then turning and running, shouting warnings to the other three about to slide their picks under a wedge. They fled, too, back towards Stan, just as the rest of the roof came crashing down, and the walls, so the air was full of dust, and shrapnel, and noise, and nothing stood firm as they hunched down, buffeted, arms over their heads, the ground heaving. They lurched and stumbled towards the roadway. Stan, too, but it was his da, he was leaving his da. He stopped, and in the thick dust he stood quite still, screaming, 'It's me da.'

Sid and Norm dragged him on. 'We know, bonny lad. We know.'

In Massingham, the accident hooter was sounding and the women ran to the pit gates. The co-op women, and those who didn't have to be on duty at the Factory left their frames, their work, and dragged on their coats as they ran, heedless of the sleet and the snow piled up against the sides of the cobbled back lanes. They ran and ran and when they finally reached the gates, they waited outside as the rescue team went down. Some of the shift would help; the rest of the shift would work on, of course they would, there was coal to produce.

The women waited, even as the sleet turned back to snow, small bairns wrapped in shawls in their arms, but its cold didn't touch them. They waited as the snow clouds seemed to suck the light from the sky, and many a pot boiled dry on the range. They waited as one shift came towards the gate, and just shrugged their shoulders, saying nothing, for they knew nothing, though of course they stood and waited too, those that weren't needed down below to help. They waited because someone was hurt, otherwise the hooter wouldn't have blown, not in Mr Massingham's pits. They waited for the hours it would take, and as the darkness fell, the cage brought up some pitmen. There was Stan, Sid and Norm, and even Ralph, and in front was Mr Albright.

From the slump of their shoulders, Annie and Maud knew. They felt for one another's hands as Mr Albright saw them amongst the women.

The co-op women went forward with them, because Annie and Maud were theirs. Madge held Annie's arm, while Audrey Smith's arm was round Maud. The others were close enough for them all to hear one another's breathing. Mr Albright led them to the security man's office, knowing better than to separate the co-op women. Here they were out of the wind and the snow, and it was quiet, so very quiet, thought Annie.

Mr Albright cleared his throat, but Stan stepped forward and took his mam's hand, and Maud's. 'They died together. It were a fall. They didn't die slowly of black lung, like

Tubby.' He looked at Mrs Smith. 'Sorry to say that, Mrs Smith, but—'

Audrey shook her head. 'Nay, lad, you're all right. Being a pitman makes one or t'other likely. They'd know that, just as we know it, and they knew which they'd prefer.'

Annie listened, and Audrey was right, her Joe had died with his Tom, and they'd have talked of the canaries, and the girls, and all their other bairns, Ben, and little Betty, and their lads, Stan and Davey. It'd have been all right. It was war, after all, and it was their pit. They wouldn't have suffered for long. So, it was all right, but still she wept deep inside, for such aching sorrow was a dark and painful thing.

Chapter Twenty-Eight

Fran and their sector were on overtime that same day. It was three o'clock when they were given a tea break, and would now work to five, when the work's bus would take them home. The shift that should have taken over from them at two was working in another sector, Lord knew where. All she knew was that she and her friends were still in the stemming room, and instead of the aloof coldness of the last couple of weeks, there was friendship as usual amongst them all.

She didn't mind the chemicals so much; perhaps the lamb had boosted them, for Sarah, Beth and the others from Massingham also seemed brighter-eyed. She stopped all thoughts of the lamb. It still made her furious that her da and Tom would do such a thing, even for their bairns.

Mrs Oborne filled the huge rubber container, holding it beneath the machine shoot, hauling on the handle so the powder gushed down, and puffed up into the air. She pushed it along the belt to Fran, who tipped the powder from the container into the funnel, with which she filled a couple of smaller containers, which they still called rubber thingummybobs. She thought of Davey, because they'd been cut off, which often happened. Perhaps there had been an air raid, or perhaps someone had damaged the phone lines. They'd all been warned about sabotage, but the trouble was they didn't know who the saboteurs were. They'd hardly walk around with signs round their necks, but he'd sounded tired, and fraught, and had shouted but the line was crackling, so she couldn't hear.

Miss Ellington had given them all a talk in the changing room, saying to look for something that wasn't quite right, something or someone doing something unusual. Fran almost laughed as she looked around. What in the world was usual about this? She poured more powder from the container into the funnel, then into another thingummy-bob, which must be going to fill something else. Who knew what? Perhaps it was a shell, which would need a detonator and a fuse pellet, and until then was almost safe and inert. Well, bloody hooray. It just made them yellow and itchy, but at least it would help end the war.

She thought again of her phone call with Davey, but if someone had damaged the telephone line they'd be noticed. Or would you just think the person fiddling about up a telegraph pole was supposed to be there? Well, she bloody wished they hadn't, and her heart still hurt because they hadn't had their conversation as usual, and it was her life-blood, and she'd wanted to tell him what had been happening, and how the girls were with her now, and they'd sort something out.

Her mask was itching, her breath was making it moist. The yellow would be claggy. Her lungs must be yel-low? She would finish her water on the bus home. She poured in more chemicals carefully, trying not to cause it to puff up, and she breathed carefully too, shallow, quick breaths, trying not to suck more than she had to into her body, knowing she must talk to her lad again and tell him about Ralph, for with Davey by her side she'd be even stronger.

She looked around. Yes, they were all getting used to it, they were handling the powder better, there was not so much in the air, and all the masks were firmly on, all were taking care. There, Da, she thought. No need to worry about me, or us. Just don't do anything so bloody stupid as to poach again. She decided then and there to tell him that tonight. She would be grateful to him, but say she didn't want him to take risks.

Miss Ellington entered the sector and spoke to Swinton with that look on her face. Fran thought back to Tubby Smith, Beth's da. Patterns, she heard Davey say. Patterns, keys, settings. Find the key and you can decode. He'd said something about a key in hospital when he'd been half asleep. But he'd not yet remembered what that was all about.

She poured more powder into the funnel.

Miss Ellington was walking towards her. Fran's hands trembled as she added more powder. She laid down her scoop and put the funnel into its stand, for one mustn't pour anything, bang anything, do anything with shaking hands, because the tremble was now a shake. Miss Ellington was coming straight for her, but then she went past and on to Sarah, who worked on Fran's right. But no, she stood between them. Why?

Miss Ellington waited for Sarah to put the funnel into its stand. Only then did she say, very quietly, 'I need you both to come with me. There has been an accident at Auld Hilda that concerns your fathers.'

Sarah paled. She wrenched her mask off, as though she couldn't breathe; her lips parted, but she said nothing, and neither did Fran. They just followed her, and behind them came Beth. All the women were watching, just for a second, but then returned to their work.

In the corridor they came face to face with Amelia, who held a sheet of paper. She looked up at Miss Ellington. 'I've just had a message. There's a car at the gates.'

Beth slipped to Fran's side. 'Let me go too, Miss Ellington.'

Miss Ellington nodded. 'If Mr Swinton allows. Give me a minute. I'll catch him before he checks on pellets.' She entered the stemming shop again.

Amelia was drawing Beth to one side, and while Fran and Sarah stood close together, Sarah whispered, 'Is it Stan too? Is Da gone? Is your . . . ?'

As the tannoy played 'It Had to Be You', they heard Amelia whispering, 'I will do what I did before, and support you. It would be nice if I could be part of the singing group, though.'

The three of them looked at her. Fran didn't feel cross, she just felt dazed. How very strange. Her da needed them and this strange girl was bargaining. How very awful. Then her anger caught up with her, and turned into a rage, worse than the rage at her da, much, much worse.

'Come on, Beth. Come on, Sarah. We have to be elsewhere.'

The three of them brushed past this girl with her piece of paper, and headed down the corridor. 'I was only trying to help. I shouldn't have . . . Damn, I've done it again,' Amelia called.

'Quite,' Fran said, but her voice was high, and shook as much as her hands.

The girls changed, took their belongings and left the Factory, walking towards the gate. They heard Miss Ellington call, 'Wait, you need a guard. He said no. I say yes.' She came after them, showed the guard at the gate her pass. 'These three have permission.' He nodded and searched them quickly. Miss Ellington was backing away. 'Hurry, the car should be there. God go with you. I will take care of he who thinks he is that God, but falls far short.'

Mr Massingham's driver, Alfie, held the door open for them. They all sat in the back, shivering from the cold and the fear of reality.

Later that night, as Stan went between the two houses, and Beth finally left Fran and returned to her mam, Ben sat in his mam's armchair, while Fran and her mam sat at the kitchen table, for no one would sit in her da's chair. Oh no. Not yet, but how could they ever? Fran cut up strips of blanket for the rug that needed to be at Briddlestone's by Monday, hearing the crunch of her scissors, the crackle of the range. 'I'm sure they won't mind if you're late, Mam.'

'Maybe, pet. But I will. The co-op is working well, we'll need the money even more since the Massingham pension covers the basics but nowt else, and we need to see to Betty's stone, and your da's, now.'

Fran put down her scissors and stroked her mam's hand, but the woman didn't look up, didn't stop working her proggy tool, or poking the short strips through the hessian. 'I am earning, and so is Stan,' Fran said.

'Aye, but he'll want to help our Sarah and her mam an' all.'

Ben piped up, 'There's Davey, he's earning something. And I can do summat for us.'

Both Fran and her mam turned and said together, 'You'll stay on at school.'

Ben was pale, his face strained and smudged. 'Then I'll run errands, so I will. You'll not stop me.'

Fran warned her mam to silence, and said, 'Aye, when you can. Da would be happy with that. You could try setting some crosswords and maybe the editor will take some. We'll talk to Davey when he comes for the . . .' Fran stopped.

Ben dragged out his crossword magazine. 'I miss him. He'd have liked the lamb Da poached.'

At that Mam dropped her proggy tool onto the hessian with a cry. With her hand to her mouth, she turned. 'Howay, lad, he did nowt such a thing. It were killed by the bus when it came off the road. Our Bert got the canary lot to fetch it in the wheelbarrow. They'd never poach a living beast, course they wouldn't.'

Ben looked at Fran, and there was relief in his words. 'I'm right glad. Don't know why I thought it of 'im, but I did and it didn't seem the right thing for 'im to do, but I liked the meat.'

The women smiled at him, as the last vestige of rage at her da was finally laid to rest in Fran. For only now she understood and dear heaven, she wished she'd known sooner. But that was that, and for now it was only the love and grief that remained. Fran said, as her mam returned to her proggy mat, 'Why didn't he, or you, tell me, Mam?'

'What, and get Bert into trouble? And Simon? Why would he do that, pet? Best to say nowt but it came off a lorry, but I know when there's summat up, course I do, and then I'm a dog with a bone. Now, we must sort out the ham tea for the funeral.' Though her voice was quite calm, Fran saw her mam's face, but she never altered the rhythm of her tooling as she talked of the arrangements. Fran cut more blanket strips, the scissor blades glinting in the lamplight, the handles sore on her itching hands.

Davey received the telegram at his digs, which was the address he had sent his mam the day after he'd received the anonymous note, thinking for some reason that she might need to get a message to him, quickly. Had he known? The news stopped the whirligig of his world, the shame of his stupidity with Daisy, and the uncertainty

416

about Fran and Ralph, for what did any of that matter in the face of this?

He took the work bus in, with Daniel sitting beside him, silently waiting for Davey to tell him what news the telegram had contained. When he did the other two sitting behind heard. Both squeezed his shoulder. Daniel said, 'Anything I can do, just say.'

They travelled on, and though these lads weren't yet marrers, they were friends, and it was enough.

The walk up the drive was silent, except for the crunching of the gravel, and when Daisy arrived and tried to slip her arm through his, he shrugged her off. Why wouldn't she be told? He'd apologised, explained, asked for forgiveness for any mixed messages countless times, but none of it mattered, not any more.

At the top of the drive he said to her once more, 'Daisy, I made a mistake, lass, and yer really got to understand that nowt happened between us. I love my lass, whatever she thinks of me. I really do.'

As usual she said, 'You can't, Davey. If she's cheating, you'll realise that you can't still love her.'

'For pity's sake, Daisy, grow up. This is not the time. I've just told you, his father's dead,' Daniel said.

'Then he needs comfort,' replied Daisy.

Davey ignored it all, just looked at the huts, his hut, and instead strode to the big Victorian house, entered the front door, and asked the man there if he could speak to whoever he had to speak to if he needed to leave. When they weren't available, he said, 'Well, you tell 'em I'm going home. It's me da, he's dead. The funeral is Monday. I am getting a taxi to the station, now. Arrest me on my return if you like, but I'm going.'

The bloke at the door pointed to an office to the left. 'Then she's available. Bang on the door.'

He did. The woman with the bun was in the office. The

417

same woman who had been in London, Miss Downes, was reaching for the telephone. He said, 'Me da's dead. I'm going. Don't arrest me until I'm back, then throw away the bliddy key if you need to.'

'Sit down, for goodness' sake. You're making the place untidy. I heard your conversation with nice Mr Simpson, if one can call it that, and am telephoning for a taxi. We will expect you back in four days. And I'm so sorry about your father. The taxi will be at the bottom of the drive when you get there. Hurry now.'

In his briefcase was a change of clothes, money and a crossword magazine, the one he used to write for. Those days seemed so good as he hurried down the drive. He had almost reached the gates when he heard running footsteps, and his heart sank. Not Daisy, not again. It was his fault, but why wouldn't she listen? Instead he heard Daniel.

'Hold up, old man.'

He did, though he could see the taxi at the huge wrought-iron gates, its exhaust puffing out into the freezing air. Daniel gripped his hand, shook it, then pulled Davey to him, slapping his back. 'So sorry. Wipe your face, old boy. It'll chap in this wind. I'll steer Daisy away once and for all. Strange girl. Bright, but strange. Got to go. Condolences, my dear pal. You've got money? Otherwise I have a bit. Only a bit.' Daniel was shoving his hand into his trouser pocket.

Davey dragged his arm across his face. 'You're a good friend, almost a marrer, and I have enough, but I won't forget it, Daniel.' He turned, walked through the gates and clambered into the taxi, wishing he could go back to Fran's arms, but he couldn't, and that was that, and what's more, his heart was sick of being broken. Oh, Da. Oh, Fran.

The funeral was at St Oswald's, high on the hill with views all around. Ben led the way with Joe and Tom's boots in either hand. Stan, Davey and their marrers spread themselves between the two coffins, as pall bearers, whilst their fathers' marrers helped to take the weight. Fran and Sarah walked behind with their mams.

'Bit of a bliddy hill, eh?' whispered Sarah.

Fran muttered, 'Bet me da's glad he's got a lift.'

Their mams turned and smiled. 'Aye, both of them, eh? Bliddy glad.'

The girls smiled at one another. A laugh was too much, yet. But a smile, oh yes, their das would expect a smile or two.

Behind them walked Beth and Mrs Smith. A small army against the world, it seemed to Fran. The gang again, tight as tight could be, for Davey had arrived last night and come to the yard and called her out. He had looked so strange she had not gone to him. Instead, with space between them, she had told him about Ralph and the threat, and that the poaching wasn't that sort of poaching. They had clung to one another then, his body trembling from tiredness and grief, but as he'd laid his head on hers, he'd said, 'I thought I were finished, because I knew summat were up.'

Fran had said, 'How could you know? No one would split on me, and they came onside for me in the end. So how?'

He'd just shaken his head, holding her so tightly that she couldn't breathe. 'Oh, I just felt it.' Then he'd had to go to his mam. But he was here in Massingham, and he'd been told.

She looked ahead as he carried his da with Eddie Corbitt, Mr Albright and Sid, for Norm was carrying her own da with Stan, Simon Parrot and Mr Oborne.

The service was short, as pitmen would expect, and the vicar ended with, 'Our pitmen are the salt of the earth, and Auld Hilda and The Pig at Sledgeford, and The Mint at Minton are good pits. But they are the few, amongst many whose conditions are atrocious.'

He'd warned them he would say as much the day before when he'd come to Fran's house to discuss the arrangements with them and Mrs Bedley and Sarah. It was because he'd have the union members on his backs, else. 'But,' he'd added, 'it's bliddy true.'

Fran's mam had sighed. 'But be quick, or else go and stand on a street corner with a bliddy placard round your neck and do it in your own time, lad. Not ours, or the offerings'll be small on the plate, and mine'll be non-existent.'

'Ours an' all,' Mrs Bedley had added, her face drawn but also strangely peaceful.

He'd grinned at that, they all had, and had left the house, ramming his hat on his head, then turned. 'Who'll take on the canaries, ladies?'

'Why, Simon Parrot, Stan and Ben, of course,' Mrs Hall had said.

'And Davey when he's home,' said Mrs Bedley. The two women had smiled at one another and watched the vicar cross the yard, his nose pink with the cold. Mrs Bedley had tucked her arm into Annie's. 'I'm right glad our lads're together, and one's not left. They'd be a bliddy nuisance, mithering about the place. What's more, one'd come and haunt t'other just to scare t'other to death.'

'Aye,' Annie had said. 'They've good bairns to go on into life, and they've had extra years when they could have drowned in the mud of Flanders.'

Fran, Sarah and Beth, standing behind them, had understood then why their mams had an aura of peace about them. Their men had lived a life when others hadn't, and were together.

The two men were laid to rest side by side, just below the graves of their families, and that meant Betty's too. All the time the bitter wind blew.

Mr and Mrs Massingham stood with Ralph, who had knocked on the Hall household's front door the day after Joe's death and been ignored. 'Now is not the time,' Fran had told Stan. 'And when it is, I will deal with it, is that clear?'

The mourners dispersed, some looking at the flowers before heading down the hill. Davey stood beside Stan, also looking at the wreaths and messages, and came across one in blue ink and handwriting he recognised. It was the same as the letter he had received telling him about Ralph and Fran.

Sincere condolences to both families, such a great shame.
Amelia.

'Is that the one who muscled in on the singing?' he asked Stan.

'Aye, the very one. I suppose she felt she must because lots of the others have sent flowers.'

Miss Ellington approached, and Davey lifted his cap. Miss Ellington gave her condolences, then called out to a brown-haired girl standing some way to her right, 'Oh, lovely flowers, Amelia.'

All the misery he could have caused Fran, and the stupidity that had led to hurting Daisy started to build in Davey, and he looked so hard at Amelia that it drew her attention. She approached.

'I received your note,' Davey said.

Amelia flushed, and pulled up her coat collar as though she wanted to hide. 'I thought it might be useful.'

'Did you, really?'

She said nothing, and as Stan and Miss Ellington looked from one to the other, Amelia moved on. After Miss Ellington had gone to talk to Mrs Hall, Stan asked, 'Well, what was that about, lad?'

Davey studied the card, feeling again the misery caused by the letter and the news it contained, wondering how he could ever have believed it. 'A well-wisher, you could say, spreading the good news of Ralph and Fran.'

Others were threading past them, looking at the flowers and tapping both boys on the back.

'So sorry, lad.'

'Such good men.'

'Thought the world of them.'

''Ow do, lads.'

The two boys dug their hands in their pockets, and if they hadn't been pitmen's hands they'd have been sore with all the handshaking. Sid and Norm joined them. The marrers were all together, Davey thought, and whispered, 'And it were right good.'

He looked at the church where he had first heard those words from Genesis, or the proper words at least, the way they'd say them down south. Well, it were right good. They turned to watch the long trail of villagers walking down the hill to their bicycles and taxis, all in a hurry to get to the ham, tea and beer set up at the Miners' Club.

Meanwhile, Fran made her way to the Massinghams, who were waiting a respectful distance from the multitude.

Fran said, as she sensed Sarah and Beth behind her, 'Thank you for coming, Mr and Mrs Massingham, and of course, you, Ralph.'

The yews around the churchyard were almost bent over in the wind. Mr Massingham had given up trying to keep his homburg on and held it instead. His wife clearly was made of sterner stuff and had stabbed hers with hatpins. Ralph stood quietly, looking from Davey, still over by the flowers, to Fran, his mouth set in a grim line. He also carried his hat, though Fran would have been happy to ram it on his head, and secure it with a powerful thrust from a hatpin borrowed from Mrs Massingham.

The pleasantries were spoken and just about heard despite the wind snatching them away. Mr Massingham sort of bowed in farewell, but before he turned, Fran said, 'Mr Massingham, you might have heard that the bus we take to work . . .' She gestured to her friends, and as she did so she saw Amelia with Miss Ellington heading away from the flowers, clearly trying to decide whether to follow the co-op ladies or linger. Did Amelia fancy a ham tea at the Miners' Club which is where the ladies were rushing, in order to take the covers off the food? Well, it was spam, so what would she think of that?

Mr Massingham leaned forward. 'You were saying, Miss Hall, or may I call you Fran?'

Fran forgot about Amelia, and said, 'Yes, of course. But I realise I don't know your name.'

Mr Massingham smiled slightly. 'Ah, that would be Reginald.'

Mrs Massingham laughed. 'Quite right, young lady. And I'm Sophia. You know Ralph.'

'Yes. I was saying about the bus . . . In the worst of the snow it skidded as a car came too fast round the corner, causing us to lose the road.'

Reginald Massingham sighed and looked at his son. 'Not you, Ralph?'

Fran shook her head. 'That's not my point, Reginald. You see, not long after, me da and Tom produced enough lamb for tea, as they felt we women needed a feed to help fight the yellow we get from—' She stopped. 'Well, I can't tell you from what.

'I thought he'd poached the sheep,' she continued, 'but he, or rather they, hadn't. It was roadkill, it was hit by the bus when yer sheep got out, and Da and Tom found it and fed all who travelled from Massingham to the Factory. I wanted you to know, for some think as how it were poaching.' She had decided to include no one else in the deed except the dead. 'But when I think of it, we all rebuilt the wall after we'd herded in the sheep, so perhaps we paid for it, don't you think?'

Reginald was looking at her intently. 'Ah, I surmised as much, when we were one short – the deep skid marks which were evident, and the blood which seeped up through the fresh snow. I mentioned it, did I not, having seen the area?' He turned to look at his family, then back to Fran. 'I agree it has been paid for, and more, for you saved the other sheep in dire circumstances, and without a second thought. So for that I am more than grateful. I hope that it hasn't concerned you greatly. I am always open to discussion . . . er . . . Fran. Another time, come to me and let me know, then secrets need not be protected, eh?'

'That's grand,' Fran said. 'So, our houses are safe then? We families won't lose them because of the roadkill, or the fact that our fathers are dead?'

Mr Massingham nodded, smiling. 'Of course, quite safe, Fran.'

Ralph was looking from his father to Fran as though he feared she would say what he'd done. She merely shook hands with Mr Massingham and his wife. They smiled, turned and headed on down the hill. Mrs Massingham was sensible, and wore sturdy boots. Fran looked after her, liking the woman and the laughter and life in her eyes. Ralph remained. She shook his hand and he squeezed hers, hard.

'Fran, I was only trying to help keep you going while Davey was away.'

She said against the wind, 'No, you weren't. I'm free of

you now. Never bother me or my family again, because *your* family don't know, and they won't, unless . . .'

Ralph stepped close, far too close, his voice low. 'Are you threatening me, Frances Hall? Best to remember I'm the one with the power. Nothing's really changed. You just watch yourself, you hear me?'

Fran didn't move, just stared up at him, eventually saying, 'If you don't step away, Ralph Massingham, I will raise my voice and tell the whole bliddy world what a right bastard you are. Is that quite clear?'

Ralph returned her stare, then swung round, making sure to elbow her, but she held her ground and didn't tell him Stan knew all about it, and what's more, could tell the pitmen, and it was they who had the power down there, in the dust and dark. No, not a word about that, for it was to be kept in case of need.

She turned round, almost smacking into Beth and Sarah. They smiled at one another, and she said, 'Time we were going.' But Sarah nodded towards Ralph. Fran turned back, for he was still there, staring with those cold, dead eyes. No, she wouldn't tell him more than she had, yet, because they were equal now: he had his status as the owner's son, but she had knowledge of his actions, the pitmen and, most importantly, was one of The Factory Girls.

She heard someone calling Ralph. It was Mr Massingham, who was halfway down the hill. Ralph waved in reply, then said to Fran, 'You should never threaten your boss.'

'Ah, but you're not my boss, are you? Your father owns the mine, and our house, not you.'

Sarah and Beth stood alongside her now as Ralph stalked off towards the path, past Miss Ellington and Amelia who had clearly decided to linger. He stopped. 'Miss Cartwright, you're a long way from Worplesdon?'

Amelia shook her head slightly. Ralph leaned closer and said something. Fran, Sarah and Beth looked at one another, and now Miss Ellington was heading towards them, leaving Amelia with Ralph.

'I'm so sorry for your loss.'

Sarah muttered, 'Never mind about that. Worplesdon? I thought she was from Guildford?'

Miss Ellington turned to look, but Ralph was striding down the hill and Amelia was making her way towards them. 'I think Worplesdon is near Guildford,' Miss Ellington said, 'but she worked in Oxford, I believe. The Massingham boy was there, wasn't he? Perhaps they were ships that passed in the night.'

Amelia had reached them. 'I'm so sorry about your fathers, I really am. And I'm sorry I've been thoughtless. Being a long way from home has stripped me of my manners. Shall we go down to the club, Miss Ellington? I think these girls have families to comfort.'

Later, after the refreshments had been cleared, Beth went home with her mam and Ben with his. He carried his da's boots, which would come in handy for him or Stan, and Mrs Bedley had taken Tom's for when Davey was back in the pit.

Davey and Fran walked round the village, Davey's arm around her shoulder, talking of the day, and how the boots placed on each coffin had somehow seemed to hold the shape and sum of the men. They smiled over Miss Ellington's words at the wake, when she'd thought they would be buried with the pitmen, and Simon's shocked reply, 'Nay, lass, good leather, good steel in the toe, what be the point of waste like that? Seems I should take some time to tell you the ways of the pitmen, and maybe canaries?'

Fran grinned. 'I thought she'd run off, but I think they're going to meet. All I heard her say, waving her stump, was,

"I can't stroke and hold a canary at the same time. You'll have to do one or t'other for me." Then Simon said, "Oh aye, I'll give yer a stroke any time you like." '

Davey laughed. 'Oh aye, he'll have the beer and she the sherry, but he's not to reckon on a stroke, or is he? Hard to tell from the twinkle she gave the lad.'

Fran held his face and kissed his lips, knowing more than ever how much she had missed him and needed him, because she couldn't bear the space that he left when he was gone. It was only now that she realised how strong he had been, how much they had relied on him. They walked on, talking of Ralph while the slag smouldered and the pithead flag flew half mast.

Davey stopped and kissed her, again and again. He needed her more than ever before now that his da was gone. He had been such a grand man, and he didn't know how any of them could bear it without him. They walked on, and as Davey gazed up at the winding gear and the cold wind tossed the smell of sulphur around like the scent of his childhood, she told him what she'd said to Ralph after the funeral, and he replied, 'It's all my fault. If I hadn't taken his damned ball . . .'

'Don't be daft, there must be something wrong with him if he's that twisted. It's as though he's gone wrong, or were wrong all along, so bitter, so angry. Anyway, I don't want to think about him any more because at the saddest time of our lives we're together, and always will be, wherever we both are, if you can decipher that gobbledygook.'

Again he pulled her to him and leaned back against the horizontal pole that guarded the allotment, where somehow they'd ended up. 'I will always love you, bonny lass, with all my heart. Do you hear? With all my heart for ever and a day.'

They kissed and he couldn't bear to leave her again, but

he must. Not this minute, but soon. Today was theirs, and tomorrow it would be the beck. It made the loss slightly more bearable, but all the while he was trying to put away the thought of Daisy, the bed, his stupidity. God almighty, what had he been thinking?

Fran said, 'Do you remember when we used to hang from this bar by our legs, all of us, all the gang?'

Tucking her skirt in her knickers, she gripped the bar and hung on it. Then she tucked her legs through her arms and up and over the bar again and was hanging by her legs. She looked up at him, laughing. 'Look, Davey, nothing's changed. I can still do it. Can you?'

He did the same, though his head touched the ground. As he stared at the upside-down world, he forced his mind away from the pain in his legs, saying, 'Aye, lass, nothing's changed, we're hanging here like a couple of bats, looking like idiots.' They hung there, laughing, until they could barely breathe, which was when Stan, Sarah and Beth found them. Within a few minutes they were all hanging like bats until the blood ran into their heads and their ears buzzed.

But Davey knew that something *had* changed. He had – well, what? Been disloyal, cried on a woman's shoulder, slept the night on her bed. *On* her bed, he repeated. He should tell Fran, but not now, not today.

Later, they walked back together, their hands smelling of rusty metal, as they always had when they were young and had been at the allotment. Sarah said, 'D'you remember when it was hot, and the earth dried and cracked? We thought we could get through to Australia if we dug and dug.'

Davey said quietly, 'And our das tanned our backsides till they stung, cos we'd dug up their baby leeks.' The days had seemed so full of sun back then, and as they talked of those times they laughed and cried, because their three fathers would not be here to dig the allotment or care for the canaries ever again, and it was good for Davey at last to bury himself properly in grief.

When the moon was high in the sky, Stan took Sarah and Beth home, and Davey and Fran clung together in her yard. The hens had been shut in, a dog barked along the alley, and in the familiarity of home Fran allowed herself to believe that everything would be all right; she and the two girls would be careful at the Factory, Stan would be safe in the pit, and Davey at wherever he was, and both would be doing as the girls were, helping to win the war.

She looked up as the cold sank into her bones, and Davey's arms held her close. 'I reckon they're up there, my da and yours, having a good laugh about being carried up the hill.'

Davey hugged her and said, 'I reckon you could be right.'

Welcome to

Penny Street

where your favourite authors and stories live.

Meet casts of characters you'll never forget,
create memories you'll treasure for ever,
and discover places that will stay with
you long after the last page.

Turn the page to step into the home of

ANNIE CLARKE

and discover more about

The Factory Girls . . .

Dear Reader,

It's such a huge pleasure to be able to write about the North-East in which my roots are firmly embedded. Though I live now in North Yorkshire, my mum was born and lived in a pit village in County Durham at the start of the First World War. Orphaned by the age of eleven, life was tough but she finally became a nurse and worked at the Royal Victoria Infirmary, Newcastle, in the early years of the World War Two. When air raids sounded, the nurses and doctors would move the patients beneath the beds. She wasn't sure how useful that would have been, but it was the best they could do.

She became a QA and was on her way to nurse in Singapore when it fell to the Japanese, (lucky her, some friends were not so fortunate). She continued to India with the convoy.

I grew up with her memories of miners as neighbours, friends and patients. Her memories became mine because she had such recall, and was so proud of 'her' people, not just miners, but her friends, some of whom became 'the factory' munitions girls. Much later they shared a great deal with her, and she shared it with me.

My mum was devastatingly attractive, hilariously funny, but along with many nurses of her generation or so I've found, as tough as old boots. I remember whingeing about feeling rough with a cold, and was told to run round the garden a few times and I would pick up. Actually I did, which was infuriating. Like most Northerners she just got on with things. She wanted a patio and dad was a bit slow in getting it sorted. She took some brick-laying classes, organised her labour force, we kids, and built it.

We frequently spent our holidays in Mum's pit village with my Uncle Stan and Auntie Isobel in the sweet shop, which had been my grandpa's. The smell, the sight, the noise of the mining community is as clear today as it was then, and so too the one-handed woman who nipped in for a visit, and brought fabulous little cakes. Mum whispered that her friend had been 'careless' at 'you know where'. We didn't then, but later learned much more about the munitions factories.

Now the mines have gone, the slag heaps used as ballast for roads and my mum's family's shop is a house. I was there not so long ago, having a look round, thanks to the kind owner who caught me peering through the entrance.

So, here is the first book in the series I felt driven to write as homage to the fabulous women, so gutsy and funny, and to the men, and the communities which hung tight and brave, and the extraordinary world of our decoders. With each page I heard Mum's voice, and her stories. She'll be up there on her cloud, as she used to say, hopefully enjoying the view I've created.

Annie x

The Munitions Factories

With the advent of the First World War it became apparent
that the country needed to move the economy on to a war
footing. This was done by changing the production of goods
in factories to munitions, as well as building new factories
to do the same. Fine, so there were the factories, but most
of the workers had gone to war. Step forward the women.
These eventually comprised roughly 80% of the workforce.

The same situation occurred in World War Two, with
one crucial difference: the government had been improving the infrastructure for munitions manufacture during
the 1930s as international crises burgeoned. However, the
problem of a disappearing workforce was repeated. Step
forward the women once more. It was these women who
helped to make survival and then victory possible. But the
very nature of munitions, which are created to harm the
enemy, means they can also damage those producing it.
These dangers were accepted by the women: women of all
ages, some with children, some whose men were engaged
in dangers of their own. But thought could not be given to
personal traumas or worries, only total concentration could
preserve their and their fellow workers' lives. In spite of the
pressures, security forbade discussion of their work with
those outside their work zone. They found respite through
their own gumption and the company of their fellow workers, and the most common sound was, allegedly, laughter
and song. We owe these workers a very great deal.

Bletchley Park

War cannot be won on munitions alone. Intelligence is crucial. Bletchley Park, this former country house fifty miles from London, became the nerve centre for Britain's code breakers: code breakers drawn from the world of mathematics, linguistics, chess and cryptic crossword setters.

It was home to some of the finest minds, the greatest lateral thinkers, who found the work fascinating, frustrating, addictive, repetitive and sometimes boring beyond belief. How fortunate for us that they stuck at it, because these were the people who saved thousands, if not millions, of lives as they decoded the enemy's messages, carried hotfoot to them from intercept sites around the country. The decoders at BP worked in huts set up in the grounds, with outside lavatories, and inadequate heaters. In winter layers of clothing were worn, and like the women in the munitions factories, they worked in huge secrecy.

But what were they doing, precisely? What I gleaned from Bletchley Park is that the Germans used a machine to encrypt (encode) messages. This was called the Enigma, which you probably know is a machine with keys a bit like a typewriter but with innards far more complicated. Alongside would be another keyboard capable of lighting up. The operator would type a letter on the normal keyboard using the setting or 'key' for the day. Inside the typewriter an electric current converted this into another letter as it passed through a rotating wheel, and temporarily lit up this alternative letter on the adjacent keyboard. This letter would be jotted down, and so on until the end of the message. This gobbledegook was then sent by Morse code to the recipient who had 'set' up his machine to match the sender's. He would type in the encoded letters and the original letters would light up on his adjacent keyboard. Voilà, the message. Of course the message would be in German, or Japanese, or whatever language the sender was using.

Now just think of that day's messages arriving from the intercept stations, and BP decoders trying to work out the enemy's setting or key – to enable them to break the code. This was Bletchley Park's role, and once the setting was deciphered (slow work and often impossible), it was distributed to all the other decoders, who could decode a stack of messages, and pass them to the translators.

Now we come to Turing and Welchman's crucial Bombe (computer) which they created at Bletchley to trawl at speed through the millions of possible alternative settings to find the right one, which could then be distributed and each intercept decoded. This became vital as the war progressed, because the setting seemed to be changed daily. Stunning, brilliant men.

But why not find your way to Bletchley Park, which is open to the public? Go and see the Bombe, visit the huts where the decoders worked, so too the translators and the clerks . . . and I expect you can tell me far more about it than I know.

Turn the page for a sneak
peek into my new novel

Heroes on the Home Front

December 1941

Fran Hall stood on the back step of her family's colliery house in Massingham, wrapping her woollen scarf over her head and round her neck before tucking the ends down inside her shabby mac. The scarf was all sorts of colours, and the latest her mam had knitted, the one her da had liked because he said that it was cheery as the days drew in. She looked down at the old chair beside the step beneath which her da's boots should have been. Aye well, they wouldn't be, not any more.

She stepped out into the yard, leaving the Proggy Rug Co-operative as they called themselves busy around the kitchen table. 'You be good, ladies,' she called. 'Not too much fun and games; you've fresh orders to finish for the department store, remember.'

She heard her mam's strained laugh. 'Howay with you, pet. Don't teach us oldies to suck eggs. You just keep wrapped up and enjoy your time with the others at the beck.' The rest of the co-op women would all be working – not just at their rugs – but at keeping things normal for her mam, and Sarah Bedley's. Their fathers had been laid to rest the day before, following a fatal accident in the mine.

She shut the door behind her. Well, keeping things normal was about right, for there had to be a new normality in the Hall and Bedley homes now. But they weren't the first in the pit village to suffer painful losses, and they wouldn't be the last.

'Aye,' she whispered to herself, looking skywards, her breath puffing out into the cold. She was a pitman's daughter and would get used to her da being up there on that great grey cloud which had settled over the pit village during the night, heralding rain later in the day. He'd be dangling his legs over the side, alongside Sarah's father, their bodies all mended after the roof fall, chatting over their big day yesterday; tucked up safe in their caskets while their sons and their marrers took their weight on the haul up the hill to St Oswald's. She reckoned they'd be laughing at the memory of the lads panting, longing for a Woodbine as they coughed and spluttered beneath the weight.

She laughed too, imagining them, two old friends – no, three, for Beth's da, Tubby Smith, would be there too – and whispered towards the cloud. 'Bad do, you old beggers chewing the cud, while you've left our Stan to take your place in the canary shed. Mark you, Da, it's the beer he'll have with Simon Parrot that's made your eldest lad take it up with a smile on his face, leaving me to do the hens. Oh, and don't either of you be worrying about a roof over our heads: the boss, Mr Massingham, says the houses are ours for as long as we need 'em.'

She stopped by the hen coop on the left-hand side of the yard, scooped out grain from the covered bucket, and chucked it through the chicken wire as they clucked about. 'Young Ben'll maybe help me, but not Mam, so don't be worrying, eh? We'll be keeping an eye on her, every minute, making sure she gets over this, like she did the babe. Don't want you pushing your nib in, checking up one dark night, and frightening everyone to death. You just rest, you've done your bit.'

Her voice faltered on the last word, but she was a pitman's daughter so swallowed and pushed back her shoulders. She put the lid back on the bucket before walking to the gate and lifting the sneck to head for the Bedleys' house where she'd pick up the girls, and Davey, her beloved lad.

She strode along the back lane, quiet now except for the

workings of Auld Hilda. She stopped, breathing in the sulphur, the air of her home town, and watched the wind whipping up the slag heap. All the same, but not the same.

She turned, looked back at the pithead, and whispered, 'You keep our Stan safe when he's back wi' yer, Auld Hilda, because you didn't do too good a job with our Da, did you? Better ratchet up yer game—' She stopped because at least her da hadn't died of Black Lung, which was his and Tom's fear. No, it was Tubby, Beth's da, who had died of that. She said now, but quietly, 'Ah well, maybe you did us a favour after all, Hilda. Da's cough was getting worse, so I'll let yer off this once. But don't you dare tek our Stan, you hear me?'

She hurried on, thinking that if anyone heard her, they'd think she'd gone mad. It was nine a.m. and the fore-shift had clip-clopped in their boots along the back alley long before it was light, their murmuring drowned by the hooter as their six a.m. shift approached. Would the seam her da and Tom had been checking when the wall and roof caved in be re-opened as planned? It had only been half worked out so was good for a few more tons once they shoved up more props. So probably – after all, wars needed coal.

What would the investigation reveal? Who knew?

She turned up her mac collar and turned right at the top of the road. Ahead was the bus shelter where she, Sarah and Beth would normally queue for the bus for their shift at the munitions factory. It would have left earlier, much earlier even than the fore-shift at the mine; four a.m. to be precise. Beth should have gone into work today, for Tubby had died a bit before so she'd had a couple of days off back then, but Miss Ellington the senior SO had given dispensation.

'Of course she had,' Fran muttered to herself. 'We three come as a package, just as the three fathers did.'

In the bag Fran carried on her shoulder were spam

sandwiches left over from the funeral tea; the corners were curling, but they'd been left outside the house in the meat safe, where the bitter cold of mid-December would keep the spam fresh enough. She turned right into Sarah's back alley, her boots clopping on the cobbles, wishing Stan, her elder brother, hadn't taken her bike to Sarah's earlier along with his own, eager to comfort the love of his life. He was all of a dither in his grief, wanting to help but not knowing how, so he'd just taken it. Daft beggar.

Ben, their twelve-year-old brother would meet them by the turning which led out of Massingham towards the beck. He was at his marrer's right this minute trying to crack a crossword that Davey had set to keep the lad's mind away from sadness, and to keep things as normal as possible.

There it was again, that word. It was normal that her mam was a widow, now. It was normal that her da was safe, out of the pit. She looked up at the clouds, grinned and shouted, 'You behave yourselves, you lot, and don't you be throwing any snow down, just out of devilment.'

She stopped because Davey, her Davey, had swung out of his back gate, and was running towards her. When he reached her he stood there for a moment, hesitating, before gripping her hands when normally he'd hug her to him. But he was grieving too, it was no more or less than that. Surely? 'Bonny bonny lass,' he muttered. 'God, I wish I could stay and never leave. I'd give anything not to get on that train today. Come on, they're waiting for us inside.' Although Davey's words were kindly meant, what she truly wanted was real words of love.

They walked on back to the Bedley house as he asked, 'Who were you talking to just now?'

Fran shrugged, knowing she'd feel a fool with anyone, except him. Well, at least she would normally, for that's how it *had* been before he left for his war work. *Normally*? Lord, she was growing to hate that word. 'I was chatting to your da, my da and Beth's. Telling them not to throw any snow down, out of devilment.'

Davey swung round surprised and laughed, a great booming laugh, his real laugh, the first since he'd rushed back from Bletchley Park. 'Aye, right enough. Devilment, eh. Careful what you say, or St Paul's likely to banish them all down to where it's dark and fiery.'

'Aye, well, they'll feel right at home there, eh?' They looked at one another, laughing, recognising the pain, the misery, but also the joy and it was again as it used to be. Or almost.

He pushed open the gate, and entered his da's, no – she stopped the thought, his mam's yard. Stan was by the bikes which leaned against the rusted downpipe on the back wall. He was smoking, watching Sarah as though he was taking a long drink, something which would sustain him through the day as she pulled the scarf up over Beth's ears, and her woollen hat down, until only Beth's eyes and nose showed. Sarah almost crooned, 'There you go, pet. Might not be the best look in the world, and you could rob a bank and not be identified, but at least you won't catch your death—'

Stan interrupted, 'We've had enough of that to last a lifetime.' All three girls and the lads smiled faintly. Beth said, 'What, robbing a bank?'

Sarah elbowed her. 'Aye, that'll be it.'

Stan dragged out his Woodbines and waved them. Davey took one, cupped his hands round Stan's match, and both lads drew on the cigarettes.

Fran looked around; here they all were, the gang that had been formed years ago, but it was almost as though they were floating, or so they'd all said to one another the evening before whilst the neighbours were scoffing the spam tea at the club. Things weren't quite real, and that's probably all it was that was wrong with Davey. It couldn't still be the trouble caused by Mr Massingham's son Ralph, who'd chased long and hard after Fran; hadn't she explained already how she had put a stop to it? She heard the question in her own thoughts.

The three girls waited like this, together, quiet, with linked arms, watching the two men, Woodbines in the corner of their mouths, untangling the bikes as they discussed how much time they had before Davey left for his train back down to the south. As the girls' breath mingled, Fran knew that even when Davey went the three of them had one another, and Ralph would continue to leave her be. She shivered at the very thought of his unwelcome advances which had tormented both her, and Davey. How could one tell the owner's son to 'shove off', especially after his threat to tell his father of her own da's poaching of a sheep? The price for his silence had been her 'friendliness' towards him, though that's all it had been, she'd at least seen to that.

She felt Sarah's arm around her. 'Are you thinking of Ralph?' Sarah whispered.

Beth muttered, 'Don't, bonny lass. He's no hold over you now.'

Fran looked from one to the other of her friends. 'But does Davey really believe in the truth of it? He's been so different, so distant, as though he still blames me.'

Sarah pulled her close, whispering, 'Or he's just bereft? Aye, well he would be, our da's just died, daft girl. We're all bliddy well struggling, all finding our way, but we're not alone, and aye, we're so lucky in that. And we've a good job an' all. With good money, which is useful to the war.'

Beth muttered, 'Oh aye, and detonators that can blow

our hands off at any time, and bliddy Mr Swinton being bossy enough to stop the bliddy Nazis in their tracks.'

Fran joined in, 'No, he wouldn't do that, he *is* a bliddy Nazi, the way he behaves.' They were laughing again and for a moment Fran rested her head against Sarah's. 'We'll all be fine, of course we will.' And Fran knew they would because she'd taken on Ralph outside St Oswald's when she'd told him his hold over her had died, along with her da. He couldn't hurt her now. She then told his father, who had attended the funeral, the truth of the sheep incident which she had just learned from her mam: that the sheep was already dead, hit by a bus, so if Mr Massingham was missing one, his pit village had eaten it.

She watched Davey as the lads ground their dog ends into the ground, seeing Stan punch him lightly on the shoulder, and heard her brother say, 'Come on, man, you've only a few hours with us, so perk up and join in. We're the cream yer know, not like that crowd yer running with down south.'

At his words she saw Davey's face stiffen, and fear washed over her. What if his distance had nothing to do with Ralph after all? Had he met someone else down in Buckinghamshire? Someone smarter, more interesting. Perhaps his time away had made him realise how small Massingham was, how boring, and she along with it . . .

Pulling Fran close to her, Beth muttered, 'Stop mithering it in yer head, Fran. I can see it writ all over your face. He knows you had nowhere to turn with the beggar. Stan's tired, and grumpy, so's Davey. Everyone's in a do, everyone here that is . . .'

Fran took her bike from Stan, while Davey dragged her bag from her shoulder. 'Lord above, what's in this, Franny? It's heavy enough to be the crown jewels.'

Sarah smiled, 'Close, Davey; it's delicious and delightful

spam sandwiches, and our Fran did as she said and snuck out some sherry, and a bottle of beer from the tea, just for us. Our Fran always does as she says, you know. You can trust her in a way you canna trust most people.'

Davey nodded, and looked down at his feet on the ground either side of the pedals while Stan held open the gate and waved them through. 'Get a move on then, sooner we get there, the sooner we can have some, eh Davey?'

The three girls rode side by side along the alley, Fran in the middle, their breath huffing out into the air, while Beth talked of the letter she'd received from her husband, Bob, who was somewhere he could not talk about, doing something he could not talk about either, but at least he was safe. 'A lot of blacked out words, but they left in, With love, Bob.'

They were laughing again.

Bob was safe, Fran thought. Be safe, that's what the wives of pitmen in Massingham Pit village said as their men headed out of the door. Be safe, be safe, for no one truly was. But at least her da and Sarah's had been with one another, marrers in life and death, and the three mothers would carry that fear no more as they went above and beyond to keep ranges burning. Or the Home Fires, as Ivor Novello had written in the Great War.

She hummed as she pedalled, keeping pace with the other two girls as Beth said, her voice juddering as she cycled over the frozen clods of earth that had dropped from the farmer's tractor wheels, 'I wonder how the others are getting on at the Factory?' which is what they called where they worked. Davey had come up with the codename himself. So much war work was a big fat secret, including their own at the munitions factory.

Sarah smiled. 'We've only been away for a couple of days, so pretty much the same, I reckon. But I wonder how Miss Poshness, our Amelia, is getting on now she's managed to get off the factory floor and into the office. Is she looking down her nose at us all, but still wanting to sing with us? Especially now Miss Ellington is arranging some canteen Christmas concerts. That's what Miss Ellington said, isn't it, at the funeral?'

Beth nodded, saying, 'By, I don't know about that Amelia, she had me right fooled, she did. So timid when she were new, but look how pushy she turned out to be, and snobby when the *Workers' Playtime* lot came along and we were the ones chosen to sing, not her. I wish we'd never helped her in her early days, that I do.'

Fran pedalled harder as they struggled up the incline out of Massingham, heading for the beck. 'Well, wouldn't surprise me if she managed to get a group together and sing instead of us. It's just something Miss Ellington said, a sort of warning about keeping a step ahead of the competition, with a nod towards Amelia.'

The other two girls gaped. 'She wouldn't?' Beth gasped.

Sarah ducked as a crow swooped, then flew on. Sarah shouted, 'I bet she bliddy would. There's a new intake, isn't there, so she'll be sniffing out some talent while we're away.' Her voice was almost a howl. 'She's a fast worker, and howay, she's so desperate to get into the bigtime, like that loudmouth on the wireless Playtime crew promised. We'd better practise, and hard. I'm not having her shoving us off the stage, no I'm bliddy not.'

Fran and Beth laughed, and Fran said, 'Then we will practise, right now.' She burst into song, there and then, as they swooped round a bend, 'You better watch out, You better not cry . . .' The girls joined in, and as they felt the wind shift and get behind them, the men hurried to catch up, joining in the chorus. 'Santa Claus is coming to town.'

Fran heard Davey getting louder and louder, and turned to look. He was pushing down on the pedals until he was alongside her, his blue eyes smiling, his blond hair, the same colour as Sarah's, but not tinged with green as Sarah's was from the chemicals. She dropped behind the two girls as he rode no-hands, sitting up straight, his cap tilted to the right, grinning as he always had. He reached out his hand. She took it, and together they rode on as Ben swooped out of the turn to his marrer's house, and joined in, calling, 'I could hear the racket miles away, you daft lot.'

Davey yelled, 'Enough of that. Have you two sorted the crossword I set yer?'

Ben came alongside, and all three of them rode along while seagulls pecked at the furrowed fields, cracking the ice. The wind was almost slicing through as Ben panted, 'Course we did. Even got the coded bit.' He overtook them, and scooted past the other two girls, yelling, 'Stop yer racket, save yer breath and catch me up, I dare yer.'

He set off on his bike, inherited from Bob, Beth's husband, and Stan tore after him, head down, shouting, 'Race you, little toerag.'

Ben's laugh was shrill, not quite right, but not too bad, considering he was only twelve and his da would not be coming home.

Davey reached the beck, still hand in hand with Fran, and all he wanted to do was hold her in his arms and never leave. Never ever leave and go back to that place, and Daisy.

Stan leaned his bike up against the leafless hedge where battered birds' nests hung, abandoned until the spring. Davey took Fran's and did the same, while the girls collected dead and rotting sticks for the fire. Davey pulled newspaper he had knotted to imitate kindling and placed it on the bank, burned black from the fire they had set just before he went to Bletchley Park. Davey built the fire with the wood the girls brought back, while Stan lit it. Beth and

Ben ran over the bridge to the rope hanging from the oak; it hung motionless on the sheltered bank.

Stan yelled, 'Don't you bliddy dare, for I'm not coming in for yer if you drop off. Come and eat. Davey's to get his train, so's we only have an hour here.'

Davey rose from the fire and walked to Fran, holding her close and together they watched the flames gain a hold. Stan and Sarah did the same, standing to the left of them. Fran whispered, 'Everything's all right, you know Davey, we have one another, haven't we?'

It was really a question, and one she had never asked him before. What the hell could he say? Did he tell her what a fool he'd been? How he'd woken on Daisy's bed when he thought Fran was going to chuck him after he'd had the anonymous note telling him she was mucking about with Ralph? How the hell could he have been such a fool to believe such rubbish?

As her eyes searched his face he said nothing, not knowing what right he had to say anything to this wonderful girl, so he just stared down at the crackling fire, treasuring every moment of her body so close to his, only rousing when Stan called, 'What the hell are you doing, Davey? The fire's going out. We need more wood.'

It wasn't just Davey he startled, but Ben and Beth who were running along the bank, and he felt Fran stiffen in his arms. He stopped, and turned. Davey saw his sister, Sarah, step back from the fire, her scarf falling from her hair to her shoulders, calling to Stan, 'Howay, bonny lad, keep your hair on, there's a few more sticks to burn through yet.'

But Stan had stormed across to Davey, and now gripped his arm and pulled him away from Fran. 'I said, we need more sticks, I'm bliddy freezing. You lasses, get the sandwiches out, eh, not to mention the beer, cos Davey has to go soon.' All the while he was talking he was tugging at Davey, who was forced to walk along the bank with Stan until they reached the gateway of Farmer Thomas' field.

It was here he backed Davey against the gatepost, so hard the gate catch dug in his back. Stan gripped his lapels, shaking him, keeping his voice low. 'For the love of God, what's the bliddy matter with you? You've a face like an armpit, and my sister has had a bliddy awful time balancing that bastard Ralph against keeping the family safe and making herself almost outcast from the village for what they thought she was doing with the boss's son. And you, what are you doing, punishing her with your distance? What do you want her to do, grovel? Well, hell will freeze over before our lass does that, and while we're about it, I've a good mind to give you a bliddy good hiding.'

He almost chucked Davey from him. 'If it's over then tell her, and don't pull the grief card, we're all feeling it. But sort it, because I'm not bliddy well having it.'

Davey fought for his balance, his boots sinking into the ploughed earth, and then he stood, ready for another go from Stan. It was no more than he deserved. There was silence between them. All Davey wanted to do was tell him about Daisy, but how? Stan would never have been such a fool.

He stared over the fields to the pit, and wanted to be back where everything was simple, where he could be here for Fran and his family. But after what he'd done with that girl . . . Thank god he had been too drunk to be anything other than a fool.

He looked at Stan who was blocking his way to the beck, and it was as though they were bairns again. Stan was the leader and knew everything, kept them safe, and in whom they trusted like they'd never trusted anyone before or since. Stan who solved all their problems.

He wanted to weep, but men didn't. He started to speak, but his voice shook. He swallowed, and Stan's voice was different now, gentle, kind. 'Come on then, our lad. Spit it out.'

Davey did, in a torrent: how he'd had the anonymous note saying that Fran was seeing Ralph, how Fran had then called the telephone box as usual and wanted to tell him something which he couldn't bear to listen to. 'I thought she were telling me it was over, so I got bliddy drunk, didn't I? Falling over me own feet I were, and this Daisy from work, she helped me, and took me back to her room—'

Stan grabbed him again. 'She bliddy what?'

Davey wanted Stan to give him a good belting, anything to dull the pain of what he'd done, or might have done. 'I woke on the bed in t'morning, not in it. On it. She were making tea or some'at, and calling me sweetheart and then when I tried to leave she were right mad, and said I'd led her on.'

Stan shook him again, so he felt like the man with the wobbly head from the cinema. 'For God's sake, Davey Bedley, are you bliddy mad? So did you? What the hell happened?'

That was the worst of it, because while Fran had done what she had to, to keep her family safe, he had done it, whatever the hell 'it' was. He was right miserable and jealous of every other bugger under the sun. He stared at Stan and shrugged, then almost shouted, 'I don't bliddy know.'

Stan let him go, and stood beside him now, handing him a Woodbine and they both lit up. 'Go back over it, bonny lad. You woke up, with your clothes on, or not?' Stan asked.

'I had me drawers on, and . . .' Davey was back in the room, seeing himself, and her, then added, 'And I had me socks on.'

Stan flicked the ash from his cigarette, and stared as the

tip glowed in the cold air. 'By, lad, you must have been a sight to behold.'

Davey stood in front of him. 'Bliddy hell, I've just thought of something else. The elastic had gone in me drawers in the morning, and the other pair were in the wash, so I'd stitched 'em tight before I went out, to keep the buggers up, and were going to have to break it when . . . Well, you know what.'

Stan nodded. 'And you've remembered . . . ?'

Davey felt as though boulders that weighed tons were lifting from his shoulders. 'They were still sewn tight. I'd forgotten. How the hell could I forget that?'

Stan shook his head. 'Because you're a bliddy fool, is why. Not safe to be let out on your own, but the thing is, you're in the clear lad. You were so drunk you would have been anyway, no way you could have done owt frisky, trust me. You'll have to tell that lass or whatever her name is, to stop being such an unholy cow making some'at out of nothing, though why anyone would fasten on you, heaven alone knows.' Stan was grinning and his arm was round Davey's shoulders now just like the days when they were bairns. 'By bonny lad, you're starting to look a sight better than you did, and I reckon our fathers're up there laughing *their* socks off at the whole sorry mess. So, best you sort it with our Franny now you're back on.'

Davey was fierce now as he ground out, 'I were never not on, I love 'er, Stan, more'n life itself but I felt dirty and I knew I had to tell her I were a damned fool, but I can now, because I know that's all it was, just me being too drunk to know which side up I was.'

Stan flicked his stub away. It arced through the air, and fell onto the ice between two furrows. 'Bet you can't get yours within a foot of mine. And let's not talk about which side up you were, eh?'

Davey's stub ended up six inches from Stan's, and they argued about how much Stan owed him as they walked towards the girls who were calling them now. They realised they had no wood to take back, so they had a quick scavenge in the hedge, grinning and talking just like they always had. But as they walked back, Stan said, 'Hang on, what about the note? Wasn't there some'at you said to me about it at the funeral? What with everything else, I'd forgotten all about it.'

'Aye, it were from that snotty Amelia. I recognised the handwriting on her flowers. I don't trust her, Stan. I've got to tell our Fran about me daftness with Daisy, but what about Amelia? Do I tell her about that?'

Stan shrugged, and in doing so dislodged a small log. He stooped to pick it up. 'They have their own ideas about her, so I reckon we let it lie, eh, unless it comes up? I'll keep an eye on 'em, and her. Don't you worry. Amelia's only an office worker so can't do any damage. Best you forget about her, and clear the air with our Fran, because we'll have to set off in twenty minutes if you're to catch your train, and finish the beer. Race yer, eh?'

Stan was off, tearing along the bank. Davey was catching up fast, because his Fran was there, *his* Fran, the love of his life. They built up the fire, they sat on their macs and ate and drank. They toasted their fathers, all three of them, and it was as they cycled home that Davey told Fran he'd been an idiot, and began the story. The wind was up, but behind them, and as they sailed down an incline she said nothing at all until he got to the part where he'd sewn up his drawers, and then her laugh soared over the wind, and probably right up to their fathers.

She held out her hand, he took it, and then, though he had said he wouldn't, he told her of the note. Again she said nothing for a while, but held his hand even more tightly, and as they came into Massingham she said, 'I'm glad you told me. It's best I . . .' She waved her hand to the girls. 'We know. As the three of us have said before, we might learn to like her again, but how can we ever trust her after all that she's done?'

Hear more from

ANNIE CLARKE

SIGN UP TO OUR NEW SAGA NEWSLETTER

Penny Street

Stories You'll Love to Share

Penny Street is a newsletter bringing you the latest book deals, competitions and alerts of new saga series releases.

Read about the research behind your favourite books, try our monthly wordsearch and download your very own Penny Street reading map.

Join today by visiting
www.penguin.co.uk/pennystreet